PRAISE FOR
Far Away from Here

"Exquisitely written, beautifully crafted, *Far Away from Here* captures Muslim American experiences with extraordinary insight and outstanding storytelling. A true literary triumph."
—S.K. Ali, author of *Love from A to Z* and *Saints and Misfits*

"A heartfelt story about faith, family, friendship, and loss, *Far Away from Here* offers great insight into the African American Muslim experience."
—Aaliyah Bilal, author of *Temple Folk*

"A big, compassionate hug of a novel, smelling of sage and coconut oil, full of tough love, honesty, and the indefatigable pursuit of hope. In this masterclass on the subtleties of character, Ambata captures the warmth and faults of the Muslim Ummah, yet dares to welcome everyone, with all that they carry. I relished it to the last drop."
—Medina Tenour Whiteman, author of *The Invisible Muslim: Journeys Through Whiteness and Islam* and *Love Is a Traveller and We Are Its Path*

"While reading *Far Away from Here*, I felt a closeness to each character as they navigated their own bumpy journeys. Ambata Kazi's debut novel honors a community hardly written about, Black Muslims post-Katrina. Life in New Orleans goes beyond the French Quarter."
—Maceo Nafisah Cabrera Estévez, author of *Amor Cubano: In a bottle, a tube and a small packet*

FAR AWAY FROM HERE

FAR AWAY FROM HERE

a novel

AMBATA KAZI

Copyright © 2025, Ambata Kazi

All rights reserved. No part of this publication may be reproduced, distributed, or transmitted in any form or by any means, including photocopying, recording, digital scanning, or other electronic or mechanical methods, without the prior written permission of the publisher, except in the case of brief quotations embodied in critical reviews and certain other noncommercial uses permitted by copyright law. For permission requests, please address SparkPress.

Published by SparkPress
www.gosparkpress.com

Published 2025
Printed in the United States of America
Print ISBN: 978-1-68463-328-9
E-ISBN: 978-1-68463-329-6
Library of Congress Control Number: 2025906229

Interior design by Stacey Aaronson

Company and/or product names that are trade names, logos, trademarks, and/or registered trademarks of third parties are the property of their respective owners and are used in this book for purposes of identification and information only under the Fair Use Doctrine.

This is a work of fiction. Names, characters, places, and incidents either are the product of the author's imagination or are used fictitiously. Any resemblance to actual persons, living or dead, is entirely coincidental.

NO AI TRAINING: Without in any way limiting the author's [and publisher's] exclusive rights under copyright, any use of this publication to "train" generative artificial intelligence (AI) technologies to generate text is expressly prohibited. The author reserves all rights to license uses of this work for generative AI training and development of machine learning language models.

To the New Orleans Ummah, for raising me well

Prologue

FATIMA, I NEED YOU.

Fatima jolted awake in her seat. She looked around to the neighboring rows in the train car but no one paid her any mind, most deep in sleep themselves. She sat up and checked the time on her iPod, Solange's voice still crooning through the earbuds. It was just after 5:00 p.m. She adjusted her hijab that had slipped back off her forehead in her sleep and looked out the window. They were crossing the Causeway, the final stretch before they arrived in New Orleans. The late-evening sun hung low in the sky. The waters of Lake Pontchartrain glistened. She'd taken the first train out of Atlanta, less than forty-eight hours after her ex-fiancé Wakeel's parents, Baba Kareem and Mama Tayyibah, had called her.

She had hoped to sleep most of the ride, but the phone call, Baba Kareem telling her Mama Tayyibah was sick, Mama Tayyibah, her voice weak, asking her to come home and be with her. What was left unsaid but understood by all, that they didn't know how much time Mama Tayyibah had, that she was dying, played in a loop in Fatima's mind throughout the entirety of the twelve-hour trip.

"Fatima, I need you, sweetie," Mama Tayyibah had said. "You know you've always been a daughter to me, even before you and Wakeel. You're my child as much as he ... was."

Fatima had been unprepared for the chattiness of the other passengers on the train when she ventured into the other cars to stretch her legs, everyone asking her where she was from and where she was going, telling her the reasons for their own travels despite her not asking and not reciprocating. They squinted at her head-scarf and tilted their heads when she said she was from New Orleans, smiling like she'd told a funny joke. She didn't know if they were better or worse than the ones who looked back and forth from her face to the emergency-exit signs.

Two men in the row in front of hers, one seated to the right of her, the other across the aisle, were engaged in an animated conversation, their voices rising above the music coming from her iPod. The man sitting across the aisle was sweating, despite the frigid air in the train car. He clutched a washcloth to wipe his forehead while talking to the man sitting directly in front of her, whose face she couldn't see. His skin was dark, so dark Fatima could barely make out the black tattoo in the shape of Louisiana on his neck. Other tattoos covered his forearm and the hand that clutched the wash-cloth. The washcloth, his T-shirt, baseball cap, and tennis shoes were all a bright, crisp white. Fatima paused the music. The man with the washcloth was speaking.

"Man, I'm bout to watch the game and then I hear 'POW!' Just one time though, right, so I'm like, Nah, it can't be. But then next day, coming home from work, I stop to talk to my neighbor and she tell me dude got shot. Killed."

"You knew him? Somebody you knew?" said the man in front of Fatima, leaning forward so she caught a glimpse of his neatly trimmed mustache and tobacco-stained lips.

"Nah, but check it, I watch the news that night expecting to hear something about it, but they not saying nothing. I check the other news channels, nothing. I go on Nola.com, nothing. So then a couple days pass and I'm walking down the street and I see these big, big white angel wings painted in the middle of the street, right there at Dublin and Belfast. With his name and the date he got shot underneath. Ain't that some shit? Street reporting."

"Damn, dude, they don't even mention it on the news no more?" The man in front of Fatima shook his head and leaned back in his seat.

"I guess not," said the man with the washcloth, looking intently at the other man. "I guess it's too many people getting shot or—or they just don't care. It ain't news no more. But, man, I felt like, like good at least to find out dude's name. Shouldn't nobody die—get shot—without nobody knowing."

Neither man spoke after that. The man with the washcloth stared out into space for a while, then mopped his face again with the cloth and tipped his hat over his eyes, leaning his head back on the seat. Fatima stared at the gold watch that glistened on the man's wrist, fixating on the pattern of links that ran horizontally and vertically, the man's words sinking into her gut: *Shouldn't nobody die without nobody knowing.*

She remembered another call from Baba Kareem, five years previously, his voice as torn with grief as it was the other day, telling her Wakeel had been shot.

"Wakeel . . . Wakeel is gone, Fatima," he'd said. "We lost him."

Her own voice, foreign to her ears, screaming, "No," over and over. No. After all those years apart when his family moved away, years of not knowing she needed or missed him, he had found her, they had found each other at seventeen, young but ready and eager to be in love. They had just found each other. He couldn't be gone. He couldn't.

Later she would learn the specifics. Wakeel had gone to visit his wayward cousin Saif, still fruitlessly trying to persuade him to stop selling drugs and do something with his life. It was there, with Saif on a porch in a quiet Hollygrove neighborhood late at night, that four bullets intended for Saif tore through Wakeel's chest and stomach, ending his life.

Fatima had vowed to leave New Orleans, forever. The city was a thief, a monster that never seemed to tire in its hunger for Black bodies. When the water came and submerged the city of her birth, drowning her roots that ran deep down in the dirt, she took that disaster as her final goodbye. She'd settled in Atlanta with her older sister, Khalilah, and her family and didn't look back.

Yet, with a phone call, she'd dropped everything and bought her ticket to return to the place she said she would never go back to. Now she wondered, why? Why was she doing this? What was she going back to?

The train car swelled with sound as people gathered up their belongings and prepared to depart. The man with the washcloth removed his hat and took out a bottle of Queen Helene cocoa butter lotion from the duffle bag at his feet. He squirted some into his palm and rubbed the lotion into his hands and arms, ending with a swipe over his bald head and his face until his skin gleamed. Fatima opened a compact mirror to look at her face. Her dark-brown skin looked ashen, her eyes tired. The weight of the past pressed down on her eyelids. Words crackled through the laughter and chatter around her like a clear channel breaking through static.

Fatima, I need you.

PART ONE

Fátima

FATIMA STEPPED OFF THE TRAIN. A BLAST OF HOT, HUMID air her welcome-home hug. It was October but it may as well have still been summer. Standing in line to retrieve her luggage from the bottom of the train, sweat trickling down her back and pooling in the cups of her bra, she regretted her outfit. Her feet felt heavy in her leather boots and her cardigan clung to her arms and back like an unwanted blanket. She'd unwisely worn a sleeveless shirtdress underneath. The porter wrenched suitcases and duffel bags from the cargo hold and tossed them inelegantly onto the pavement. Fake Louis Vuitton, a bulky blue duffel bag held together with duct tape, an army rucksack, two large, heavy-duty trash bags closed off with zip ties. They looked as pitiful as the people waiting to claim them. Bags were getting snatched up quickly; nobody was checking tags. Somehow Fatima had gotten pushed out of the row of passengers hovering around the growing pile of luggage. Just as she caught sight of one of her red-and-black plaid suitcases, she saw a hand reaching for it.

"Excuse me," she whispered, trying to push through the tight crowd. Nobody budged. "Excuse me!" It came out harsher than she intended. The woman in front of her turned, looking indignant. Fatima's bag was moving away from her. She ignored the sour looks and shoved her way through.

"Excuse me. Excuse me. That's my bag. I think that's my bag."
Now she was shouting. Was it her imagination, or did the man dragging her bag away speed up? She ran after him. People turned to watch but nobody tried to help.

Fatima made eye contact with a man in a gray uniform standing at the sliding doors that led into the main lobby and pointed fiercely at the man walking away with her bag. The guard hesitated, then stood in front of the doors, blocking the man.

Fatima ran up out of breath. "My bag," she panted. She wrenched the handle and pulled at the tag, pointing to her name. "This is my bag."

The man holding it scratched his head. "Oh, my bad." He shrugged and walked away into the lobby.

Fatima gaped at the disinterested security guard. She gestured toward the man who stood in the lobby with his hands in the pockets of his sweatpants.

"You're not gonna check and see if he has a ticket? You're gonna let him stand around like that?"

The security guard looked over his shoulder toward the lobby, his hands on his heavy belt loaded with various attachments. He sighed and sauntered through the doors toward the man. He took a few knock-kneed steps toward him. His pants were too tight; he couldn't run in them even if he could muster the energy or care to do so. The man caught sight of him and turned swiftly toward the exit, hop-stepping out the door. The security guard walked back. He looked over lazily at Fatima and raised an eyebrow. He stood just to the side of the door, splayed his legs wide, and folded his arms. Fatima rolled her eyes and went back to the train to get her other bag.

Baba Kareem was supposed to be picking her up. She walked around the lobby wheeling her bags, looking for him.

They'd all loved Baba Kareem when they were kids. All the

FAR AWAY FROM HERE 9

babas were their babas, but Baba Kareem was extra special. Tall, brown, and massive as the big oak trees that studded City Park, he was the most gentle and playful. Fatima remembered Saturday afternoons at Wakeel's house, all of them sprawled out on the burnt-orange shag carpet in the living room watching cartoons. Her, Wakeel, his cousin Saif, Tahani, and her younger brother Hadi. Khalilah would be there too, sitting on a chair reading a book, her legs crossed at the ankles, her lace-trimmed white socks without a speck of dirt on them, bored and grumpy because she had to watch the younger ones.

Baba Kareem would come in from work, calling, "Hey, hey, salaam alaykum," in his rich baritone, and suddenly the room would shrink, his muscular body blocking out the light that filtered in through the porch. "Baba Kareem!" they'd all shriek, forgetting whatever show they were watching and running to him. Wakeel, who always took the seat closest to the front door, would hop up, shouting, "Baba!" and jumping into his father's waiting arms. After a long hug, Baba Kareem would lean forward and let go of Wakeel, making them all squeal in fear that Wakeel was going to fall. Then with one arm he'd swoop Wakeel around onto his back and carry him around the room. All of them, even prissy Khalilah, bounced on their toes with their arms raised. "My turn! Me next!" they'd shout, and Baba Kareem made sure they all had a turn to ride on his back, never once dropping any of them.

"Fatima?"

Fatima looked up from digging through her purse for her phone and dropped her shoulders, relief coursing through her.

"Baba Kareem," she sighed.

He stood in starched blue jeans and a charcoal-gray T-shirt, tucked in, and the tan suede boots he always wore. His beard was a bit grizzlier, with more gray than brown, and he wore glasses now, but he still looked the same. As he walked toward Fatima, she wanted to run into his arms the way she did as a child. Instead they stood and faced each other, arms at their sides, and smiled at each other. She yearned to be a kid again and hug him, but she was a woman now. If she were Wakeel's wife, maybe then it would be okay, but they were forever in this strange space, family, but not. They exchanged salaams.

"You look . . . well," he ventured. "Healthy."

"So do you," Fatima said. She scratched at a spot on her hand, a mosquito bite, she realized too late, a red bump already forming.

"I'm parked right out front," he said.

He reached for her bags, ignoring her protests, and started for the exit. She had to practically jog to keep up with his long strides.

"You still have the truck," she said, as they stepped outside.

His emerald-green four-door Ford had always been his pride and joy. He hoisted Fatima's bags up and set them down in the bed. He wrestled the keys out of his front pocket and unlocked the passenger door, holding it open so Fatima could climb in.

Baba Kareem pulled the truck out of the horseshoe driveway and turned right onto Loyola Avenue. The city was quiet on a Sunday evening, the sky strips of dark, smoky oranges and blues that wrapped around the tall downtown buildings. The WDSU clock tower rose up from Howard Avenue, reflecting the setting sun's rays in blinding waves. They stopped at a traffic light and a woman pushing a rusted shopping cart filled with torn, white garbage bags ambled across the street. She stopped at the median to rifle through a discarded McDonald's bag that had landed next to the overflowing trash can. Not finding anything to her liking, she continued on under the bridge, where people were setting up tents for the night. Across the street, Fatima saw the man who'd tried to run off with her bag— walk off, really, because why run when "security" would just let you do it?—strutting out of a corner store on Simon Bolivar, a brown paper bag tucked under his arm, the other arm swaying behind

FAR AWAY FROM HERE

him. He dapped a few men off who stood in front of the store. They shouted at his back but he kept going, disappearing around the corner. Whatever he had, he wasn't sharing.

Baba Kareem cleared his throat. "Mama Tayyibah's at home, not resting like she should be. Sister Amatullah comes by to help out when the nurse can't be there, but that woman won't let nobody help her." He chuckled.

Fatima laughed with him. Behind his smile there was a tightness in the corners of his eyes, a droopiness that didn't have anything to do with age. Baba Kareem skipped the interstate on-ramp and continued on down Earhart Boulevard. Maybe this was the way he always took, or maybe he was instinctively taking the scenic route so Fatima could look around. They passed the back side of the station where several unused trains sat, their insides invisible in the dark. This was where city officials had set up cages for a temporary jail right after Hurricane Katrina. Fatima shuddered thinking about the stories she'd read about how people had been treated.

After they crossed South Claiborne, Fatima leaned forward. "What's that?" She pointed to a brick building to the left.

"The old Booker T.? They tearing it down," he answered without looking.

"Building a new school?" she asked.

Baba Kareem huffed. "You would think, huh? Nah, condos, I think."

Fatima laughed, thinking he was joking. "Condos? Next to the projects?"

He gave her a wry look that snuffed out her laughter.

"You're serious?"

"Mm-hmm."

Next to the gutted school sat nothing but piles of rubble from there to the Broad Street overpass.

"Wow," was all Fatima could say.

"Yep," sighed Baba Kareem. "Welcome to the new New Orleans. Condos and mixed-income housing in the hood, or what's left of it." He made air quotes with the words "mixed income." He explained the concept to her.

"Well," she shrugged, "that could be good, right?"

"Hm. That's what they say. They call it revitalization. We'll see."

Baba Kareem didn't trust them, them being local government, the mayor and the city council. When had they ever cared about poor Black people, he said. Fatima remembered these projects from when she was a kid; her mom or dad took this stretch when they had to go uptown or downtown, no stoplights till Claiborne so it was a fast detour. She'd marveled at how many people lived in the stolid, brown brick buildings. There were always lots of people outside, kids running around in the patchy grass, the adults crowded on porches playing card games, shouting at each other over loud music. On the news the projects were always described as dangerous and full of criminals, but to Fatima they just looked like places where families lived.

Baba Kareem took the on-ramp to the overpass. The courthouse still looked the same, but there was a tall shiny building behind it Fatima didn't recognize. It was pale gray, almost white, with a thick orange stripe going up one side and a wall of windows, floor to ceiling. More new condos or a fancy office building, she assumed.

"That's Gusman's Paradise," said Baba Kareem. "The new jail."

Fatima gaped at him. Twenty minutes in the city and things were all so surreal.

"We're only beginning to see the changes," said Baba Kareem with a shake of his head.

Broad Street was an odd mix of old and new. The Popeyes across from the courthouse was now a health food store and the old boxing gym was now a movie theater. There were a lot more beauty-supply stores than Fatima remembered, plus a bike store. But

Tastee's and African Vibrations remained in their prominent locations, and Baba Kareem confirmed that Umoja Bookstore was still holding it down on Esplanade. The corner store at St. Bernard, where Khalilah (not too bougie to eat hot chips) and Fatima used to sneak after school for snacks, was still there, as was the McDonald's across from it, though it had gotten a facelift. The combination of old landmarks and strange new ones was jarring.

Baba Kareem crossed Florida Avenue and turned right onto Treasure Street. A few blocks down he pulled up in front of a two-story peach-colored brick house with vibrant blue shutters. Baba Kareem kept the house fixed up, but it had been that color forever. Downstairs was a garage on the left that led to what could have been a small studio apartment, but Baba Kareem used it to store his many tools. The right front side of the house next to the stairs was designated for Mama Tayyibah's flower garden. Signs of her illness showed in the lack of attention to it. Her begonias drooped and the African violets' deep-purple petals wilted. Weeds peeked through the white awning that skirted the perimeter. Fatima's immediate thought was that she wanted to fix it, coax all the flowers back to life. She didn't know a thing about gardening, but she did know Google.

The neighborhood looked the same. The house across the street that they called the Sanford and Son house because of all the random items strewn in the yard was still as junky as ever. Mr. Jim, the owner of the house, was a white man who'd been old since they were kids who repaired appliances and also bought used cars— "classic," he insisted—and fixed and sold them. An electric saw screeched from the backyard. Mr. Jim was still at it.

The double shotgun next door, white with green trim, had a wreath decorated with red, orange, and yellow leaves, with pinecones and fake mini pumpkins nestled among the leaves, Ms. Carter's handiwork. She worked at a bank and had two daughters and always wore pantyhose and high heels, even on the weekends. A pair of dusty work boots sat on the porch mat. That was new. Ms. Carter must have finally got herself a man.

On hot summer nights, Wakeel and Fatima used to sit outside and find Ms. Carter sighing on her porch swing clutching a sweaty glass of iced tea. She called them lovebirds, then launched into stories about how Mr. Carter brought her flowers every day of their marriage, and how you couldn't find men like Mr. Carter anymore. Fatima and Wakeel would glance at each other in the dusk and try not to laugh. Wakeel always joked that there was more than tea in those tall, sweaty glasses Ms. Carter always kept by her side.

Gutted houses dotted the streetscape though. Two on Baba Kareem and Mama Tayyibah's side and three on the other, their insides, visible through broken windows, black and cavernous. X's had been slashed across their fronts and sides with red spray paint, numbers squiggled in the top and bottom, one for the number of animals found, the other for people. Most of the ones Fatima could make out were zeros, but the one on the corner, the sprawling one where the Wallace family had lived, Mr. and Mrs. Wallace, their five kids, and Mrs. Wallace's mother, bore a three. Fatima turned away. She didn't want to look anymore.

Baba Kareem lugged Fatima's suitcases up the stairs. Fatima wrapped her arms around her torso despite the clinging heat. She took the stairs slowly. How many times had she run up and down these stairs, how many times had she tripped, how many times had she and Wakeel sat at the top dreaming about their future? Not about money, clothes, or cars, but what they were going to do, who they were going to be. Wakeel slicing the air with his palm while he talked. He was going to have his own art school, fund a community center, hell, run for city council, maybe even mayor. Fatima was going to be a journalist, an editor for *The Times-Picayune*, start her own magazine. A community-focused power couple, he'd say, his wrist bumping up against Fatima's, her heart beating impossibly fast, feeling the heat from his body.

"You coming?" called Baba Kareem.

"Hmm?" Fatima looked up at his face, shrouded in darkness. She blinked, coming back to the present. She'd stopped in the middle of the stairs, lost in memory.

The smell that greeted Fatima when she crossed the threshold reminded her of visiting her great-grandmother at a hospice center after she'd had her third stroke. The stale smell of sickness. She wanted to go back outside. She wanted to walk and walk until she got back to the train station and onto a train headed anywhere but there. Baba Kareem set her bags down by the coffee table. His movements had slowed, grown weary. Any room he was in had always seemed smaller to Fatima when he entered it, but now it was the opposite. He shrank and the room swelled.

"I'll go see if she's up," he said, the same whispered tone Fatima's family had used when they visited her great-grandmother, as if the volume of their voices could add to her pain.

Fatima tugged off her boots and set them next to Baba Kareem's on the shoe rack by the front door. It had always overflowed with shoes, Mama Tayyibah fussing at them to straighten their shoes as she did it for them. Now Fatima's and Baba Kareem's were the only pairs. Fatima padded around the living room, dimly lit by a lamp with a shade draped in a cream-colored doily crocheted by Mama Tayyibah. Other, larger doilies draped the tops of the sofa, the same squishy blue one Baba Kareem brought home many years ago. Fatima remembered him and Wakeel lugging it carefully up the stairs after carrying out the old burgundy velvet one the children had jumped on till its stuffing exploded. The ivory chairs that sat on either side of the mahogany coffee table also held a doily. She crocheted blankets too. Fatima still had a pink-and-yellow one Mama Tayyibah had made her for her tenth birthday. Wakeel had boasted to his friends about the red, black, and green one his mother made with a zigzag pattern for him, trying to convince her to start a business selling them. "Boy, I'll go blind trying to do that," she'd said.

Above the entertainment center (covered with a doily, of course) sat several framed photos. Fatima squinted at them in the dim light. Baba Kareem and Mama Tayyibah on their wedding day. Baba Kareem in a white dashiki with matching pants, an elaborate gold pattern trimming the neckline, sleeves and pant cuffs, a gold domed kufi perched on his head. Mama Tayyibah wearing a white dress of the same material as Baba Kareem's, a sparkly chiffon headwrap like golden cotton candy whipped around her head. Two-year-old Wakeel, also in white, stood in between them, his arms wrapped around Baba Kareem's leg, staring at the camera. Photos of young Wakeel nestled into a pile of freshly raked leaves, throwing them in the air; another of him trying to look fierce, his fist raised defiantly, with just the faintest wobble of a stifled giggle on his lips; a candid one of him around six or seven years old, sprawled across a sofa reading a newspaper with a furrowed brow. Toward the back Fatima lifted one in a rust-red wicker frame, the six of them on Mama Tayyibah and Baba Kareem's porch swing, taken one hot summer afternoon. Fatima in white shorts and a Grover T-shirt she wore till it fell apart, her hair in cornrows and a smile so big her eyes folded into her face, Khalilah in a purple plaid ankle-length dress with a tie belt and shiny pearl-shaped buttons that went all the way down, her hands in her lap and her head tilted to the side, smiling angelically. Tahani and Hadi, their thick, golden hair shimmering in the sunlight, and Wakeel in a tank top with red stripes across the front and blue jeans, his arm draped around Saif, his lips drooping, wearing black despite the heat. Saif. Even then Fatima didn't like him, and he didn't like her either. Even then they were battling for Wakeel's attention. Saif had won, and they had Wakeel's body in the ground as his trophy.

A door whined open down the hall. The wood floors creaked with Baba Kareem's approaching footsteps. Fatima put the picture back, sliding it behind another photo to block out Saif.

"She's up now," Baba Kareem said in a voice straining to be upbeat.

Fatima followed him silently down the hall to their bedroom at the very end across from the bathroom. She'd been all through this house but never in their bedroom, never even seen the inside. Mama Tayyibah sat on one side of a king-sized bed propped up on pillows, wearing a black stretchy turban and a plush terry cloth robe the color of raspberries wrapped tightly around her. Fatima's throat caught when she saw Mama Tayyibah's face. Mama Tayyibah. Mama. She wanted to slap her own face for the tears that puddled in her eyes. She was supposed to be strong for Mama Tayyibah, and here she was crying. Mama Tayyibah sat up and raised her arms to Fatima, her own eyes brimming with tears. Fatima fell into her arms. There was no room on the side of the bed so she slumped down on the floor on her knees, wrapping her arms around Mama Tayyibah's torso, and laid her cheek in the soft space between Mama Tayyibah's breasts. Beneath scents of menthol and laundry detergent was a faintly rancid oily smell. She took it all in.

"Baby. Oh, my baby." She pulled at Fatima's chin. "Let me see you."

Fatima lifted her head up, her chin still in Mama Tayyibah's hand. Fatima's hijab was sliding off. Mama Tayyibah laid a finger on Fatima's baby hairs that had surely gone frizzy from all the sweat of the day. She grabbed a tissue from the nightstand and put it over Fatima's nose for her to blow. Fatima grabbed the tip of Mama Tayyibah's index finger and pressed down on the pale-blue nail. Mama Tayyibah wiggled her fingers at Fatima.

"You see me, huh? Lord help me, I'm still vain."

Fatima laughed and pulled Mama Tayyibah's hand to check out

her manicure, little ovals of sky on each nail, and two rhinestones on the bed of the ring finger.

"You go to the nail salon, Mama T?"

"The nail salon comes to me. Tahani comes once a month and fixes me up. You know she got her certificate from cosmetology school?"

Fatima shook her head. She couldn't remember the last time she'd spoken to Tahani.

Mama Tayyibah patted the back of her head. "Mm-hmm, I'd have her do my hair too if I had anything left."

Her throat caught on her laugh and brought on a fit of coughing. Fatima sat back on her haunches to give Mama Tayyibah some room. Baba Kareem, who'd been standing by the door, rushed forward to pour water from the pitcher that sat next to a glass on top of the dresser, but Mama Tayyibah waved him away.

Her face had lost all its plumpness, but with her velvety, cocoa skin, it brought out her cheekbones and jawline. There was a milkiness to her eyes that made Fatima's own water from looking at them. Lines fanned out from the corners, disappearing under the band of her turban. Fatima rustled a small jar of coconut oil from her satchel that she'd tossed on the floor when she knelt to greet Mama Tayyibah. The oil had softened into clumps from the heat. Fatima crushed one between her thumb and index finger and patted some on Mama Tayyibah's cracked lips and around the corners gray with ash. Mama Tayyibah pressed her lips together and tilted her head back, her eyes fluttering shut for a moment. She opened them and smiled at Fatima, her mouth shiny and pink again.

"See, that's why I wanted *you* here. Paying attention to the details."

Baba Kareem shifted behind Fatima. Fatima felt the air in the room shift. Mama Tayyibah blinked her watery eyes and smiled tightly at Fatima. She wanted to look back at Baba Kareem but was scared of what she might see. Mama Tayyibah pressed her thumb to the center of Fatima's forehead, to the V forming there, then tapped her nose. Their eyes held each other. Mama Tayyibah winked at her.

Fatima took a shower and dressed in the steamy bathroom, lotion wet on her skin. She washed her hair, although she'd just washed it the other day. She needed to get the train completely off of her. She forgot she wasn't at Khalilah's though, where she had her own en suite bathroom. Now she'd have to wrap her wet hair back into her headscarf until she got to her room. And that was another thing she wasn't sure of, where she was sleeping. If Baba Kareem had already gone to bed she might have to sleep on the sofa, something Mama Tayyibah never allowed. But things were different now; maybe she didn't care about that anymore.

Fatima hadn't known what to expect when she finally got to see Mama Tayyibah. Baba Kareem said she was dying, but she didn't look so bad. She looked good, considering. Maybe because she'd stopped the chemo, or maybe she was having a good day. Fatima had heard about that, how people with terminal illness would have short spells where you almost couldn't tell they were sick. But that usually happened just before they died. Fatima's mouth watered like she was going to throw up. She made a quick dua for Mama Tayyibah to be healed. That's what she was supposed to do, but she didn't believe it would work. That was one of the things about faith she struggled with. She believed Allah could heal Mama Tayyibah from stage four cancer, but *would* He? Why? If it wasn't the cancer, it would just be something else.

Fatima bunched her dirty clothes into a plastic shopping bag and tiptoed out of the bathroom and down the hall to the living room. The house was silent. Her stomach growled. She hadn't eaten since afternoon, when she'd trudged a second time through the train cars enduring stares to get a kosher hot dog from the snack kiosk. She stuffed the bag of clothes into her half-unzipped suitcase and headed to the kitchen. There was a light on over the stove and a plate covered in foil. She drummed her fingers on the countertop, studying the covered plate. If she ate it, nobody would say anything about it, but what if it wasn't for her? She pulled at a corner of the foil, stopped when it crinkled, then tried to lift up an edge to see what was underneath. The foil tore jaggedly off the center across the plate.

"Salaam alaykum," rumbled Baba Kareem, entering the kitchen.

Fatima jumped and tried to lay the torn foil piece over the other piece. She waited for him to say something about the plate but he walked over to the fridge, opened the door, and started rustling through it.

"Is this for me?" she asked.

"Hmm?" Baba Kareem said, still going through the fridge.

She waited for him to straighten up and close the fridge door. He shook a bottle of Martinelli's apple juice, one of those little bottles Fatima used to pretend was a fancy perfume bottle, holding it out from her neck and squeezing an imaginary atomizer pump.

"Is this for me?" she asked again, too hungry to be shy.

"Oh, yeah. The sisters are real good about bringing food a few times a week. I cook sometimes too." He shrugged. "Mostly eggs though." He popped the top on the apple juice and sipped it. "I think Sister Iris brought that one."

Fatima pulled back the foil she'd massacred. A whole baked chicken leg quarter with rice smothered in okra and tomato gravy. It looked homemade, the okra crisp and bright green, the tomatoes fresh and cooked down till they were small and soft. She set the plate to warm in the microwave and leaned against the counter with her arms folded. Baba Kareem finished the juice and sat back, running his thumb along the condensation that gathered on the bottle.

FAR AWAY FROM HERE

He hadn't offered her any. He'd drunk his straight out of the bottle. She had to ask for food. The table wasn't set. A twilight zone feeling crept in. She'd never had to ask for food in this house, and anything anybody had was offered around. If there wasn't enough for all, there wasn't enough for any. She caught the microwave before it beeped and brought the steaming plate to the table.

"Have some," she offered, sliding the plate over.

"Nah, I'm good," he responded without taking his eyes off the bottle, which he still clutched in his fist. He finally let go and rubbed his hands roughly over his eyes.

"Tired?" Fatima tried. She pierced the chicken with her fork and a chunk slid neatly off the bone. The skin was crispy the way she liked it.

Baba Kareem shook his head vigorously like he was shaking himself out of a trance and hopped up.

"I'm sorry, you want some bread?"

He pulled a crinkly white paper bag out of the bread box next to the toaster. Fatima recognized the red-and-blue Leidenheimer label. Baba Kareem opened the bag and rolled the paper down, revealing a half loaf of perfectly golden French bread. He set it on a wooden cutting board and cut a few slices with a sharp knife, then brought it to the table with a white ceramic butter dish and a butter knife. Now this was the Baba Kareem Fatima knew.

The first bite of food made her ravenous. She tried not to shove the food in her mouth since Baba Kareem was sitting across from her. She sipped at the large glass of ice water he brought her and cleared her throat. She had to ask him about where she'd be sleeping. She knew they had a guest room, but with all that was going on she didn't know if they'd fixed it up for her. Finally she asked, awkwardly, insisting she didn't need much, just a bed, like she was the one who had asked to come to stay with them and not the other way around.

Baba Kareem shifted in his seat and scratched under his chin. "If it's okay, we were going to have you sleep in Wakeel's room. The guest room is, uh, not available."

"Oh."

She wasn't prepared for that.

"Yeah, sorry. I should have told you before but . . ."

He looked like his words caused him physical pain. She was supposed to help him out, clearly. Tell him it was fine, which she eventually did. The sleep she'd felt coming on evaporated.

Baba Kareem left to bring Fatima's bags to Wakeel's room then came back to tell her goodnight. She washed her plate and glass and wiped down the table and countertops. She found the broom in the utility closet by the side door and swept the floor. She would have mopped it, cleaned the cabinets, done whatever made-up chores she could find to avoid the inevitable, if not for the noise she would make. Finally, with a deep breath, she faced the darkened hallway that led to Wakeel's room. She had spent a lot of time in Wakeel's bedroom before he moved to Chicago, then none at all when he came back.

Fatima stood at the threshold, the maroon carpet springy beneath her feet. Wakeel's posters still hung on the walls, maps of Africa, the US, the world, Malcolm X kneeling in prayer in a nearly empty musalla, gilded lanterns above his head, a profile of Marcus Garvey in military costume, keyhole nostrils flaring, the Djenne Mosque in Timbuktu, its gritty facade that made Fatima rub her fingertips together as if she could feel the dust.

Wakeel's prized drawing desk sat in the corner, a lamp clipped to it, the backless swivel stool. Fatima crept over to it and swept her hand across its bare surface, imagining it covered with paper, Wakeel hunched over it, his dreads covering his eyes. She remembered when he had brought out his drawings once when she was at his house. He had dozens of drawing pads filled with pencil sketches, lines and etchings that showed a lot of effort and time had been put into them. He had a cartoon character he created when he was twelve. A crime-fighting Black duck named Splatter Duck modeled after Shaft. Splatter Duck had a mission to restore Black communities, exposing corruption and police brutality, getting rid of drugs and dealers that destroyed the vitality of once-prosperous neighborhoods. In one series of drawings, Splatter Duck used his powers of intimidation to shut down a liquor store that was a hotbed for illegal activity. Looking at Wakeel's empty desk, she could imagine him sitting at it, working. She could see the bones of his hands, his long fingers, the knuckles jutting up and down as he worked his pencils, erasing and adding over and over till he got a detail just right, an eye with the right slope, the irises wide and glassy, a mouth with the precise curve of a snarl, the sinewy arm and leg muscles, veins pulsing. Fatima looked away, trying to push the image out of her mind. The corkboard above the desk held scraps of paper thumbtacked to it, a phone number on a torn piece of hot-pink paper with no name attached, drawings and scribbles on loose leaves, random words: "kingdom," "rapture," "Adinkra." To the right a calendar dated 2004.

She looked at Wakeel's bed. Her bags sat at the foot of it. The red, black, and green crocheted blanket Wakeel loved so much was draped over it, its colors still as vibrant as when Mama Tayyibah had made it. A folded prayer rug rested on top. She imagined Wakeel sprawled in that bed during their late-night conversations after he officially started courting her. She'd been so shy with him at first, knowing nothing about being in a relationship other than the snatches of affection she witnessed from her parents when they thought no one was watching, her father holding her mother at the waist, burying his face in her neck as she washed dishes, her mother tossing her head back, eyes closed, enjoying it, or what passed for intimacy that she saw among her schoolmates, boys who wrapped their arms around their girlfriend's shoulders in a grip that looked more like a loose chokehold or groped their bodies as if they were their property, not-so-surreptitiously pinching their breasts and backsides. No boy had ever shown any real interest in her and that had been fine, until Wakeel. She'd been so scared and uncertain of what to say over the phone with him, but his honesty chipped away at her fear of being vulnerable.

He liked to talk about the future, using the word "we" instead of "I" in a way that made Fatima tremble. She hadn't thought much beyond her life at this point in time, but that was all Wakeel talked about.

"You gotta think big, Fatima," he said in one of their breathless conversations. "This world is ours. We gotta take it."

"And how do we do that?" she asked.

"By making a lotta noise. Scream our heads off until everybody hears us."

Fatima still didn't know what he meant, but his words made her feel alive in a way she had never felt before.

He became bold in expressing his love for her. He sang to her over the phone. "You" by Jesse Powell and "All My Life" by Jodeci were his favorites. Like everything else he did or said, there was no irony to it.

"I really have prayed for you all my life," he said.

"What do you mean?" she'd whispered into the phone.

"I mean I thought about you all the time while I was away. Wondering what you were up to. When I knew we were coming back, I was praying I would find you here."

"But we were just kids, Wakeel."

"So? Kids have feelings. I knew I wanted you in my life."

Fatima had blinked back tears, grateful he couldn't see her. She was embarrassed to admit she hadn't thought much about him, had forgotten about him really.

"You don't remember, do you?" he'd said. "How I used to follow you around everywhere? How I always had to sit next to you when we all watched cartoons together? It was always you, Tima."

She closed the door of Wakeel's room and picked up the prayer rug. She shook it out and was about to lay it down but she couldn't remember which direction was northeast. Lake Pontchartrain was north. She closed her eyes and turned left, facing the lake, then right and a little more right as she followed it down past the airport and boats to Haynes Boulevard, east. She laid out the green rug. It was old, with grooves at the feet, knee, and hand spaces. She wondered if it, like everything else in the room, had once belonged to Wakeel. She slipped her bare feet into the grooves, wider apart than she would normally stand. She prayed, standing, then bowing, then kneeling, her palms touching Wakeel's, forehead and nose pressing into his.

Afterward, she released her hair from the elastic she'd used to tie it up before putting on her hijab. It was damp and warm. Her hair products were in a ziplock bag at the very bottom of her suitcase. She was too tired to dig for her moisturizer, although she'd regret it in the morning.

She pressed the home button on her phone. She'd already sent texts to her parents and her older sister, Khalilah, letting them know she'd made it in safely. Khalilah had responded, *I still think you're making a mistake, but alhamdulillah.* Fatima had rolled her eyes at the text, such a perfectly Khalilah response. She'd been vocal in her disapproval of Fatima going back.

"I can't believe you're even considering this," she'd said, standing in her kitchen preparing dinner, impeccably dressed in a silky peach blouse and black slacks underneath a pristine white apron, her locs swept up in a neat bun at the top of her head, tiny gold-and-pearl hoops glistening from her ears. Though Fatima and Khalilah shared the same umber skin tone and perfectly arched, thin eyebrows that never needed to be groomed, Khalilah had an elegance about her that was unmatched. "I mean, things are finally picking up for you. You just started that internship."

"It's just an internship," Fatima had retorted.

"An internship that could lead to a job. Tell me, are there any Muslim women's magazines in New Orleans? Is there a vibrant Black Muslim social scene that you can write about like we have here?" Khalilah pushed the cutting board aside and pulled a pan of chicken drumsticks toward her, the skins pulled back, revealing the plump raw meat. "This is a step back, Fatima. A step way back."

Fatima had pursed her lips. "She's sick. And lonely, I guess. Baba Kareem is working two jobs just to try to pay the mortgage and the medical bills."

"You're not a nurse," Khalilah chided.

"They have home care. She just wants somebody to keep her company."

Khalilah had stopped talking for a while. She rubbed her special seasoning blend, a mix of cayenne, garlic, thyme, and other spices and herbs she kept in a small glass jar, into the chicken pieces. She lifted up the chicken skins and laid them back over the meat with the same gentle precision that she used to tuck her children into bed at night. When she spoke again, her voice was soft as melted butter.

"We all love Baba Kareem and Mama Tayyibah."

She looked timidly at Fatima.

"And we all loved Wakeel. But . . . going back won't change the past. You need to move on with your life."

Fatima had chewed on her bottom lip, considering her sister's words.

"I know. But they need me. I can't say no."

She'd rolled her shoulders back, unconsciously trying to mimic her big sister's cool poise.

"And it's not about Wakeel."

Fatima scrolled through old texts. Ishmael's was toward the bottom. Khalilah didn't know about Ishmael; nobody in her family did. She and Ishmael hadn't messaged each other in weeks, not since she told him she was going home. She typed *I'm here* then deleted it. Her thumb hovered over the keyboard. She closed out the text thread without reading any of the old messages. She turned the ringer off and set it on the nightstand.

She still hadn't sat on the bed, was scared to even touch it. Instead she walked over to Wakeel's dresser and slid open the top drawer. His clothes rested in the drawers, neatly folded. She pulled a gray T-shirt out from the top and held it to her face. It smelled stale, like old perfume. She took off her own T-shirt and put on the gray one, Wakeel's. She ran her hands over the sleeves of the shirt. The nubby cotton became silk on her skin. She turned back to the bed and pulled back the blanket. Sky-blue cotton sheets. They looked new but she still imagined Wakeel's limbs tangled in them. She crawled into the bed. She wanted the sheet and the blanket, even though it was too hot for that. She pulled them up high so they covered her neck and the bottom of her face. She pulled till she had both sides tucked under her, a shroud. Her eyelids heavy, she imagined the heat generated from the blanket came from Wakeel's body. This was the closest she would ever come to lying with him.

Fatima spent the next few days puttering around the house. A nurse came in the morning just before Baba Kareem left for work. One night Fatima tiptoed to the kitchen for a glass of water and saw light coming from underneath the guest-bedroom door. The shadow of footsteps interrupted the light, then she heard the groan of mattress coils and Baba Kareem sighing. She understood then why she couldn't sleep there.

The nurse, Beatriz, was efficient. She wore colorful scrubs that swished when she walked and spotless white shoes. She smelled of coffee and peppermint, her brown hair in a neat bun. From her bed, Fatima could hear Beatriz swishing down the hall, opening the bedroom door, saying, "Buenos días, girlie," in a sing-song voice. She'd sing Mama Tayyibah to the bathroom and start the shower, her laughter audible above the gushing water. Fatima had tried to help her dress Mama Tayyibah once, but Beatriz looked offended. "My job, miss," she'd said, taking the nightgown from Fatima's hands.

Fatima stood back feeling useless. Beatriz rubbed cocoa butter lotion onto Mama Tayyibah's feet and legs while Mama Tayyibah grunted her approval. Her strong arms worked the lotion into Mama Tayyibah's skin until it glowed. Fatima fought to keep her face flat and not look away when she saw Mama Tayyibah's bald head for the first time. Beatriz rustled through a drawer and scattered a few turbans over Mama Tayyibah's lap. "Which color you want today, mama?"

After she finished grooming Mama Tayyibah, Beatriz headed to the kitchen to make oatmeal, which she called porridge. Fatima had always hated oatmeal, but she couldn't refuse the bowl Beatriz brought her. Beatriz's oatmeal was like nothing Fatima had ever tasted, creamy and sweet, with tiny chunks of green apple and raisins. Beatriz made coffee, too, café con leche with a dusting of cinnamon on top. Fatima asked once if it was okay for Mama Tayyibah to have coffee and they both looked sternly at her but didn't respond. No one wanted to say what they all knew; Mama Tayyibah was dying and could have whatever she wanted.

Fatima didn't know what she was doing there, and there was no one she could share this feeling with. She already knew what Khalilah would say, and her parents had been confused when she told them, her mother sounding slightly jealous that she was dropping everything for Mama Tayyibah, her father concerned about

FAR AWAY FROM HERE

29

her safety. He wasn't comfortable with her traveling alone and told her she should have a mahram with her, a not-so-subtle hint that she should be married by now. They didn't know Ishmael existed, and if they did, they'd be calling all the masajid in Atlanta to line up suitors for her.

Fatima quickly grew restless in the house with Beatriz handling Mama Tayyibah's needs. After breakfast, Beatriz and Mama Tayyibah bickered over Mama Tayyibah taking her medicine, a cocktail of giant pills that made Fatima's own throat close up when she saw them. Beatriz wouldn't back down though, and Mama Tayyibah relented in the end. Beatriz left in the afternoon. Fatima lay in the bed with Mama Tayyibah watching old shows, *Cagney and Lacey*, *Miami Vice*, and *Colombo*, trying to solve the mysteries. They hashed out the plots until one or the both of them dozed off, waking up at the sound of Baba Kareem returning home. Khalilah would smirk so hard if she saw what Fatima did all day.

Tahani came by one evening, dressed in black scrubs, her salon uniform. She wore thick black liquid eyeliner that went past her eyelids and swooped up in a flourish and made her hazel eyes stand out, and red lipstick. Her nails were long and painted a deep purple. She dug her nails into her hair while she talked, fluffing her golden spirals. Fatima barely recognized her. She had been such a plain Jane when they were growing up, with her white hijabs and long dresses. They hugged each other awkwardly.

"You skinny," Tahani greeted Fatima, in a way that expressed admiration.

Tahani had always been chubby growing up but now she had a grown woman's body.

"You look good," Fatima said.

"I look fat," Tahani laughed, proud of her curves. "Two babies back-to-back will do that to you."

"I didn't know you got married."

"I didn't."

Her voice carried no bitterness or shame, just a statement of fact.

"Oh, I . . ."

Tahani leveled her eyes at Fatima.

"What do you have?" Fatima asked.

Tahani whipped out her phone and tapped the photo app, her face beaming.

"Two girls," she said. She moved next to Fatima to show her. "Aliya's four years old, and Safia's about to turn three."

They had her light-brown complexion and crinkly blonde hair, both in neat Afros.

"They're adorable," Fatima cooed. "You gave them Muslim names."

"Well, yeah, they are Muslim."

She gave Fatima a "duh" look and swiped through several more pictures. She stopped at one of a dark-skinned young man sitting on a sofa, gold grill shining, Tahani next to him in a black mini dress, her fleshy legs crossed toward him, his hand protectively gripping her hip. She turned the phone off and slipped it in her back pocket.

"So, what about you?" she asked. "What's new?"

Fatima told her about school and Khalilah, her abandoned internship. She left out Ishmael.

Tahani nodded absently. "So, you gonna get a job here?"

Fatima stammered. She hadn't considered it, hadn't thought about what she'd actually be doing with her days other than being with Mama Tayyibah. She told Tahani maybe.

"I would tell you to go by *The Times-Picayune* but I hear they shutting down," Tahani said.

"Yeah, I heard something about that but I thought it couldn't be true."

"Girl, these days, anything that seems like it can't be true prob-

FAR AWAY FROM HERE

ably is." She took in a tired breath. "This city ain't what it used to be. You'll see. Speaking of, you been out? I know you here to look after Mama T and all, but let me know if you wanna hang out."

"You have time with your babies and work?" Fatima gestured toward her work clothes.

Tahani shrugged. "I still get out. I'll see what's popping this weekend for us to get into."

"Okay," Fatima responded.

Fatima didn't know what Tahani had in mind, what "popping" meant to her. Fatima's nightlife in New Orleans had only ever been community events, Eid picnics, Kwanzaa festivals, and Sunday school at the masjid. The stuff she heard her schoolmates talk about in high school—house parties with no adults around, hole-in-the-wall bars in the Lower Ninth they snuck into—had always sounded like a different world. In Atlanta she had started going to clubs, but all she ever did was stand around awkwardly and laugh and pretend to have fun with the girls she came with—she couldn't really call them friends—and pretend the clear plastic cup she clutched had more than Coke in it.

Tahani had pulled her phone back out of her pocket and was scrolling through Facebook, pausing every few scrolls to like an image or a post. The screen bathed her face in a white glow. She had an emptiness in her eyes Fatima recognized among her peers at school and in the clubs, the laughter that didn't reach their eyes, the fake cheer when cell phones came out for selfies, the same emptiness she checked her own face for every morning when she looked in a mirror.

Once at a club the guy friend of one of the girls Fatima was with, a short guy with a ponytail, had squinted at her, his lip curled with mild distaste. Startled to find him looking at her like that, she asked him what was up. He kept the stank look on his face. "Why are you here?" he asked. "What?" she asked, trying to match his rude attitude. He repeated himself. Fatima shook her head and turned back to her group. The girls hadn't heard what he said but they raised their eyebrows at Fatima. She rolled her eyes at them, like what he'd said was too silly to even repeat. In fact, he'd read her mind, or rather dug deep to the question she tried to bury. Why was she there? Why was anybody there? She'd looked around and seen a bunch of drunk, high, lost souls, dancing and laughing to keep from crying, filling themselves with emptiness. She'd wanted nothing more than to join them.

Fatima met Ishmael in her senior year of college at the campus bookstore where she went to wander through the shelves after classes. She didn't have time to read with all her coursework, but it comforted her to pretend to have a life where she did and encouraged her for what she might have after graduation. Ishmael worked the cash register. The bookstore was empty that afternoon; it was the post-midterm slump when no one needed textbooks anymore and it was too early for scantrons and blue books. The partitions were still up, the ones they used to control the long lines during the first few weeks of school when lines snaked around the store, so Fatima had to walk a long zigzag to get to the register, feeling like a mouse in a maze studied for human entertainment.

Ishmael kept her waiting, his elbows on the counter, his hands linked behind his neck, face buried in a thick book. His skin was a warm brown like maple syrup. He wore a rumpled orange plaid shirt with the cuffs sloppily folded up. He had hair fingers could get lost in, Fatima noticed. Thick and wooly, uncombed but not dry, purposely unkempt because his lining was fresh. His goatee was also neatly trimmed.

He stirred when Fatima cleared her throat, sliding slowly away from his book, his eyes still on the pages. Fatima decided to be a jerk and pick up her book she'd laid on the counter and drop it back down on the counter with a thunk. His head shot up; he glared at her behind his thick black frames. She arched her eyebrow at him. He slapped a palm on her book and slid it toward him, their eyes locked as they smirked at each other. Fatima was aware they looked ridiculous, but she was determined not to let him win. Ishmael broke the staring contest to look down at her book, *Dreams from My Father* by Barack Obama. He chuckled. She didn't take the bait, so he spoke.

"You riding the change wave too?" he asked, his voice deep and raspy.

She tapped her debit card on the counter.

"You know you can get this way cheaper at B&N, right?" he said. "They mark these books up for gullible students."

"Your salesmanship is impeccable. Where's your supervisor so I can rave about you?"

He grinned at her and shrugged. "Suit yourself."

She paid and started to walk away.

"Hey," Ishmael called.

Fatima turned in time to catch him sizing her up. His eyes flicked up quickly to her face. "It's a good book." He jutted with his chin toward the book she clutched to her chest. "I'd like to know what you think."

His eyes told her he was serious. She felt something then, low in her belly. His smile grew and she flushed, cleared her throat, and looked down at her feet.

"Maybe," she said, trying for coolness.

He leaned down and folded his arms on the counter, his cocky grin returned.

"Yeah, maybe," he responded.

Fatima turned on her heels, willing her hips not to sway as she walked.

A few weeks later she returned to the bookstore, having avoided it using the excuse that she needed to save her money. She saw Ishmael as soon as she walked in, at the counter in the same posture, head ducked into his shoulders so all she could see was the top of his head. She walked around the partition this time and went straight to the front, laying the Obama book down lightly on the counter, not looking at him. He glanced at the cover then looked up at her. She kept her eyes down, then flicked them up to him. His face spread in a slow smile.

"I finished it," she said with a shrug. "You said you wanted to talk."

He stood to his full height. His eyes on her made her heart beat fast. She could turn away. Grab her book and walk swiftly out the door. She shouldn't be there. What was she doing?

He leaned toward her and folded his arms over the counter, his biceps bulging beneath the thin gray T-shirt he wore. She leaned toward him, resting her elbow on the counter, their faces almost close enough to touch. She wasn't going anywhere.

Fatima couldn't tell Tahani about Ishmael. She would understand. She might gossip about her, but she would understand. But the reason Fatima didn't tell her about Ishmael was because he wasn't a factor in why she shouldn't have left Atlanta; he was part of why she did.

Not that Tahani seemed to care. Fatima could tell they wouldn't be swapping secrets late in the night. Tahani yawned and switched off her phone.

"Anyway, I just stopped by to check on Mama T. You need anything?" she asked, turning toward the hall before Fatima could answer.

"Nah, I'm good," Fatima said to her back.

Tahani opened the bedroom door and shut it behind her. Tahani's indifference stung. When Fatima had opened the front door to her, she'd looked vacantly at her, a tired smile on her face, and given Fatima a perfunctory hug, like it had been just weeks since the last time they saw each other. Years ago, after the storm, they'd cried over the phone when Fatima finally got in touch with her. Tahani's grandmother on her dad's side had stayed behind and hadn't been rescued in time. They'd promised to stay in touch, but Fatima couldn't remember a single phone call after that first one. She could see now that Tahani had a lot going on raising two babies by herself. Still, there was something standoffish about her behavior that Fatima couldn't understand, a carefully concealed hostility, it seemed, in the way she looked her up and down. Something unspoken lingered in the air, not just with Tahani but everybody in this house. Secrets everybody seemed to be tiptoeing around.

Tahani

TAHANI DROVE AWAY FROM MAMA TAYYIBAH AND BABA Kareem's home distressed. The nerve of Fatima, showing up, smiling, acting like nothing had ever happened—well, after she got over the shock of how Tahani looked, how she had changed, her eyes growing wide, then blinking several times before they settled on a spot over Tahani's shoulder. Tahani had stuck her chin out at Fatima, leveling her eyes, the defiant posture she'd perfected over the last five years when anyone questioned her about how she was living her life. She turned the music and the AC up, the air blowing the ends of her curls back and forth over her collarbone, making her feel briefly young and carefree, not a bone-tired single mom going to pick up her kids.

How dare Fatima come home and act all nonchalant, like she hadn't left and stopped calling shortly after the storm. Asking Tahani questions about what she'd been up to like it was all perfectly normal, like they'd never been close friends. But okay, had they been, really? Sure, they spent a lot of time together, so accustomed to each other's houses they could walk around them with their eyes shut (one of their favorite games) and not hit a wall, but she couldn't recall them ever sharing secrets or anything deep like that. They just always hung together. They'd known each other all their lives; what secrets did they even have?

Tahani remembered when Wakeel started courting Fatima. She'd been as excited as Fatima was when he came back, seeing the two of them together picking back up seamlessly, like two separate puzzle pieces finally finding each other. Some things just look right together, and that was Fatima and Wakeel. They had the same dark-brown skin color and tallish, slim bodies, but it was more than just the physical resemblance. Some couples you could just look at and see their whole lives play out in the smiles they shared, the way they set their eyes on each other like no one else was around.

Tahani couldn't recall any special moments with her and Wakeel, but he was a fixture of her childhood. He was always so easy to get along with; he knew everybody and everybody knew him. Tahani remembered how the elders' faces lit up whenever Wakeel came around. He was a promise of the future, a sign that the next generation was going to be okay. And then he was gone, snuffed out. Tahani knew it wasn't right, that Allah never took a soul as punishment, that every life taken held a lesson for the living, but still she asked sometimes, why? Why Wakeel? They were all so hurt by it. And then Fatima just picked up and left, like only she had lost somebody, like they weren't all hurting.

Tahani humphed again under her breath at the magically returned Fatima. And had the nerve to act pious. On some benevolent air. Uh-uh. Tahani didn't trust it. There was something behind the serene smiles and vague alhamdulillahs about her own life in Atlanta. Fatima was hiding something.

Tahani pulled up at her coworker Danielle's house in Gentilly just as the sun reached its lowest point, blinding everybody and washing everything in gold. Danielle was in her thirties and didn't have kids, but she offered to help Tahani with hers on her days off from the salon, and she even picked them up sometimes depending on her shifts. She wouldn't accept payment; instead Tahani repaid her by running errands, picking up lunch on workdays and making grocery and drugstore runs on her way to get the girls.

Between Danielle and Mama Jennifer, who ran a twenty-four-hour daycare out of her Uptown home and had "raised half of all Hollygrove children for decades," Tahani was able to juggle work and childcare and just make rent, utilities, and food, despite the gas she burned to get from Gentilly to Uptown and across the river to the Westbank and back again six days a week. Aliyah starting school next year would bring some ease financially but would also mean another daily stop in addition to making arrangements to pick her up from school. Tahani sometimes convinced herself she could take on a second job, but as it was, other than the few evening hours and the five hours a night she slept, it seemed she was always working already. She had only Sundays to rest and snuggle with her babies, and even then, sometimes she took in an extra head at her home, but only if it was somebody she really liked and trusted.

Danielle's was half of a red brick shotgun house off Mirabeau and Elysian Fields. A black Corolla Tahani didn't recognize was parked in the driveway behind Danielle's white CR-V. Walking up the cobblestone path, she noticed the front door was slightly ajar. She stepped up to the porch and tapped lightly on the door with her fingertips before entering.

"Hello?" Tahani called into the darkened foyer.

Seeing lights flashing from the living room to the left, she headed that way and found her daughters close together on the couch, TV light bathing their faces, Aliyah clutching a remote in her lap.

"Umi," they cried, sliding off the couch like noodles.

The living room was also dark. Tahani switched the light on.

"Where's Ms. Danielle?" she asked.

"She's with the man in her bedroom," Aliyah replied.

"The man in her—?"

FAR AWAY FROM HERE   39

Tahani stopped short and tried to compose herself. She smiled tightly at the girls.

"Where's your bags? Let's go get some ice cream."

The girls scrambled to gather their things and were in their shoes in rapid time. Tahani hustled them out and slammed the front door behind her extra hard. If her girls hadn't been on the lawn looking at her, their little spidey-sense detecting something not quite right, she would have done it again for good measure. She smiled at them again and struck her tickle-monster pose, hands curved into bear claws in front of her face, pretending to chase them to speed them up. They squealed and ran to the car, hopping into their booster seats. She peeled away from the curb without even buckling her seat belt, her breath ragged between her clenched teeth. She drove two blocks before she felt her chest begin to rise and fall, air actually entering her lungs and loosening her limbs.

At Baskin-Robbins, she picked up her phone from the cupholder and saw she had three missed calls from Danielle. She swiped past the notifications and sent a text to Mama Jennifer. Not having to run errands for Danielle anymore wouldn't make up for the extra childcare costs, but she'd figure something out. She ordered a double scoop of Gold Medal Ribbon for herself and kids' cones of mint chocolate chip for Aliyah and strawberry for Safia and sank into the booth, scooping a heaping spoonful of ice cream into her mouth. The sweet and cold of the ice cream hit the sensitive nerve on the tooth that had been bothering her lately, the one that needed to be checked but she didn't have insurance beyond Medicaid, and she welcomed the pain as an opportunity to feel something other than despair. She closed her eyes while the girls bounced in their seats, high on a sugary cloud.

Tahani pulled up to her apartment, a duplex tucked into a cozy corner off Elysian Fields near the University of New Orleans. She loved the area, a tidy mix of apartment homes like hers—occupied by college students (the quiet kind, many of them older), small families, and young professors from the university—and older two-story single-family homes.

Her apartment was on the second floor. Ms. Terri, the older white woman she rented from, lived in the more spacious apartment below. Tahani had gone to check out the apartment with Aliyah on her hip and Safia big in her belly, sure she would never get such a nice apartment in a nice neighborhood looking the way she did, but Ms. Terri seemed to like her immediately. "Promise me you'll keep quiet and clean, pay your rent on time, and that you won't leave anytime soon, and the place is yours," she'd told Tahani.

Tahani had made good on her promise, training the girls to walk on quiet, socked feet and entertaining them with crayons and Play-Doh and silent dance parties and moonwalk competitions when they needed to get their sillies out. Ms. Terri pretended not to like children but sent up plates of home-baked chocolate chip cookies and petit fours several times a month. Tahani responded with containers of soup and gumbo when the weather got cold and Friday-supper plates from the masjid with a slice of bean pie on the side.

The apartment was spacious, with two large bedrooms facing the backyard and an open living room and dining room with windows that took in lots of sunshine. It even included a front balcony that overlooked the street. The girls loved to sit out there and blow bubbles and watch them float off over the balcony. The space allowed Tahani to indulge her passion for decorating. With permission from Ms. Terri, Tahani had painted the walls a warm sage. She spent her free time carefully acquiring pieces of furniture from garage and estate sales she learned about in the paper and through Facebook groups, and at hidden-gem thrift stores in

Harahan and Old Metairie. Tahani did her research, learning about how to spot quality antiques. She'd even considered a class she'd learned of through one of her groups but talked herself out of it. She couldn't afford the cost (she could), or she didn't have time (well, that was mostly true), and, finally, it was silly, who did she think she was taking an antiquing class like some middle-aged wealthy white woman? The result of her efforts was a space she loved to exist in, a space that, while she spent more time away than present, gave her peace of mind and room to breathe.

When Tahani arrived home with her daughters after getting ice cream, she went straight to the kitchen to get dinner started. She pulled a glass pan of baked chicken drumsticks out of the fridge and set a plastic produce bag of broccoli on top of a cutting board. She cut the oven on to warm the chicken and scanned the pantry next to the stove. It would have to be box mac and cheese tonight; she didn't have time to make it from scratch. The girls wouldn't mind.

In her bedroom, she took off her work clothes and slipped into black sweatpants and a stretchy neon-pink exercise hoodie. She joined the girls in the living room where they sat reading a book with their LeapFrog. She laid out her dark-red prayer rug and pulled her white cotton prayer dress over her head. As her toes sank into the rug, she took what felt like her first real deep breath since the dawn prayer several hours earlier. Tiredness rushed in with her exhale.

It was all she held in throughout the day to get through it. Sometimes when she finally sat for a break at work, the fifteen minutes or so between clients when she ate a salad or sandwich, she found her jaw ached from the unconscious habit of clenching her teeth. It was the clients who complained if she'd been late getting them started, or if they had to wait longer because *they* were the ones late. The ones who didn't know what they wanted and insisted she decide, then sniffed and frowned at their reflection when she gave them the mirror. Or, her favorite, the ones who hemmed and hawed when it was time to pay, grumbling about so-and-so who was cheaper and better, or doing their hair themselves, while they dug through their purses and of course never tipped. They'd tag her or the salon on Facebook in their selfies taken just minutes after leaving the shop, and Tahani would smile despite herself watching the likes and comments roll in. She was good at what she did, making things look beautiful.

Soon after she began reciting the fatiha, the girls started arguing over the LeapFrog pen. Safia was hogging it, insisting Aliyah pick the story she wanted to read and let her press the words, even though it was Aliyah's turn to control the pen. Tahani snapped her fingers behind her back and tried to maintain focus in salah, but Aliyah was heated, and the disagreement soon turned to a tug-of-war for the pen. At first Tahani tried to push on, but then she paused and mouthed, "Allah, Allah, Allah," focusing on the tip of her tongue as it clicked against the roof of her mouth. Like a switch her mind zeroed in on the evening prayer, and the sounds of her daughters fighting vanished from her ears.

She moved through the motions of the prayer and felt herself emptying—the endless six-day workweeks, the constant budgeting and re-budgeting, numbers running circles in her head, cut here, add here, just barely get by month to month—all gone, released, at least for the moment. By the time she moved into jalsah position, sitting back on her haunches, her shoulders had dropped and rolled back on their own, her calf muscles relaxed, her palms limp on her bent knees. She salaamed out slowly, reluctantly, wanting to savor the feeling of rootedness to the earth in communion with God.

Sated, she turned and found the girls perched on the sofa like dolls, their heads bent together over the book they shared, their hands jointly clasping the pen, a tenderness between them like they

FAR AWAY FROM HERE

hadn't just been on the verge of drawing blood. Tahani almost felt she had imagined the fight. They both looked up at her at the same time, sweet smiles stretching across their faces.

Tahani motioned with her head and the girls jumped up and into her lap, one on each leg. She wrapped her arms around them and planted kisses on their foreheads, lingering over the faint scents of hair oil they gave off. This was what it was all about, she thought. This moment right here, these two little humans Allah had entrusted her with. That word, "trust," sent a spark through her. It was both thrilling and terrifying to be a parent, to be a mother.

"My pearls," she sang, rocking them from side to side.

They tucked their heads into the crook of her neck, taking in her smell of various sweet-scented oils and creams, then Safia popped her head back up.

"Is the macaronis ever gonna be ready?" she asked in an exasperated voice.

Tahani laughed and blew a raspberry into Safia's powdery neck, sending her into a fit of giggles. She tapped their bottoms to get them off her lap and then stood up with a grunt, shaking off the numbness in her thighs from the girls' weight.

"You girls are getting big. I won't be able to do that much longer. Come on, let's eat."

At the table, the girls wiggled and danced in their seats as they ate. If Tahani would have let them, they'd have hopped out of their seats to really jig, but she drew the line at staying seated. "You can sing your lil hearts out as long as you eat all your food," she told them, "but tushies must remain glued to seats." Safia ate around her plate in circles, grabbing one bite of each item till she was done, but Aliyah, despite the many times that Tahani suggested she sneak in some veggies in between bites of meats and grains, left her broccoli for last. When she got to the vegetables, she would sigh and set her chin in her palm, scowling at her plate.

"Aliyah," Tahani cooed, "don't you wanna eat your dinosaur trees so you can grow big and strong?"

Aliyah sat up. "No, I want a brother."

Tahani's eyes widened, startled. "A what? A brother? Where in the world did that come from?"

"Mina at Mama Jennifer's school is getting a brother," she replied.

"And you have a sister," Tahani said, nodding toward Safia.

"But I want one of both."

"Each," Tahani said. "And you don't 'get' a sibling. It's not like there's a store that sells them. They're not fruit."

Tahani felt tired. The conversation irritated her, like a bee buzzing around her head that she couldn't swat away. Aliyah looked hurt. Tahani took a breath and tried again.

"Listen, habibti, it's beautiful that Allah is blessing Mina's family with another child, a boy, but . . . they have a family, a mama and a daddy." Tahani gestured into invisible space. "We don't have that, not right now at least. It's just me right now. But you know, maybe, insha'Allah, it could happen later. Who knows what Allah has planned for us."

She patted Aliyah's leg under the table and looked over at Safia, who took in the conversation in stoic silence, as if she could sense the seriousness of it. Tahani smiled at her in a way she hoped was reassuring to her, to them both.

"Who knows," Tahani repeated, the words echoing in her chest.

After a beat of silence, she cleared her throat and pointed to Aliyah's plate.

"Now eat your broccoli," she said.

"Dinosaur trees," Safia sang. "Make you grow big and strong."

"Yep," Tahani said, her voice distant. "Big and strong."

Later, after bathing the girls, reading them their chosen two books each, tucking them in and having them recite three short surahs from the Qur'an, Tahani laid on the floor of her bedroom on an exercise mat, staring up at the ceiling fan, following the blades' slow, even rotations till they began to cross in her vision. She lifted her torso up and did ten more sit-ups, then collapsed back onto the mat, her hair spilling over the top of the mat and onto the floor. She gathered her hair into the hood of her shirt, forming a little pillow that tickled her neck, and rested her arms above her head.

She was thinking about Aliyah, what she had said. It had blind-sided her. Weren't they enough, the three of them? Their father, he wasn't a bad guy, but distant, always had been. Tahani had thought he was cool at first, like she was dating Batman or James Bond.

Darius was seven years older than her, had his own place and a good government job. But when she found out she was pregnant with Safia so soon after Aliyah, that knowledge forced her to look closely at her and Darius's casual relationship. She confronted him and told him he needed to step up, and surprisingly he did, inviting her to move in with him. But as they played at making house, dancing around the possibility of marriage, it quickly became clear to the both of them that it wasn't working. They'd built a relationship off fun and sex, but they had nothing in common. He wasn't a family man, and though Tahani's relationship with her own was beyond complicated, it bugged her that he was so okay with not meeting them or knowing them, that he couldn't understand her pain at being separated from them.

She envisioned a reunion, maybe, if she and Darius got married. He wasn't Muslim, but her family might warm to him and soften toward her if they made it official. Darius only wanted her though, and he shook his head when she asked him if he'd go to the masjid with her sometime, just for a community event. He'd never once asked her a question about her religion, saying nothing when she excused herself to pray. "I'm about this life right here," he would tell Tahani when she asked open-ended spiritual questions.

He talked often about leaving New Orleans, leaving America period. He envisioned them living big in some cosmopolitan European city like Amsterdam or Stockholm. Tahani could not see herself at all in those settings and didn't want to. New Orleans was her home. She knew the streets with her eyes closed, could conjure the faces and hear the voices of the people at will. She didn't want to be a stranger in a distant land, and Darius wanted just that.

When she was six months pregnant with Safia, he told her he'd been offered a job working for an independent military contractor. The job required him to move to Afghanistan.

"Afghanistan?" she'd said. "What would I do there?"

"You wouldn't, Tahani," he'd replied, his face tight. "It's not a place for a family. I wasn't—I'm saying it could be a good opportunity for me, for us, but I'd be going by myself."

"For how long?"

"I mean, it's the kind of job you can build a career off, a solid retirement, if you can stick with it. But I'd be able to send you money, for the girls . . . And I'll be able to visit. Probably just once a year. But I will."

He went on and on about opportunity, and Tahani knew he had made up his mind already, was mentally already there watching his bank account grow. They were breaking up without breaking up, just letting the relationship fizzle out.

He'd kept his promise financially, wiring her money every month, money she never touched, putting it into a savings account she had set up for the girls. But he'd only visited once, a little after Safia's first birthday, bouncing the girls awkwardly on his knees and fumbling through small talk with Tahani. The girls knew their father only from pictures and cards he sent, birthday gifts and Christmas gifts that confused them since they didn't celebrate the holiday. They studied the photos he sent from the government compound he lived in, his tan uniform blending in with the endless

FAR AWAY FROM HERE 47

sand and rocky terrain around him, or from his many exotic travel destinations, snorkeling in Cape Verde, eating gelato in Rome, or hiking in Nepal, always scribbling a promise on the back of the snapshots to take them with him when they got older. He was a mystery man to them, a shadowy figure all the more so strange as they bore no trace of his features, looking like Tahani had spit them out of her own mouth fully formed.

As far as Tahani knew, Darius had no serious girlfriend or wife, which seemed to fit his personality perfectly. She was baffled sometimes that she'd had two children with a man who she knew so little about.

The last thing she needed in her life was a man. She had too much to figure out, was too caught up in work and her children and being in the present to consider a life partner, let alone a potential stepfather for her girls. There was time. She was only twenty-three, even if she felt much older for how distant her teenage years seemed, that blip of time that leaped from high school to motherhood so fast she had whiplash.

She rolled over onto her belly on the exercise mat, then pulled herself into plank pose. Her hair slipped out of the hood and fell over her eyes. She tried to blow it off her face, only for it to fall right back down. Still she held the pose as long as she could, alternating the weight on her triceps until her arms and shoulders burned. She launched into a set of push-ups, grunting with each rise.

Her mind went back to Fatima. There'd been a few phone calls after the storm, but it was such a chaotic time. And Fatima's concern for Tahani's family and their shared tears over Tahani's grandmother had been genuine. Tahani knew she was being petty. It wasn't like she had lost sleep thinking about Fatima. She let her thoughts travel, the what-if thoughts: What if she had left New Orleans like Fatima— no, not really that, but what if she had let herself be a young woman? Gone to college, made friends, had experiences that didn't potentially lead to babies. Her heart did a little guilty ping, but she allowed herself the question, the alternate-story possibility.

She ended her push-ups and curled into child's pose, her torso resting on her thighs, her arms straight out in front of her, forehead pressing into her knees. Maybe that was her bone with Fatima. A feeling that Fatima's return cast a shadow on her own life that forced her to look back, something she never liked to do. And something else, the possibility of friendship.

Tahani didn't have any friends. There were the other hair stylists at the shop, but they were messy, liked to gossip too much, and she felt scorn in their gaze, the way their eyes roved over her body, the bit of acid in their words when they spoke to her, or about her more so, her lighter skin and hazel eyes. But ultimately it was her silence. She was quiet, didn't indulge their thirst for gossip, didn't chime in when they talked about men. They knew she was Muslim. Whenever she had to give her name, that was the first question she was asked: "You a Muslim or something?" Her coworkers never mentioned her religion beyond not offering her certain foods they brought to share. "I know you don't eat pork," they'd say, their words carrying an accusation. "No," she'd respond, slightly flustered, holding back the urge to apologize while also wondering why they never bothered to bring foods she could eat. They thought she was uppity. So be it. She had her girls; they were her world. But maybe she did need a real friend, one older than five, and one who came from her way of life.

Fatima

FRIDAY ARRIVED AND MAMA TAYYIBAH SURPRISED FATIMA in the morning with an invitation to jummah.

"I never miss it if I can help it," she said.

Fatima hadn't seen Mama Tayyibah outside of her bedroom, but when she came out of her room after getting dressed, there she was at the kitchen table dressed in a plum-colored abaya that hung off her frail body, a black turban, and a pale gray scarf draped over her shoulders, sipping tea. A wheelchair sat folded like an accordion by the front door.

Fatima had wanted to say no but knew she couldn't. She had to see everyone eventually. Friday prayers at Masjid Al-Ghafur had always been a treat growing up, only being able to go during the school holidays. They were lively spiritual and social gatherings led by Imam Hassan, whose powerful sermons made the grown-ups laugh and cry and filled them with righteous indignation at the wrongs inflicted on Black Americans but also strengthened them to fight back within an Islamic framework. Even for Fatima as a kid not knowing half of what was being said, Imam Hassan's booming voice commanded her full attention.

After the khutbah and salah, everybody gathered outside in the grassy area next to the parking lot where folding tables were set out and a long line stretched to the kitchen, where plates of fried fish or baked chicken, and Sister Iris's bean pies, were sold. Those who had to go back to work skipped to the front to grab a plate and go; everybody else took their Styrofoam containers to the tables, one side for the men, the other for the women, though they shouted, laughed, and teased across the tables to each other. Every jummah was like a mini-Eid, the food, the laughter, the clothes—dashikis, abayas, kufis, and khimars in a rainbow of colors and clashing, dizzying patterns. The children sneaking candies the elders gave them, chasing each other in tag.

Fatima knew every corner of the masjid, could see it in her head, the thin green carpet, hard and bristly beneath her feet, lines of tape stretching across on a diagonal for the prayer rows. "Shoulder to shoulder, toe to toe," the imam would call just before the start of prayer. The rumble and shuffle of bodies making space for those that trickled in late. The ceiling fans whirring above their heads, causing the flyers pinned to the corkboards on the walls to ripple, though they provided little respite in the summer months. The white plastic blinds, slots missing or broken, too small for the windows, exposing gaps on either side. The rickety wooden shelves stuffed with Qur'ans and books of hadith. The large black velvet tapestry that hung above the mimbar, "La illaha il-Allah, No god but God" embroidered across the front in gold. A part of Fatima yearned to be back in that space that was as familiar as her childhood home.

Baba Kareem came in dressed in dark-brown slacks and a white short-sleeved tunic with gold embroidery. Fatima smiled to see him outside of his work clothes. He nodded to Fatima and Mama Tayyibah and hoisted the wheelchair down to the truck. He came back up for Mama Tayyibah, lifting her gently from the dining chair. Mama Tayyibah wrapped her arms around Baba Kareem's neck, clasping his shoulder with her bony hands. She looked so small in his arms, so girlish with her head ducked into the hollow of his neck.

Fatima imagined them as bride and groom on their wedding day.

"My shoes," Mama Tayyibah cried.

"I'll get them," Fatima offered.

"The black slingbacks," she called over Baba Kareem's shoulder as he whisked her out the door.

Fatima tittered as she went to look for the shoes. No one was even going to see them, but still the woman was specific.

She rode squeezed into the back cab, behind Mama Tayyibah, who rested her head against the seat. Fatima touched Mama Tayyibah on the shoulder. She reached up to hold Fatima's hand.

"You okay?" Fatima asked.

"Mm-hmm," Mama Tayyibah mumbled, her voice tired.

Mama Tayyibah's hands slipped from Fatima's. Her head dipped low; snores whistled from her nose.

Fatima sat back and watched the streets through the tinted back window. Baba Kareem leaned forward, one hand on the wheel, peering through the windshield like he was maneuvering through a downpour. It was sunny though, and hot as July even with the air conditioner blasting. It was a short trip down Broad to Esplanade Avenue. The old John Mac school building sat empty, crumbling red brick and busted-in windows, surrounded by houses that looked like a bag of Skittles. Lime green with bright yellow trim, ocean blue with rich purple. The more stately ones stood in stark white, competing with the sun's brilliance. Thick green foliage curled up and over the facades, concealing some of the houses till all you could see was a peek of a door or a window. Vines spiraled around wrought iron fences and crawled up brick walls and ate into the fronts, like a hand from the earth taking back what once belonged to it. Still, there were blighted homes amid the color and sparkle. The landscape reminded Fatima of the big cardboard clowns at carnivals, the smiling, bright-red painted lips spread wide revealing pearly whites but with gaping black holes where some of the teeth had been kicked in. Corner stores were ubiquitous, as were the brown paper bags carried in brown hands by brown-skinned people trotting out through their doors and into the street. This street, like so many streets in this city, was schizophrenic, hood and chic, dripping with wealth and sagging with poverty, every turn a mystery, splendor or squalor, who knew.

They crossed Claiborne and made a right onto Villere. Two blocks down, Baba Kareem parked. Fatima squinted and ducked her head to look across the street through the sliver of window through the space in the headrest. She couldn't get a good view from her seat, so when Baba Kareem got out and went to the truck bed to get the wheelchair, she slid to the middle and leaned over Mama Tayyibah to get a better look. She didn't recognize it. The squat little masjid she remembered had grown into a stately two-story building the color of buttercream frosting, with sparkling windows and a high wrought iron gate enclosing it. Young palm trees sprouted from patches in front of the gate, one on either side of the entrance. The little grassy area where they used to set up folding tables now had a paved patio with a pergola covering the whole area.

Mama Tayyibah woke up when Baba Kareem opened her door. She groaned like she'd been taken out of a good dream too soon. He opened the hatch for the back seat and Fatima slid out, stealing furtive glances at the masjid, not ready to take it all in yet.

She stood to the side holding the wheelchair steady as Baba Kareem slipped an arm behind Mama Tayyibah's back and hooked his hand under her armpit, his other arm tucked under her legs.

"Come on, old girl," Baba Kareem whispered, pulling her from the seat.

He held her, his face so close to hers his nose touched her cheek. Mama Tayyibah pressed her forehead to his temple, her eyes closed. He took a few measured steps back and eased her into the wheelchair, then turned back and grabbed a blanket from the floor of the back seat, another one of her crochet pieces, this one in thick blue and yellow vertical stripes with skinny white threads in between. He settled the blanket over her legs, tucking the edges in at the sides. Fatima stood back as he backed the wheelchair out of the grass and onto the sidewalk. As they walked to the front entrance, the double doors leading to the masjid sprung open. Two men, tall and bearded, stepped out and opened the doors wide, securing them with bolts that drove into the porch floor.

A wind caused Fatima's lavender jersey hijab to billow out around her head. She grabbed it and wrapped it tighter around her head, wishing she had also worn an underscarf. She was glad she had worn her denim jilbab. In Atlanta she would never have been seen wearing a jilbab, but in New Orleans she didn't care. Any stares she got were on familiar turf.

Fatima gave salaams to the men at the door. They nodded and whispered the greeting back to her. She slipped her shoes off and placed them on a rack by the door and stepped inside. The ruby-red carpet was cool and springy beneath her feet. The musallah was one big room, studded with white pillars throughout the space. A dusky red velvet rope ran across the width of the room, separating the men's and women's spaces. The side of the room closest to the far wall had white folding chairs; the other side was bare. Baba Kareem wheeled Mama Tayyibah down a plastic-covered walkway, the wheels crinkling the thick plastic. The prayer room was empty save for one man, a black-and-white kufiya draped over his head covering his face, a grizzly gray beard peeking out, a Qur'an open in his lap. He rocked slightly as he read in a faint voice. Fatima followed Baba Kareem till he settled Mama Tayyibah at the end.

"Thank you, dear," Mama Tayyibah said in a husky voice.

"Alhamdulillah," Baba Kareem replied, his eyes glowing.

He walked to the front and stood to pray his sunnahs. Fatima sat on the floor next to Mama Tayyibah, who worked a string of dhikr beads in her hand, her thumb sliding the smooth amber beads down her palm one by one. Fatima was in awe of the space, the plush, new carpet, gleaming honey-toned wooden beams, the cream-colored walls and the neatly painted white trim, the skinny bamboo blinds stained an earthy red that blocked out the sun and provided a close, cozy feeling. Calligraphy posters with the ninety-nine attributes of Allah, and Allah's name and the Prophet Muhammad, all in Arabic with gilded letters, hung from the walls in tasteful frames. The only thing familiar was the black shahada tapestry above the mimbar. Everything else was new. It was a grand space, clean, bright, elegant . . . and empty.

"We must be really early, huh?" Fatima whispered to Mama Tayyibah.

Mama Tayyibah clicked the beads and looked around the empty room. "Not really. The khutbah starts at one o'clock."

The antique wooden clock by the door showed it was twelve fifty.

"Where is everybody?" Fatima asked.

Mama Tayyibah sighed. "Things have changed, baby girl. Something happened. Our congregation's not the same anymore." She stopped and shut her eyes. The clicking of the beads ceased. She looked pained, and Fatima knew it had nothing to do with the cancer.

"I—I . . ." she tried.

Fatima placed her hand over Mama Tayyibah's foot. "It's okay. We don't have to talk about this now."

Mama Tayyibah looked relieved but continued.

"Imam Hassan tried to step down last year, and all hell broke loose. Suddenly every brother wanted to be imam, and every sister thought it should be their husband at the mimbar, never mind the shurah. A lot that had their pride hurt left. Now we got just random folks coming through, cabbies and store owners, no commitment to our masjid, they just want to pray and go."

Fatima looked at the empty mimbar, a little wooden cove at the front where the imam sat until it was time to give the sermon.

"So who's giving the khutbahs now?"

"The council sent a few men. An Arab brother came and left, two Pakistanis from I don't know where, trying to push the sisters upstairs, out on the grass for all they cared. They didn't know our community and just wanted to come in here and change us, giving lectures on how to dress and talk, wagging their heads at our recitations. With attendance already low we really didn't need that, so Hassan started calling on volunteers. It's a mixed bag, but we have a few good ones."

She stopped talking when the doors opened. People were starting to trickle in, mostly men but a few older women too. Fatima recognized a few. Sister Mariam, a plump, stern-faced woman with wire-rimmed glasses and who always had butterscotch candies for the kids in the bottom of her purse. Sister Iris, whose long gray dreadlocks stuck out below her headscarves and who made the desserts and therefore always smelled like brown sugar. And Sister Amatullah, who wore thick polyester jilbabs with matching-colored hijabs and whose skin shone like a new penny even though she had to be close to her eighties. Today she was head to toe in pale yellow, and when she saw Fatima and Mama Tayyibah, she raised her hands above her head and opened her mouth wide in a silent shout then hurried over with her arms spread, ready to hug.

Fatima stood up to greet Sister Amatullah. She held a finger up to Fatima and stooped down to embrace Mama Tayyibah, gripping her shoulders as she kissed both cheeks, then draping her arms around her.

"How you feeling, sister?" she asked, patting Mama Tayyibah's arms like she was frisking her.

"Alhamdulillah. I'm here and it's jummah."

"I know that's right," said Sister Amatullah.

"And I got my daughter here with me."

Mama Tayyibah reached out to squeeze Fatima's hand.

"Oh, yes." Sister Amatullah turned to Fatima and grasped her forearms. "I had to check on my friend first, but now let me look at you." She rested her palms on Fatima's cheeks. Her hands were dry and rough, her fingertips cool. "Oooh," she cooed, pulling Fatima in for a hug. "Masha'Allah, masha'Allah, Allahu Akbar."

Fatima had to stoop down to hug her around her torso. She nestled her chin against Sister Amatullah's shoulder while Sister Amatullah rubbed her hands up and down Fatima's back. It was uncomfortable crouching down to hug her, but Fatima also didn't want to let go. Sister Amatullah's body was so soft and familiar. She pulled away, gripping Fatima's elbows, repeating "masha'Allah" over and over again, while Fatima stood and smiled awkwardly.

"So how's Atlanta, dear? I hear you a big-time writer out there."

Fatima laughed at the embellishment. It was a habit of the elders, their penchant to boost anything the younger ones were doing into something bigger. If you had one trumpet lesson, you were a musician; if you had a tiny role in a school play, you were an actor; if you were considering studying chemistry, you were a scientist.

"No," Fatima demurred. "Just a freelance journalist for some tiny publications. Nothing major."

"That's all right, though, you just keep at it," Sister Amatullah said. "You know, I have a project I'm working on, been working on really." She clasped her hands to her chest, and just as she opened her mouth to speak, the man with the black-and-white kufiya over his head stood and began the adhan. His voice boomed out over the microphone even though there were only a handful of people in the room.

FAR AWAY FROM HERE

"I'll tell you about it later," she whispered and moved to sit down next to Fatima.

A tide of people came in, the men and women parting at the door. Fatima was surprised to see Tahani duck through the door, a smoke-gray scarf draped loosely over her big hair, which stood out of the front. She wore a knee-length white tunic over black leggings, her daughters trailing behind her in sleeveless yellow cotton dresses over white capri pants, wearing white two-piece headscarves, the knobs of their pigtails bulging under the sides, dainty white lace-trimmed socks on their feet. Tahani settled them down at the end of the row, whispering salaams to the women. Aliyah sat down next to Tahani; Safia draped her body across her mother's back, staring at the women in the room. The women cooed and wiggled their fingers at her, but she didn't smile. Still the women beamed like she had blessed them with a show of teeth.

Fatima watched them, smiling, when a flash of white passed her peripheral and the room went quiet. Salaams bellowed out from the congregation. The guest imam had arrived. A young dark-skinned man with a smooth, hairless face, wearing a white thobe and a white turban wrapped around his head, walked briskly over to the mimbar, bending down to shake hands with some of the men, who smiled warmly at him. He carried a Qur'an and a spiral notebook, papers sticking out from the edges, tucked under his arm, his head bowed. He set his books down and rifled through his papers, getting them in order. A man walked over and adjusted the mic for him. He smiled distractedly at the man then looked around to the congregation. Fatima's eyes locked on his. Saif.

Fatima stared openly at him, not caring if anybody saw her. It was like everybody in the room vanished and it was just her and him. She was frozen in anger, shocked. She could have gotten up and left, but she didn't trust her legs. Every heartbeat was a hard thump in her chest.

She blinked and looked around. Everybody's eyes were on Saif, patient, attentive, lips slightly curled in anticipation. Their smiles were fond. She could see Baba Kareem's upturned head in the front row but not his face. Why didn't he—anybody—get up and grab Saif and pull him away like the imposter he was? Fatima looked up to Mama Tayyibah. Her face was stoic, her eyes steady on Saif. She didn't look surprised though. This clearly wasn't his first time being imam.

She breathed in and out heavily. Sister Iris, sitting next to her, looked over at her, her eyes concerned. Fatima forced a smile and tried to stop her raspy breathing, an effort that brought on coughs. Sister Iris reached into her handbag and placed a cough drop into Fatima's hand.

Saif. In her masjid. She didn't stop to ponder the audacity of calling it hers. What was he doing there? How dare he show his face there.

Fatima had spent almost as much time with Saif as she had with Wakeel growing up, more if the time after Wakeel moved away was counted, but they had merely shared the same space, not talking or playing. Saif existed on the periphery, the kid in the corner, Wakeel's shadow. He didn't talk much, and when he did, it was to butt into Fatima and her friends' conversations and disagree with them. Anything Wakeel said he agreed with; anything the girls said he disagreed. They could say it was raining outside; he'd argue them down that it was sunny. They all stiffened when he came around, rolled their eyes and smirked when he spoke. They tolerated him only because of Wakeel.

It was worse after Wakeel moved away. Then they really couldn't get rid of him. He'd find them at the playground and crush their daisy chains with his foot or jump into their double Dutch

FAR AWAY FROM HERE 59

ropes and tangle them up. His favorite thing was to walk up behind them unsuspecting and knock his knee into the backs of theirs. "Stop it, Saif!" they'd shriek. "I didn't do nothing!" he'd shout and run away. Then they didn't see him anymore.

When Wakeel came back to New Orleans and he and Fatima began their courtship, Fatima saw Saif only a few times outside Wakeel's house. By then Saif the chubby bully had become someone else and he and Wakeel's relationship had changed. Saif's unannounced visits were brief. He only came in the evening and never went inside to speak to Baba Kareem or Mama Tayyibah. He would tip his head up at Fatima from where she sat on the porch, and she would nod back. When he left, Wakeel would return to the porch agitated and quiet. He'd shake his head and rub his face like he was exhausted. Fatima knew not to ask him what was wrong. Everybody knew Saif was involved in bad things. She wanted to rub Wakeel's back or wrap her arms around him and lay her head on his shoulder, but all she could do was sit quietly and curse Saif for ruining their evening. Then Saif crushed the seeds of Fatima's happiness like the flowers of their youth, leaving nothing but anger at him in the debris of her heart. His presence now licked the flames of her lingering hurt and grief.

He tapped the mic.

"As salaamu alaykum wa rahmatullahi wa barakatu," he began.

"Wa alaykum as salaam wa rahmatullahi wa barakatu," the congregation returned.

Fatima parted her lips but didn't speak. Saif's thobe reached down to his ankles. He had bulked up, but his face still carried the round chubbiness she remembered.

"I greet you all today," he continued, "with the best of greetings. Peace be upon you, and the blessings and mercy of Allah."

"Wa alaykum as salaam," a few voices repeated.

"Today, I want to talk to you about forgiveness." He didn't look at Fatima, but he was turned in her direction. "Allah is merciful, and He loves when we show mercy to His creations."

The congregation lapped up his words, nodding and saying mm-hmm every time he paused to take a breath. The cadence of his speech lulled them; they rocked and swayed to its rhythm. But Fatima sat rigid, unmoved. She didn't hear most of what he said beyond her own heart thumping in her chest. The man who killed the man she loved was alive and telling others how to live right by Allah. She didn't care what his message was or how he packaged it; it all screamed "fraud" to her. Fake, phony, liar, murderer. Only because she didn't want to disrespect Allah or His House did she stay sitting. She clenched her fists in her lap until he finally finished. Her jaw ached from gritting her teeth.

The man in the black-and-white scarf walked back up to the microphone and hurriedly called the iqama.

Allahu Akbar, Allahu Akbar
Ash-hadu an la illaha il-Allah
Wa ash-hadu ana Muhammadur rasulullah
Haya ala salah, haya ala falah
Allahu Akbar, Allahu Akbar
La ilaha il-Allah

"La ilaha il-Allah," the faithful repeated in unison as they stood and formed rows.

"Shoulder to shoulder, toe to toe," said the man with the scarf, walking back and forth between the rows, stopping here and there to move people closer together.

"Prayer's ready, prayer's ready," he called.

Satisfied, he assumed a spot to the right of Saif, who stood in the center of the row, getting ready to lead the prayer. All heads were bowed except Fatima's. She was looking at Saif. Sister Iris cleared her throat and gently nudged Fatima with her elbow. Fatima bowed her head, wishing unsuccessfully for tears to cool her anger, and folded her hands over her chest.

The room stayed quiet after the prayer. People stood to do extra prayers. Baskets were passed around the room for donations to the masjid. "Jazak Allah khair, May Allah reward you" was written in Arabic and English transliteration on a piece of paper in black marker and taped to the outside of the basket. Fatima pulled ten dollars from her wallet and dropped it in. Several women gathered around Mama Tayyibah, whispering and laughing, their voices rising as the room began to swell with activity. They hugged Fatima and welcomed her back. She softened under their motherly touch; thoughts of Saif slipped away. They asked about Khalilah and her parents.

"It's time for them to come visit," said Sister Clara.

"How long has it been?" asked Sister Juwayriah, peering at Fatima over her glasses.

"Oh, I don't know," Fatima said, "About a year."

"Too long," said Sister Bayyinah, shaking her head. "Too long."

Tahani walked over with her daughters. The women turned their attention toward them.

"Come here, my baby," called Sister Clara to the older one, who was in a better mood now. She squealed and ran behind Tahani's legs as Sister Clara made to chase after her, then popped her head back out to see if she was.

Sister Iris asked Fatima about what she'd been up to in Atlanta. She gave her the same answer she had given Tahani: school, internship, writing.

"No boyfriend?" asked Sister Bayyinah, raising an eyebrow at her.

Fatima stiffened, her face growing hot, and Sister Bayyinah swatted her arm.

"I'm just teasing," she said. "You gotta be careful out there though. Pretty young thing like yourself."

The women laughed and resumed their chatting. Tahani squinted at Fatima. Fatima looked away from Tahani's gaze but felt her eyes still trying to read her face.

Baba Kareem came up to get Mama Tayyibah. The women's smiles withered and they stopped talking at his approach, their eyes measuring him.

He knelt to unlock the wheelchair. Tahani pulled Safia gently off Mama Tayyibah's lap, where she sat perched after climbing up to give her a hug. Mama Tayyibah's face looked ashen, her smile droopy, the circles under her eyes darker and heavier. The women surrounded her once again to hug and kiss her goodbye, their duaa and ameens overlapping each other.

Outside, Saif stood at the gate talking to a group of men. Fatima wanted to turn around and go back inside, pretending she had forgotten something, but Baba Kareem was already wheeling Mama Tayyibah down the ramp. She had no choice but to follow them, and she whispered a silent prayer that they could somehow get by Saif without him seeing her. No such luck though as Baba Kareem stopped and he and Saif shook hands. Fatima knew Saif was Baba Kareem's nephew, but Wakeel was his son. How could he stand to even be in the same room with the man who had caused his own son's death? The other men walked off with Baba Kareem to help him get Mama Tayyibah back into the truck. Fatima was left standing in front of Saif. He looked at her but didn't say anything. She opened her mouth, then closed it. She turned toward the truck.

"You just gonna walk off and not speak," he said to her back.

Fatima stopped and turned around. He grinned. She glared back at him. He huffed and shook his head.

"Still stuck-up, huh?"

"You're unbelievable," Fatima said.

"Cool off, sis. I'm just playing with you. Welcome back."

"I'm not back."

He chuckled. "Whatever you say. So how's Atlanta? You a Failcons fan now?"

Fatima shook her head. "I'm not doing this."

Saif's grin faltered, his bravado diminishing.

"Doing what?"

"You know what. This." She gestured toward the space between them. "We're not friends, Saif. I'm not about to pretend we're two old neighborhood buddies catching up. Do I have to say his name?"

Saif stepped back. He looked pained. Fatima's punch had landed. She turned and left him standing there.

Saif

SAIF TUGGED AT THE BANDED COLLAR OF HIS THOBE AS he watched Fatima walk away. It hadn't felt tight till he saw her sitting with the women. He had considered stepping down from the mimbar and running away, but Allah and the reminder of his responsibility to the community stopped him. He'd swallowed down the choking feeling and made it through the khutbah, the eyes of the believers holding him steady.

There was something about standing in front of the ummah that made him feel good, at least while he was up there. All eyes were on him, but all ears were on the message. He was just a vessel, an instrument, like his father was always telling him in his letters. It was a beautiful thing. He could be there but not there, there in his body, but inside of him gone, just a shadow. For a short period of time, he was with The Unseen, in His Realm.

But now he was back on Earth, watching Fatima walk away from him with disgust, her scorn coating him like mud. Saif turned back to the masjid and saw Brother Abdullah walking across the parking lot toward him, his pace slow and even. He was dressed in a three-piece suit with a tie and a black-and-gold star-and-crescent tie pin, a high, pointed kufi on his head, and shiny wing-tip loafers on his feet. He wore gold-rimmed glasses and kept a neatly trimmed salt-and-pepper mustache and goatee. His cocoa-brown skin bore

FAR AWAY FROM HERE

no marks of age. He walked with one hand in his coat pocket, the other dangling at his side, tapping his thigh.

"As salaam alaykum, young brutha," he drawled, extending the hand that had been in his pocket toward Saif. Instinctively they both extended their other hands too, cupping them around their shake.

"Powerful khutbah, young brutha, powerful khutbah."

"Shukran, Jazak Allah khair, brother," Saif replied, his mood lifting at the compliment.

Brother Abdullah stepped close to Saif, his chin pointed up as he squinted at Saif behind his glasses.

"You know, you used a word during your talk," he continued, "'element.' You talked about the elements of faith. And in that word, 'element,' you have the e-l-m, the elm, like the Arabic word 'ilm,' meaning knowledge. And, see, the ilm is an element of faith. That's what some people forget. We have to *know* our faith, and we have to *know* Allah, the one true God. And we know it, and we know Him, by living our religion. You see? We pray, we fast, we read our Qur'an, yes! But we also have to live it out in these streets. We have to have the ilm, the element, in our daily lives. You feel me, brutha?"

"I feel you, Brother Abdullah, I do. You dropping that science."

"That's 'cause the science is the ilm," he said.

"The element," Saif replied.

"There it is," he said, tapping his lapel with his palm. He wore a thick-banded ring with an onyx stone, Allah's name in Arabic fossilized in silver at its center. "Now, that's what I'm talking about in my new book. Got a few copies with me right now, right here in my car."

Saif smiled and walked with him over to his Lincoln. Brother Abdullah was more than a spoken-word artist or a poet; he was a true wordsmith, always taking words and twisting them and turning them, pulling out letters to tell a story or give a message. It was difficult to keep up with him though. A lot of the younger brothers steered away from him, fearing a convoluted lecture that would leave their heads spinning. Saif had always appreciated the man's conversations, though, and looked forward to them, mostly because it was a treat to have anyone speaking positively to him, giving him real guidance, but also because a part of him knew to hold on to this, even if Brother Abdullah's words were slippery as feathers. They were a gift; they wouldn't always be there.

Saif had all Brother Abdullah's books and tapes, some from as far back as his childhood. He used to hide them in a shoebox under his bed, away from his younger brothers who might try to use them as toys, pulling the strings out then trying to wind them back in with a pencil, but mostly he hid them from his stepfather. If his stepfather had found them, he would have thrown them away as soon as he heard a mention of Allah or Islam. Saif's rap tapes, and later CDs, full of curse words, could be out on display, but anything Islamic or suggesting "that Arabic voodoo" had to be tucked away.

Brother Abdullah opened the trunk to reveal a large crate of books. The trunk, like his car and his suit, was impeccable, the carpet inside clean like it was brand-new. "Tread lightly on the Earth" was one of his frequent sayings. He pulled one of the paperbacks out and placed it in Saif's hands.

"I'm selling these at a discount. Twelve dollars or two for twenty. Comes with a CD. Gotta share the knowledge."

Saif turned it over to the back cover and saw "$8" in the top left corner. He chuckled to himself and pulled out his wallet, giving Brother Abdullah a twenty. Brother Abdullah handed Saif another book and took the money.

"All right, all right," Brother Abdullah said.

They shook hands and Brother Abdullah walked off with a few books tucked under his arm to talk to a group of women who stood together in a tight circle. Saif looked around at the small gathering of people, the clusters of men and women here and there, the few kids, the homeschooled ones, who'd fidgeted through jummah and were now free to laugh and play basketball or run and chase each other. The girls in their white two-piece hijabs and dresses over leggings, their sandals clacking against the pavement, the boys in button-down shirts their mamas and daddies had forced them into, the formerly tucked-in edges now wrinkled and exposed.

Before the storm there had been swarms of people spilling in and out of the masjid doors and trickling out into and down the street, the parking lot too small to hold all the cars, long lines for the supper plates. It was a lot smaller and quieter now. Saif could feel it every time he stepped into the masjid, a sleepiness in the congregation, a tiredness over everything. He thought sometimes maybe he could be the one to wake them up, get the blood pumping again, but Fatima had reminded him of something he didn't like to think about in this space, this one space where he felt a little bit free. He was a fraud. If they knew the truth of who he was, they'd never let him stand at their mimbar, maybe not even let him through the doors.

Saif's phone buzzed. He pulled it out from the slim pocket of his thobe. He saw the name and silenced the call. A mistake, but he needed a minute. He returned salaams from some of the brothers and a few sisters and hurried through the gate toward his car. Cocooned behind the black tint of his windows, he returned the call.

Dupe answered but didn't speak. Saif took in a breath through flared nostrils.

"I'm on my way," he said. "Thirty minutes."

Dupe hung up without saying a word. Saif tossed the phone onto the seat next to him and rested his head back on the headrest, his eyes closed. He needed to keep this up until he had a way out. But that was the problem. He couldn't see any way out. When he thought back on it, the picture of that first time he had gone up to

Dupe and told him he wanted to work for him, that memory so clear like it was yesterday, it was like somebody taking his heart right out of his chest. He wanted to cry but couldn't produce any tears. He started the car and looked back through the rearview mirror; the gold light fixtures above the masjid doors glittered in the afternoon sun.

Before the storm, the whole building would be lit up late into the night. Always a few old heads in there reading Qur'an and praying, dozing in corners for a few minutes here and there, then back at it. Saif used to drive by but never go in. On nights after one his stepfather's tirades, Saif would pull up and watch the light peeking through the blinds, the shadow of movements caught in the corners.

It wasn't like that now though. Sometimes he drove past at one or two in the morning, hoping, but all the lights, except for the ones above the door, were out. Sometimes he wished he could climb in through a window and lay out on the floor on his back, looking up at the dark ceiling, imagining the angels floating above his head, falling asleep with their comfort around him. Sometimes he imagined them swooping down in the night and lifting his soul up with them, leaving his body on the floor. Saif didn't even think he would look back at it, just let himself be carried away.

The only way out he could see would be to leave. New Orleans, he could leave. But this community, this ummah, it was all he had. If he left, he'd have to go far away, and he might not ever be able to come back.

Saif took off his thobe and headed to Dupe's place. Dupe lived way out in Kenner, a one-bedroom apartment in a small brown brick complex behind a strip mall a block off Williams. Inside the gate there was a courtyard with lots of plants and small potted trees and some old patio furniture, battered kids' toys scattered around. The apartments formed a horseshoe around it. The residents were mostly working-class immigrants: Mexicans, Hondurans, and Vietnamese. Saif could hear sounds from televisions and faint thumping beats from Spanish club songs as he made his way back to Dupe's, but he hardly ever saw anybody when he came by, and if he did, they didn't really speak, just nodded at him cautiously.

Saif knocked and a man answered, one of Dupe's associates. The man wore a white undershirt and gray jeans. He had thick, prison muscles. He stepped back from the door and let Saif in, then closed the door and stood to the side of it. Another man sat at a table in the dining area on the other side of the open room. He sat sideways in a chair with one elbow resting on the back of the chair. He watched Saif with no expression on his face.

Dupe sat on one end of the couch in the darkened living room. He wore a black T-shirt and black jeans with starched creases, with red-and-black Air Jordans and a red Chicago Bulls cap with a black brim. A thin gold rope chain hung from his neck. He didn't look at Saif when he came in. The television was on but muted. Saif's feet made no sound on the shag carpet as he walked over. It felt awkward, his sneakered feet on carpet, after being only in socks at the masjid. Had he slipped off his shoes, though, Dupe would have sneered and asked him what was wrong with him. It was one of many small things that reminded Saif he was far from Allah in such a place.

An old Looney Tunes cartoon played on the television, a black-and-white episode with Bugs Bunny tiptoeing through some type of forest, Elmer Fudd in the distance behind a tree with his shotgun, his eyes giddy. He thought he had Bugs trapped, but Bugs smiled at the screen, his raised eyebrows letting the viewers know he knew Elmer was there.

Dupe's apartment was sparsely furnished; the living room held just the couch, a tan wood coffee table, and the television perched on a matching wood stand. A round table with four chairs sat in the connected dining area. No art hung on any of the walls. The door that led to what was likely the bedroom was always closed. The kitchen off the living room sat quiet and dark; Saif never saw any food or dishes on the counter. It was spotlessly clean and freezing cold. He couldn't tell if Dupe really lived there or not. It didn't feel like anybody lived in it.

Still not looking at Saif, Dupe pulled his phone out of his pocket and tapped the screen a few times with his thumb. He set the phone on the coffee table and slid it to the center of the table so Saif could see the screen. Five unanswered calls to him. Saif looked over at Dupe's profile. He wore his beard like Method Man, thin along the sideburns and jawline. He had a tattoo behind his ear, a music note and initials, and more tattoos peeked out from his short sleeves. Saif knew Dupe liked to work out; his arms were all muscle, no fat. Arms that told Saif he could have him on the ground with one punch to his jaw.

Saif swallowed. He knew he had to answer, and fast.

"I had something to do. I got a couple of things on Friday afternoons," he said.

Dupe balled and flexed his fists, causing the veins in his forearms to bulge. He looked at Saif, or rather turned his head in Saif's direction, and spoke over his shoulder.

"Used to be you didn't have nothing to do unless I said you had something to do." He sniffed. "People changing. People changing and thinking they can just do what they want, ain't gotta answer to Dupe no more."

He turned back to the television then sat back, spreading his arms across the back of the sofa. Now he looked at Saif fully.

"You 'bout that life," he said, both a question and an answer. "Way I see it, you gotta be. Only way out is . . ."

FAR AWAY FROM HERE

Dupe wouldn't finish the sentence. There was no need. Out meant lying face down in the dirt somewhere out in the high grass of an abandoned neighborhood in New Orleans East, one of many unofficial graveyards for things no longer deemed useful—old or stolen cars, broken refrigerators and washing machines, sellers who were no longer efficient—hoping in their last breaths that somebody found them before the stray dogs did.

Saif had known that when he approached Dupe when he was sixteen and had nothing to do with his life. But he had never thought that would be him. All he had wanted was a way out of his stepfather's house, away from his mother and her disappointed eyes.

When Saif's pastor stepfather wasn't calling him the son of a jailbird, or throwing out his Qur'an's, he was telling him he needed to apply himself in school, get an education to overcome his low, heathen origins. Saif actually believed his stepfather at one point, tried to shut out the noise of his classmates and listen to his teachers and read the books, but he grew restless. He made decent grades, B's and a few C's, but none of it connected to the real world for him. The only class he liked a little was world history, for the few times the books and the teacher went past Europe and Asia, the few times they opened the door to Africa. That class was the first time he learned about Mansa Musa. He remembered when the teacher said Mansa Musa was a Muslim. An African Muslim. It was like telling him flying elephants existed. For the first time he felt like he might actually be connected to something, like he might have a history, a lineage.

But just as fast as the door had been opened, it had closed back, back to Europe and "civilization"; the oasis returned to a mirage. Saif even wrote to his father about it, figuring he would know and tell him more, but if his father got that letter, he never responded. Saif knew between his stepfather and the prison officials he was missing some letters. It didn't matter though, it wasn't enough. He had all these pieces, his father, Wakeel, Mansa Musa, but they didn't come together to make any kind of picture for his life. All he knew was he needed money, real money, and he needed it fast. As far as he could see, which wasn't further than the end of his own block, this was the only way.

But then Wakeel died. Saif returned to that night on the porch often, before the bullets had stopped flying and he had opened his eyes, realizing he was still alive. Before he'd looked up and seen the other young men crawling across the porch floor toward one figure splayed in a corner. Before he'd heard them say, "It's Wakeel. He ain't breathing."

Wakeel hadn't wanted to be there that night. He'd sat off to the side while the others played spades and smoked, flipping his phone open and closed, probably wishing he was with Fatima. Saif knew Wakeel only still hung with him to try to talk sense into him, bringing him copies of *The Autobiography of Malcolm X* and *The Souls of Black Folk*, talking about Saif's potential and his talents. Except Wakeel didn't talk that night or bring him books. He'd just sulked in the corner.

Saif had been annoyed by Wakeel's presence, barely holding his tongue from telling his cousin to fuck off. That's what made his heart hurt so much; that his last memory of Wakeel was wanting to curse him. He'd been so caught up in his own frustration he hadn't noticed the gray Camry with illegal tint pull up at the corner with its headlights off. When the car sped off from the curb toward them, it was too late for him to react. Shots popped off like firecrackers, spraying the porch where they sat. Saif had thrown himself to the ground, knocking over the card table. The car screeched off around the corner and disappeared, the squeal of its tires soon replaced by the wail of sirens. He remembered crawling over to Wakeel and putting a hand on his cousin's chest, feeling the warmth

FAR AWAY FROM HERE 73

leaving his body as his precious blood leaked out onto the floor. Not realizing till someone shook him that he was screaming, "No!" at the top of his lungs.

It took Saif killing his own cousin to find a reason to live. But by then he found himself stuck in a life, another life, that wasn't his, and this one was even harder to get out of, because he had chosen it. He went from one prison to another. He had really thought at first this job would take him places, and it did, but only to the ugliest corners of this city, places most people didn't go even in their worst nightmares.

Sometimes, a lot of times, being in the dirt didn't seem so bad. It seemed a lot freer than where he was now. Except for the soul. If the dirt was all there was, if it was just an eternal sleep, he would gladly take it. But he knew it like he knew the pulse in his neck: he would have to stand and face Allah, and somehow, some way, he needed to clean the dirt off of him before that time came. Let that be what killed him, his effort to cleanse his soul. So there he went from prayer at the masjid to selling for Dupe, from heaven to hell and back again in an endless loop that he knew would eventually break him.

Saif rubbed his fingers roughly across his forehead, felt the low, pulsing pain beneath his fingertips, the constant tiredness. He took a breath and swiped his palms down his cheeks, steeling himself.

"I'm here, man. What you need me to do?" Saif asked.

Dupe looked Saif full in the face then, his eyes glinting with satisfaction. He had Saif. He knew he had him. They were like two bulls, their horns locked in an endless embrace.

Fátima

TAHANI CALLED FATIMA IN THE EVENING AFTER JUMMAH TO ask her if she wanted to "kick it." There was a spoken-word event at a café in the Warehouse District. The attendants often hung out together afterward, sometimes hitting up a few clubs or a house party. Real casual, she said.

"Black people in the Warehouse District?" Fatima asked.

"Yeah, that's how you know you're in the right location. Look for the brown faces," Tahani replied.

Fatima was hesitant about the venue. It was a coffeehouse by day but served alcohol at night. She didn't go to bars.

"Me neither," Tahani shot back, her voice indignant. "So you wanna go?"

"Umm . . ." Fatima stalled.

"What, you and Mama T got big plans? A *Murder, She Wrote* marathon? Or is it *Matlock* night?"

Fatima snorted with laughter. "All right, I'll go. What should I wear?"

"Girl, wear what you want. You'll see it all out there. Dashikis and miniskirts, sweatpants and halter tops. Dude out there last time I was there had on a whole boubou with the leather slippers and a Big Bird–yellow kufi. It really don't matter."

She told Fatima to be ready by nine thirty. Fatima balked at the time but kept it to herself. She didn't need another old-lady joke.

FAR AWAY FROM HERE 75

She was strangely comfortable with her slow daily routine with Mama Tayyibah. It was like she had checked out from life when she was home with Mama Tayyibah watching old TV shows, lying in bed with her, eating Beatriz's pan dulce or sipping her hot chocolate with crushed dried chili peppers. Beatriz was Mama Tayyibah's nurse, but she was spoiling Fatima. Fatima knew she shouldn't get used to it; it wasn't healthy cooping up in their home like that. Mama Tayyibah knew it too. When Fatima told her she and Tahani were going out, her eyes lit up.

"That's wonderful, baby girl," she said, nestled deep into her bed with a pile of blankets and pillows, only her head peeking out. "Tahani needs some good company too," she added. She grimaced. "I don't know what happened to that girl. Something happened after the storm. She ain't been right since her grandmother died."

Tahani had seven brothers. She was the only girl and the second-to-youngest child. Her mother was strict with them all but especially Tahani. Mama Sajeda didn't seem to like any of the girls in the community really. Anytime she saw one of them she'd give them a sour look. If they even glanced at a boy for longer than one second she'd scowl and chastise them, calling them fast. "You need to put them eyes in a book, girlie," she'd say. Fatima had never known Mama Sajeda to say a kind word to any of them, and definitely not to Tahani.

Tahani was her mother's mirror image. Mama Sajeda kept her hair covered even inside her house, so Fatima never saw it, but she could tell from her light eyes and pale eyebrows that her hair was blonde like Tahani's. Her fleshy, pink lips pressed into a tight line whenever somebody complimented Tahani's eyes or hair. Fatima had witnessed several of Tahani's grooming sessions with her mother. She attacked Tahani's wild, kinky curls with a vengeance, Tahani hunched between her legs, flinching in silent agony while her mother raked a skinny comb through her hair, coaxing it into a tight ponytail since a bun was impossible. She greased and gelled and pinned to flatten Tahani's mane to her scalp. Not surprisingly, Tahani was the first to wear hijab, long before she got her period. On the playground, she'd tugged at the neckline of her headscarf, smacking her teeth and rolling her eyes, but she didn't dare take it off.

Fatima asked Mama Tayyibah about Mama Sajeda.

"She comes by to visit every now and then, brings one of those casseroles that make you sleep a whole week trying to digest them." She stopped and cleared her throat, swallowed painfully. "Get me a sip of water."

Fatima reached for the tall glass Beatriz kept on the nightstand with a covered pitcher of ice water. She held the straw for Mama Tayyibah to sip.

Mama Tayyibah sighed. "Thanks, baby girl." She continued, "Her and Tahani had a falling out though. I tried a couple of times to talk to her about it, even played my cancer card, but that woman is so stubborn. Anytime her daughter's name comes up she turns to stone. All tight-lipped, won't say a word. She always was a tough woman. Can't say we ever been friends. She was real shook by Wakeel's death though. Came over to sit with me, but I ended up having to comfort her, crying like it was one of her boys. But not a lick of sympathy for that girl. Don't even mention Safia and Aliyah when she talk about her grandbabies. She already got twelve, can you believe it?"

Her eyes grew wistful. She would never have grandbabies. Fatima knew from Wakeel that she endured several miscarriages and a stillbirth after having him. She reached for Mama Tayyibah's hand and held it. Mama Tayyibah smiled sadly and squeezed Fatima's hand. If Wakeel had lived, maybe he and Fatima could have given her a grandchild by now. Maybe then she wouldn't have cancer. It was a stupid thought, but Fatima couldn't help but think

FAR AWAY FROM HERE 77

it. One incident, one loss, could shift the future in unfathomable ways. What if Fatima never got married? What if no man could ever replace Wakeel?

Back in Wakeel's room, Fatima rifled through her suitcases. The closet and dressers were full of Wakeel's clothes, so she didn't have anywhere to keep hers. Baba Kareem had overlooked it, and she didn't know how to bring it up. He never mentioned Wakeel. He wasn't Baba Kareem's biological child, but he was the only father Wakeel had ever known. Somebody tried to call Baba Kareem his stepdad once, but Wakeel sternly corrected them. "He ain't my stepdaddy, he's my daddy," he'd told the person. You could never tell he wasn't either. Baba Kareem loved him like he was his and disciplined him like he was his too.

Tahani hadn't given Fatima much to work with in terms of what to wear, so she went by how she felt, tossing aside her jeans. She wore sweats most days now, so she felt like dressing up a little, just for something different. She pulled out a pair of black pants and black suede ankle boots. She paired them with a black sweater dress. She wrapped her hair in a crinkly purple chiffon scarf and applied a deep mauve lipstick for a pop of color.

Tahani called Fatima when she was outside. Mama Tayyibah had long been asleep, so she couldn't greet Tahani, but that wasn't why she didn't come to the door. Fatima saw Tahani's fishnet-clad legs when she opened the car door. Tahani wore a black dress with a cropped leather jacket and knee-high boots.

"Um, okay," Fatima said, taking her in. "I thought you said everybody'd be wearing whatever."

"They will," she said, looking in her visor mirror, dabbing at a corner of her eye with a tissue. "This is my whatever."

Fatima shook her head. "Riiight."

"So who's your boyfriend?" Tahani asked as soon as they took off.

"What?"

She pursed her lips at Fatima. "Don't try to play me. I know a guilty look when I see one."

Fatima groaned. "He's not my boyfriend. He's . . ."

"A friend with benefits?"

"No! He's just—I don't know what he is. He's just a guy."

She wasn't lying. She didn't know what Ishmael was, what this thing was they were doing, or had been doing. She still hadn't called him and he hadn't called her.

After that time at the bookstore, they met up at a café near Five Points. It wasn't a date. Ishmael and his friends met there regularly, he said. "Come hang out" was the invitation sent via text, "if you like intellectual stimulation." Fatima was skeptical but intrigued. It sounded like something set out of a novel in Brooklyn or the movie *Love Jones*. It sounded grown-up.

Erykah Badu's "Next Lifetime" was playing when she walked into the café. Posters of album covers for some of Atlanta's most famous musicians hung on the walls. Next to Outkast's *Aquemini*, someone had stuck a Post-it Note that read, *Where were you when Aquemini dropped?* She spotted Ishmael and his friends in a corner at a large table strewn with paper cups of coffee and small plates of half-eaten pastries, newspapers, notebooks, and books tossed about. Ishmael had his arm around the chair of the girl sitting next to him. His other arm shot up in the air when he saw Fatima, waving to her like she was a football field away and not just a few steps. She waved and walked over.

"Everybody," Ishmael said, "this is Fatima. Fatima, this is everybody."

They all chuckled. There were two women and three men seated. Ishmael proceeded to name everybody. Fari was dark-

FAR AWAY FROM HERE 79

skinned with a close-cropped natural and features that made Fatima
guess she was from the African continent. She smiled warmly at
Fatima. David wore his hair in twists and had on a bright-colored
dashiki. He tipped his head at Fatima when Ishmael introduced her
but didn't look at her. Jaquan had the milky-white skin of the seriously melanin-challenged, long dreadlocks, and a patchy beard. He
put his hand over his heart when Ishmael said his name. "As salaam
alaykum, my sister," he said in a serious, solemn tone. Fatima held
her breath to avoid laughing.

"Over here we have Wild Wayne." Ishmael pointed at the man
seated at the foot of the table closest to where Fatima stood. "Wild"
Wayne was light-brown skinned with glasses and looked, despite
his nickname, mild and bookish. He smiled weakly at Fatima, his
eyes sleepy behind the thin wire frames he wore, and mumbled hello.

"And Rashida," Ishmael finished, gesturing to the young
woman sitting next to him. She had long, straight hair and warm
brown skin. She spread her mouth and showed her teeth in a careful
way, like smiling might mess up her makeup. She tilted her head
toward Fatima and said hi in a soft voice.

"Come sit," Fari said, patting the seat next to her, which would
put Fatima at the head of the table, between her and Ishmael.

Fatima couldn't refuse it, though she had hoped to duck into
the more-discreet seat between Jaquan and Wayne. She clutched
her denim jacket to her chest and pointed in the direction of the
café counter.

"I'll just grab a coffee first," Fatima said, hoping by the time she
came back she could slip into the seat she preferred without anybody noticing.

Ishmael lifted his arm from Rashida's seat and stood up. "No,
I'll get it for you," he said. "Cappuccino?" he asked.

Fatima shrugged. "Sure."

She draped her jacket over the back of the seat and sat down.

She smiled at Ishmael's friends and clutched her purse. "So you're at the university, yes?" asked Fari. She had an interesting accent, a mix of African and British.

"Yes," Fatima responded.

"What are you studying?" asked David, in a tone that suggested there were right and wrong answers.

"Communications."

He bobbed his head slowly, eyes heavy lidded. She had passed the first round, if only barely.

"What about you guys?" she asked around.

"Biology," Rashida said, her face serene. "I'm premed."

David was history, Jaquan African studies, Wayne was English, though he turned the word up at the end like it was a question.

"Maths," Fari declared with a smile.

Jaquan laughed and repeated Fari's answer, mimicking her accent. "It's ma-*th*, girl, not math-*s*."

Fari pursed her lips and chuckled. "Only in America, Jaquan. And you're the African studies major? Tsk."

Jaquan rolled his eyes and faked a yawn. Fari reached over to pinch his nose. Fatima smiled at their playfulness. Ishmael returned with Fatima's drink and a blueberry muffin. He set them both on the table in front of her. Fatima thanked him, surprised. He shrugged in response. He pulled his chair out and over closer to her, on purpose or incidentally, she couldn't tell.

"Hey," teased Fari, pouting at Fatima's plate. "I don't recall getting a muffin when you brought me into the group."

"Yeah, Ish," David chimed in, furrowing his brow as he looked around the table. "I think you owe us all some muffins."

"Hmm," said Fari slowly. "Methinks Fatima might be a special friend."

Fatima pressed her lips together, feeling her face flush. Ishmael smacked his teeth.

"Maaan, Fari," he started but didn't finish, looking off to his side. Jaquan and David grinned, waiting. Wayne looked pained. A flicker of something passed across Rashida's face; she blinked a few times and studied her nails.

Finally, Ishmael said, "That's grown-folks business," and he spread his legs, his thigh brushing against Fatima's. He leaned back and lifted his arm, this time resting it on the back of Fatima's chair.

Fatima couldn't say she wasn't attracted to Ishmael. She definitely was. But it was more than physical attraction that drew her to Ishmael. He was different. Different from Wakeel, different from the life she had known. He was from Chicago, and not Muslim. He wasn't tied to her family, her community, or her traditions.

But to Tahani, all Fatima could say was that he was just a friend, just somebody she knew and hung out with. Ishmael would challenge her to look at the world in different ways, but he would also hurt her and shame her for who she was, to push her toward who he thought she could—or maybe should—be. He was passionate and imaginative, but he was also cruel. She'd come back to New Orleans with the hope of getting him out of her head and heart.

Fatima shook her head. "He's . . . nobody," she said with finality.

"Yes, ma'am," said Tahani. "I hear you on that one."

They rode fast on the highway headed toward downtown, windows down, cool wind causing Fatima to hold on to her headscarf, but she liked the feel of it on her face. It was decidedly unlively for a Saturday night, just a few cars on the interstate. Before she knew it they were at the Tchoupitoulas exit.

"My ex didn't know how to be in a relationship," said Tahani. "Took me two babies to figure that out."

Fatima didn't know what to say. She almost forgot she and

Tahani were the same age. Her issues with Ishmael were a teen drama compared to the heavy stuff Tahani was dealing with. She couldn't relate, so she just listened.

Tahani huffed. "I don't even know how I got caught up with him. First nigga to tell me I'm pretty and I lose my shit. He ain't even all that cute. Alhamdulillah, my babies took after me." She laughed but it was thin, hollow. She smacked her teeth. "I went and did everything my mama said I'd do. Hmm. Turns out she was right all along."

Fatima bit her lip. "Don't—" she tried, "don't say that about yourself. Don't beat yourself up. You can still, you know, do something with your life. I mean, you know, meet a nice guy who'll be good for you and your daughters."

Tahani shifted away from her in her seat, her eyes intent on the road.

"I'm not trying to meet nobody," she said, defensive. "And I am doing something with my life. I'm working and raising two daughters all by myself. I may not have run off and gone to a fancy college, but I'm doing something."

Fatima bowed her head. So this was what it was about. She had "run off." This was what they were now, those who left and those who stayed. She had heard that a lot from people after the storm, people who weren't from New Orleans but had a lot to say about people who were. "Did you leave before or after?" they'd ask, a litmus test for sensibility that determined their level of sympathy. If you left before, you were smart, and worthy of pity for your losses. You were welcomed and offered clothes and food and sometimes shelter, jobs, maybe some money to get back on your feet. If you left after, you were shamed, tsk-tsked for making stupid choices, for ignoring the warnings until it was too late, given all the same things offered to those who left before, but with scorn. You might stay past your welcome. Never mind that it cost money to leave the city for what might end up being nothing. Money for gas that burned endlessly on backed-up highways, for hotels that raised their rates because they knew you were coming, money for food, water, and diapers. Did you get stuck in that awful Superdome with those rapists and murderers? Or rescued off your roof in those helicopters, or off your porch in one of those little canoes? Oh, what a shame, what a tragedy. Fatima heard it for months after the storm, and now it manifested itself differently among the people of her hometown—those who returned, and those who didn't.

"I didn't run off," Fatima said.

"I didn't say you did," Tahani shot back. "But you didn't come back either."

"What was there to come back to?" Fatima asked in a huff.

"Yeah," Tahani said, "wasn't nothing worth coming back to."

They were quiet after that. Tahani's words stung. Fatima hadn't thought about leaving her friend and what that might have meant to her. She hadn't thought about leaving Mama Tayyibah or Baba Kareem, any of the community, really. All she had thought about was the memory of Wakeel, leaving it behind. Fleeing the dead, she had forgotten all about the living.

They passed in front of the spoken-word event. A diverse crowd of people spilled out from the entrance and in clusters up and down the block, their heads bathed in yellow light from the street-lamps above. Rumbles of laughter erupted and various voices rang out. The time on the dashboard read nine fifty. It either hadn't started yet, or the real entertainment was taking place outside. Tahani parked two blocks up on Chartres Street. She kept the car running while she touched up her makeup in the visor mirror.

"Want some eyeliner?" she asked, holding up a skinny black eye pencil.

"Do I need it?" Fatima asked, pulling down her own mirror.

"Let me see," Tahani said.

Fatima turned to look at her. Her eyes close up reminded Fatima of Christmas lights, honey-colored with flecks of green. The cinnamon freckles that dusted her nose and cheeks showed through her foundation.

"Eh," Tahani said, tossing her head. "It's so dark in there I guess it don't matter."

"So I do need it?" Fatima asked, making Tahani laugh.

"Nah, you good, girl," Tahani said. "Looking all fresh-faced."

She closed her visor and opened her door. Fatima climbed out and shut her door. Tahani walked behind the car toward Fatima, tugging the hem of her dress down till it was just above her knees. Fatima walked a little behind her, ducking her head and looking out from under her eyelashes, pulling the loose edge of her scarf across her chest and around her neck. It was mostly an artsy crowd that reminded Fatima of the places she started going to in Atlanta. Mostly everybody was drinking, holding clear plastic cups with dark and light liquids or amber glass bottles of beer.

Ishmael and his crew would have fit right in with a crowd like this, though Fatima didn't know what they'd make of the guys wearing sagging jeans and Cash Money T-shirts, huddled in tight circles twisting their short dreads and passing blunts around, a cloud of smoke above their heads. The weed smoke mixed with the slight overripe-fruit smell of incense burning from a table in front of the wide-open double doors that led into the venue.

A petite light-skinned woman with a mane of thick, curly dark hair sat on a tall chair next to the table, a cash box at her elbow. She wore a long paisley-print skirt and a yellow T-shirt tucked in that accentuated her impossibly tiny waist; half a dozen colored bracelets snaked up her wrists, and long, heavy silver necklaces hung around her neck. She smiled when Tahani and Fatima walked up, revealing crooked teeth.

"Peace, sisters," she said in a voice too deep for such a small person. "Five-dollar donation to get in."

Tahani and Fatima paid and stepped inside. The place was packed. "Natural Mystic" was barely audible over all the people talking and laughing. Fatima followed Tahani, who moved through the crowd like she knew exactly where she was trying to go. People parted for her without her having to say a word. Men looked at her hips hungrily. She stuck her hand behind her, reaching out for Fatima. Fatima grabbed Tahani's hand and let her pull her along. She folded her other arm over her breasts. She could have gotten through the crowd faster if she turned sideways, but then guys would have moved up to press their bodies onto hers. Instead they got her shoulders as she whispered "excuse me" and pushed through. She squeezed her eyes and mouth shut when one man accidentally blew smoke in her face. "Sorry, beautiful," he crooned. She ignored him and kept going. Finally they got through the crowd and arrived at a sofa just to the side of the stage where three men sat. One of them jumped up when he saw Tahani. He was tall, over six feet, with light-brown skin and kind eyes that made Fatima think of Winnie-the-Pooh. His short dreads were held back with a black cloth hair band.

"Whoa, what's happening, Tiger?" he yelled, a big smile on his face.

Tahani smiled sweetly at him, a bounce in her step Fatima hadn't seen before. They hugged chastely, their bodies far away from each other, only their arms and shoulders touching.

"Asaad, this is my friend Fatima. She's from here but she just moved back from Atlanta."

Fatima held her hand out to shake but Asaad placed his over his heart.

"Salaam alaykum, sis," he said.

Fatima returned the greeting to him.

"How you feeling, ma? You want something to drink? Coke, ginger ale? I got the hookup at the bar." He looked around and leaned toward Tahani and Fatima. "Don't tell nobody. I'ma get y'all some Reed's," he said in a dramatic voice.

He left them to get the drinks. Tahani sat on the sofa, and Fatima squeezed in next to her. A burly man next to Tahani frowned at them when she scooched over to make room for Fatima, but she ignored him, flicking her hair in his face.

"You VIP around here?" Fatima teased Tahani.

She shrugged but smiled secretively, raising her eyebrows. Asaad returned and set two tall green glasses with napkins wrapped around them down on the coffee table in front of them. He sat on the edge of the coffee table, his knees knocking the burly man's.

"My bad, dude," he said, holding up a hand.

The man nodded appreciatively. Asaad was charming. His warm smile never left his face while he talked and teased everybody around him.

"They treating you all right in the ATL?" he asked Fatima.

Fatima shrugged. "It's all right."

"Yeah, I was up there for a hot minute after the storm. Cool place. Not New Orleans though. Had to get back home, better or worse." He bounced his shoulders up and down. "The energy, you know?"

Fatima nodded along, although she had no idea what he was talking about. Asaad turned his attention back to Tahani, tugging on the top edge of her boot.

"Looking like a Mad Max Tina Turner up in here." He started singing "Private Dancer" in a hilariously accurate imitation. Tahani laughed and slapped at him.

"Shut up, boy. You stupid," she said.

Fatima sipped on the ginger beer Asaad brought her. The gin-

FAR AWAY FROM HERE 87

ger burned her throat and warmed her belly. She blinked several times as her eyes teared up.

"Good stuff, huh?" Asaad said to her.

"Yo, Saad," a man behind them called. Fatima looked over her shoulder to see a man in glasses with a face like a beagle tapping at his bare wrist.

"Oh, my bad," said Asaad, standing up. "I'ma see y'all ladies later. All right, Mad Max." He tapped the heel of Tahani's boot, winked at her, and walked away.

"He seems nice," Fatima said.

"Yeah," Tahani said, watching him walk away, her voice dreamy.

The lights in the room dimmed and brightened several times until the room quieted down. The stage lit up to reveal the deejay tucked into the corner of the stage, his headphones covering one ear.

"What's happening, folks? Y'all ready for the show?" he asked.

People clapped and whistled.

"All right then, give it up for your booooy, Asaaaad Amiiiiir!"

The theme from *The Price Is Right* boomed out from the speakers. Asaad jogged onto the stage grinning, his fists raised.

"How y'all feeling out there?" he asked the crowd.

More whistles and claps. "We aight," somebody shouted, causing more laughs.

"Who that is?" Asaad said, putting his hand above his eyes and peering out at the audience. "That better not be Malik." A burst of laughter and shushing. "I done told that fool not to come back around here."

"All right, folks," he continued. "We got some cool folks coming up to the mic tonight. But before we start calling them up, I gotta tell y'all a little story."

"Aw, lawd," somebody groaned.

Asaad whipped around, scowling at the audience. Giggles

erupted. This was part of the routine. Asaad launched into a convoluted story about going to the grocery store for his grandmother on his bike, watching the bike get stolen while he stood in line to check out the groceries because he didn't realize the bike was his, not having enough bus fare to get back to his grandmother's, and having to walk all the way there only for his grandmother to tell him he got the wrong items and send him back to the store. He rubbed his forehead and walked in circles around the stage while he told the story, acting out the parts and voices to comedic effect.

It all made sense now. The smiles, the jokes, the people's response to his teasing, their eagerness to receive it. He was the perfect host. Tahani watched him from her seat, her eyes following his every move, a smile dancing on her lips, ready to laugh at his every joke. Fatima looked at Tahani and then up at Asaad. They seemed an odd pairing, but for the way Asaad made Tahani light up, she said a dua for them.

They stayed for the whole show. It was long, two hours, but never dull. There were poets, singers, musicians, and comedians; a monologue was performed and a short play. It was lively and interactive, with the audience encouraging and sometimes participating when a particular poet or singer performed a popular piece. Though Fatima had never been to this event before and didn't know anybody, by the end she felt like part of a family, like they were all gathered together in somebody's living room.

"Thanks for bringing me," she told Tahani after the show.

They were standing outside. Tahani eyed the door. She chatted with a few people, but Fatima knew she was waiting for Asaad to come out. He did finally, long after the crowd outside had thinned and it started to feel awkward standing there. He came out lugging crates of records for the deejay, whose load was significantly lighter.

"Waaaa, what's happening?" he said when he saw Tahani and Fatima. Talking on the mic for hours, entertaining the audience,

FAR AWAY FROM HERE   89

and he was still a bundle of energy. He set the crates down onto the sidewalk with a thud and put a hand on his lower back, his face a caricature of pain. The deejay walked past him and headed over to a white van parked in front.

"This dude bout to have me at the chiropractor. Man, I'm too old for this mess," he shouted at the deejay's back.

The deejay raised his arm and flipped the bird at him. Asaad shook his head and turned back to Tahani and Fatima.

"So what y'all ladies getting into?" he asked.

Tahani shrugged. "I don't know. What's popping?"

"Malik's having a little something at his house. I'm probably gonna grab something to eat then head over there. Y'all welcome to come. You know where it is, huh, T?"

"He stay in Mid-City, huh? On Saratoga? Yeah, I know the spot."

She looked at Fatima and raised her eyebrows. Fatima was tired, but she knew Tahani really wanted to go. She shrugged in acceptance. Tahani smiled and turned to Asaad.

"Okay, we'll pass through."

"Fa sho." He waved at Fatima. "You gon' stay awake, sis?"

Fatima rolled her eyes and smiled. "I'm good."

Asaad walked with them back to Tahani's car. He stood on the sidewalk with his hands in his pockets, looking up and down the sidewalk, his face unexpectedly drawn. It was a kind gesture, him waiting for them to leave, but it also reminded Fatima how unsafe the city was. His action was more than just gentlemanly; it was necessary vigilance.

"Who's Malik?" Fatima asked as they eased into the sleepy Mid-City streets.

"Asaad's cousin, I think. Probably a play cousin though 'cause they don't look nothing alike."

"So where do Aliyah and Safia stay when you go out?" Fatima asked.

"Used to be my coworker Danielle. My auntie's watching them tonight. Her kids are grown, and she don't have grandkids, so she's always asking to keep them. Finally took her up on it. I don't ask my brothers, even though Khalil and Jamii both have girls."

"Why not?"

"They wives stuck up like Umi. I don't know what she told them about me, but they act just like her when I come around, turning up they nose at me and my babies."

Tahani parked on a quiet street that made Fatima think of an ice cream parlor, rows of tightly packed double shotgun houses in an assortment of sherbet colors lining both sides of the street. You could stand on a porch at one end of the street and look down a row of identical porches to the other corner. Fatima already knew which one was Malik's because of the people packed on the porch and in the front yard. It was a peach-colored house with a peach-and-white-striped awning hanging over the porch. The yard was not well-kept, the grass patchy with thick weeds sprouting around the house and in between the cracks in the walkway. Juvenile's "Ha" blared out from inside the house and mingled with harsh laughter and shouts. This crowd was different from the one at the spoken-word event. They stared openly at Fatima and Tahani, looking them up and down. They were overdressed; everyone else wore jeans, T-shirts, and sneakers. Fatima wanted to pull Tahani back and tell her they should go, but there was no way to do it without being obvious. So Fatima looked straight ahead like she belonged there, like she knew where she was, and ignored the stares.

Inside was hot with bodies, the air thick with the smell of sweat, weed, and stale fried chicken. Sade's "Couldn't Love You More" crooned out of the speakers remixed over a bounce beat. A few people greeted Tahani. She waved and hugged a few as they made their way through the house. She stopped in what must have been the dining room just before the hallway, next to a folding table covered in liquor and soda bottles. She stood against the wall and Fatima did too. Tahani swiped her hair out of her face and folded her arms. Fatima leaned back and looked around.

"So what's the deal with Asaad?" Fatima asked.

"Huh?" said Tahani. "Nothing. What you mean?"

Fatima cocked her head at Tahani. Tahani laughed.

"We're just friends."

She was being coy. Fatima was tired and bored and didn't want to be there so she pressed her.

"You seem like you like him. And he seems to like you."

Tahani rolled her eyes and leaned against the wall. "He don't want me. I got too much going on."

"You're not the first woman to be a single mom," Fatima said.

Tahani sighed and shook her head. "It's not that. You don't understand. Look, let's just go. I'm tired."

Fatima was following her back out of the house when a guy stepped in front of her, blocking her path.

"Excuse me," Fatima said without looking at him, then again, louder, too loud because this time a bunch of people turned around to look at her.

"My bad, baby," he said. "You a Muslim?" He pronounced it "Moozlim."

Fatima nodded absently. "Yeah, excuse me. I gotta catch up with my friend."

By the time she got around him, Tahani had vanished. She was heading for the door when she noticed someone in a dark corner of the room who looked familiar, his head bent down looking at a phone. He looked up, and Fatima saw it was Saif. The thobe and turban were gone. He wore black jeans and a red T-shirt with a white cap, a thick gold chain around his neck, and a heavy gold watch on his wrist. He didn't see Fatima and she should have kept going but she was so surprised to see him there. She stepped behind a circle of people and watched as a young man walked up to him and whispered in his ear. Saif nodded and put his hand in his pocket and the other man did the same. They dapped and put their hands back in their pockets, then took them out again. The other man walked off. Fatima stepped away from the people she'd been hiding behind and watched until Saif noticed her. She could have walked on out the door, but her feet carried her over to him.

"Well, if it isn't Mr. Imam," she said. "What are you doing here?"

"I could ask you the same question," he said, looking away from her.

"You selling?" she asked.

He stepped off the wall and stood to his full height.

"What's wrong with you, girl? What the hell you talking about?"

He spoke in a gruff whisper, looking around to make sure nobody was listening to them.

"You still selling."

It was a statement, not a question.

"I don't have time for this."

He pushed past Fatima and walked out the door. She followed him out of the yard and down the street.

"Wakeel died because of you, and you still doing the same stuff. He lost his life trying to save you, and you don't even care, do you?"

He whipped around. "Shut up," he growled at her. "Shut up. You don't know what you're talking about. You think you the only one lost Wakeel? He was my brother. You think I don't wake up every day and feel guilty about his death? I wish it had been me, okay? Every day I wish it had been me."

Fatima shook her head.

"You got everybody thinking you different," she said. "That

you changed. And you got the nerve to stand in front the ummah and tell them about how to make they lives better."

"'Cause you perfect?" he spat back. "The ummah know you out here?"

"Don't try to make this about me, Saif. I'm not the one who got Wakeel killed."

He pressed his balled fists into his forehead. "Look," he said, his voice strangled, "I can't just stop selling. It don't work like that. Once you in this life, you gotta stay in it. Niggas don't just let you go. I'm trying, okay? I'm trying to do right by my brother and not make his death be for nothing. It just take time."

"Time, huh?" Fatima said. "Funny, that's the one thing Wakeel and I both lost because of you."

She turned and walked back down the sidewalk toward Tahani's car. Tahani sat in the driver's seat looking at her phone. Fatima rapped on the window with her knuckle and she unlocked the door.

"Hey," Tahani said when Fatima got in. "I was halfway to the car when I realized you wasn't behind me. You okay?"

"Yeah," Fatima said, buckling her seat belt.

Tahani switched on the inside light and looked at Fatima. "You sure?"

This girl could be a detective. Fatima shook her head.

"Yeah, I'm just tired. Let's go."

Tahani pulled up to Mama Tayyibah and Baba Kareem's house, her tires crunching against gravel on the quiet street and making loud popping noises. She put the car in park, her hand still on the gearshift.

"Good night," she said.

Fatima put her hand over Tahani's. Tahani looked at her.

"I'm sorry," Fatima said. "For leaving you and for . . . not being a good friend."

Tahani's shoulders dropped. She tilted her head and opened her mouth, then closed it. Fatima squeezed Tahani's hand.

"You don't have to tell me it's okay," Fatima said. "It's not. But I'm sorry for leaving like I did and not keeping in touch."

Tahani bobbed her head. A strand of hair was stuck to her eyelashes. Fatima reached over and pulled it away.

"Welcome back," Tahani said.

Fatima couldn't tell Tahani she wasn't back, so she just reached over and hugged her. Tahani's shoulder dug into Fatima's neck and her hair tickled Fatima's face but she didn't care. It felt good to hug Tahani and she didn't want to let go; she didn't ever want to let her go.

Tahani

TAHANI ENTERED THE STAIRWELL THAT LED UP TO HER apartment and slipped her boots off at the threshold so the clacking of her heels wouldn't disturb Ms. Terri, tiptoeing up the stairs for good measure. She flicked on the lamp next to the front door and dropped her keys on the table, an old wooden nightstand she had converted into an end table and stained a pale blue after watching a DIY staining video on YouTube. It was weird coming home to an empty house. The girls had never slept out. Tahani had told her aunt Kim she would come get them, she didn't care how late, but when she called her after dropping off Fatima, her aunt told her the girls were already asleep and Tahani may as well let them stay.

"But they don't have sleeping clothes or toothbrushes," Tahani had protested.

"Ooh, they actually do. I picked up a few things for them at the T.J. Maxx this morning, and I always keep a few extra toothbrushes around."

"Auntie Kim," Tahani groaned, "you know you didn't have to do that."

"I know," she said, "but I was already there picking up a few things so I figured why not. They had the cutest little zip-up footie pajamas in a nice soft cotton with adorable patterns. I picked out two of each, one yellow with teddy bears, the other lavender with clouds, in case they wanted to mix them up. They both wanted the clouds though. I took some pictures of the two of them cuddled up on the couch. I'll send them to you."

"And you know," she continued, "I could send the pajamas back with them if you need them, or I could . . . keep them here with me, in case you need me to watch them again."

Tahani smiled and shook her head as if her aunt could see her. She was so used to doing things on her own she forgot what a treat it could be for a family member to get to spend time with her children, and ditto for her girls. She really had to do better. It wasn't right to deprive them of these connections just because of her own issues.

"You can hold on to them, Auntie, just in case. Just call me, you know, if they wake up fussy or anything," Tahani said. "If it gets, you know, too much to handle." She was floundering; her girls weren't the fussy type, and they went down at night like a stack of bricks. "Just, just call me if you need anything," she finished.

"Mm-hmm," Auntie Kim replied in a way that told Tahani she was being silly and she would do no such thing. "Enjoy your night off, baby girl. You just relax and take you a bubble bath or something."

Tahani ended the call and turned the volume up on her phone and made sure her text notifications were on, as if she were really worried about her daughters. She sat down in the armchair next to the lamp and end table, a bouclé wingback with a red-and-blue ikat print she had snatched up at an estate sale on Magazine Street last winter. She kept an ivory linen footstool tucked underneath, and after she dropped her bag on the floor and took off her jacket she pulled out the footstool and rested her legs on top of it, rotating her ankles a few times. Her calves and ankles were often sore from all the standing she did at the shop. The older stylists were always telling her, when they saw her doing leg lifts and stretches in be-

FAR AWAY FROM HERE   97

tween clients, "Just wait. You gonna feel it all the way up your thighs and in your lower back." Now that she thought about it, she couldn't remember the last time she had actually sat in this chair she'd been so excited to find, or if she had ever even used the footrest. Her daughters mostly used it in their pretend play, propping stuffed animals up on it like a bench when they played school.

Tahani tapped her fingers on the arm of the chair, thinking. She didn't know what to do. Should she make herself a cup of tea and read a book, pop popcorn and watch a movie, or take a bubble bath like Auntie Kim had suggested. She wasn't really a bubble bath type of person. She liked quick, steamy showers that left her skin rosy, but a soak in the tub did sound nice. She had just decided on the bath and was mentally scanning her bathroom cabinet for some bath oil when her phone rang, the jarring ring almost making her fall out of the chair. Okay, maybe the raised volume was a bit much. She looked at the screen and her eyebrows shot up. She pressed the phone to her chest, then pulled it back, biting her lips that were already curling into a smile.

"Hello," she said, trying to keep the tremble out of her voice.

"Whoa, what's happening, Mad Max?"

Tahani laughed. "Asaad? You a mess. What you doing calling me?"

"Ay, you the one gave me your number."

"Because you insisted!"

"Insisted, huh? So, 'Come on, girl, you know you want me to holla at you,' is insistent. Y'all ladies need to make us work a lil harder now, don't you think?"

"Whatever, Asaad! You know that's not how that went."

"Yeah, I'm just messing with you. I just called 'cause I didn't see you at Malik's. Wanted to make sure you got home safe."

Tahani smiled. Despite his banter, she knew Asaad was genuine.

"Yeah, I'm good," she replied.

"Hamdulillah, hamdulillah, that's what's up. Can't have my girl saying I ain't got no home training."

She shivered at "my girl" and found herself at a loss for words.

"Hello? Tahani? You still there? What, you fell asleep on me?"

"No, I'm still here. I just, um, got distracted."

"Yeah, fa sho," he said, his voice turning somber. " I've been known to have that effect on women."

She rolled her eyes. "Boy, you stupid."

He made a sound like he was stretching.

"You at home?" Tahani asked.

"Yep, bout to fall asleep on this couch," he said through a yawn. He began to sing in a sleepy voice. "Tahani, Tahani, ain't got no ta-himey for me."

She chuckled. "What you want, boy?" she asked, leaning her head on the back of the chair, her own voice tired.

"You," he mumbled.

She lifted her head back up, suddenly very awake.

"What did you say?" she asked.

"Mmm," he said, in a voice that sounded like he was already in dreamland, "you heard me."

Tahani pressed her lips together. Her face was hot. Thank God he couldn't see her.

"I—I gotta go, Asaad."

"Yeah, fa sho. Salaam alaykum," he replied.

"Walaykum as salaam," she responded.

She pulled the phone away from her ear and just as her thumb hovered over the end-call button, she thought she heard him say, "Sweet dreams." She brought the phone back to her ear, but he had hung up.

"Sweet dreams," she whispered.

She slid down the chair until her head rested comfortably on the back, her phone clutched to her chest. She propped her legs back up on the footrest and closed her eyes. In her mind, she threw out the tea, the bubble bath, and the popcorn too. Instead she saw Asaad kneeling down in front of her, holding her tight calves in his warm hands and rubbing them with his fingers, his thumbs starting at her ankles and dancing up the front of her calves, hitting all the right spots, his palms cupping the fleshy part just below her knees, kneading her skin till it softened, became pliable as dough. She held that image and let it rock her to sleep.

The thing with going out at night, getting dolled up and pretending to be a regular young adult, was that in the morning Tahani's real life sent her crashing back to Earth. Her alarm woke her at her usual Monday-through-Saturday time, 5:00 a.m. She was always up before dawn for the morning prayer, but at least on Sundays she could go back to sleep for a few hours and experience waking up with the sun high in the sky. But this wasn't a Sunday. This was Saturday, her busiest day of the week. She had to pray, eat, shower, dress, pack bags for the girls and lunches for them and herself, pick them up from Auntie Kim, get them to Mama Jennifer's, and get herself to the shop before nine for her first appointment of the day. The drive to Auntie Kim's and then to the salon would be her only quiet times, but her mind would be racing through all the things she had to do that day. When her alarm went off she shot up in bed. She threw back the covers, and when her feet hit the floor she allowed herself one deep breath. *Bismillah, let's go.*

The salon was housed in a salmon-pink Creole cottage with pale-blue shutters in Algiers Point. A big white sign hung above the front door, CHEZ LA ROSALIE, painted in French Quarter green script with little red rosebuds dotted around the curves of the letters. The owner, Jalisa, was from an old Creole family. She had inherited the house from her grandmother and turned it into a hair salon that she had operated for over twenty years. She lived only blocks away.

Algiers Point was one of Tahani's favorite parts of the city because not a lot of people knew about it, or if they did they didn't think to come out, especially not if it meant crossing the river, even on the ferry that went back and forth from the French Quarter to the Point. Tahani took Aliyah and Safia on a ferry ride once. They had lunch at a restaurant and walked along the Mississippi River Trail, picking daisies to make flower crowns. Sometimes, if the weather was good and she had a little extra time in the afternoon between clients, she walked out by the river to watch the water. Its lazy brown lap soothed her and made her feel a part of something timeless.

She pulled into the gravel parking lot behind the salon at 8:45. Alhamdulillah, she beat Ms. Shelly, her first appointment, so she wouldn't be able to hold that over Tahani's head, talking about "these young girls don't understand responsibility." She'd also beaten Danielle, who's calls she had not returned, but who she would have to face soon enough. Tahani parked next to Jalisa's gold Cadillac Escalade, dwarfing her own practical blue Honda Civic.

She'd picked up a smoothie on the way, one of those super-protein and vitamin-packed drinks with juiced beets, spinach, and celery, blended with fruit juices and yogurt. It would keep her up and on her feet till noon, but with the coffee she'd had earlier, it would also keep her running to the bathroom between clients. She juggled the smoothie and her lunch bag in one hand while she used the other to unlock the shop door.

She stepped in and locked the door back behind her. The lights above the mirrors were on, but the rest of the shop, the seating area and the shampoo and hair-drying areas, were dark. Jalisa sat in her

FAR AWAY FROM HERE   101

booth seat, the one closest to the front door, reading a newspaper, her legs crossed with one Sketchers-clad foot lazily swiveling the seat back and forth. Despite the showiness of her car, Jalisa was always dressed simply in black pants and a black top, her dyed jet-black hair in a neat bun, and her signature red lipstick and black eyeliner.

Tahani had never been in the shop when Jalisa wasn't there; she was always there before Tahani arrived and when she left, even if Tahani had the last client in the shop. She never yawned or seemed tired, and she hardly ate beyond a few bites of salad or spoonfuls of yogurt or oatmeal she kept perched on the top shelf of her workstation. She wasn't one of those zip-around-the-store micromanager types; she moved through the whole day with a cool ease, never flustering or raising her voice. She looked up over her newspaper and smiled at Tahani.

"Good morning, doll," she drawled.

She pronounced the word "dawl." Everyone was either "dawl" or "hawt" or "hun." With her pale skin and dark, straight hair she looked more Spanish or Arab, but when she talked what poured from her mouth was 100 percent New Orleans Creole.

It might seem they weren't about to open by how leisurely Jalisa sat, but with the shop immaculately clean, every tool in its place and all the shelves stocked with products, there wasn't much for her to do. She'd been doing this work for decades so she made it look easy.

Tahani took her phone out of her bag and tucked it in the back pocket of her work pants. The stylists didn't have to, but Tahani had six sets of black scrubs that she wore to work every day, so she wouldn't have to worry about choosing outfits or spilling hair oil or hair dye on them. She washed them and pressed them every Sunday along with the girls' outfits for the week. She knelt down and slid her bag to the very back of the bottom shelf behind the extra bottles of hairspray. She checked her hair in the mirror, fluffing out her curls. She shook out her half apron—where she tucked combs and scissors while she worked—and tied it around her waist.

"Ms. Shelly's coming in at nine," she said.

"Bless your heart," Jalisa replied, her voice deadpan.

Tahani laughed. Ms. Shelly had a reputation for being difficult. She hardly had any hair left, but though most of the ladies her age and with her hair loss accepted it and transitioned to wigs, she came dutifully twice a month for a wash and set, complaining always at the end that the silver curls were too loose and didn't hold.

Jalisa folded up her newspaper and perched it on her workstand. She stood up and stretched, her hands on her lower back.

"You know, hun," she started, "I've been watching you, watching how you work, and I just wanna say you're doing an amazing job."

"Oh, thank you," Tahani said, surprised.

"I'm serious, doll," she said. "Don't tell my other ladies, but you're the only one I trust because you always keep your calm. You're just the type I'd want to turn my business over to."

"Wait, what?" Tahani said.

Jalisa held her hands up like she was being stopped by the police.

"I'm not saying anything, but I'm just saying, I wanna retire at some point, but I wanna see this place keep going, you know? I don't have no kids or nothing, this business has been my life, but I'm kind of wanting to do something different. I've been running this place for thirty years now. You know I'll be sixty next year, right?"

"I did not know that."

Tahani wasn't lying. Jalisa always talked like she'd been around forever, but Tahani thought Jalisa was in her late forties to early fifties at the most.

"Black really don't crack, huh?" Tahani said, causing Jalisa to cackle.

She opened her mouth to say more, but somebody rapped on the door, Ms. Shelly likely.

"We'll talk more later," Jalisa said, then turned to answer the knock. She peeked through the glass then looked over at Tahani. "Get ready," she said in a low voice.

Tahani managed to get Ms. Shelly in and out of her chair with only minor complaints and one or two unreasonable requests. She even mentioned maybe finally getting a wig, at least for special occasions, and having Tahani style it for her. Tahani was writing down recommendations for wig shops for her to try, and thickening (miracle, Tahani thought) shampoos at Ms. Shelly's insistence, when Danielle breezed in carrying the scent of vanilla, her hair glossy in new microbraids, her mahogany skin glowing with bronzer. Whoever this new guy was that had Danielle ditching Tahani's kids clearly had her attention. By then the shop was pretty busy. The two women nodded to each other and kept their backs to each other while they worked on their respective clients. It wasn't until Tahani was sweeping up after her last client, who had moved to the dryer, that Danielle cleared her throat. Tahani stood to her full height and looked at Danielle.

"You was wrong for leaving like that," Danielle said, her tone belying her words to avoid capturing the attention of the few clients still in the shop. They were always hungry for gossip or drama.

Tahani resumed her sweeping. "You are not serious," she said.

"So I had a friend over, so what? The girls were safe and sound on the couch watching cartoons. They didn't even know I was gone."

"The front door was open, Danielle," Tahani hissed. Her heart hammered in her chest. Just like that she was almost shaking with rage, all the more so because she had to contain it.

Danielle flinched like Tahani had hit her. She blinked several times and looked at the floor.

"I'm—I'm sorry," she mumbled. "It won't ever happen again."

"Of course it won't," Tahani spat. "I'm never letting you watch my kids again."

Danielle shifted her weight onto her hip. "Let me? I was doing you a favor."

"Some favor," Tahani said.

Danielle dropped her stance. "Look. I'm really sorry, T. I would never want to hurt your girls."

Tahani softened despite herself. Danielle's phone buzzed. She picked it up and looked at the screen and grinned. She leaned on the counter and began texting, her eyes giddy. Tahani rolled her eyes and untied her apron. She folded it and put it back on the shelf, then grabbed her bag and said goodbye to Jalisa and the other ladies in the shop. She stepped out into the night. It was just past seven o'clock. Her stomach growled loudly just as she spotted the crescent moon, thin as a baby's fingernail. She had skipped lunch, busy with clients.

The next new moon would bring winter, which didn't mean much in New Orleans, but right then it was chilly. Just months before, during Ramadan, she had prayed to Allah late into the night under each phase of the moon, praying for change in her life. Was what Jalisa hinted at, Tahani taking over the salon, was that the change she had prayed for? She wanted to be excited about it, she wanted it to be the spark in the night sky, the possibility, the beginning of something new, but . . . something was missing, a feeling. She couldn't put her finger on it. She probably shouldn't put too much thought into it; it might not even be anything. Jalisa might just be blowing smoke, dreaming out loud.

FAR AWAY FROM HERE 105

Tahani shook her head. She should just let it float away like all dreams.

When Tahani finally arrived home with her girls, she found a thick, creamy envelope in the mailbox, her name and address written in black ink and an elaborate script. The return address held a name she didn't recognize. As curious as she was, she had to tuck it away. The girls were hungry and she had promised them they would have a movie night. As much fun as they'd had with Auntie Kim, they complained as if they had been away from their mother and home for weeks and had not been happy when Tahani picked them up from her aunt's only to shuffle them over to Mama Jennifer's. They had clung to her for several minutes and only let go when she told them they would make their own pizzas and cookies for dinner. They all fell asleep cuddled up on the couch. Tahani only remembered the envelope she had left on top of the television when she went to shut off the lights after she had carried the girls to their beds and tucked them in.

Tahani sat at the foot of her bed and slid her thumb under the flap of the envelope. She pulled the contents out, and a confetti of gold and silver glitter dusted her lap. The first thing she saw before she even slipped the tissue paper covering off was the Arabic script at the top printed with gold ink: "In the name of Allah, Most Gracious, Most Merciful." A wedding invitation. Bilal Abdus-Salaam and Jamilah Muhammad. The last of her older brothers was getting married, and she was cordially invited by her parents, Musa and Sajeda Abdus-Salaam, to witness her brother and Jamilah's union under the Mercy and Blessing of their Creator.

If she was tired before opening the envelope, she was both wide awake mentally and emotionally blindsided from the blow of its contents. With the exception of her younger brother, Hadi, and occasional, stilted conversations with her father, whose gentleness bent like a blade of grass in the wind against her mother's scornful presence, she rarely encountered her family, despite living just a few miles from them. She might see them at Eid prayers or masjid events, and she'd endured a few aqiqahs for new nieces and nephews, but they didn't speak beyond salaams and a bland "how are you." In a city of less than five hundred thousand people, they had managed to avoid each other quite well.

Her heart didn't race, and her breath came slow and steady in her chest. The piece of paper she held pinched between her fingers carried a weight that rooted her to the spot where she sat. She read the invitation from top to bottom three times. Her eyes scanned the lines, examined every letter, looking for clues or some secret code to explain how this message had arrived at her doorstep. She probed her heart, trying to determine how she felt in that moment, but despite how deep she delved, it came back to her empty. She didn't know how to feel.

Fatima

FATIMA SETTLED INTO A ROUTINE. DAYS WITH MAMA Tayyibah, taking her out to the porch late mornings with her tea and her blankets. Afternoons lounging in their bedroom watching old TV shows or movies. The heat finally began to let up a little, the air thinned, promising coolness still just out of reach. Baba Kareem shuffled in and out of the house, ghostlike. That he slept in the guest room was a quiet-as-it's-kept fact that went unmentioned. He and Mama Tayyibah didn't talk much. Fatima heard his soft knock at Mama Tayyibah's bedroom door—*their* bedroom door—in the early morning hours. Sadness cloaked the room when they were together, heavier than anger.

Tahani came by in the evenings, sometimes with her daughters. Fatima bought puzzles, blocks, and coloring books from the dollar store so they could be entertained when they came over. She and Tahani sat on the rug on the living room floor with them, talking while they played, nothing too heavy, but they tried to make up for the lost time, though their conversations were constantly interrupted by the girls. Tahani was good with them, attentive and patient, nurturing. Fatima liked when they came over, the swell of energy waking up the house that creaked with quiet throughout the day.

Fatima continued to go to jummah on Fridays with Baba Kareem and Mama Tayyibah. Sometimes Saif gave the khutbah, sometimes not, but he was always there. He and Fatima didn't speak to each other if they could help it, and when he was at the mimbar, Fatima stared openly at him, unmoved by his words that stirred everyone else. He never looked back at her, his eyes refusing to meet hers when he gazed out at the congregation. She watched him, though, and made sure he knew she was watching him. He wasn't a bad man, she recognized, but she couldn't quell the anger that flared when she saw him. The fact that he was trying only seemed to make it worse. She blamed him, still. *It should have been you*, she thought as she watched him. It was cruel, she knew, she didn't really want him to be dead, but that was the ending that made sense. Fatima comforting Wakeel through his grief and his realization that Saif had dug his own grave, nursing him through the hurt with her own body as a healing balm. She and Wakeel, together, Saif out of the picture. She stood in prayer with the believers, the warmth of her sisters' bodies holding her close, yet her anger at her love's murderer just a few rows ahead of her blinded her. *Why him, Allah? Why did you take Wakeel and leave him?*

Fatima was in the kitchen making tea one evening when Baba Kareem came in. The hard steps of his heavy boots on the wood floor, the sigh as he sank into the chair by the door, his grunts as he pulled off his work boots. Fatima poked her head out from the kitchen to greet him. His head was tipped back onto the chair, his hands folded over his stomach, legs stretched out and crossed at the ankles. Fatima filled two mugs and carried them into the living room, setting one on the table next to Baba Kareem. He opened his eyes and looked over at the steaming mug. His eyes lit up in delighted surprise.

"Shukran," he said, lifting the mug and cupping his hands around it.

He held it like it was too precious to drink. Fatima wondered how long it had been since anyone had brought him anything. She sat on the edge of the coffee table across from him. It was a thick, solid-wood table, so she knew it could hold her weight. He sipped when she did and peered into the mug.

"Mm," he said, "What kind of tea is this?"

"Chai," Fatima said. "Sister Amatullah taught me how to make it. She uses almond milk, but I just used regular milk."

"It's spicy," Baba Kareen said.

Fatima named the spices in it. He nodded his head slowly.

"I like it," he said. "Thank you."

Fatima smiled. "I thought you would."

He asked after Mama Tayyibah.

"She's doing okay. Resting," Fatima said. "Beatriz takes good care of her."

He smiled. "Alhamdulillah," he whispered.

Fatima studied his face. She took another sip of her tea.

"I'm not sure why I'm here," she confessed.

Baba Kareem took a slow sip of his tea. She heard him swallow. He held the mug under his nose and breathed in deeply.

"Hm. I don't even like tea, but this is good."

He chuckled. She didn't laugh with him.

"I screwed up," he said.

Fatima looked at him, surprised. He set the mug down on the table and rubbed his fingers across the lines on his forehead.

"I took another wife."

It was a good thing Fatima was gripping her mug with both hands; otherwise she might have dropped it. She put it down next to her. So many questions flooded her brain, but she was too stunned to speak a single one.

"I didn't tell her. I knew she wouldn't go for it."

"You're old," Fatima blurted out.

He was unfazed by her rudeness. He didn't even blink.

"I loved Wakeel as my own," he said. "It wasn't hard at all. Some men talk about marrying women with kids and talk about how they can't love something they didn't produce, but I never felt like that with Wakeel. The minute I looked at him he was mine. He was so pure, his face wide-open and trusting. Everything about him said, 'Take care of me, love me.'" He stopped and looked down at his hands, his face tight. "It was stupid. Yeah, I was too old for it, but I thought, I don't know, if I could bring another child into this house, it could heal us, you know?"

He looked at Fatima, his eyes pleading with her, begging her to understand. He dropped his head.

"I've never seen her so angry. She yelled and screamed and threw things at me. She didn't throw me out though. Didn't bad-mouth me neither. Just, this quiet rage took over her. I annulled the other marriage, but it didn't change anything. She shut me out completely. I came into the room and she looked at me like I was a stranger. Then she got sick. She let me be there with her, let me take care of her as best I could, but she wouldn't let me hold her. Closest I get to holding her is when I'm lifting her in and out of that wheelchair."

He looked at Fatima again, shaking his head.

"I made a mistake. I did a stupid thing. Thought another baby could make everything right. Foolish old man. That's what she called me. And she was right, that's just what I was. Trying to make up for one loss and now I'm about to lose the best thing that ever happened to me. And the worst thing is I broke her heart. Every day I watch her struggling, getting sicker, and all I can think is none of this compares with how I hurt her. I'm the cancer that's killing her."

He ran his hands roughly over his head and then down his face. Fatima could hear the rustle of his beard as his hands raked over it.

"Thanks," he said. "For the tea. And . . ." He waved his hand in the air.

He got up slowly. The joints in his knees popped as he stood. Fatima listened to his soft footsteps as he went down the hall, the bathroom door opening and shutting, then the sound of water running, the flow starting and stopping over and over. Cupping the water in his hands and running it over his forearms and face, then filling his mouth and spitting it out, sniffing it in then out of his nose. Over the head, neck, and ears, then, lastly, rinsing the feet. He was making wudhu, cleansing himself, preparing for prayer.

Fatima sighed and looked into the milky well of her tea mug, her emotions pulling her down to the bottom with the dregs. She would rise after Baba Kareem came out and they would pray together, her behind him, his voice a low rumble in the quiet living room, calling to Allah, beseeching their Lord to forgive them.

This was what they were left with, the rituals to keep them going, through pain, shame, hurts caused and endured, on and on until Allah called them home. They stood to face Allah, heavy with their shame and guilt, giving it to their Creator, and yet carrying it still, so that when they stood again to face Him, after this life, they might finally be relieved of their burden, lifted and light.

The next morning Fatima woke to sirens. The doorbell rang and she heard Baba Kareem rushing to the door, his choked voice, the thud of many footsteps pounding down the hall. She hurried out of the bed and pulled a sweatshirt over her pajamas and stuffed her hair, wild from sleep, into the hood. She stepped into the dark hallway. Mama Tayyibah and Baba Kareem's bedroom door was open. Baba Kareem stood at the foot of the bed; two EMTs stood at either side of it, bent over Mama Tayyibah, who laid silently. Fatima couldn't see Mama Tayyibah's face, only her feet covered in thick woolly striped socks and her boney legs. Her robe was open and her flannel nightgown rose above her knees. Fatima wanted to run to

Mama Tayyibah and cover her with a blanket. She wouldn't want to be exposed like that.

One of the men, his arms and neck covered in tattoos, blue latex gloves on his hands, pulled a stethoscope from around his neck and bent down to check Mama Tayyibah's heartbeat. Baba Kareem was talking furiously, the other EMT, hands on hips, nodding absently, his eyes on Mama Tayyibah. The one checking her vitals finally stood and Fatima could see her. She was small, sunken into the bed, her face ashen, pinched with pain, eyes squeezed shut.

"We're going to take her in," the EMT said. "She needs fluids."

He turned, saw Fatima standing there, nodded shortly, and walked past. He came back pushing a gurney. Fatima stepped back into the entrance of the bathroom to make room for it, then walked around to the foot of it to watch, clutching the cold steel in her hands. The other EMT placed his hands under Mama Tayyibah's shoulders and thighs and lifted her onto her side, while the first slid a board onto the bed, then laid her back down. Their moves were effortless and considerate, lifting Mama Tayyibah gently and with great care. Fatima fought tears as she watched them carry Mama Tayyibah down the stairs, straps tight around her body. People up and down the block had gathered on their porches to watch, their faces tight with concern.

Baba Kareem handed Fatima the keys to his truck and stood hesitantly at the door.

"I'll call you soon to let you know what hospital we're at," he said.

Fatima put her hand on his shoulder and he looked at her. She cast aside propriety and wrapped her arms around him. He lifted his arms then patted her back awkwardly. She let him go and stepped back. She wished her own father were here so she could have strong arms holding her.

She went inside the house and closed the door and leaned back against it, wrapping her arms around herself. She surveyed the dark rooms, the living room that opened into the dining room that led to the kitchen. The quiet pressed in on her, not threatening but not inviting either; it was just there, indifferent. She pictured Baba Kareem alone in this house and an unfathomable sadness washed over her. They were like a fading picture, its colors washing away, Wakeel, Mama Tayyibah, Baba Kareem, Fatima, vanishing one by one. Who would remember them? Who would call their names and tell their stories so they didn't completely disappear?

PART TWO

Fátima

MAMA TAYYIBAH ENDED UP STAYING AT THE HOSPITAL for three days. The doctor said this was a normal progression of the cancer. Fatima pictured the cancer cells in Mama Tayyibah's body like an angry Pac-Man, gobbling away at her, going up and down and in every corner of her body, taking away all the good. The words "hospice" and "terminal" were brought up. They needed to prepare for her end, the doctor said. End, The End, it gurgled in Fatima's throat. She pictured Mama Tayyibah in the bed, floating, then sinking, sheets turning to water, pulling her down below the surface, folding in like a V, midsection, legs, chest, shoulders, hands, face, and, last, feet, swallowed up into a hole. This was her end.

Mama Tayyibah returned home, but it wasn't the same. She was quieter, she stared into the distance, peered sometimes so intently over Fatima's shoulder that it frightened her. Beatriz was replaced by Penny, a solemn, efficient intensive care nurse. No more singsong laughter and café con leche, no smells of cinnamon and brown sugar. Only rubbing alcohol and disinfectant, smells of decay. Pills were replaced with needles to administer pain relief, drugged comfort that caused Mama Tayyibah's eyes to flutter and roll back into themselves, sinking into painless stupor.

No more jummah. The sisters came to visit, circling Mama Tayyibah in prayer, reciting Qur'an for strength and comfort, for endurance. *La hawla wa la quwwata illa billah.* There is no strength nor might save with God. *Inna Allaha ma'a sabireen.* Indeed, God is with those who are patient. *Inaka kadi'u illa rabika.* Indeed, you are toiling toward your Lord.

Sister Amatullah came every day, her willowy frame wrapped in thick shawls, her starchy polyester abayas perfectly tailored so that the hems touched the tops of her heels. She sat and held Mama Tayyibah's feet in her rough hands, whispering prayers. Fatima was reminded of Sunday school classes, lessons about Azrael, the angel who comes at death and pulls souls at last breath, with ease for the believers, with force for the ones who turned from God. Fatima imagined Azrael with hands as gentle as Sister Amatullah's, Mama Tayyibah's soul slipping from her body like a fish returned to water.

Sister Amatullah found Fatima in the kitchen one afternoon, making a sandwich. Fatima offered her one.

"Chile, I can't have bread during the day unless I want to sleep all the rest of it." She laughed huskily. "That's something you won't understand till you're older."

Fatima looked through the fridge to see what else she could offer her. There was a foil-covered pan with roasted zucchini and squash and smothered chicken that Sister Mariam had brought the day before. With all the women coming by bringing food, Baba Kareem and Fatima could barely get through it all. They told the women they didn't have to, but the women nodded and ignored them, coming every other day with a new dish. Sister Amatullah was delighted by the offering. Fatima fixed her a plate and went to put it in the microwave, but Sister Amatullah stopped her and asked her to warm it in the oven.

"I don't eat microwaved food if I can help it," she said.

Fatima filled a small glass baking dish with the vegetables and chicken and set the oven to preheat. She sat back down across from Sister Amatullah at the table.

"So how you doing with all of this, baby?" She waved her hand behind her toward Mama Tayyibah's room.

Fatima fiddled with the crust of her sandwich. "I'm okay," she said, but this was Sister Amatullah; she didn't have to lie. "Not good."

"You know I lost my mama when I was sixteen," Sister Amatullah said.

"I didn't know that," Fatima replied.

"Mm-hmm, and I was an only child, only living child. My daddy had to take over raising me hisself, he didn't never marry again, too sad. Lasted ten years then he passed on with her. Died of a heart attack while he was working at the pharmacy."

"I'm sorry," Fatima said.

"That's just life. Alhamdulillah. Allah knows best."

"So how long have you been Muslim?" Fatima asked.

Sister Amatullah sat back in her seat and looked up at the ceiling. "Oh, going on about fifty years, I'd say."

"Wait, so that means you were . . . how old?"

"Now you know you not supposed to be asking people about they age." She laughed and patted Fatima's hand. "I'm just kidding. I was about your age, maybe couple of years older."

"Really? I didn't know they had any Black Muslims that far back."

"Well, we started out with the Nation, you know. That's how most of us learned about Islam. People talk about Elijah Muhammad, and he certainly did some unhonorable things, but you gotta give credit where it's due. Wouldn't a lot of us be Muslim today if it hadn't been for his teachings."

"That's actually what I wanted to talk to you about," Sister Amatullah continued. "My project I've been working on. My step-daughters been pushing me for years to write my story down—I think 'cause they tired of hearing me talk about it," she laughed. "But I found myself one rainy morning reflecting on Allah's verse commanding the Prophet to recite and, I don't know, I was inspired. So I wrote a few words down, then I wrote a few more, and well I just been chugging along ever since. Writing in the morning after prayer. I find that I like it."

Fatima nodded along. She had heard these stories so much growing up but had mostly dismissed them as unimportant. The Nation was Black Muslims' past; they'd shaken it off and found real Islam. Fatima hated when people asked her if she was in the Nation, and she vehemently denied having anything to do with it. She responded that she was an orthodox Muslim, a term that made her cringe now.

"But that's where you come in," Sister Amatullah said, causing Fatima to blink and refocus. "I was thinking maybe you could read it and tell me what you think, if it's any good. You think you could do that?"

Fatima pressed her lips together in a weak smile. Her instinct was to say no, but she knew she couldn't do that. She had the time, certainly. She worked up a more genuine smile.

"Yes, of course I can do that for you," she replied.

Sister Amatullah clapped her hands.

"Oh, I'm so excited to have a professional reading my writing. And I want your honest opinion, don't hold back. I'm a tough old woman."

Fatima chuckled. She wasn't enthusiastic about the project. But at least it could give some purpose to her days, some activity, something to point to when Tahani teased her or Khalilah questioned her. She would read Sister Amatullah's story and indulge her with a pleasant review and then be done with it.

FAR AWAY FROM HERE

Fatima's mother called her early the next morning. Fatima had been dodging her calls.

"Salaam alaykum, baby, how's everything?"

"Everything is fine," Fatima said.

She was lying on her back in Wakeel's bed. She sat up and leaned against the headboard, pulling the blanket up over her chest.

"I wanted to check on you," her mother said. "I heard Tayyibah took a turn for the worse."

Fatima filled her in on what was going on.

"And what about you, baby? How are you holding up?"

"I'm fine," Fatima said.

Her mother was silent, holding her breath for more that Fatima wouldn't give her, even now, years after losing Wakeel. Her dejection as her waiting turned fruitless fizzled out down the line.

Fatima didn't know why she shut her mother out. It hadn't always been like that. She had always been a mother Fatima could talk to, share things with. When Wakeel started courting Fatima, her mother became her confidante and advisor, the two of them sitting on Fatima's bed, their legs folded, knees touching, like two schoolgirls. Together they dreamed about the wedding Wakeel and Fatima were going to have, the dress Fatima would wear, the cake and decorations, whether or not she would kiss Wakeel after they exchanged rings, her mother's understanding that Fatima didn't want her and Wakeel's first kiss to be in front of everybody. The fear and thrill of being alone with him for the first time, having him touch her. Then her mother took her back down to Earth to talk about the practical things, the work of marriage, long after the wedding, when the real love kicked in, as she called it. Fatima listened, a little.

She had always idolized her parents' marriage, the affection between them that was palpable, that made her feel like she was intruding on their intimacy, even at the dinner table, the way they looked at each other, into each other so intently, taking each other's words as sustenance for their souls. Her parents' love had always been a little intimidating to Fatima, a little bit frightening to witness, intense but in an unconscious way. It was something that carried its own heartbeat, something big that filled every room they occupied together. They were high school sweethearts, intended to marry after they both finished college, but then Fatima's father found Islam and introduced her mother to it, and amid the fervor of new religion, they married during their junior year. Khalilah wouldn't come till many years later. It was a fact that troubled Fatima. Ostensibly it was because her mother wanted to continue her education, going to graduate school to study social work, but Fatima always felt that wasn't the real reason. Her parents were full with each other, sated just the two of them. Some couples needed children to complete them, to solidify them, but not Fatima's parents. When they looked at each other, rooms, walls, furniture, children could fade away unnoticed. Fatima didn't resent it, never felt unloved. On the contrary, she basked in the warmth of their love. Snuggling between them was the safest, most loving place in the world. Yet she knew from as early as she could remember, without ever being told, to knock before entering their bedroom, to clear her throat before entering any room they shared together, for it would be an energy too powerful to witness. She didn't grudge them that; she wanted it for herself. She craved it without even knowing it, so that when she saw Wakeel, after years of not seeing him, she saw the spark of the fire her parents kept burning for each other, fed daily with kisses, tender glances, light touches. She saw the possibility of deep, boundless love, and she wanted it more than anything in the world.

Fatima didn't grudge her parents their passionate love, but

when she knew it was lost to her, when Wakeel's beautiful soul was carried away with the angels, she couldn't bear to be around them anymore. Their love was a perfume once sweet, turned noxious. She couldn't breathe around them.

Her mother didn't understand. She was hurt by Fatima's rebuffs when she tried to comfort her, stung by Fatima's dismissal of her advice. Fatima's father stayed away, became shy, a line of concern like a smudge of ink on his forehead. Fatima could have pressed her thumb on it to smooth it out, but she didn't. They spent a few months in Atlanta after the storm, in Khalilah's home with her husband and children. Huddled around the television all day and night, endless footage of New Orleans underwater, only the roofs of the homes in their neighborhood visible, their shouts and breath snatched from their throats as they watched the devastation unfold, Black faces screaming for help—Fatima watched it all with indifference. Her parents' agony as palpable as their love, they held each other, clutched tight, two bodies entwined into one. Even in their grief, they had each other. Fatima had nothing. The one she would have held to get her through this grief was the one who had been taken from her. Her empty arms lay limp in her lap. She was numb to the tragedy occurring, only her anger reminding her she was alive.

Fatima balked at her parents' suggestion that she go with them to Houston, the closest place where they both found suitable work. She could transfer to a school there, just give it some thought. Fatima shook her head. The thought of being around them repulsed her. She could tolerate the chafe of Khalilah's bossiness more than the silk of her parents' coddling.

They needled her for details of her life, in their gentle way. She told them she was busy with school, which was true. Her mother, for whom work and family had never been in battle but who insisted on education first, even suggested she meet a man, through the proper channels of course. Khalilah's husband could be a proxy for her father, vetting possible suitors. Fatima reminded her mother of what she had always taught her daughters about finishing school. "I just want you to be happy," her mother had said, her voice heavy with melancholy. Fatima could tell her mother she was fine a million times but she would never believe her; she knew Fatima better than she knew her own self, despite Fatima's belief that she could hide her emotions.

Yet hiding Ishmael from her parents and Khalilah had proved to be easy. They couldn't imagine she would have a boyfriend, and he wasn't Muslim, so their networks knew nothing of him. Besides, Fatima stayed away from the masjid as much as she could help it, only going for Eid with Khalilah's family. She missed standing in prayer with the congregation, the press of bodies squeezing her like a hug, though she convinced herself it wasn't necessary for her faith, even as her relationship with Ishmael grew. She had it under control, she told herself. He was just a friend, and she was mature and enlightened enough to have a friendship with a man. She wasn't doing anything that the young people around her weren't also doing, and actually far less. They were exploring their possibilities, creating themselves, trying on and discarding personalities like clothes until they found the right fit.

Fatima realized then as her mother's sadness pulsed over the phone that she could tell her this, just like she'd shared her fears and desires with her throughout her girlhood. Her mother might not fully understand, but she would hear her, she had always heard her. Fatima took a deep breath and tried.

"Umi, there's this guy," she started. She told her about Ishmael, how they met, how long they'd been seeing each other. Her mother was quiet, unnervingly quiet, but Fatima pushed on. "Umi, are you still there?"

"Yes, of course I'm here." She paused. "I—I had no idea. Well, do you love him?"

FAR AWAY FROM HERE   125

"I don't know. I mean, is it even possible? Can I love someone who isn't Muslim?'

Her mother sighed. "Well, only you can answer that, baby, but I'll tell you what I know. Your faith can wax and wane like the moon, turn from gush to tiny trickle and everything in between. That's normal in life. The person you share your life with, you want them to be there holding you up through all the phases. If you can't find it in you to get up and pray at dawn, or fast another day of Ramadan, will he push you? Will he remind you of what your life purpose is? Before you talk about love, before you even think about it, you need to find out who you are, and who you want to be. Then you find someone who embraces your fullness, who lets you be but never leaves you down."

When Fatima thought of Ishmael, she thought of his gaze on her, the slight smirk in his eyes that stirred something deep in her belly but also infuriated her later when she was alone. He was always studying her, had been studying her since that first day at the bookstore. Fatima had lapped up the attention like a kitten, thrilled to be seen, but it hadn't occurred to her till much later to wonder what it was he saw, and what it was he was looking for.

The first indication came shortly after she met his friends at the coffeehouse. They were at the campus library, just the two of them, studying for midterms. Fatima was shuffling through index cards of notes for her African American literature exam when she looked up and caught his gaze scrutinizing her headscarf. She had it wrapped snugly around her face that day. It was one of her bigger scarves that draped across her chest and shoulders.

She raised her eyebrows at him.

He shook his head. "I don't get it," he said.

"What?"

"It's so . . . patriarchal. Hiding your beauty because a man told you you should be ashamed of what God gave you. Don't you find it ironic?"

Fatima's face burned. She looked down at her study notes. She was so flustered the words just looked like ants crawling around the paper. The words in her head, the response she wanted to give, similarly crawled around, her thoughts scattered crumbs. She could have said, "What man? What man picked out my clothes this morning?" But instead she launched into a history of hijab, how Allah sent down the commandment for covering after the women believers during Prophet Muhammad's time reported being harassed in public. She told him the hijab was meant to mark the women as believers, of an elevated class that were not to be bothered. She went on and on about respect and nobility and honor, ignoring the boredom on his face, the humoring smile he gave her like one would give a small child. When she finally finished he only nodded and pulled his history book toward him. People at other tables had caught Fatima's monologue and looked at her with pity. She blushed and slid down in her seat, trying to hide behind her notes.

She'd thought—hoped—they were done with this line of conversation after her botched lecture, but it turned out Ishmael was just getting started. They'd gone to see a play at the campus theater, Fatima, Ishmael, Fari, David, and Jaquan. "Wayne's having another existential crisis," David said with a scratch of his head as explanation of Wayne's absence. Everyone bobbed their heads in response, clearly used to this. Rashida, who, in addition to studying to become a doctor, also played tennis, painted, and was a member of the drama club, played the lead in a modern rendition of *Othello*. Fatima didn't know what to expect of Rashida's performance and was surprised at how good she was onstage, how she came alive in the role, exhibiting way more personality than what Fatima had experienced during their first meeting. They were waiting outside

FAR AWAY FROM HERE 127

in the cold for Rashida, hopping from foot to foot, and began to discuss the storyline of the play.

David and Jaquan were worked up about the theme of race and interracial relationships in the play. David rejected the whole premise.

"A Black man thirsting over some white woman," he grumbled. "That's some bullshit right there. Classic case of 'getting got' if you ask me. If he hadn't been messing with that white woman, he wouldn't have ended up dead."

"And, see," Jaquan jumped in. "That's how you know Shakespeare was Black."

They all burst out laughing.

"Y'all laughing, but think about it. He ain't saying, 'Don't get with a Black man.' He's telling Black men—*other* Black men—to stick with the sisters." Here he gestured toward Fari with a conspiratorial wink, who responded with a shake of her head.

"You have a point for all your ridiculous claims, Jaquan," Fari said.

Jaquan's eyes grew wide. He pointed at his chest and mouthed, "Me?" Everybody turned in surprise to Fari. As a rule, she and Jaquan never agreed on anything.

"Yes, you do," she said. "However, you're not quite right."

Jaquan's shoulders dropped.

"Haven't you heard of Shakespeare's 'dark lady'?" she asked.

Jaquan shook his head. Ishmael opened his mouth to speak but Fatima was faster.

"Yeah, my African American lit professor mentioned that. There's all this talk of Shakespeare plagiarizing. Apparently it was pretty common for the times. And it's a well-known fact that most of his plays aren't original. Even *Othello* was inspired by a play by this Italian guy, who got it from someplace else too. They all did it. But Shakespeare has all these 'dark lady' poems about this woman he loves but she's too dark and therefore 'ugly' but he still loves her. The one we read in class went something like, 'dark wires be her hair.' But yeah, some legit scholars believe that it was really a Black woman who wrote his plays for him, or he stole them and took credit because women couldn't do stuff like that at the time. I mean even all the actors at that time had to be men, so it would have been a man playing Desdemona."

"White people so weird," Jaquan stated.

Fari nodded her head, beaming at Fatima.

"Yep," she said. "See," she wagged her finger at Jaquan, David, and Ishmael. "Behind every 'great' man is actually a Black woman doing all the work who's had her work stolen by a mediocre man." She smirked at them.

"Mediocre *white* man," Jaquan contended.

"Oh, so you're changing your argument?" Fari teased. "Already?"

"I'm just saying. Real Black men don't compete with Black women and don't steal their shit. So no, I'm not claiming Shakespeare no more. He ain't invited to the cookout."

"But what's really interesting to me, though," Fatima interjected, "is that all the conversation on *Othello* focuses on race and interracial marriage, but nobody talks about religion in the play. I mean, he's called 'The Moor.' That means North African and likely Muslim."

"Hmm," Fari hummed appreciatively. "So what do you think that angle adds to the story then?"

"Well, a big thing that stands out to me is how Brabantio, Desdemona's father, accuses Othello of using witchcraft to seduce Desdemona. It pretty much goes unchecked but that's classic Islamophobia, that Muslims are evil and Islam is a religion that practices devil worship."

They all nodded, except Ishmael, who had gone strangely quiet. Fatima was too worked up to really notice. This was the most she had said to the group, and definitely the most she had said related to her religion probably ever. Everyone else was watching her. She had never had such a captive audience, so she kept going.

"But what really gets me is the violence," she continued. "Othello's so quick to believe Iago, so easily swayed from love to jealousy. I don't know. It bothers me that he's depicted as being weak and easily tricked."

"It is an interesting interplay," Fari said. "I have to say I've never really considered that part of the story, Othello's possible Muslimness. It's surprising Shakespeare didn't reveal Othello's religious identity, one way or another."

"And playing into the stereotype of Muslim men as violent," Fatima added. "Of Islam as inherently violent and oppressive to women. It's noticeable there's no Muslim or 'Moorish' women in the play."

"But isn't it though?" Ishmael finally spoke.

Fatima's face hardened. She knew instantly where this was going, and she began to feel uncomfortable, the spotlight now too bright and punishing.

"Isn't *what* though?" she asked.

Fari and David exchanged looks. Jaquan looked down at the ground and shuffled his feet as if he wished he could make a hole in the sidewalk and slip away through it. In her mind Fatima was thinking, *Don't do it, don't do this.* But it was too late. Ishmael was fired up, and he had an audience too.

"The point of Othello's story as I see it," he said, "is that Islam doesn't fit in modern societies period. That's what kills Othello. His fear that his wife can assert herself over him, be in society he can't, not because he's Black but because of old, barbaric customs he clings to. Killing Desdemona is an honor killing. He's trying to restore some false sense of dignity, trying to assert his authority over her. He's not a stereotype; he's a classic example of the backwardness that is Islam. The only option for him other than rejecting his false religion is to die by his own hand."

Fatima shook her head. "You don't know what you're talking about. Your analysis and reading of the work is all wrong and biased, skewed by your attitudes about religion and religious practice."

"Is it?" Ishmael asked. "One could make the same argument about your own grandiose claims. All this flexing to appear objective when really you just want a positive and false fairytale version of this old religion you insist on clinging to despite all reason against it." He laughed mirthlessly. "What are you even in school for if your religion only allows you to be a housewife? Excuse me, 'prefers' or 'glorifies.' What is even the point?"

"Ishmael," Fari hissed, her face a contortion of disgust.

"No, it's okay, Fari," Fatima said. "I don't need anybody to come to my defense." She turned to Ishmael. "Or ridicule me or try to take me down under some false pretense of knowledge and concern either," she spat. "I have to go," she said. "I've got some useless studying to do."

No one said a word as she turned and stalked off into the cold night. She felt Ishmael's eyes boring into her back, but she kept her head high. Tears stung her eyes but she blinked them back. It wasn't until she was across campus and far away from them that she allowed the tears to fall.

This was the person she was giving herself to, her time and attention, she had thought with disgust and loathing of herself. It didn't make sense. She had thought him mature and worldly but his behavior after the play had been childish and borderline bullying. Why was she punishing herself under the guise of something like love? *What would Wakeel make of me if he were alive?* she thought with horror. But that was the point, right? If he were alive they would be married by now and building a life on shared beliefs and ideas, surrounded by family and community to nurture and support them.

She went home, turned off her phone, made wudhu, and prayed. Her forehead on the cool prayer mat restored her in a way she hadn't felt in a long time. At the feet of her Lord, at His threshold, she felt whole and complete, good as she was, not needing to change a single part of herself. This, this moment alone with her Lord, was right and true and free. She cried again, but this time she felt relief in her chest, lightness and coolness washing over her.

The call from Baba Kareem and Mama Tayyibah came just weeks after that clash with Ishmael. "There's a lesson in everything," her father had told her when Wakeel was taken from her. "Allah never sends any hardship our way unless He intends to teach us something about ourselves."

Recalling this memory while on the phone with her mother, Fatima became angry. She realized how Ishmael had manipulated her, how she had allowed him to manipulate her and make her defensive, when really she should have pointed out that the real irony of his statement was that he as a man was criticizing her personal decisions as a woman. It wouldn't be the last time he would make digs at her faith, calling her submissive, scoffing when she excused herself during outings with the group to go pray. It was coming to Fatima as she spoke to her mother that Ishmael's issue wasn't with her faith, it wasn't that she was submissive to God, it was that she didn't submit to him.

Did Fatima love Ishmael? Most times, she hated him for how he looked at her, that measuring gaze that said she didn't add up. She didn't even know why he sought her out, and she couldn't help but think it was because she was Muslim, because of his ideas about Islam and Muslims, especially Muslim women. She was vulnerable, but not in the ways he thought. The fullness of Fatima? Ishmael didn't know and likely didn't care to see that, let alone embrace it. He would be glad if she gave up prayer and fasting. He wanted to break her, that part of her. She knew that. Yet she was still drawn to him. That was the part that confused her.

It was her own fault, she figured. She could have left him alone, never stepped foot in that bookstore again. He wouldn't have sought her out. No, she laid herself down, a willing prey. With Wakeel she had never had to play these mind games, didn't have to be anything other than who she was, didn't have to hide or fake or pretend to be strong when she wasn't. "Your weakness is your strength." Wakeel told her that once. They gained power when they revealed their weakness, not allowing others to reveal it for them.

"I wanted what you have, Umi," Fatima confessed to her mother. "A great love like yours and Dad's."

Ishmael. What was she trying to do with him? Trying to make him fill shoes he would never be able to? He hurt her with his words, but at least he was honest, brutally honest. She was the one withholding the truth, leading him on. She had tried to shrink herself, shed the important parts of herself, but it was impossible, it would lead nowhere, she risked exploding. People cannot squeeze themselves to fit into someone else's tiny box. She needed to breathe, and, worse, she had cut herself off from her own oxygen supply.

"Why is it so hard?" Fatima groaned.

Her mother laughed and sighed. "Oh, sweetie, it won't be, I promise you. When you know, you know. It won't be hard at all. It will be the easiest and most natural feeling you've ever felt. That's why they call it falling in love. You'll just slip right into it." Her voice dropped. "Now, it's after that slip that the hard work begins."

Falling, slipping into love. Fatima had done that once. She had felt that. But could she ever feel it again? Could it be possible again? Fatima shook her head. She just couldn't see it for herself.

Tahani

SHE HAD TO CALL IN HER BROTHER HADI FOR THIS ONE.

Come over, she told him via text, on her first day off after receiving the wedding invitation.

Per Aliyah and Safia's demands, Hadi was perched on their little pink stool they used when Tahani did their hair, his arms wrapped around his gangly legs. They were playing hairdresser, and Hadi with his golden Afro had the perfect lion's mane for them to work with. Aliyah stood at his left side spinning tufts into two-strand twists while Safia stood at his right sliding a pretend flat iron down his hair. Safia had pinned the front of his hair back with a hot-pink bow at his crown, making him look like a present. He didn't know about the bow, so Tahani had to keep a straight face while they talked. "No peeking," the girls had demanded when they pulled him onto the stool by his legs.

Hadi and Tahani were just over a year apart. When Tahani felt really uncharitable toward herself, she thought Hadi was a consolation prize for her mother after having birthed a girl. Tahani told him as much once, and he'd laughed without mirth. "Some prize," he'd said. Though he was a boy and super smart in all the right subjects, they'd mostly ridden out their childhood in the same boat. They looked so much alike they were mistaken for twins, and Tahani thought for that reason their mother treated them both as castaways, and their older brothers followed suit.

Growing up, whenever someone complimented her mother on her looks, it was like a dark cloud moved over her face. She wouldn't smile or say thank you; she just went stony silent. Everyone said she looked like Vanessa Williams. Even with her tight, white head-scarves, or maybe because of them, her hazel eyes stood out. Tahani didn't think her mother hated her looks, she just despised having to talk about them in any way. They were facts that had nothing to do with who she was. But still, there was something about Hadi and Tahani resembling her, especially Tahani, that bothered her. Compliments, beauty, makeup, and adornments were all things Tahani's mother placed no value in. "Humble yourselves in this world or be humbled before your Lord" was her favorite saying. So after Tahani got over the shock of being invited at all, she and Hadi marveled at the details emerging of their brother's impending wedding.

"A hotel?" Tahani asked Hadi, studying the invitation.

"Yuuup," Hadi replied. "With a live band."

"Shut up."

"Shut up is bad words, Umi," Safia said.

"Yes, habibti, you're right. Umi was just joking," Tahani said.

Safia either didn't know how to or didn't feel like opening the flat iron, so instead she ran the back of it across Hadi's hair, hitting him each time she brought it back down to his head.

"Ouch?" he called, tilting his head to look up at her.

"Sorry," she said. She smiled and pushed his head back down.

All of Tahani's brothers had been married in small ceremonies at a masjid. Only the food had been plentiful, and that was because of the custom of feeding the people. Weddings were traditionally communal events where all were welcome. It wasn't uncommon to see people in the food lines who hadn't attended the ceremony and may very well have walked off the street just to get a plate. After the ceremony and dining the brothers from the masjid would take Sty-

FAR AWAY FROM HERE
135

rofoam containers filled with food and walk around the neighborhood passing them out to people who might be hungry. If there was still more food left over, they'd box up plates and drive out to the homeless communities under the I-10.

"How did Bilal convince Umi?" Tahani asked.

"I don't think he gave her much choice. Apparently it's all Jamilah and her family's doing. They insisted on paying for it all."

"Wow," Tahani said.

The invitation in her hand had to be Jamilah's doing. Tahani wondered how much Jamilah knew about her and her status with the family. She didn't know how to interpret any of it.

"You going?" Hadi asked.

"I guess I have to," Tahani said.

The wedding wasn't until spring. Tahani had plenty of time to prepare herself. She set the invitation on the coffee table.

"So what else is going on in your life?" Hadi asked, stretching his legs out under the coffee table. His knees creaked.

"All right, girls, I think Uncle Hadi's getting tired," Tahani said.

"Beauty takes time," Aliyah stated, her fingers still deep in Hadi's hair. Safia nodded solemnly.

Tahani shook her head at Hadi, who started to shrug, but Safia put a hand on his shoulder and leaned over to look in his face. She wagged a finger at him, her face dead serious. Tahani and Hadi both laughed. Tahani really didn't know where they got this stuff from.

She told him about Jalisa's kind-of, sort-of business offer.

"Word," he said, his eyes widening. "That's dope, sis."

"Yeah," she said, considering.

"What?" he asked.

"I just . . . I don't know." Tahani twisted a strand of her hair around her finger. "I know I should be excited by the possibility of running my own salon, but . . ." For some reason her mother's face popped into her head, a look of disapproval. But that wasn't it. "I just don't know if I see myself doing that, like committing to doing that. Jalisa is always there, like sunup to past sundown. The shop is her life. I don't know if I want it to be my life. I started doing hair because I was good at it, but, I don't know, maybe I could be good at something else, you know?"

"So what do you see yourself doing?" he asked.

Tahani sighed. "You know, I never thought about that." She untangled her fingers from her hair and rested her hands in her lap. "I don't know. I just don't feel like being a hairstylist is it."

"Well, you got time," Hadi said, pulling his legs back toward his chest. He leaned his head back till it was resting on the couch behind him, turning his head back and forth between Aliyah and Safia until they were forced to let go of his hair. "I know what don't got time though. My booty going numb in this tiny seat." He rolled over out of the stool and onto the floor, stretching himself out flat on his back. The girls squealed and jumped on top of him. He grabbed Aliyah and started tickling her belly. Safia tried to squirm away but he reached an arm out and started tickling her belly too. Tahani couldn't do anything but laugh.

Later, Hadi, his 'fro distended from Aliyah and Safia's styling, sat on a chair at the kitchen table while Tahani made them tuna fish sandwiches. The girls had retreated to their room to prepare for a play they were going to perform. Tahani could hear them discussing costumes, who would wear what, and she kept an ear tuned in case their discussion turned into an argument. Safia played her role as younger sibling to her advantage at every opportunity, demanding her way, but lately Aliyah proved she could hold her own.

Tahani chopped a boiled egg and added it to the tuna, then spooned in relish. She looked over at Hadi, who was silently rubbing the stubble on his jaw with the backs of his fingers.

"What you thinking about over there?" she asked.

"Honestly?" He stopped and looked at her, his eyebrows raised. The seriousness of his face made her feel a little cold.

"I'm thinking about how you left the family," he said, his voice soft. "I'm thinking about how Aliyah and Safia don't know their grandparents."

Tahani set the knife down on the cutting board and laid her palms on the cool tiles of the counter.

"Hadi," she started, though she had no idea what she planned to say.

"I'm not blaming you, sis. Trust me. I know how Umi and them can be, but it's just . . . not right. I mean . . ." He leaned forward and rested his elbows on his thighs, then sat back in the seat. "You just don't know how you leaving left a hole in everything."

"I doubt that, Hadi." Tahani leaned back against the wall, watching him. "I seriously doubt that."

"It's true though," he continued. "No one will say it. No one will say anything. But it's true. I feel it. I know it. Especially Abi. When Shaheed and them bring they kids to the house and they all get to crawling around, Abi's smiling watching them but there's a sadness in his eyes. His eyes running over them like he's counting something and he knows there's some missing . . . Umi, too, in her own way."

Tahani didn't know what to say. Hadi, quiet, shy Hadi, too sensitive for his tough older brothers, always watching and reading everybody. It was why he and Tahani connected so well. He could read her without a word. They'd grown up in the house speaking with their eyes, holding each other up when their mother scolded one of them or their brothers teased one of them till they left bruises only they could see in each other. Tahani wanted to say he didn't know what he was talking about, but who better than he would know?

"You don't just leave without leaving a mark," he said, looking squarely at his sister.

Tahani turned back to the counter and finished making the sandwiches, even though her appetite had vanished. She sliced the sandwiches in half and laid them on two small plates and brought them over to the table.

"Thanks," Hadi mumbled, pinching the edges of the plate.

Tahani sat down and put her hand on top of his, felt the warmth of his fingertips against her palm.

"You're right, okay? You're always right," she said, rolling her eyes.

He smiled and slid his plate closer to him.

"Uuuummi, Uncle Haaadi," Safia called from the hallway.

"We've been summoned," Hadi said solemnly, rising from the table.

He took his plate and walked into the living room where the coffee table had been moved to make space for the girls to act out their play. Tahani sat where she was for a minute, pulling crumbs from the corner of her sandwich, what Hadi had said running circles in her mind.

Her life with her family was severed quickly after the storm and the news of her grandmother's death. Her father's mother lived out in Plaquemines Parish, in a little house close enough to the river that Tahani could see it glistening when she stood on her tiptoes and peeked out the little window in the bathroom at the back of the house. She didn't visit her grandmother often, usually only a few times a year. Those visits were awkward with her brothers barely concealing their bored faces and her mother clearly uncomfortable around her mother-in-law, who wore jewel-toned caftans and low-heeled satin slippers embroidered with tiny gold beads and sequins in a wavy design that Tahani traced back and forth with her eyes. The radio was always tuned to a blues

FAR AWAY FROM HERE 139

station, too low for Tahani's mother to turn down under the pretense of disturbance but loud enough for Tahani to hear the scratchy voices rich with yearning. Tahani was fascinated by the cool, dark house and the cool, dark woman who inhabited it, but sandwiched between her brothers and stifled by her mother's watchful presence, she was too stiff to respond to her grandmother's questions about her life beyond a few sentences. Those trips to the bathroom were her only time to peek around the house and try to find its secrets.

One ordinary Saturday morning in early fall when Tahani was about ten years old, her father told her over breakfast to pack an overnight bag. She was going to stay the night at her grandmother's. She looked to her mother, who sat at the far end of the dining table with her eyes down, intently stirring her tea. Tahani nodded solemnly at this news while delight rippled inside of her. She ate her breakfast as slow and neat as she could manage, not wanting her mother to recognize her eagerness and give her any reason to scold her and call off the sleepover. Her older brothers reacted with typical indifference, but Hadi looked pained at the thought of a long weekend without his one comfort. Tahani apologized to him with her eyes, then slipped away to get ready.

Her grandmother greeted her at the door swathed in sapphire and a silky brightly patterned scarf wrapped around her head, thick gold hoops hugging her ears. She bent at the waist to fold Tahani into her arms. Tahani's face was enveloped into the soft fabric of her grandmother's dress, her scent of tobacco and lavender leaving Tahani slightly dizzy when she let her go. She clasped Tahani's chin in her palm and looked at her son.

"I'll be back to pick her up late morning," he said.

"Take your time," she called back, winking at Tahani.

He tapped the porch railing lightly with his fist. "You know—" he started.

"I know she don't eat no ham and ain't no wine in this house, Musa."

She exaggerated the vowels in his name. Whenever they visited she called him Michael, a name that had confused Tahani at first until she realized that must have been his birth name. Her father chuckled and bowed his head.

"Yes, ma'am," he said.

He stooped to kiss Tahani on her forehead, his large palm cupping the back of her head, causing her white headscarf to slip back toward her hairline.

"Be good, honey bear," he said.

They watched his truck back out of the driveway, the gravel under the tires popping and crunching as he pulled away, his shadowy figure behind the windshield getting smaller and smaller. He tapped the horn once and was gone. Tahani looked up to her grandmother. She was the tallest woman Tahani had ever seen, almost as tall as her father, she now realized.

"You ate?" her grandmother asked.

"Yes, ma'am," Tahani nodded.

"Well let's go down to the water and pick some blueberries," she said. "I got some peaches to make a cobbler. You ever had cobbler?"

"No, ma'am," Tahani responded.

Her grandmother chuckled. "Yes, ma'am, no, ma'am. Chile, I hope you know more words than that."

Tahani felt her face flush. Her grandmother chuckled again and said, "Come on and put your stuff down and I'll get us some buckets."

They walked down to the riverbank where, among the tall grass and thick weeds, bushes full of blueberries bloomed wild. Tahani didn't think she liked blueberries, but when her grandmother coaxed her to try one, the warm sweet burst in her mouth was like nothing she had ever tasted. The juice stained her fingers and splattered the hem of her headscarf. She ate as much as she picked and still the bushes were heavy with fruit. She had never had so much fun outside, getting dirty and not caring.

Later, they sat at her grandmother's large wooden kitchen table while her grandmother showed her how to prepare the peaches. Tahani watched as her grandmother set a large pot of water to boil then dropped half a dozen peaches into the water, then after a few minutes scooped them back out with a slotted ladle and into a bowl of cool water. Warm in Tahani's hands, the peaches were so soft the skin mostly slid off under her fingers without the need of a knife.

Tahani had never liked helping in her mother's kitchen, where everything had to be precise and she was often corrected and criticized for doing something wrong. With her grandmother the work was slow and quiet, just the breeze coming through the open windows and the radio playing. Tahani caught a line from a song that she repeated in her head till she'd never forget: *Lover man, oh where can he be?* Despite her grandmother's teasing her quietness, she didn't speak much herself, and Tahani found it was easy to follow her grandmother's motions and made fewer mistakes.

They made dough for the cobbler, cutting a stick of cold butter into tiny cubes and dropping them into a bowl of flour, grabbing fistfuls and blending the butter and flour together with their fingers to make a grainy mix. Then they sliced the peaches and added them to the large bowl of blueberries with brown sugar, cinnamon, and nutmeg. Lastly her grandmother took a jar with a golden-brown spice and shook some into her palm, sprinkling it over the fruit.

"Always put a little ginger in whatever you cook," she told Tahani. "Keeps the heart warm."

After they put the cobbler in the oven, her grandmother set a cast iron skillet on the stove next to a simmering pot and took out

142 AMBATA KAZI

bread and cheese. She told Tahani to sit down at the table and "rest her dogs."

Among the scents of baking fruit and toasted bread, Tahani smelled something familiar but too complex to grasp. Her grandmother set a small plate with a grilled cheese sandwich in front of her, then a steaming bowl of gumbo.

"Had some containers in the freezer," her grandmother said. "That's turkey sausage in there." She pointed toward the bowl. "I told your father I don't mess with pork."

Her grandmother set her own bowl down, minus a sandwich, and sat down. She cupped her palms over her food and mouthed something silently, then picked up her spoon.

"Amen and ameen and let's eat," she proclaimed.

Tahani blinked over the food in front of her, not touching anything. The smells brought her back to school where, every fall, the cafeteria line buzzed with a particular excitement. Her schoolmates stood in line with their trays, impatient to grab a small paper bowl filled with gumbo, then a plate with a grilled cheese sandwich cut diagonally. And every fall, Tahani stood wearily in line, setting a sandwich, and only a sandwich, down on her tray. She sat at the table with her classmates giggling with glee, dipping their sandwiches into the broth from their cups of gumbo. She watched it all like watching a show on television, wondering how it tasted, the toasty buttery bread soaked in broth mixing with warm, gooey cheese. Her own sandwich was dry and tasteless in her mouth.

"I never get to have this," she told her grandmother, who laughed heartily.

"Well now you do, sweetness. Eat up."

Tahani picked up her sandwich and dipped a corner into the rich dark-brown broth. She took a big bite. It was better than she ever imagined.

After that glorious lunch, her grandmother told her to sit on a cushion on the floor of the living room in front of her armchair. She loosened Tahani's hair, now free of her scarf, from the elastic that held it together in a bun. With a wide-toothed comb, her grandmother eased the tangles out of Tahani's hair from ends to scalp, then used the teeth of the comb to gently scratch her scalp, a sensation that made Tahani think of how cats must feel when humans scratch behind their ears. It was the best feeling in the world. With Bessie Smith crooning from the radio, her grandmother rubbed oil that smelled faintly of roses into her scalp, then braided her hair into two French braids.

They ate more gumbo for dinner, then her grandmother spooned cobbler into chipped porcelain bowls with scoops of vanilla ice cream. The combination of warm fruit and sweet, cold ice cream was so good Tahani regretted that she had to brush her teeth, wanting to savor the tastes on her tongue.

The day with her grandmother had been such a dream she wondered if she would be able to sleep that night. She wished she wouldn't have to when she learned where she would be sleeping. Her grandmother had a twin-sized daybed in the corner of her own bedroom, outfitted with pink satin sheets and several white and pink throw pillows.

"I didn't want you to get scared in the night, so I thought you might sleep here in the room with me. I use this little bed for when I'm reading," her grandmother said, somewhat sheepishly.

It was perfect. She laid awake after her grandmother's breaths had evened out, reveling in the feeling of being alone and vaguely womanish with the cool, silky sheets against her skin, while studying the moonlight beyond the tree branches from the uncovered window.

There were other visits after that one, but never alone and never again overnight. The only mention of the time they had spent together was the paper bag filled with blueberries her grandmother gave her at the end of each visit. Tahani ate them one by one in the car ride home, savoring the juice of the berries on her tongue as she pierced the skin with her teeth.

Tahani learned of her grandmother's death weeks after the storm. Her body was found among the rubble of her destroyed home. She was surprised herself by how much the news devastated her and felt stunted in her grief as no one else seemed very affected, even her father. She suspected it had something to do with her grandmother not being Muslim.

Returning to their home in New Orleans after spending several months in Houston, the stifled feeling she'd accepted as her lot began to feel like a chokehold. She began to rebel, refusing to wear her headscarf and staying out late into the night with friends, then not coming home at all. She and her mother fought about her comings and goings, her disrespect for the house rules, and then her mother resigned. "I've washed my hands of you," her mother told her.

Tahani had packed her bags and moved in with a friend, then met and quickly hooked up with Darius. She had convinced herself she had won a battle and was now free, but the victory had felt hollow.

It struck her then, sitting in her kitchen, how they all left marks of themselves in the lives they left behind—Wakeel, Fatima, Darius, her grandmother, herself. She had blamed Fatima for leaving, for not considering who she left behind, and here she was being faced with who she had left behind, the mark of her exit like a stain on wood that could never be rubbed out, a shadow in the corner of the frame, more visible for the absence it reflects. Hadi said Tahani had left a hole. Who else could fill it but her?

Saif

DUPE SENT SAIF TO THE NINTH WARD NEAR THE OLD
Florida projects to make a drop. As punishment for Saif's insubordination, Dupe sent him to spots farther and farther on the outskirts of the city doing the small jobs he typically gave new guys. The drop was in front of a vacant lot across from a faded yellow single shotgun house on Gallier Street. There were only four houses on the whole block, spaced out between empty lots, the ghosts of old homes showing in the thin, patchy grass in the centers, and a small Baptist church on the corner. Even with the sun dipped low, the church gleamed bright and white, sitting on a raised platform. No doubt it had to be one of the churches rebuilt after the storm, one that church groups from other states came to the city for a couple of weeks to revitalize. Wooden steps led up to a wide porch and a single door with thick glass panes.

Saif imagined the cool and stillness of the interior, the polished dark wood pews, white Jesus on a cross at the altar, his head bent to his chest, arms splayed, red droplets at his thorn-wrapped wrists, wax tears pouring down his sunken cheeks. Saif put himself in Jesus's place, pictured himself tied to a cross, sacrificing himself for his people. Better way to die than the way he was living. No altars for him. His body slipped off the cross and collapsed in a heap on the floor where it belonged, turning into ash to be swept away.

It looked a lot like the church Saif's stepfather ministered at, where Saif was stuffed into a shirt and tie and forced to attend with his mother and brothers, the one time they had to act like a family. They sat in the front pew, Saif's mother rigid, her eyes fixed on her husband as he droned on and on, or rocking and swaying with the congregation when the choir punctuated his sermons with songs and collective hums, Saif and his stepbrothers squirming and sweating in the hot room, elbowing each other in boredom and frustration. They all fidgeted, but Saif's mother only ever looked at him.

Saif was seven years old when his mother remarried. He was young, but he knew something strange was going on; there was a shift in his mother. He didn't know if she had ever actually accepted Islam, but she stayed with her head wraps and long African-print skirts for a couple of years after Saif's father went to jail, then it was like one day she came home with her hair swinging down her back, wearing skinny skirts as straight as her hair with pantyhose and heels. She went from talking about when Saif's father got out to not talking about him at all. Next thing Saif knew he was sitting across their dining table from a man in a suit who studied Saif behind thick black glasses, watching his mother fidget over her plate, her eyes flicking back and forth from the man's face to Saif's like she was watching a tennis match. The man won and Saif's mother got a ring and they moved into a three-bedroom house in the Ninth Ward off Almonaster. In just a few years the house filled with one, two, then three more boys who touched and climbed over every surface and filled Saif's stepfather's eyes with a pride he never showed with Saif. Saif moved from the bigger bedroom in the back of the house next to his mother and stepfather to the smaller one near the front door to accommodate his three half brothers. It never seemed to occur to his mother or his stepfather that Saif could have shared a room too. No, it was Saif by himself and the three brothers together, and Saif was treated like a house guest that wouldn't leave.

His brothers were okay, rambunctious but okay, but it was like an unspoken rule, one that they knew and Saif accepted, that he was a stranger in the house, to be acknowledged only when necessary, never brought into the fold. The shunning was one thing, but the scolding from his stepfather grew and grew with the birth of each child. Saif wouldn't have cared if he had Wakeel, but Wakeel moved the same year Saif's first half brother was born. By the time Saif turned thirteen, he was out of the house more than he was in it. He escaped every chance he got, which was plenty since his stepfather preferred him gone, but without Wakeel, without a solid place like Baba Kareem and Mama Tayyibah's to go, he only had the streets to turn to. By the time Wakeel came back, the streets were all Saif knew. The dark and all its dangers had become his home.

Saif couldn't see any lights on at the yellow house. The front door had a block of wood covering what used to be a square of glass. The torn screen door over it hung off its top hinge. A piece of an old rag was stuffed into a broken pane in the window next to the door. It looked like it could be abandoned but Saif had seen worse with people living in them so he couldn't tell. He shut his car lights off but kept the engine running.

The shadow of a tall, stooped figure emerged from around the back of the house, then shrank as it moved closer to the street. He wore a short-sleeved button-down plaid shirt that hung loose on his frame, his jeans saggy and old. Saif couldn't see the man's hands. From the way his elbows stuck out it looked like he had them tucked into the back pockets of his pants. Saif had expected someone younger to come out and meet him, but this man was older, his unkempt Afro flecked with gray and white hairs, bits of it like dust in his scraggly beard and on his chest where it was exposed through his half-buttoned shirt. As the man got closer to Saif, a cold feeling crept into his chest. He knew this man, and when he reached the edge of the grass and the streetlight hit his face it hit Saif where he knew him from.

Saif pulled his hat down lower and wished he had his shades. He couldn't remember the man's name but he recognized him as one of the older brothers that were always present at the masjid. The ones who were there for every function, every nikkah and aqiqah, every janaza, standing in corners in their worn jalabiyas and kufis, bringing chairs for the men and women who could no longer sit on the floor during the khutbahs, emptying the trash cans, serving food at community feedings, only eating or drinking after everyone else, and always away from everyone else, perched on folding chairs in a corner near the kitchen door, plates clutched in their hands. The helpers and the doers, the quiet, hidden ones who seemed to have no lives outside the masjid, no wives or children. The ones who disappeared sometimes and came back, a little worse for wear, but still standing, helping and doing for others.

Everyone knew they had drug or alcohol problems, had probably done some time, lived their lives doing odd jobs, gathering a wardrobe from old clothes donated to the masjid, accepting whatever handouts came their way, cash and canned goods to keep them going. When the pain of their existence became too much they slipped away, unnoticed by most until they returned. How long had this brother been away?

Saif's hands gripped the steering wheel. He could drive away. Pull off before the man crossed the street. But his feet wouldn't move. The man was at Saif's window now, hands still in his back pockets, his body trembling for that hit that would take away his pain, just for a little bit. And there was another presence, in the car and all around Saif, presences swirling and pressing themselves all around him, taking up all the air to where he felt he couldn't breathe. They were watching him, waiting to see what he was going to do.

Saif yanked his hat off and opened the car door, startling the man, who took several steps back, his hands out of his pockets and out in front of him, like he was preparing to block a blow.

"I'm not gonna hurt you, man," Saif said.

The man's name came to Saif then.

"Brother Umar?"

The man stayed in the same position. His wet, black eyes widened, bewildered.

"Imam?" he said.

The word was like a punch in Saif's gut. He shook his head.

"No, brother, no. Not imam. Just Saif." He looked over at the house. "Is this your house?"

Brother Umar scratched his head.

"It's . . . where I'm staying. My brother's old house. He still own it but he live in Florida now."

"He know you here?"

Brother Umar scratched his head again, his body twitching. Saif took that as a no. Umar had found a way into an abandoned home, likely living without water or electricity, sleeping and waking in the dark, slinking away before the sun came up, pacing the streets, getting a few dollars here and there till he could get another score. Saif breathed and took in the darkening sky above them, the twinkle of the stars like question marks, asking him, interrogating him, what he was going to do, as if there really were a choice. He rubbed the back of his neck.

"Come on, man," he said, gesturing toward his car.

"What?" Brother Umar asked.

"Come on, brother," Saif said. "Let's get you some help. I ain't about to leave you out here like this. Come on."

Brother Umar looked back toward the house, rubbing the inside of his elbow and forearm.

"Ain't nothin' there for you, man," Saif insisted. "Come on."

Brother Umar took one more look back, then turned to the car, his feet dragging on the asphalt toward the passenger side. Inside, he sat rigidly, his hands folded in his lap, rocking slowly back and forth like he was cold and trying to warm up. Saif sent a text to a few older brothers. Told them in as few words as possible that he had Brother Umar with him and to meet him at the masjid. He knew they would know without him saying. If Saif didn't notice Brother Umar's absence, they had, in that silent way of keeping track of every single person who walked through the masjid's doors, anticipating their questions before they even fully formed them in their own heads, attending to their needs.

Saif drove slowly out of the neighborhood, up Law Street toward North Galvez, which would take him out of the Ninth Ward and straight to Treme and the masjid. When they hit Galvez, Brother Umar, who had been leaning so far forward he looked like he might fall through the windshield, finally sat back, knocking his head back into the headrest. An ease settled in the car as they crossed Almonaster. Instinct made Saif look right in the direction of the old house where his mother and stepfather still lived and where he hadn't stepped foot inside for the last five years. His mother hadn't even called him during or after Katrina, and when Saif finally called her she'd sounded flustered, her voice faltering when he said it was him. "Yes, we're fine," she'd said. "We're in Saint Rose with Gene's brother's family until we can get back to our home." After a few minutes she said she had to go and ended the call without asking Saif how he was making out or if he needed anything. The few times Saif called every year, the conversations were about the same. He thought about not calling anymore, seeing if she might call him, but he knew she wouldn't.

"I know what it's like to feel alone," he said, not looking at Brother Umar. "Feeling like don't nobody care whether you live or die, like you could just vanish off the Earth and nobody would notice. I wish I could tell you that's not true, that people do care, but . . . they might not. But . . . I don't know, maybe that's not what it's about, maybe that's not why we live. Fact is Allah put us here, in these bodies and in these lives, and we supposed to do something with them, but we gotta find out what that is."

"We serve."

Brother Umar's voice came out like a roll of thunder. From the way he'd been leaning into the passenger door curled into himself with his head smashed on the window, Saif hadn't even thought he was awake. He didn't move from that position.

"What?" Saif asked.

"We serve." Brother Umar's voice was weaker now, fading. "That's what we do. And try to hold on in the in-between."

"In between what?"

Brother Umar didn't answer. Saif put a hand on his back and felt his body clenching and quivering.

"Let's get you some help, brother."

Saif pulled into the parking lot of the masjid. It was long past isha, the night prayer, by then. The lights were on inside and Saif could see the empty prayer space through the blinds. Four elder brothers stood in a huddle under a lone light by the basketball hoop. Imam Hassan was one of them. Saif felt a weight shift deep in his gut.

"Salaam alaykum," he said to the men.

"Walaykum salaam," they returned as one, their voices low and solemn.

Brother Jamii bounced on his toes. He was one of the brothers who was always in the center of the front row at jummah, his face upturned, eager to hear the message.

"Thank you, young brother," he said. "It's a miracle, just a miracle, you finding him. Allah made that happen. Masha'Allah, alhumdulillah."

Saif bobbed his head, not knowing how to respond.

"How did you come to find him?" Imam Hassan asked.

The white light beamed on his forehead, casting the rest of his features in shadows. Saif couldn't see his eyes. Still he felt them on him, studying him, suspicious.

"I . . . I . . ."

"I called him."

Saif turned. Brother Umar stepped silently out from the side of the car and took a few steps toward them, staying in the dark at a distance, his torso tipping sideways.

"See?" Brother Jamii said to Imam Hassan, looking at him then quickly looking away. He cleared his throat.

"Uhm, come on, brother." He held out his arm to Brother Umar. "Let's get you on your way. Closest clinic we could find was in Lafayette. Got a bit of a drive."

"Y'all need me to bring him? Take the ride?" Saif asked.

"No, young brother, we got this," Brother Jamii replied.

"Yeah," Imam Hassan chimed in, his eyes still cloaked in darkness, "we got this. You go on ahead home . . . or wherever it is you going."

The accusation in his voice buzzed in the air between them. Saif stepped back like he'd been hit. His knees felt like rubber. He made it to his car and collapsed into the driver's seat. He would have stayed there resting his head on the back of the seat till his heart stopped hammering in his chest, but Imam Hassan hovered in the distance, waiting for him to leave. Saif started the car and backed out. The back end was close to Imam Hassan, but he didn't move. Saif waved as he turned the wheel toward the gate, but Imam Hassan didn't wave back. Saif watched the imam's shadowy figure shrink as he pulled into the street and drove away.

Fátima

FATIMA WOULD NEVER HAVE GUESSED SISTER AMATULLAH lived alone by the interior of her house. Her oak dining table, where Fatima sat reading through her manuscript, was a massive piece of furniture that seated twelve. She lived in an old-fashioned two-story Uptown home, off Louisiana Avenue, with big, cavernous rooms that could accommodate her timeless, antique furniture. In addition to the table, a china cabinet rested against one wall, a serving table along the other. The window behind Fatima, draped with heavy silver jacquard curtains, washed the room in sunlight.

It was a frigidly cold December day, in the midthirties, the sky cloudless and so starkly blue it hurt Fatima's eyes. She was excited to finally break out some real winter clothes; she had dressed in her bulky oatmeal-colored sweater and gray wide-legged jeans. It wouldn't last long though. The weekend forecast predicted rising temperatures up to the high seventies.

The comfort and familiarity of the house, its warm, creaky wood floors, fresh with the scent of Pine-Sol, the hum of silence broken by the crackle of the heater, like someone rattling a door-knob before opening a door, rustling to life, felt like an embrace. It was, like its owner, ancient and timeless.

The manuscript was handwritten in loopy cursive on yellow legal pad paper. Despite the coffee Fatima had that morning, the words blurred together as she fought off drowsiness. Her laptop sat cold on the table beside the stacks of legal pads. Sister Amatullah had said she wanted her to read it, but when Fatima called her to set up a time to come by, she mentioned having Fatima type up the manuscript too, as if she had asked that from the beginning. Shuffling through the many pages of writing, Fatima felt the enormity of the assignment she had naively agreed to do press down on her eyelids.

Sister Amatullah shuffled in from the kitchen holding a mug, steam curling out from the top. She set it down in front of Fatima.

"Assam with sage," she said, ceremonially. "And a pinch of mint."

Fatima took a small sip of the tea. It was robust and refreshing, like a breath of fresh air burst into a stuffy room.

"Good, huh?" Sister Amatullah said with a smile. Her skin was a warm brown like hot cocoa, shiny as a new penny, without a wrinkle despite her almost eighty years of life. She could easily pass for sixty. She wore a sky-blue cotton abaya, navy blue flowers embroidered around the neckline, and a brown wool cardigan with deep pockets. Fine bones of white ran through her steely gray hair, gathered in a neat bun at the nape of her neck. Dainty pearl earrings jingled from her ears; her eyeglasses, thin pale-pink plastic frames, hung over her sunken bosom from a gilded chain around her neck. Instead of putting them on when she wanted to read something, she held the folded glasses over her eyes, her head bobbing up and down as she scanned the pages. Her fingers were long and thin with nails filed into perfect ovals. They reminded Fatima of piano keys when she tapped them on the table. Sister Amatullah sat sideways, facing the window, one arm resting on the table, her other on the top of the chair. The afternoon sun that came through the window splashed across her face and made her amber eyes flash yellow, her eyelashes glitter gold. She rested her head in her hand, but not in a tired, worn-out kind of way, more like a person in the throes of contentment, her eyelids droopy with fullness. She didn't speak, didn't even seem to notice Fatima in the room with her anymore, a smile dancing on her lips in a quiet reverie. The tea had revived Fatima's senses. The letters on the page fused back into solid, unmoving words. She folded her legs onto the seat of the chair and tucked back into the pages.

I was born in 1935 in New Orleans, Louisiana, named Amalie Jean Wilkins for my maternal and paternal grandmothers, respectively. My mother, Patricia Ann Blache, came from an old Creole New Orleans family, roots older than New Orleans itself. She was milky brown just like café au lait and soft and round as the sweet, puffy dough on the inside of a beignet. My father, Robert Gerard Wilkins, was from Mississippi and black as molasses, very tall and very thin with a long, skinny face.

Last of the four children my mother bore, I was the only one to survive past my baby years. Miracle baby, everybody called me. My mama loved me, thankfully. Sometimes women go through things like what she went through and have so much grief they don't know how to love the ones that's alive, but not my mother. She went the other way. Cared for me like I was one of them rare porcelain vases from the Ming dynasty and she had butter on her hands. I couldn't hardly do nothing. My daddy said, "Leave that girl alone. Let her run and skin her knees. It'll make her strong." He lost that fight though. Mama wasn't having it. So I snuck away as much as I could and hid my scars.

My mama went to St. Paul Catholic Church on Chef Menteur Highway every Sunday. Volunteered for Sunday school too, even though those bad kids ran her ragged till when she got home she had to lie down in the dark on top the covers, her arm thrown over her eyes like she couldn't stand to see the world anymore, at least for an hour or so.

She went to the church smelling of Dove soap and Chantilly Lace and lit those short red glass candles, stood in the communion line, white-gloved hands clutched to her chest, lips trembling to receive those funny little white wafers and drink the red liquid from the shiny gold goblet the church boys held out, wiping the goblet with a white cloth after each sip. Oh my mouth watered to try it too. Was the juice sweet or tart? Was the wafer chewy or hard? I never saw anybody turn back to the aisle chewing. Did they just swallow it down or did it dissolve on their tongue like an Alka-Seltzer in water? Or did they suck on it like a peppermint, maybe? I wanted to know but my mama only frowned when I asked. Said I was thinking about the wrong things. I was one of the only few who didn't stand for communion. I wasn't allowed to go up to the altar because I wasn't baptized.

I wasn't baptized because my daddy wouldn't let me. I realize now my father was a unique man for his time, or at least more outspoken and obstinate than the other Christians we knew, who just wanted to keep quiet and keep to tradition. He wore a shiny gold cross every day, never took it off for nothing. You could see it in the little hollow space of his throat, just above the buttons of his shirt. Wore it till his grave. But I also never saw him step foot in any church, not my mama's nor anybody else's, except for weddings, baptisms, and funerals, or if he was fixing something in one. It was him and my mama's "bone of contention," as my mother put it when I asked and she forgot to stop me for being "impertinent," which was her way of saying "minding grown folks' business."

FAR AWAY FROM HERE 157

She was always reading the dictionary and made me look up every word I didn't know when I read to her from one of our encyclopedias, which I did every evening while she cooked dinner. We had our twenty-six-volumes encyclopedia set, our big red Merck medical manual, a Merriam-Webster dictionary, and the Bible. My daddy had his National Geographic magazines, but I wasn't allowed to look at them because they had people without clothes in them. So of course I smuggled them under my shirt and hid in the bathroom—the only place I could ever have privacy, and even then my mama came knocking after five minutes. If only she knew the pictures in the Merck were way more shocking. But I digress.

My father was a Mr. Fix-It. An electrician, officially. And a carpenter. But he also worked on cars, fixed plumbing, painted houses, whatever you can think of that needed hands. He could fix anything and did a lot of odd jobs around the neighborhood. Anyway, he said he didn't need to go to church because God was everywhere. He was as close to God with a hammer and nails on somebody's roof or under they house with a wrench as he would be stuffed into a suit sitting on one of them hard pews. My mother shook her head and crossed herself, kissing her knuckles for good measure.

He let me go to church—"only if she wants to," he told my mama—but wouldn't let me get baptized till I was old enough to decide for myself. That meant eighteen years old, and wouldn't you know by then I wasn't interested in wafers and goblets, or candles and kneeling anymore. By then it was the fifties and the only thing I wanted to kneel for was the anthem at our football games. Instead of National Geographics, it was a black beret I had tucked into the waist of my skirt when I left my parent's house. That's something my mother and father agreed on. They didn't want no daughter of theirs marching the streets raising a fist, chanting and singing. My mother, though, she was quietly proud of the student activists, led by the words of the Alabama preacher Dr. Martin Luther King Jr., despite asking where their mothers were. I saw that pride in her eyes, wet and shiny, lit up by the lights of the television. The little twitch of a smile amid the horror of watching young people dragged out of restaurants, their clothes and faces smeared with thrown food and condiments but still beaming defiantly. Sicced by dogs and hit with water hoses that bit into their skin but still they stood up. She was proud, yeah?

But I was still her only child, her daughter and her miracle baby. I never wore the beret. But I liked the feel of the coarse wool rubbing against my ribcage, just below my heart. Now I think of it, that scratchy feeling carried the zeal of the old Christian monks with their hairshirts, not that my mother, with her strict religious enthusiasm, would ever appreciate such a comparison. May God have mercy on her soul.

What would she think of me now, dressed in a way that people mistake me for a nun? Her only child, her miracle, a Muslim. She didn't live to see it. Died the same year I first heard The Minister speak. Minister Malcolm. And guess who hipped me to his words? My father. Sitting in his armchair at the radio nursing a whiskey, pretending he was reveling in new bachelorhood and didn't miss my mother so badly he cried like a whooping cough every night.

My daddy, who believed in choice, distrusted the church, had no patience for protests and sit-ins, grunted in grudging appreciation of The Minister's words because he knew they carried action, not just the threat or promise of action but the inevitability of it. I heard it too. I didn't need a beret. I

FAR AWAY FROM HERE 159

donned a scarf. Covered my arms and my legs. Stood tall.

My daddy didn't like it. Not one bit. But with one reminder from me, the first time I ever spoke up to my father, conjuring my mama's quiet, confident spirit, he backed down. I had decided for myself. He'd said all those years ago to my mother, "Let the girl choose." Well now the girl had chosen. Allah and His Messenger.

My birth name, Amalie, means someone who works hard and with eagerness. Most people now know me as Amatullah, which means a female servant of God. I never officially changed it though. I considered it, but it was the one thing my father asked me not to do. Said my name had been chosen with love to honor my ancestors, and it was important to stay connected to my heritage. I respected his request and I can see the wisdom in it now.

There was always something strange about my father. He was so tall and dark and slender. Folks never thought he was from New Orleans, even from this country, till they heard him speak. They called him "The African." I heard it, but I never thought much of it till much later when my feet were in African soil, my ankles and calves and the hem of my long skirt caked in mud and dust. Senegal. First thing I noticed, I was surrounded by my father. He was dead but all around me. All the men looked like my daddy.

And I remembered something, once. Something I'd buried deep in my mind, tucked away as a dream. A cold night, many, many years in the past. I'd woken in the night afraid. Despite the cold I threw back the covers, wanting, needing my father right at that moment. My mother lay alone in my parent's bed, my father's side dented but filled only by moonlight. Finally I found him in the living room. He was standing with his back to me, looking down at his feet. I called, "Daddy," I'm sure of it. But he didn't answer. I became afraid and my feet felt like they were stuck to the ground. He bent down at the waist, a low bow. Then he stood and then he was on his knees, pressing his face into the floor. Something in my head told me this was not for me to see. I backed away and ran back to my room. I buried myself in blankets and at some point slept.

The next morning, shyly, I asked my father about what I had seen him doing during the night, thinking maybe he had a secret exercise he only did after everybody else was sleeping. He laid the backs of his fingers against my forehead, then my cheeks, then under my chin. He thought I had a fever. He said I must have been dreaming. I said okay.

But there I was, in Africa, surrounded by African men and women, tall and slender and dark as my father, "The African." Their backs to me as I stood in the recesses of the dark, cool prayer hall, bowing at the waist, then dropping to their knees, foreheads kissing carpet, at the threshold of Allah's mercy. And then I knew. I hadn't dreamed it. My father went home in his dreams, to the home his ancestors had been taken from, the home he had never known but that his soul remembered. I felt his soul in that African, Muslim soil. I had come home.

Fatima put the papers down.

"So, how bad is it?" Sister Amatullah asked with a chuckle.

Despite her grin she looked truly apprehensive of Fatima's assessment. She hadn't shared her writing with anyone before.

"It's . . ." Fatima started and stalled. She shook her head, her eyes dreamy. "It's . . . amazing," she finished.

Sister Amatullah's eyebrows shot up. She smiled brightly as a schoolgirl.

FAR AWAY FROM HERE

"Really?" she asked, unbelieving.

"Really," Fatima confirmed. "I mean, wow, that's so cool about your dad. How you connected with his possible ancestry and heritage like that. And I didn't know you had traveled to West Africa."

"Oh yeah, child. Senegambia, Mauritania, Mali. I even went to Timbuktu and touched some of the oldest handwritten Qur'an's in all of Africa."

"Is that in your book?" Fatima asked.

"Mm-hmm," Sister Amatullah answered. "Got lots of stories about that."

"How did all that come about? You doing all that traveling?"

"Oh, well, when I met my husband, just, you know, when he was courting me, he asked me, you know, what most people ask someone they're thinking about building a life with, did I want children. And of course I should have known he would ask that, should have thought about that myself, having kids, but truth be told I hadn't. Before accepting Islam I hadn't thought about marriage, period. But everybody said, 'Sister, you gotta get married. It's what Allah loves from us, to join together and be partners.' So anyway me being young and a little mouthy, so my mother always said, I just said the first thing that popped in my head. 'I want . . . to travel,' I said. And I tell you I did not expect those words to come out my mouth. Wanted to swallow them right back down, but it was too late. He must have seen it on my face 'cause then he laughed, a little child giggle. That made me soften to him, like. Like, 'Hm, I kinda like this fella,' 'cause like I say this whole marriage thing was new for me. And he said, 'You know what? I wanna travel too.' And so that's what we did. Got married and instead of setting up house we packed up and set off. Said we was holding the babies off for a little while but then at some point we realized we liked it like that. Just the two of us going off on adventures."

"Did you ever . . ." Fatima ran her thumb along the curled edges of the papers, hedging her words. "Did you ever regret, you know, not having kids?"

"That's a fair question," Sister Amatullah responded. "I thought about it, when he got sick. Thought he should have, you know, someone to keep his name alive, his legacy. But . . ." She stopped and looked down at her feet, crossing and uncrossing her ankles, then crossing them again. She shrugged. "We had a good time, me and him. A good life. He lives on in my memory. He's alive in my heart. I don't know if that's enough for him, but I feel it's so. He didn't look a wink sad when he passed, or even once leading up to it. Smiled through it all."

"Course I did surprise myself by getting married again later. Saw that one coming less than I saw the first. But I knew he didn't want me alone like that. He said as much before he passed on." Sister Amatullah smiled wistfully. "Anyhow, he's all in them pages." She tipped her head toward the writing pads. "Lots of stories involving him. So, insha'Allah, he lives on in my pages, my book, whoever cares to read an old lady's stories." She grinned at Fatima.

"That's beautiful," Fatima said. "And your writing is really beautiful too. I can't wait to read more."

And she meant it. She'd been skeptical and dubious about the whole project, but now her mind was alive and curious. Sister Amatullah, like most of the elders, was always telling stories. And Fatima, like most of the younger people, was always nodding along impatiently, listening with only one ear. She had always taken the elders at face value. They were old and had always been old, to her mind. But they had been young once, too, as Sister Amatullah's manuscript reminded her. With all the same potential for mistakes and having to make decisions with lots of uncertainties and doubts. Fatima thought about how it felt for her to move about in the world, in New Orleans and in Atlanta, other places she had been, as a Muslim woman, a Black Muslim woman. The stares, the fearful

FAR AWAY FROM HERE 163

gazes, the looks of disgust and hostility. But someone like Sister Amatullah was doing that at a time when no one else was. *What was it like?* she wondered for the first time. Being Muslim, being Black and Muslim in the fifties and sixties, when all that—bus boycotts, sit-ins, marches, protests—was going on? She saw the elders in a new light and was awed by their courage to be themselves, to be true to their new beliefs—or maybe not new, maybe old and ancestral too.

"You guys were so brave," Fatima said in whispered reverence.

"Hm?" Sister Amatullah said.

Fatima shook her head. "Nothing. Just thinking about something. I really like your story though."

"Well, good, you can help this old woman type it up and fix up my words and make it nice." She set her hands on the arms of the chair she'd sunk into and started to pull herself up. "Now if you'll excuse me, I think it's time for my nap. Do you nap?" she asked.

Fatima made a face then shook her head. "I don't think I have since kindergarten, unless falling asleep in class counts."

Sister Amatullah shook her head. "See you young folks. Y'all don't know the power of a nap. Don't burn yourself out. Them books always gonna be there and this world gonna keep turning even if you close your eyes. Learn how to rest."

Fatima laughed. "Yes, ma'am." She packed to leave, nestling the sacred pages she'd been entrusted with safely into the belly of her bag. Sister Amatullah pulled her in for a hug. Fatima bent into Sister Amatullah's warm, fleshy arms and let the elder woman wrap them around her torso, resting her chin on her shoulder. She closed her eyes to capture this moment, to hold fast to the feeling of being held, of feeling at home, safe in these arms that had supported so many. She pressed her palms into Sister Amatullah's back, feeling the bones safely tucked into solid flesh, wishing to never have to let go.

Outside, just as she was opening the passenger door of Baba Kareem's truck to set her bag down on the floor, an emerald-green Honda Accord pulled up behind her. She looked up to see Saif behind the wheel. She turned back to the truck. Could she just walk away? Slip in through the passenger side and peel off, like Saif was no one she knew? Not knowing what to do, she mindlessly rifled through her bag. The trunk of the Honda popped open and Saif stepped out and walked over to the back. He closed it and walked up to the curb carrying reusable tote bags filled with groceries. He bent and set them on the sidewalk, standing to hoist his jeans up his waist, though they instantly slid down to their original position. He wore a gray Saints hoodie and tan Timberland boots, the suede unscuffed. Fatima pulled her phone out of her bag like that was what she'd been searching for.

"She got me in the store with the recycled bags," Saif said, gesturing toward the groceries. "Talking about, 'Don't bring me none of that plastic, boy.'"

His voice was a perfect imitation of Sister Amatullah's gruff directives. Fatima smiled despite herself.

"You shop for her," she said.

Saif smirked at her. "I'm not an ogre, Tooma."

She startled at his use of her childhood nickname. She hadn't been called that in ages.

"I know you're not a monster," she replied.

Saif looked away. "I got milk in here," he said. He gathered the bags and walked past Fatima to the front steps. He stopped and turned around.

"I'm just going to drop these off." His fists opened and closed around the handles of the bags. "Wait for me?"

Fatima stiffened. She stuffed her hands in the pockets of her coat and shrugged. He turned and jogged up the stairs, groceries rattling in the bags at his sides. Fatima leaned back on the truck and watched him.

She'd asked Wakeel once why he hung with Saif. He'd stiffened immediately at her question.

"I mean, y'all are so different," she had backtracked.

"He's family," Wakeel had responded, his voice surprisingly firm.

She had left the conversation at that, understanding that she had touched a nerve.

Saif came out carrying bottles of organic apple juice and granola bars. He handed one of each to Fatima with a shrug.

"You know you can't leave Sister Amatullah's without food."

Fatima smiled and took the offerings.

"So, what's up?" she asked.

Saif looked off in the distance and took in a breath that made his broad chest rise. His ebony skin was plump and unblemished, like a baby's. Not a trace of facial hair. His hair was so close-cropped he looked almost bald. He stuffed his hands in the front pocket of his hoodie and finally looked at her.

"Can we—I wanna show you something." He gestured with his chin toward his car. "Take a ride with me?"

Fatima shifted from foot to foot.

"I—it's not proper," she blurted out.

Saif raised his eyebrows at her, his lips a gentle, teasing smirk.

Fatima was right, it wasn't proper to be in a car alone with him, but that wasn't really what troubled her. It was that she didn't fear him or his intentions, that she had never feared him, that—dare she say it—she felt safe with him. He carried a sadness in his eyes, but it brought about a strange sense of calm that drew Fatima in. Time seemed to slow around him, become irrelevant, and she felt like nothing bad could happen when he was around, which didn't make sense considering what he did for a living. This thought jolted her. Is this what Wakeel had felt—before? Is this why he had stuck around Saif, even when things were going wrong?

"Okay," Fatima agreed, letting out a breath she didn't realize she was holding. "I gotta drop Baba Kareem's truck off first."

"I'll follow you," he said.

Fatima drove down Napoleon to Broad, the late-afternoon sun low in the sky, evening approaching. It washed everything in shades of pink and orange. Through the rearview mirror, all she could see was the shadow of Saif behind the intense sunlight, a face without eyes, a phantom presence. The whole way he was right behind her, in the same lane, past the rows of bail bonds offices, the old Popeyes at Tulane, and the old Whitney Bank, now a dollar store, the new Whole Foods shining like an oasis in a desert.

Fatima parked and climbed out of the truck. Inside, the house was quiet. She tiptoed to the hallway entrance. No light shone under the doors, but she could hear Baba Kareem's muffled voice, a tinkle of laughter from Mama Tayyibah, coming from their bedroom. The sound, the knowledge that they were in there together, soothed her. She set the keys on the coffee table with a soft clink and slipped back out of the house.

Saif's car carried the sweet, smoky smell of incense, Nag Champa, Fatima recognized with an appreciative sniff. It was dark and cavernous on the inside, the windows tinted. When she shut the door, the outside world grew hazy, like a cloud passing over the sky. The black leather interior was spotlessly clean, the faux wood grain details shiny. A nasheed trilled from the speakers, a love song for the Prophet Muhammad, only a duff drum accompanying the Arabic words. Fatima glanced at Saif's profile, his eyes intensely focused on the road. He was truly an enigma.

Saif turned right and entered I-10 East at the on-ramp just before Gentilly Boulevard. At that time of day there was no traffic, just a steady flow of cars, and the sanest of New Orleans drivers, not yet those in a rush to pick up children from school or get home from work, speeding and cutting into lanes without signals as if only they had somewhere important to be. Now the flow was smooth and well coordinated and in no time they were approaching the high rise revealing all of New Orleans East, the Industrial Canal and the towering buildings of the Folgers factory. The heady smell of roasting coffee beans filled the car despite the windows being rolled up.

It was the smell that signaled you were entering the East, the once-thriving, predominately Black and middle-class area, so expansive it could be its own city, with long, wide streets and sprawling homes set far back from the streets with immaculate lawns and landscaped gardens. Hidden behind fences were large backyards, some with kidney bean–shaped swimming pools and hot tubs, barbeque grills ready to be fired up for weekend birthday parties and family gatherings. Tucked into the subdivisions with winding roads that curled into spirals were small, human-made lakes and ponds.

The surrounding wilderness, uncultivated and wild, housed all matter of wild swamp animals. Fatima had heard stories from friends and schoolmates of wild boar sightings and nutria, those cat-sized rodents introduced to the land by ambitious and short-sighted farmers and traders hoping to harvest them for their fur, not considering until it was too late their rapid reproduction and thus infestation, so common some folks feared leaving their homes at night lest they encounter the hulking, orange-toothed, disease-carrying creatures.

Saif put another CD into the player. "Exhibit C" by Jay Electronica streamed out from the speakers. As they continued on down the highway, passing the Bullard and then Little Woods exits, the last of what could be considered New Orleans territory, Fatima understood where they were headed, her gut turning with dread. The only place beyond that point that concerned either of them was the Muslim cemetery in Slidell. After the flat forestland past Little Woods was the Causeway bridge. As they hit the Causeway, the panoramic view of Lake Pontchartrain unfolded like a blanket around them, the surface of the baby-blue water glittering against the afternoon sun. There were only faint streaks of clouds in the sky. The sight of all that achingly beautiful blue and silver dazzled Fatima like a fever dream, distracting her attention from their destination. How could she think of anything while surrounded so completely by this ancient water, only the thin strip of highway at the center that connected New Orleans to other lands interrupting its majestic flow? She followed the flight of the seagulls, wings spread wide as they dipped down low, their bellies skimming the water searching for fish. They rose and fell from sky to water in effortless, timeless motion. Their harmony with all the elements of nature, their rhythmic movements, resonated with Fatima's spirit. To move with God, not against His will and force, was her aspiration.

All too quickly they were back on land, from water to trees to concrete. The endless blue of Lake Pontchartrain gave way to the green of forest then the hard gray of industry. Gas stations, car-repair shops, small locally-owned grocery stores, diners, and restaurants. People thought of Louisiana as a Black-and-White state, but the sight of a Chinese restaurant tucked into a small Slidell neighborhood disrupted that false dichotomy. They crossed train tracks and drove past an extensive boatyard and marina.

"Whoa," Saif said, shooting an arm out in front of Fatima as he made a sharp turn onto a slim, forest-lined road with steep ditches on each side. Coming directly at them was a large dump truck. Fatima gasped and Saif moved to the very edge of the road to give the truck more room. They both leaned to the right away from the truck as if that could protect them from a blow. The truck driver was completely unbothered, pushing past them as if he didn't see them at all. Saif looked at Fatima, both their eyes filled with fear.

"My bad," Saif said. "I always miss this turn."

"Yeah, I can see why," Fatima said, laughing uneasily. "All these trees, you can't see the side roads."

Her heart pounded in her chest from the jolt. It quickened again at the sight of the cemetery. The surrounding neighborhood was serene, with neat ranch-style homes far off the road, wide wraparound porches with ceiling fans and rocking chairs, plants hanging down from beams along the edges of the porches, some concealed by screens. Forest loomed beyond their backyards, no fences sectioning off space.

Saif turned into the gravel parking lot on the left side of the entrance before the burial grounds. A discreet green sign marked the entrance. Nothing indicated from the front that it was a Muslim cemetery. There were no standing headstones, only flat bronze markers in the ground, many of them studded with flowers still fresh from recent visitors. Fatima stepped out of the car, her knees popping as she stood. She was tired from the long drive, the blur of water and trees bringing heaviness but not the ease of sleep. Her body was stiff, especially her legs. She pressed her heels into the gravel to stretch her calves. She took in a deep breath, the scent of pine cooling her nostrils and reviving her senses. With only the chirping of birds and the rustle of leaves from the surrounding oak trees, peace washed over her. This was a place to rest the body and the soul.

Saif walked over to where Fatima stood and leaned back on the passenger door. He looked out at the burial grounds.

"This is where I come to clear my head and just . . . I don't know, just get some energy, you know?"

Fatima had thought he would say "peace" or "quiet." "Energy for what?" she asked.

Saif shrugged and scratched at the back of his neck. A mosquito jumped off and flew away.

"Energy to live," he said. "To keep going when all I want to do is stop. Dig a hole for myself and just climb in."

Fatima studied his profile. The softness of his plump cheeks and jaw. Only the sagging, puffy skin under his eyes suggested the hardness of his life. He had the face of a boy but the tired eyes of an old, old man. He stood to his full height and stepped away from the car. He stuffed his hands in his jeans pockets and pointed with his chin toward the graves.

"Come on," he said.

Fatima followed him. Small white markers directed visitors toward the right graves. They walked at the edge of the rows to the fourth row. Saif stopped and pointed toward the far fence.

"He's a few spaces from the end."

They walked a few paces to the center of the rows where the path was more worn.

"Try not to walk over the graves," Saif said over his shoulder, pointing toward the ground.

Fatima nodded. She walked slowly and read the names of the deceased and their birth and death dates, subtracting to figure out their years lived. Sixty, seventy-five, eighty-two . . . Full lives. Most of the plaques were small and basic, just names and dates. A few had small vases bronzed into them to hold floral bouquets. Fatima touched the petals on one. They were artificial flowers, the fabric petals silky and faded a pale pink. Some markers had *La illaha il-Allah* carved into them. One grave had a large black marble plaque below the standard one, about the length of a full body. A hand-carved message, the letters all caps and uneven, had been written into it. "Loving father and grandfather," it read. "Shining example of what it means to be a Muslim. Thank you for teaching us Islam." The message was signed with love by five names in different scripts. Fatima was moved by the sincerity of the words and the effort in having it placed as a cover over the dearly departed loved one. She stooped and ran her fingers over the engravings and asked Allah's mercy for the souls of all who rested in the earth beneath her feet. She prayed their presence as fellow believers comforted those who rested waiting to meet Allah. That was all they really did as believers, those living and those no longer of the world—waited, patiently and impatiently, to return their bodies to the dirt and start their new, eternal lives, their real lives as spiritual beings shed of their human trappings. They didn't fear the inevitable, only the meeting with their Creator coming when they were not in their best state as they should be.

Will I be ready when my time comes? she wondered. *Am I ready now?* The thought sobered her, sinking into her chest as a heavy anchor rooting her to the ground. She wasn't ready to fly. This life was a heavy burden for the believers. That was why they prayed for light to illuminate their graves, light to lift their spirits and their path to their Lord. She thought of something Imam Hassan had said in one of his soul-stirring Friday khutbahs. "If this life feels like a prison to you, take it as a sign of faith, a sign that you are a true believer in Allah and His message to humanity. And let that heaviness drive you to your knees in submission and acceptance of Allah's power over you. That's where the light is. We have to kneel and let go of our pride and arrogance before we can stand and be free."

Saif stopped at a grave shaded by trees. It held no flowers but was spotlessly clean. Fatima had noticed some plaques so heavily caked with dust and dirt that the names were fully concealed, almost hiding the entire marker. This upset her. One she had rubbed and rubbed vigorously with her palm, pebbles scratching her skin, frantic for the name to resurface beneath the dirt, her breath only coming when the letters reemerged. She wished she could come every day and wipe down every grave marker till they shone in the sunlight. Every name should be known and read, never forgotten or hidden.

She did not need to rub Wakeel's marker though; the letters shone with recent, consistent attention. She regretted she hadn't brought flowers. She regretted avoiding coming here and refusing to go to Wakeel's burial for what she now recognized as her own selfish purposes. She hadn't even known flowers were allowed. She knew so little of the practices around death and the departed. She had always shunned those rituals, ignoring them as if they weren't relevant to her, as if death wouldn't come to touch them all, eventually.

Wakeel had been the first young person she had known to die. It had seemed so unnatural to her, so revolting. His death had angered her for how it upset the balance of things for her, disrupted her understandings of the world. It angered her still, now, as she stood at his grave for the first time. She asked now not why had he been taken from her but why she had ever thought of his death that way, as something, someone, who had been taken from her. Taken by whom? Allah did not steal, nor punish, not like that. And who was she to think she was so special to receive Allah's personal vengeance? No, it was so much bigger than that, she now realized. Wakeel's death was bigger than that and it was a test and a lesson. A lesson Saif, in all his imperfect actions, had learned and was trying to implement by changing his life the best he could under complex, complicated circumstances Fatima knew she could not begin to understand.

Fatigue washed over her. She felt she could lay across one of these plots, curl her legs into her chest, lay and sleep and rise, covered in grass. Saif stopped at a grave, one with a plaque in the ground, and stood over it, his hands in his pockets. Fatima walked over and stood next to him. The wind whipped the edge of her scarf up and over her mouth and chin. The flutter over her lips felt like a kiss. She knelt and ran her hand across the letters, then pressed her palm against them. She dropped her hand and sat back on her haunches. Saif kneeled silently next to her.

"I grew up in a house full of people," he began. "My mama, my stepdaddy, my three younger brothers. Half brothers I guess but it still don't feel right to call them that. Running and crawling over everything, laughing, but I couldn't never join them. If I tried then the noise became a problem and we all had to be quiet. Till I learned my place. We could've been cool but my stepdaddy didn't want that. After a while they learned to keep their distance from me if they wanted to play, and eventually I stopped trying, just sat there wanting to be seen but at the same time not. To be in that house was to be in a place where all the light had been sucked out, blacker than behind your eyelids, just empty.

"Being with Wakeel, and Baba Kareem and Mama Tayyibah, even being with y'all annoying-ass girls was heaven. Playing outside or watching TV together, Baba Kareem rubbing my head and wrestling with me, Mama Tayyibah feeding me and pulling me in for hugs I pretended to only tolerate. *This is how life can be,* I used to think. *I'm not crazy. I'm not a monster or a ghost.* After being with y'all I'd go home and try to pray like we did at the masjid in my bedroom, but my stepdaddy caught me once on the floor then told me I couldn't close my door no more. Only place he couldn't tell me to keep the door open was the bathroom. So that's where I'd pray, when I could. Praying and praying so I could feel close to y'all.

"Wakeel was my brother. Mama Tayyibah and Baba Kareem were more mother and father than my mama and stepdaddy could ever be. With them I could be safe, I could be loved. I was jealous sometimes, of all y'all, Wakeel too, because I wanted to have that feeling all the time. When Wakeel left, my whole world broke apart.

I stopped praying and started selling. Then Wakeel came back, but it was too late, I was gone. Dude wouldn't give up though, kept coming around. He never said it, but I know he blamed himself.

"That bullet was supposed to be for me. I wish every day it had took me instead of him. And every day I have to live with what happened. That's my punishment. Now I'm all mixed-up. Selling and praying."

He laughed emptily, then rubbed his head back and forth.

"I'm gonna get out. I have to. But I can't just stop, you know? It don't work like that."

He stopped and bowed his head. Fatima looked up to the darkening sky.

"We have to pray," she said. "What time is it? Can we make it home in time?"

Saif gestured to the grass around them.

"Why we gotta go? We can pray right here."

Fatima looked around, unsure. They were the only people there.

"I don't have wudhu. I need to wash up."

Saif looked around then stood up and walked over to a patch of dirt in between two grave markers. He bent over and rubbed his palms over it, then swiped them over his hands and face. It was a practice called "tayammum," a way to wash up for prayers when there was no water. Fatima had never actually done it before though. She kneeled awkwardly and rubbed the coarse dirt lightly over the backs of her hands and face and followed Saif to an empty row that led to the rows of graves. They stood, Fatima a few steps behind Saif to his right. She took the loose end of her scarf and wrapped it snugly around her neck, tucking the edge under her sweater. The sun was low, preparing to depart, no longer giving warmth.

Saif whispered the iqama, *hayya ala salah, hayya ala falah,* come to prayer, come to success. He paused for a moment, then raised his hands to his ears. His call, "Allahu Akbar," crackled through the wind, beginning the prayer. Fatima followed and folded her hands over her chest. Praying outside, at Wakeel's grave, being led by Saif, it was a transportive experience, lightness and a binding to the earth, the rough grass tickling her palms when they lowered themselves to the ground, pressing her nose and forehead into the cool earth, hearing nothing but knowing it teemed with life beneath them. Saif recited from Surah Al Infitar. "A time will come when the sky is torn apart; when the stars scatter, and the ocean drains away; and when the graves are tossed about, and laid open. At that time every person will be told what they have done, and what they have failed to do."

Fatima had never visited Wakeel's grave, not even after the janaza. She had slipped away after the prayer, her last time attending Masjid Al-Ghafur. After she and Saif completed the prayer, she opened her palms to the sky and prayed for Wakeel's comfort in his grave, for a peaceful rest until the day when all the graves are opened and every soul faces its Lord. "Inna ilahi wa inna ilayhi ra-ji'un," she whispered into her upturned hands. To God we belong, and to God we all return.

Tahani

TAHANI PULLED UP AT SISTER IRIS'S HOME IN NEW Orleans East early Sunday afternoon, her trunk and back seat loaded with bags and boxes. Sister Iris lived in a four-bedroom brick-and-stucco ranch-style house with an immaculate front lawn in a quiet neighborhood off Chef Menteur. For the last month Tahani had been coming by every Sunday helping her go through home decor magazines and catalogs and come up with an interior design plan. She had cornered Tahani at the masjid one Friday after prayers.

"A little birdie told me you're a design guru," she had said, her lips spreading into a sly smile.

The only person she could have heard that from was Imam Hassan's wife, Khadijah. Tahani had helped her pick out the paint colors, curtains, and carpet for the masjid renovation the previous year.

Sister Iris came from Trinidad. You could see it in her copper skin and high cheekbones, and hear it in the accent she still carried after all these years in the US, her consonants clipped and her vowels drawn out. "It's easy to keep an accent in this third-world country of a city," she'd say with her hearty laugh. She was short and heavy bosomed and she always wore long, flowing brightly patterned skirts and white cotton tunics; her short graying locs

FAR AWAY FROM HERE

and jangling silver earrings peeking out from the thin, gauzy scarves she wrapped loosely over her head. Like a lot of Caribbean people, she'd spent time up north but found the feeling of home she craved in New Orleans. "I hear the horns and the drums and see the people dancing in the streets with their colors and umbrellas and I forget what country I'm in," she said. She did a mean whine at their ladies-only parties too, her hips moving with a mind of their own that made the elder women squeal and fake chide her.

She and her husband were new empty nesters since they're youngest child had just moved out. Caught up in work and raising children, they'd kept the same sturdy but drab furniture for the last twenty years and the walls were still the same eggshell white they'd been when they first moved into the house. "But that's not my style," Sister Iris had insisted at the masjid to Tahani, the word "style" coming out a hiss between the gap in her teeth. "I'm ready to show off my style now."

"Well I'm no guru, Sister Iris, but I do like decorating and I'd love to help you," Tahani had said. "I'm pretty busy with the salon but I can come by on a Sunday as long as I can bring my girls with me."

"Of course!" Sister Iris exclaimed. "I have a big playroom for my grandchildren and a nice backyard for them to run around. Yes, I should say that now, whatever redecorating we do has to remain functional for the children."

Her tone went firm on "functional." She had worked as a librarian at the Gentilly branch for decades, and she was the one you could count on to provide carefully selected, high-quality educational toys and books for the masjid's annual Eid toy giveaway. Tahani had even passed on a few of Sister Iris's picks that she'd kept from her own childhood to Aliyah and Safia, sturdy wooden block puzzles and hardcover copies of *Mufaro's Beautiful Daughters* and *The People Could Fly*.

This time Tahani came alone, since they'd be moving around the furniture Sister Iris and her husband had ordered and going through the decorative pieces Tahani had bought. She'd left the girls home with Fatima, her friend's first time alone with them. Fatima came over with her laptop and a tote bag full of books. Tahani pressed her lips together to hide her grin. As she walked out the door she heard Safia say in her boss-lady voice, "So, the first thing we're going to do . . ." Tahani giggled and said a prayer for Fatima; she doubted her friend would crack the spine on any of those books.

Sister Iris's husband, Brother Hakeem, answered the door.

"Salaam alaykum, sister," he said. "Come in and get this woman off my case, please."

Tahani laughed. Brother Hakeem grew up in the Lower Ninth Ward, and it was reflected in the rhythmic way he spoke, his words coming fast and crashing into each other. For all the years they'd been married, Sister Iris still laughed at the way he talked. "It's like a song," she said. "I barely understand a word."

Brother Hakeem was average height and wiry, not an ounce of fat on his body. Even though he was almost seventy, he walked with a bounce in his step like a young man, his hand always on the cell phone he kept in a case clipped to his belt along with his keys. He worked as a repairman—washing machines was his specialty but he fixed other things too—and his phone rang often. Tahani never saw him in anything other than freshly pressed jeans, a polo shirt, and a beanie over his short dreadlocks. He was dark-skinned and kept his facial hair trimmed in a neat salt-and-pepper goatee.

Tahani would have been surprised he was even there since he was a sunup-to-sundown type of working man, but he and one of his sons were there to do the heavy lifting, something she could tell he was excited to do by the way he bounced on his toes. "The man can't sit down to save his life," Sister Iris often quipped, though her voice was proud when she said it. And not like she could talk because she was always up and going too.

Sister Iris and Brother Hakeem's house didn't look like much on the outside, as nondescript as most of the homes were in the East, but the inside was surprisingly bright and modern, with lots of open space.

The process, the weeks of visiting different stores, flipping through binders of fabric swatches, picking out patterns for curtains and rugs, deciding on color schemes and furniture styles, all of it had invigorated Tahani. This was better than hair and makeup, she had to admit, and she had never thought anything could be better than that. Who knew Home Depot could be more exhilarating than Sephora? She'd consulted with Sister Iris throughout the whole process, despite Sister Iris's insistence that Tahani had her full trust. But Tahani had read in one of the design books she had checked out from the library—she had almost maxed her number of checkouts in her excitement over the new project—that the client should always be a part of the decision-making, from small to big. That control led to more client satisfaction and less headache. Sister Iris imagined herself easygoing, but she was a strong, opinionated woman. Brother Hakeem had warned Tahani in his playful way one afternoon at their house. "Don't be fooled by that woman," he'd said while "that woman" went into the kitchen to fix a snack tray. "She got to have her hand in every pot."

"What he saying in there?" Sister Iris shouted from the kitchen. Her accent became more pronounced when she was excited. "There" became "dere."

Brother Hakeem shouted back, "I said I love you with all my heart."

They both heard her scoff.

"See how much she love me," Brother Hakeem had said with a grin.

Now as Tahani witnessed the fruition of all the weeks of planning and prepping, hunting for deals and antiques, painting, the placement of furniture and carefully selected pieces, she felt sad because it was coming to an end. She would leave and not see the work she had done, not experience it except through the copious photos she had taken throughout the process. Funny she'd never felt this way at the salon. Not this longing to continue. But then again, there she didn't have to wait for the next experience because there would be another woman waiting to get in her chair.

Jalisa had officially made her offer the day before, as she and Tahani had closed down the shop together. Tahani had the last appointment of the day. It had been a whirlwind of a Saturday, customers coming in nonstop, the doorbell constantly jingling, then everything slowed to a crawl in the evening, with the other stylists giddily packing up their bags, making plans with their unexpected time off. Tahani had been surprised that Jalisa let them go, but then she recognized why. The look of satisfaction on Jalisa's face, the serenity of her brow, was one Tahani had never seen on the woman who was a steady force. Her mind was already on a beachfront villa.

"So what do you think, doll?" Jalisa had said, adjusting her rings and studying her immaculate manicure. She looked up at Tahani with a sleepy smile.

"I . . . I don't know what to say."

"Oh, come on, hun," Jalisa said. "You're a natural. You've got the knowledge, the talent, the clients all love you, even if they hate all that gorgeous blonde hair you've got." She winked at Tahani. "And most importantly you've got the savvy. The, what they call it, 'stick and move' abilities to be a hands-on boss like me. Keep the stylists on their toes without wanting to stab you behind your back. And even if they do want to, that just means they respect you."

Tahani pictured herself as a boss. Certainly she did well under pressure. Knew how to keep her cool where others melted. She wanted to say she'd learned that from working for Jalisa, watching her manage the meltdowns and catfights. But she realized with a jolt that she really learned that coolness from her mother, who could dish out any critique or order without even a faint trace of a line on her brow, just a slight rise of her eyebrow and a curl to the corner of her mouth. At work, out and about in the streets, she had a little of her mother in her, minus the imperious attitude.

"What's got you smiling like that?" Tahani had asked Jalisa as they finished tidying up, expecting to hear about some new man in Jalisa's life. She always had a romance brewing, a new "fella" in her life, as she called them.

"I thought you'd never ask," Jalisa said, smoothing her already-sleek hair back into its tidy bun. "I did it," she continued.

Tahani cocked her head at her boss. "Did what?" she asked.

"Bought myself a condo in Destin," she said, beaming. "Thought about California, maybe Santa Monica or Tahoe, but," she raised her arms and fluttered her fingers in the air, "those earthquakes, you know? Give me a hurricane over the ground breaking beneath my feet any day of the week that ends in y." She cackled with laughter.

"Wait, so . . ." Tahani started. "You were serious? About quitting the business? You're really leaving, all of this?" She waved her hand around the shop.

"Yep," Jalisa said. "Adios, au revoir, and goodbye. Beachfront condo, honey, with a balcony and French doors, marble countertops, stainless steel appliances, and gorgeous oak floors. It's already furnished and everything. I just gotta pack my bags and hop in my car." She tipped her head back and spun around the chair. "I'm off, darling."

"Wow," Tahani said, taken aback. She had never seen Jalisa like that before. "But what about your family? How do they feel about you moving?"

She knew Jalisa came from a sprawling Creole family with

roots back in Louisiana hundreds of years. They mostly all lived in or near Algiers and popped in at the salon so often Tahani joked that every second person who came through the door was a relative of Jalisa's. Jalisa remained professional in front of the customers, but her narrowed eyes showed her irritation when one of her family members came in. "What now?" was her typical greeting to any of them except her elders.

"Aw the hell with them," Jalisa said with a wave. "They're all telling me I'm crazy and aren't I too old to be running off like this—'running off' like I'm some kind of teenager or something or leaving some lug of a husband—but they're really just jealous 'cause they don't have the courage to actually leave and try something different. I mean these are folks, you tell 'em, let's maybe not have red beans this Monday, let's, I don't know, have steak fajitas, and they look at you like you suggested taking a trip to Mars or something. But you watch, couple of years after me, they'll be following behind me, doing the same thing and acting like they did it first. You just watch." She smacked her teeth. "They can all eat shit is what I told them."

Tahani burst out laughing. "Miss Jalisa!" she shrieked. "You did not!"

"You think I didn't," Jalisa smirked.

Tahani shook her head. With Jalisa this was not hyperbole. The woman had no filter unless there were clients around.

She sighed now. "I love them, but my God," she groaned. "They're insufferable, you know?" She looked at Tahani. "You come from a big family, right?"

Tahani stiffened, her mirth deflated at the mention of her family.

"Yeah," she nodded, hoping that was the last of Jalisa's questions about her family. She was always asking, but Tahani only gave her the bare minimum for responses.

FAR AWAY FROM HERE   183

"So you know, right?" Jalisa continued. "Always meddling in your life, no such thing as your own business." Jalisa shook her head. "First they were mad because I didn't go the marriage-and-kids route—how dare I not be miserable and complaining all the time like them—then I had the nerve to think I could start my own business. Now it's, oh, I'm abandoning the family, being reckless, even betraying my hometown and my ancestors!"

She laughed then sighed with a shake of her head.

"Ah, but I guess I'll miss that sometimes, at least knowing they're nearby, seeing them every day. I mean literally, everywhere I go, one of them is there too. Last night I ran to Walmart in my jammies to get milk for my morning coffee and literally bumped into my aunt Debra. She was all smiles till she saw my pj's and her face got all pinched and sour, like she smelled something bad. Her mouth shriveled up to where I couldn't hardly even see it anymore. Before I even got home my mother's calling my cell and giving me an earful about parading in the streets in my sleeping clothes. I mean my God, it's Walmart. I was probably the best dressed in there, counting the staff—except my aunt Debra. The woman wears heels every day and I've never seen her without makeup. Anyway, so I tell my mother, 'Ma, you do know I'm fifty-nine years old, right?' And she's all, 'Yeah and I'm eighty-two, what's your point?'"

Tahani managed to keep a small smile on her face but inside she was crumbling, thinking about her own "big" family that really shrunk down to three, her daughters and Hadi. She wished she could banter with her mother the way Jalisa did with hers, give as good as she got, but she had never had that type of relationship with her mother, no playful sparring, no sweet and sour, just burn, after burn, after burn, each wound fresh and stinging, no cooling relief.

She had cousins, aunts and uncles, grandparents, mostly from her mother's side, but they weren't Muslim and, so her father quietly hinted when she asked him about them, were pretty hostile toward the religion. Tahani hadn't ever considered until that moment how that estrangement might have impacted her mother and maybe hardened her. If it hurt her mother, she never mentioned it, and in that silence, that avoidance, lay the essence of her issues with her mother that trickled on to her brothers, even her father, everyone who grew up in that household affected by her bitterness. They didn't talk, Tahani and her mother. Tahani couldn't remember a single time when she and her mother sat down together and had a conversation. No nostalgic stories from her childhood while her mother combed her hair, no words of wisdom culled from teenage years or early adulthood passed on with her mother perched at the foot of the bed. Her mother was a closed door. Always had been.

Tahani was tempted to join Jalisa's family in criticizing her decision to move away from the family and start a new life. Why walk away from a good thing? She knew despite Jalisa's scroll of complaints that the woman loved her family and they were her backbone. Why leave that comfort and familiarity, that love?

But she was also impressed by Jalisa's bravery and boldness, stepping into the unknown. It wasn't easy to be on your own. She had done it out of what had seemed a necessity that she now questioned.

"So look, hun," Jalisa continued. "I'm planning to be out of here by the end of May. I'll be in and out of the city for a little while and hopefully settled in Florida by the end of the year. I know I mentioned to you about taking over, and I want to officially make you an offer. Chez Rosalie is yours if you want it."

Taking over the shop had been at the forefront of Tahani's mind since Jalisa first introduced the idea to her. She had tried to convince herself that Jalisa was only dreaming out loud, or making plans for a very distant future, to keep herself from diving into any fantasies. Now in a blink it was here and it was a real opportunity in

FAR AWAY FROM HERE

front of her for the taking. Ideas came to her often. At work, at home with her children, while trying to pray, when she finally laid her head down to sleep. She could convert the back storage area into a spa where the ladies could get facials and massages. She could hire nail technicians to do manicures and pedicures and bring in a makeup artist. She herself dabbled in oils and creams and had entertained ideas of making her own skin- and hair-care products. She could bottle them and sell them out of the shop. There was a lot she could do and it was exciting.

But . . . she wasn't sure. It was a big decision. She didn't know why she was so unsure about the opportunity until she sat in Sister Iris and Brother Hakeem's newly painted and redecorated living room, surveying the work she had put together just in her own mind and taking in the feeling the redesigned space gave off. It was so satisfying, a breath of fresh air. That's what she would call her interior design business, if she had one. A Breath of Fresh Air Home Design.

But she wasn't supposed to be thinking about an interior design business. This was about Chez Rosalie, the salon she started at, just a few years ago, as a shampoo girl and now had her own booth and had been handpicked by the owner to take over. Jalisa trusted her, despite her young age. She recognized something in her, her potential. She had worked so hard to prove herself and now was her chance. It was a natural next step and several steps beyond her expectations. She could always do design work on the side or just as a hobby for friends. Jalisa was expecting an answer soon, by the end of the following week because otherwise she needed to start the process of hiring a manager. Chez Rosalie must continue on.

Tahani went home with her mind racing, feverish to make a choice that either way would impact her future. This could be everything she needed to build the life she wanted. For her and her daughters.

Tahani shut off all the lights in the apartment and headed down the hall toward the bedrooms. She stopped at Aliyah and Safia's room and turned her ear to the whisper of space in the crack of the door and listened for the purr of her daughters' even breaths. Her own breath swelled and slowed to match theirs. She could picture the rise and fall of their delicate chests as they lay on their backs taking in and releasing air.

Aliyah would sleep the night like that, flat on her back and her hands resting on her ribcage, as calm in sleep as she was in life. Safia, once in full sleep, would thrash about and by morning be in any number of odd positions. On her belly with her head stuffed under the pillow, curled in a ball at the foot of the bed, sideways with her torso and legs hanging over the edges. Tahani rested her forehead on the cool painted wood of the doorframe and smiled, picturing their peaceful sleep-soothed faces bathed in moonlight. She kissed her palm and blew the kiss into their bedroom, then turned toward her own.

She didn't bother to turn on the light. She sat on the side of the bed and looked at what she could see of the moonlit sky through the half-closed blinds. She rolled out her exercise mat and looked down wearily at it. She grabbed at the layer of loose flesh on her belly and squeezed it, her bittersweet companion, always there. Her phone buzzed from inside her purse at the foot of the bed where she tossed it hours ago.

Asaad's name flashed across the top of her phone screen. Why was he calling her? More importantly, why did her heart quicken at the sight of his name on the screen? As her thumb hovered over the answer button, the phone slipped out of her hand. Like a game of hot potatoes, she caught and dropped the phone from hand to hand

FAR AWAY FROM HERE   187

till just before it hit the ground. With all the fumbling she'd accidentally accepted the call without an opportunity to decide.

She heard Asaad yelling, "Hello," before she'd even brought the phone to her ear.

"You in a tunnel or something?" Asaad asked with fake exasperation.

"Why you calling me all late?" Tahani asked.

She looked at her alarm clock, ready to make an accusation. Nine thirty, it read. It was Saturday night. She closed her mouth.

Asaad surprisingly didn't make a grandma joke. His voice turned grave.

"I, uh, wanted to talk to you about something."

"Oh?"

"Yeah . . ."

She waited.

"So . . . ?"

A rustling sound came through the phone and outside her window simultaneously. The familiar scrape of magnolia leaves against concrete.

"Where are you?" Tahani asked.

A pause.

"Um . . . I'm not saying I'm outside your house, but I might be outside your house."

"What?"

Tahani hopped off the bed and looked around her room. She tugged at the hem of her sleep shirt, a threadbare Bob Marley T-shirt softened by many washings, a gaping hole along the neck band.

"This is stupid," Asaad mumbled. "You know what? Forget I called. My bad." His voice grew distant like he was pulling the phone from his ear.

"No, wait," Tahani said, her voice nearly a shout. She surprised herself with her outburst and was embarrassed by her eagerness but kept going. "It's okay, give me a minute and I'll come down."

She flew around the room, changing her clothes, fluffing her hair and touching up her lips with tinted lip balm. She finished the quick change with a spritz of rosewater then fluffed her hair once more for good measure. She looked down and realized in her haste she had put back on her favorite black abaya with red embroidery that she kept hung on a hook inside her closet. She called it her Saturday-night "fit" because she only wore it at the end of her long workweek. The accommodating width of fabric, her curves vanishing into its folds, signaled comfort and relaxation. That she didn't opt for something sexy, that she shrugged off her unconscious choice with the thought, *It's Asaad*, not diminishing him but aligning him with what brought her comfort, was another surprise that she didn't have time to think about.

Tahani tiptoed down the stairs on bare feet. Asaad stood at the bottom of the porch steps, his hands in his jeans pockets, shifting from foot to foot. Tahani pushed the screen door open and looked up and down the quiet street.

"You should probably come up," she said.

"You sure about that?" Asaad asked.

"No."

Her hands shook and she let go of the screen door and turned back toward the stairs, making him move quickly to catch the door before it slammed. No man other than her brother had crossed the threshold of her home.

"But come on," she continued, gathering up the hem of her abaya so she didn't trip.

"Your babies sleep?" he asked, walking up the steps behind her.

The heat of his body so close to hers brought warmth to her exposed calves. She lowered her dress to cover them.

"Yeah," she replied.

It felt weird hearing Asaad mention her children. He of course knew she had them, but they never talked about them; he had seen them at the masjid but never met them. For the first time she considered how he might be with her girls and wasn't at all surprised in her confidence that he would be great with them and they would take to him like sugar to tea. And for that reason she didn't want them to meet him. So as soon as they tiptoed their way up the stairs and into the apartment she shunted him back outside onto the balcony and shut the door.

"Marry me, Tahani."

She hadn't even turned from the door. She paused with her back to him.

"What?" she whispered, not trusting her ears.

He reached over and gently tugged her by her elbow to face him. His face was in the shadows, she could only make out the contours of his cheekbones and jaw, the milkiness of his eyes. She wanted to touch his face, run her thumb across his bottom lip. She stepped back. She needed light to guide her to what was right but at the same time was grateful for the dark that concealed her desires.

"I know I'm doing this all wrong," he said. "I had a whole speech prepared, but I'm so nervous I knew I was going to mess it up so . . . I love you, Tahani. And I want you to be my wife."

She stood and took in his words. She needed to sit down. She held her trembling knees and rocked. Marriage. To Asaad. Color schemes came to her mind. Fabrics. Ivory, lace, tulle. A sprig of baby's breath for her hair, or a crown of flowers tied together with satin ribbons. Baskets of rose petals for her daughters to hold in their gloved hands, sprinkling them before her footsteps. Asaad in a cream-colored Nehru suit, standing underneath a trellis of lilies waiting to receive her. The image glitched. Asaad's suit replaced by the jeans and T-shirt he now wore. The lilies and rose petals dried up, the silk and lace turned back into the polyester of her work uniform. This was real life. Her and her two children who had only a shadow of a father, no grandparents or cousins, in a little two-bedroom apartment she barely slept in and struggled to afford. No, no, no. This was the life she had made and that she must stay in, alone. She blessed the darkness that covered their faces.

"Asaad, I can't marry you."

Asaad laughed. His eyes twinkled in the moonlight.

"I knew you would say that," he said. "I prepared for that. I know you're thinking, 'This dude's a lil comedian tryna be somebody. He ain't nobody, ain't got no money, talkin' 'bout wanting a wife.' But I got plans."

Tahani shook her head. Either he didn't see it or ignored it and kept going.

"I'm in school. Studying arts and education. I got a job and, insha'Allah, I'll get a better one when I graduate. I got plans, T, and I want you, and your daughters—who I haven't met but I know I'll love—in those plans."

His chest rose and fell rapidly but he didn't stop to breathe. Tahani held her hand up.

"This isn't about money, Asaad."

"Then what is it? You don't have feelings for me?"

This was her chance. She could tell him she loved him. That she dreamed about him. That his face in her mind made her smile. That she had to seek Allah's forgiveness for all the times she yearned for his touch on her skin.

"No," she lied. "Not like that. Not like, you know, that kind of love."

Asaad's chest sank. His shoulders dropped.

"Yeah, okay," he said, his laughter hollow. "So I made a fool of myself, again. Shit, I could write a whole comedy off that topic."

Tahani wanted to put her hands on him, to comfort him, but

she knew better. She had caused enough confusion. "I'm sorry" rested on her tongue, useless.

"Well, this is awkward," he said, a feeble attempt at his stage voice. Even he couldn't force a laugh.

He stepped closer to her. She forced herself to look up and take in his defeated face. He looked back at her and smiled, a hint of mischief in his eyes. He took a curl of her hair and spun it around his finger, then unraveled it.

"Tiger," he whispered.

She shivered. Her body and her heart screamed for him. She stepped back and lowered her head. And then he was gone and she was alone, again, in the dark.

Fatima

FATIMA AND TAHANI ARRIVED AT THE LAKEFRONT IN the early afternoon. It was a disorienting balmy winter day, made stranger by news reports warning of a coming freeze. Tahani's daughters squealed in the back seat. The freakish weather meant they could dress for summer in February. They sported matching heart-shaped sunglasses and rainbow-striped bathing suits—they weren't going swimming but they begged Tahani to let them wear them—with white cotton capri pants, their hair bound in Afro puffs with pink and yellow plastic hairballs, their scalps shining with coconut oil through perfectly even parts down the middles of their heads. Fatima reached back and tickled their bellies.

"Hello my little koala bears," she cooed.

The girls slapped playfully at her hands, giggling. They'd been shy with Fatima when she first met them, only answering her questions or responding to her greetings with Tahani's prodding; now they called her "auntie" and ran to her when they saw her, jumping up for hugs.

Tahani got out and opened the back door. She'd pinned her limp curls back in a swoop across her forehead and covered the rest of her hair with a white chiffon scarf, pinned to the crown of her head with a silver rhinestone clip. She wore a large white T-shirt with "Q93" emblazoned in red across the front over loose black jersey pants, and now she shook out a long denim shirt and put it on. Fatima had never seen her so dressed down, without makeup or earrings. She was moody and standoffish, ignoring the girl's attempts to get her to play with them, the fingers they dangled in her face for her to plant kisses on, their faces that they plunged into hers to nuzzle noses. She hadn't spoken during the car ride, only muttering that she was fine in a tone that kept Fatima from pestering. Her eyes remained hooded; she wouldn't look at Fatima.

Fatima let the matter drop. She had her own edge, wondering if Saif would be there. The masjid was hosting a crawfish boil, but there were a lot of other people out too, as there would be for many months, with spring approaching. It was a charged environment for Saif to be in, that much Fatima understood now, a mix of the sacred and the secular, the past he was trying to leave behind and the future he was trying to build on rough territory. She was disturbed to realize just how much she could relate to this attempt to straddle worlds. Isn't that what they were all trying to do?

The air was smokey and filled with smells of charcoal, barbecue sauce, the briny scent of beer, and the unmistakable burnt-grass aroma of weed. Fatima and Tahani walked through the parking lot holding the girls' hands tightly. A gray pit bull with a smudge of white across its chest sat unleashed on its haunches in the back of a truck with a steely gray paint job that matched the dog's coat so that it looked like it was part of the truck. The dog's owner, sporting a bald head and mirror sunglasses, a thick gold rope chain around his neck, stood next to the truck, his body rigid. Both man and dog had stolid faces. Strangely, they reminded Fatima of the soldiers at Buckingham Palace, but she didn't know what the man and his dog could be guarding.

Safia and Aliya clutched Fatima and Tahani's clothes as they inched past the dog that didn't even look at them. The parking lot was packed with cars and trucks and people, some sitting in the beds of the trucks, others draped across the hoods or sunk in fold-up chairs. On one spot of grass a banner announced a family reunion. Several people stood in rows doing the Bus Stop while a DJ played "We Are One" by Maze and Frankie Beverly. The song competed with Luther Vandross singing "Never Too Much" booming out of speakers from underneath a tent where a group of men and women sat playing cards.

The masjid event was easy to spot mostly for the profusion of colors from the women in their scarves and wraps that fanned out in the breeze wafting in from the lake waters, and the men in their brightly patterned African outfits and their peaked kufis. Fatima spotted Brother Kabir first, standing on a patch of grass before the tables. He was tall, well over six feet, and wore a tunic and loose pants with a high, square kufi. The entire outfit including the hat was bubble gum pink; black leather sandals adorned his feet. Brother Kabir taught the young children's Islamic studies classes at the masjid, which Safia and Aliyah attended, like Fatima and Tahani before them. In fact, Brother Kabir had been their teacher as well, though he looked no older now than he had then. He was a relic, a fixture of the masjid. The girls ran to him, shouting his name. He bent to them like a tree come alive from a fairy tale, his face opening into a smile.

"You look like cotton candy!" shouted Aliyah, bouncing on her toes.

"Salaam alaykum big and little sisters," Brother Kabir said in his deep, rich voice, taking in Fatima and Tahani as well.

His smile revealed a gap between his teeth, almost wide enough to fit another tooth in between. Fatima used to fixate on that gap in Sunday school classes, imagining what objects could fit in that seemingly vast space, a kernel of corn, a raisin, one of those erasers you stick on the end of your pencil when the original one runs out.

FAR AWAY FROM HERE 195

Then she'd get called on and called out for not paying attention, but even that was a treat because she'd be blessed with the gap's appearance in its full glory, for Brother Kabir could never stay stern with them for too long; his reprimands were always followed by a joke.

"Fatima," he would say, "stop daydreaming about your future husband and focus on your studies. Your true prince will want a smart woman."

The class would erupt in laughter and Fatima's cheeks would grow warm with embarrassment. Her complexion concealed the flush, but her bulging eyes gave her away, and she'd be giggling behind her hands, too, because how did he know that's exactly what she had been thinking about?

"Tahani," he said now, his hands laced together at his waist, "masha'Allah, your daughters are so intelligent. They are my top performers every class."

He had always been tougher on the girls, pushing them to do their best and challenging them to work harder and not give up.

"And your Safia, that girl is a firecracker. I call her my vice principal. She keeps everybody in check, shushing them and pointing her finger at the board."

Here he jabbed at the air in front of him, his brow deeply furrowed, mimicking the girl's actions in a comically accurate imitation that made Fatima and Tahani laugh. Safia was only four years old, but she had the makings of a future leader. Her favorite word was "why," and she wielded it like a sword. Tahani had shown Fatima Safia's school progress reports that were sent home at the end of each week, the behavior section blooming with red. But Fatima could tell by the way Tahani grinned while shaking her head that she was also proud of her strong-willed daughter.

"You are doing a fine job with those girls." Brother Kabir gave her a thumbs-up. "Keep up the good work."

Tahani looked stunned by the compliment.

"Alhamdulillah," she mumbled, ducking her head.

The girls had run off into the grass to join the other children in line for the bounce house. They were already yanking their sandals off and tossing them in the grass. Aliyah and another girl stood face-to-face in line, their arms wrapped around each other's waists, foreheads almost touching.

"Your Aliyah and my Munira have become good buddies," Brother Kabir observed. "Masha'Allah. They remind me of you two." He wagged his finger back and forth at Fatima and Tahani. He ducked his head and glared mock angrily at them. "Insha'Allah, they won't give me as much trouble as you two. Anyway, come by and see my wife and new baby later." He gestured out into the distance with his chin. "We'll be having her aqiqah soon, insha'Allah. She just turned three months."

Fatima nodded effusively at him. He turned and walked away. When he was a few feet away, she sidled closer to Tahani, who stood with her arms folded, sharp eyes following her girls' every movement.

"Girrrl," Tahani purred, already knowing what Fatima was going to ask.

"Baby?" Fatima asked.

"Mm-hmm, you heard him right," Tahani replied, raising an eyebrow. "And new wife too."

"Shut up."

Tahani chuckled.

"So, wait, this makes—?"

"Three," Tahani supplied. "And he's got five kids each from the first two, and the third one may not be done yet. She's only like thirty-eight."

"But how old is Brother Kabir?" Fatima asked.

"I don't know, in his late fifties gotta be by now."

"And he's still . . . ?"

Tahani smirked. "Brother Kabir got that thunder."

"Ew!" Fatima swatted at Tahani. "I don't even want to think about Brother Kabir like that."

Tahani laughed then stopped short, sucking in her breath sharply. Fatima looked up in time to see Asaad walking in their direction, though from the way he hunched his shoulders forward, hands stuffed into his pockets, his dreads hanging over his eyes, he didn't look like he planned to stop or even slow down. As he got closer Fatima could see his eyes were sad and tired, so different from how he had been at the open mic event.

"Salaam alaykum," he mumbled as he shuffled past so quickly he stirred up a breeze that ruffled Fatima's scarf. He didn't look at Fatima; his puppy dog eyes stayed on Tahani, who blinked rapidly and lowered her own.

"What was that about?" Fatima asked.

Tahani watched the kids with stony eyes, a light sheen of sweat glistening on her forehead. Her pale skin was already turning rosy from the heat. Fatima forgot Tahani didn't tan in the sun and wondered if it was the same with Safia and Aliyah, although they were a shade darker than their mother. Tahani finally spoke in a whisper after a long pause, her lips parting and shutting.

"He asked me to marry him," she said.

Fatima held her breath. "I thought—isn't that a good thing?" she ventured.

"I told him no."

"Why?"

Tahani pouted her lips and let out a sigh. "I can't. I can't do that to him."

Fatima shook her head in confusion. Tahani rolled her eyes and huffed.

"He's twenty-two. I can't saddle him with two kids."

"Isn't that for him to decide?"

"What does he know?" she snarled. "What do any of you know?" She glared at Fatima. "You all with your degrees and your futures. What do I have? He thinks he wants me, but it would be a mistake. Talking about how he wants to travel, wants to go to Africa. He's starting grad school in the fall. It would never work." She stopped. Her voice dipped low, as if she were talking more to herself than to Fatima. "He deserves better."

Fatima reached over and took her friend's hand. Tahani's eyes grew watery but no tears spilled; her chin quivered, revealing a dimple. She squeezed Fatima's hand back, then let go and walked over to her daughters, who in the midst of all their play turned to her like sunflowers to the sun. She knelt to them and raised her face to accept the kisses they showered on her cheeks. The other children crowded around them observing their joy. She opened her arms to them all.

The men set to work, unfolding long white tables and setting them out end to end in the grass, with a gap in the middle to separate the men's side and the women's. They spread newspapers across the tables and stacked napkins and tubs of wet wipes on a side table in anticipation of crawfish-juice-stained fingers. They hauled heavy bags of ice from truck beds and threw them down on the concrete, breaking the blocks into smaller pieces, then tore the bags open and dumped the contents into coolers of soda and bottled water. Brother Salim manned a huge, fiercely bubbling metal pot, its bottom heavily blackened with soot from several years of use. Blue flames licked the sides of the pot, flashing orange when they were fed by the boiling liquid that bubbled out from the top. A few other men stood around a grill cooking hamburgers and hot dogs, smoke from the grill rising in shivery waves around them.

Fatima walked around greeting people. They all asked about

Mama Tayyibah. She gave her standard response, alhamdulillah, she's . . . okay. Alive, was what she wanted to say but never did, the word a gut punch, a sobering reminder. Though just the mention of Mama Tayyibah's name made the air still. Death, or even its potential, its nearness, the ruiner of all pleasures.

Brother Kabir's eldest wife, Shakeela, insisted Fatima come sit with her and her co-wives and fill them in on her life. Shakeela lived out in Slidell and rarely came into the city if she could help it. "So much crime," she hissed. Her eyes swam behind her thick glasses, which slid down the bridge of her nose, her nostrils flared as if to keep the frames from sliding off her face. She wore a sage-green head wrap high on her head, a sprinkle of salt-and-pepper gray visible above her forehead.

The wives sat together in a circle on an old quilt; Daleel, the third wife, sat with her baby, who laid on her back on the blanket, tugging her bare toes toward her mouth, causing herself to rock back and forth. Daleel was homely and shy. Her skin was milky white, her eyes shockingly blue, shocking perhaps because she rarely raised them. She wore a gray abaya and white hijab, an old-fashioned cotton one with a lace trim, pinned below her chin.

Sherie, the second wife, shook a plastic giraffe above the baby's head. The toy squeaked when she squeezed it, to the baby's immense delight. Sherie wore a long, straight brown skirt and a loose flowery tunic with bell sleeves that fluttered out a few inches before her plump wrists, her hair covered in a brown cotton scarf tied tightly behind her head, the ends trailing down her back, small gold hoops hanging from her ears. She was a quiet, serious woman, both her and Daleel so different from the boisterous Shakeela; then again, Fatima didn't know them like she knew Sister Shakeela, who had been a fixture of her childhood in the masjid.

Fatima asked her about her children. Shakeela happily obliged to share their accomplishments. Not to be outdone, Sherie launched into details of her own children. It quickly became a cordial battle of bragging that Fatima observed like a tennis match between Venus and Serena, the lines between friend and foe bending and blurring. Daleel focused on her baby and her two-year-old running around in the grass with the other kids, her wild, crinkly light-brown hair, streaked with gold, lifting and falling behind her back as she ran with the children, she and Safia trying to keep up with the others. When finally there was a lull in Shakeela and Sherie's accomplishment sparring, Fatima excused herself and snuck away.

She was at the snack table loading a Styrofoam bowl with tortilla chips and salsa when a pair of sneaker-clad feet came into her line of vision and she heard a throat clearing in front of her. She looked up to find a gangly young man standing in front of her clutching the handle of a heavy-looking black messenger bag, its strap dragging in the dirt. He had sandy-brown hair, thick and spongy like new carpet, and pale, almost yellow eyes with girlish lashes; his cheeks, rosy like pink-paint-stained fingers had squeezed his face, were heavily freckled. His face was so much the same as Tahani's that Fatima knew instantly who he was but was still surprised.

"Hadi?" she said, squinting at him.

Hadi smiled shyly at Fatima, dropping his eyes. His already-red cheeks grew redder.

"As salaam alaykum," he said in a surprisingly deep and starkly serious voice.

Fatima hadn't seen him in many years. She remembered him as a quiet kid, always reading, tagging with her and Tahani reluctantly when his mother insisted he ditch his video games and comic books and go outside and play. He would typically stuff a book into the front of his jeans and squirrel away under some tree while the other children played, or walk several paces behind them when they trawled the neighborhood, tripping along the pavement, his nose in his book. He was only a year younger than Fatima, but she still thought of him as a kid, Tahani's kid brother. His voice said otherwise.

"What's up?" Fatima asked.

Hadi hoisted the bag up onto the edge of the table and pulled out a bulky black camera.

"It's loaded," he said. "I've got some others at home, and a recorder in the trunk, but I think this one is best for what Tahani says you're trying to do."

Fatima took the camera in her hands. "I don't know anything about cameras," she said, holding it awkwardly to her chest, looking at all the knobs and buttons on the panel.

"It's easy. Just point and shoot. You can see the images here," he said, pointing to the viewing screen. "Try it."

She held the camera up to her face and looked through the viewfinder, scanning the crowd around her. There was Tahani fixing the strap on Aliyah's sandal. Aliyah stood with her foot pointed out toward her mother, who kneeled dutifully in front of her daughter, who danced to a jig in her head, her upper body tilting and swaying, watching her friends play, anxious to rejoin them. Tahani looked up, probably to tell Aliyah to be still, but in a playful way, her eyes revealing a smile that made her daughter put her hand over her mouth and giggle. Fatima snapped a shot and looked at the image on the screen; the sunlight washed their faces out, only a shadow of their smiles visible. She went back behind the lens and found Brother Kabir holding his baby daughter up to his chest, one hand cupped protectively over her head. She caught that one too.

"These would be great in black-and-white," she said.

"You can do that," Hadi said. "It's easy. You can do all kinds of things to manipulate the photos."

Fatima lifted the camera back and scanned over to where the elder women sat in folding chairs, their arms folded over their chests or fanning themselves with napkins and pieces of cardboard. She caught Sister Amatullah looking at Sister Mariam, her hands folded gently in her lap, listening intently as the other woman spoke. Sister Mariam squinted out into the distance as she talked. Two other women leaned in to listen. Fatima wondered what the women were talking about that had them looking so serious.

"Do you have video cameras?" she asked.

She turned the camera toward Hadi and snapped a picture of him before she realized what she was doing. His face was caught in shadows from the trees behind him, causing the freckles to spread out like ruddy stars across his cheeks. They emphasized his youthfulness, but the shadows revealed a strong jaw and chiseled cheekbones. Wisps of fine hairs grazed his jawline. Looking at him through the lens, at everyone, made Fatima feel emboldened to study them. With her own face hidden behind the camera, she could look at them in a way she couldn't in real life, and also, they looked different, open and exposed, vulnerable, without even knowing it. In the picture she caught of Hadi, he looked back defiantly at the camera, at the person taking the picture. His gaze was steady and unflinching.

"Maybe you could help me," Fatima said, still looking at him through the lens. He extended his hand and gently lowered the lens from her face. "Oh, oops. Sorry. Everything looks so cool from behind the camera, so different. Know what I mean?"

He had a glazed look on his face, his eyes fixed on Fatima's mouth. She waved her hand at him.

"Yeah," he said, dreamily, then snapped out of whatever trance he was in, his golden lashes fluttering. "So what do you need help with?" he asked, back to business.

She explained to him what she'd been thinking about, about Sister Amatullah's manuscript, the stories they, as kids, had heard countless times, and the many they didn't know. He nodded, not exceptionally interested, but with respect for her idea. He had time. Now was a good time before he started graduate school. He asked Fatima about school and life in Atlanta, about being away from home.

"I think about leaving New Orleans," he said. "I know there's more opportunities for me elsewhere."

"The first year is hardest," Fatima said, which sounded like the right answer, "but it gets easier."

It hadn't been hard for her, but she couldn't say that. But if she was honest with herself, looking around at all the familiar faces, she realized what she may have been missing without even knowing it.

"So, are you going back?" he asked. "To Atlanta?"

Fatima looked around and felt a sadness creeping in that surprised her, and made her afraid.

"I don't know."

There was tremendous relief in speaking those words. They carried the weight of confession in them, and Fatima had finally set them down for a moment to rest. Why she said them to Hadi, though, she wasn't sure. But he seemed to understand something of their heaviness, detected a deeper meaning below the surface. He lowered his eyes, as if giving her some privacy, or perhaps he was embarrassed by this show of vulnerability.

They were interrupted by Tahani, who came up carrying a whimpering Safia.

"Here, you wanna tell your uncle about it?" she said.

Before Safia could answer, Tahani hoisted her into Hadi's arms. He took her with trepidation. He was the fun uncle, not the cuddly, comforting one. Fatima and Tahani giggled. He bounced her awkwardly in his arms and patted her on her back. Safia reared back and looked grumpily at him, but she relented and rested her head on his shoulder.

"What are y'all up to?" Tahani asked. "Y'all been over here for a while smiling and sharing cameras, acting like y'all ain't at a public function, a masjid one at that."

Her tone strained for seriousness but her joy was evident in the way she smiled at them.

Fatima rolled her eyes. "Whatever," she said, "it's just Hadi."

Her voice came out sharper than she intended, more sarcastic and dismissive, and they both picked it up. Hadi looked wounded. Tahani glared. Fatima tried to laugh it off but neither of them indulged her with even a smile. She cleared her throat.

"I just meant he's your brother. He's family."

They softened a little, and Fatima took it as an opportunity to gush about how Hadi had agreed to help her with her project. She smiled at Hadi in a way she hoped was sweet and apologetic.

"Yes, sure," he said. "I'd be delighted to help."

Tahani snorted. "Delighted?" she teased. "What are you, British?"

"Oh, right, my bad." He dropped his shoulder back in a gangster lean. "Fa sho, baby."

They all burst out laughing.

"That was actually pretty good, Poindexter," Tahani said.

Fatima laughed, but not too much. She didn't want them to gang up on her again. She lifted the camera back and snapped a few shots of Tahani and Hadi talking. She played around with the zoom features and looked out into the parking lot, searching the rainbow of brown hues warmed by the sun's glow, people laughing and dancing, playing card games, working grills, kids blowing bubbles and chasing each other with water guns. They were all out there together, enjoying the warmth of the sun and the refreshing presence of the water in a city that had drowned and revived itself countless times, a city that wasn't supposed to exist, filled with people, many of whom weren't supposed to exist either, yet here

FAR AWAY FROM HERE 205

they were and here the city still was, defiantly standing, storm after storm after storm.

Through the lens, scanning the crowd, a flash of white on black caught Fatima's eye. She turned back and looked out above the camera, then back behind the lens. Saif, dressed in a white thobe, walked through the crowds in the parking lot, head down, hands stuffed in his pockets, looking like a schoolboy hiding out, trying to avoid being seen and caught. She snapped a few shots of him loping along toward the barbecue.

A young man sidled up to him. Saif stopped, looked around, seemed to look right at Fatima through the lens. The man wore a red baseball cap, his face hooded by the brim. His shirt and sneakers, Jordans, were also red. His black jeans were stiff; his whole outfit looked fresh. A thick gold chain and gold watch glinted in the sunlight. Saif leaned back from the man. He rubbed his palm roughly across his forehead and kept looking around. He was fidgety, on edge, not at all like his usual self. Fatima's finger hovered over the capture button, but she didn't press it. This wasn't a moment to record.

The man in red betrayed no emotion. He kept his hands in his pockets and held a relaxed pose, legs splayed wide, shoulders back, yet Saif appeared threatened by the man. Finally the man relented in whatever hold he had on Saif. He stepped out of Saif's path and allowed him to continue on. Saif walked away, looking behind him several times at the man, who watched him. Again Saif seemed to be looking right at Fatima, though she knew he couldn't see her yet. She put the camera back down to her chest, her palm over the lens, and turned back to Tahani and Hadi.

She had witnessed something she shouldn't have, that much she knew. She was embarrassed to have seen Saif like that. Her feelings for him were complicated. She didn't like him, she didn't think she ever would, but she sensed he was in serious danger.

New Orleans was a small city where everyone seemed to know each other or at least have seen each other, but somehow Saif managed to keep his two lives separate; only Fatima knew of their dual existence.

But he wouldn't be able to continue like that forever; the two would come to a head, and the man in red was a crucial piece, an obstacle on the bridge between the two, the bridge Saif was trying to cross and then burn. Fatima couldn't help him, no one could. He was on his own, and she could see this turmoil in his eyes as he approached the picnic area. They locked eyes. Saif slowed in his steps, bobbed his head in greeting, and continued on.

Tahani turned to see Saif walking off toward the men. She turned back to Safia, who was now back in her arms. She broke off half of a tortilla chip from her bowl and handed it to Safia.

"He is so strange," she mumbled.

Fatima wanted to ask Tahani what she meant, but Safia began to whine as she set her down.

"Let's get you some food, mama," Tahani crooned.

"Can I have a hot dog?" Safia asked, hopping on her toes.

"Of course, binti."

Tahani kneeled and hoisted Safia on her back, who wrapped her legs expertly around Tahani's waist.

"She's getting so big," Fatima said wistfully.

Hadi nodded absently. She grinned at his disinterest in children. Picturing her own self as a mother seemed so far off in the distance. In all the time she spent with her niece and nephew in Atlanta, the endless games of Chutes and Ladders and interminable pushes on the swing or trips down the slide at the playground, and now lately with all the time spent with Aliyah and Safia, still it was a world that seemed foreign to her, a place she might never travel to. She felt old sometimes, like some things—marriage, motherhood— were lost to her, sealed away like winter clothes in the tropics. She couldn't imagine being any other way than she was now, alone, a thought that filled her with an unbearable sadness. This failure of her imagination seemed permanent, unchangeable.

She understood Tahani's refusal of Asaad as a failure of imagination, too, even when faced with an opportunity for change. Why were they all so set in their minds about what their adult paths would be? Why couldn't they accept happiness as a possibility for themselves? What made them think they were unworthy?

Fatima looked at Hadi as he munched contentedly at a handful of grapes he'd plucked from a bowl of fruit at the table. That was what made him seem so much younger than her, the freshness of possibility that hadn't been snatched from him by unfortunate circumstances. He had done what the adults always said to do: focus on school, enjoy your youth. If Fatima had never reconnected with Wakeel, if he had just stayed a fixture of the past, she would probably be like Hadi, young, youthful, not carrying adult baggage. Tahani too. If she had made different choices, perhaps the pursuit of happiness would be a given.

Deep love at a young age had changed her, just as young motherhood had changed Tahani. But then they wouldn't have the experiences they'd had, wouldn't have learned what they could endure at such tender ages. Was it worth it? Were the sacrifices to youth and adult happiness worth the love they now knew that carried them, haunted them, kept them up at night, held them and imprisoned them at the same time? Fatima didn't know, and what was the point in pursuing the answer? Here she was. Here they were. Now.

They feasted. Hot, spicy crawfish and boiled shrimp was tossed across the newspaper-covered tabletops. Whole baby red potatoes and corn on the cob, halal spicy beef sausage. There were burgers and hot dogs, coleslaw, and Sister Mariam's should-be-famous potato salad. Sister Juwayriah made a dozen of her crawfish pies. Fatima managed to snag a slice before they were gone, which didn't take long. The men complained about not getting any.

The children continued their play, grazing food from their parent's plates or being snagged by their shirts and having food stuffed in their mouths while they kept one foot out, ready to run off again. They would play till sunset and maybe later, and not till everything was packed up and it was time to go would they declare themselves hungry, starving, and beg for food immediately, their tired eyes blaming their parents for depriving them of nutrients.

The men and women stuffed themselves, ate themselves silly, yet they sprang up with ease when it was time to pray. Brother Anwar rose to call the adhan. Plastic sheets were spread across the grass, weighted down with chairs and table legs. They passed around jugs of water filled at taps. "Not too much, not too much. Use what you need. Use only what you need," was shouted as the jugs exchanged hands, till everyone stood in rows, water dripping from ears and elbows, hemlines soaked. Children who took the rows for play spaces were quickly snatched up, their howls snuffed out with threats of lost toys and no candy, or a promise to go home immediately, canceling quickly arranged plans for sleepovers. Finally the noises settled down and they could pray.

Saif was called up to lead but he shook his head. "Maybe he's sick," folks whispered. "He must be feeling ill," a few murmured. Fatima could not see him, but she felt his agony. The only illness nested in his soul's yearning to be free. Where was escape? Let him hold it for a minute, let them all, a tiny moment of peace, of connection with their Lord.

Brother Anwar gave a duaa after the prayer: "Ya Rabb, Ya Allah, deliver us from evil, protect us from shaytaan, block us from his grip, plug our ears from his call, his taunt. Audhu billahi min as shaytaanir rajeem. We seek refuge. Cover us, protect us. Ya Allah. You are Mercy, You are the Most Merciful. Cover us with Your Mercy. Ameen."

Saif

SAIF SAT ON HIS HAUNCHES IN THE FAR-LEFT CORNER OF the masjid, his eyes downcast but still taking in the filling of the room. Brothers gave him hearty salaams but quickly retreated, eyes questioning and concerned, catching a hint of his weariness but giving him space. He forced himself to breathe slowly when he really wanted to grab and gulp the air. Was he bobbing at the surface or slowly sinking? Only he knew the answer. A few steps away, an elder brother in a tan thobe rose slowly and stepped to the mic, raising his hands to his ears. The elder paused and in the silent room Saif heard him gather his breath to begin the adhan. Saif closed his eyes against the trembling of his heart.

It was his time now. The whole room stilled in anticipation. He rose and stood at the lectern and forced himself to look fully at the congregation, the faces, the upturned eyes, tired, bored, eager, hungry for the word. Most of them would never stand where he stood, never see what he saw, never feel what he felt—that mix of fear, excitement, and anxiety to fill their minds, hearts, and souls with something good, something from the Creator.

He saw Brother Umar among the helpers in the far-left corner near the door. They propped him up, physically and spiritually. There was a slight brokenness to his posture, but he was still and resolute, tilted at the waist with his head inclined toward the mimbar, determined to catch every word. He wore a tattered gray

FAR AWAY FROM HERE

jalabiya and a black striped knit kufi crooked over his Afro. There was his uncle Kareem, his father's younger brother, Wakeel's beloved stepfather, sitting patiently in the last row at the edge, ready to assist Mama Tayyibah if needed. Many times his uncle had reached out to him after Wakeel's death, offering him food, inviting him to the masjid, even hinting at a place to stay, but Saif had ignored or shrugged off all attempts, deeming himself undeserving of love and care. Still he knew if he were to step to his uncle today, right at that very moment, his uncle's arms and heart would be open to him. If only he would take the step.

He glanced over at the women's section, a crayon box of color shimmering against the drab browns and grays of the men, intensified by the sunlight that crawled through the blinds, bathing them in gold. The mothers, grandmothers, aunties, and sisters, the love that measured beneath heavy lids, seeing all and excusing nothing, merciful, compassionate, and exacting. Among them was Fatima, who he knew was there, could feel her presence and her gaze, but he didn't look at her. He welcomed the reminder she brought, the shame he needed to strive.

He began his greeting to the congregation when the door to the main prayer hall opened. He was used to this happening at the start of the service, but something about this interruption made him turn toward it. Three young men entered the room. They wore jeans slung low at their hips, T-shirts revealing tattooed arms and wrists, gold chains winking out from the neck bands, baseball caps that were quickly removed. To everyone else there was nothing remarkable about their appearance. Many of the young men, new to Islam or straddling the secular and the sacred, the masjid a brief respite from the streets, didn't take on the jalabiyas or kufis, though a few wore beanies or dhikr beads strung around their necks or wrapped around their wrists, things to be slipped into their back pockets when they left. So no one else batted an eye at the newcomers. But Saif caught the pressed black jeans and red T-shirt and cap of one of the young men, and his breath thinned.

At the quiet urging of an elder, Dupe and his associates, the same two who were always with him, slipped their shoes off and placed them on a shelf by the side of the wall. A flash of tension passed through Dupe at this unexpected command, an unwillingness to obey in the set of his spine. He tilted his chin at the elder then slowly bent down to remove his shoes. He was not a man who humbled himself.

Dupe and the other men tried to sit by the wall near the exit door, but another elder pointed them to the third row in the men's section, which put them at the center of the mimbar, right in Saif's line of vision. Sweat seeped into the collar of Saif's thobe. He looked down at the Qur'an in front of him on the lectern next to his notes, the Arabic words he knew well now blurring together on the page, swirls of indecipherable script.

Allah's first revealed words to the Prophet Muhammad came to Saif like a whisper, "Read in the name of your Lord." The letters stopped swirling and locked into place. Solid black lines that had withstood the test of time, traveling from the desert of seventh-century Arabia to twenty-first-century America to flow off the tongue of a young Black man in a little neighborhood masjid in New Orleans.

Like the alif, the beginning letter of that first prophecy, Saif must stand tall and face his challenge. With a quick intake of breath that expanded his chest, he looked up and looked squarely at Dupe. He had been called to this religion and called to the mimbar to speak to the people, his people. He had something to say, something they all, Dupe included, needed to hear.

"I greet you all with the best greeting," he began. "As salaamu alaykum wa rahmatullahi wa barakatu. Peace be with you and the mercy and blessing of the One God, Allah."

FAR AWAY FROM HERE

213

The rumble of voices returning his sincere greeting strengthened his heart. Though many of them saw him often, at the mimbar or sitting among them, they had never witnessed the smile he gave them now, the opening of his heart that brought light to his face. They smiled back at him, warmed by his glow.

"I want to talk today about forgiveness. Istighfar is a powerful concept. We know Allah is eager to forgive us any fault within us, any wrong we commit. Allah in His infinite mercy wants nothing but to share that mercy with us, His greatest creation. But too often, something gets in the way of that path to forgiveness. We say it's Shaytan, and yes, that's part of it. We say it's dunya, the trials and traps of this world laid down by Shaytan and his helpers, and that's part of it too. But the greatest obstacle to reaching Allah's mercy is sitting right there in your mirror.

"Allah is ready to forgive you, but are you ready to forgive yourself? You've done wrong, you've made mistakes. We know, because Allah tells us in this book, that not a single soul, not even our blessed prophets and righteous teachers of Islam, our dear scholars and imams, will enter paradise without His mercy.

"But the path to that mercy starts with us, facing our mistakes, facing our sins, admitting our wrongs and then forgiving ourselves and committing to doing right. I've done wrong. I've done harm. I seek Allah's forgiveness and I accept His forgiveness. I accept that I am worthy of His forgiveness. We say, 'La hawla wa la quwwata illa billah,' 'There's no power or strength except with Allah,' and if we accept that Allah has all the power, we must accept that what we seek of Him, what only He can give, is given to us."

"And forgiveness is transformative," he continued, "in a most unexpected way. It's a gift that keeps on giving." A few squinted at him, curious where he was going with this logic. "What happens when we seek Allah's forgiveness and accept tawakkul, the trust that we are forgiven, and then forgive ourselves. Then we reach another, greater level in which we can forgive others who have wronged us and seek forgiveness from those we have wronged."

He looked to Brother Umar, looked into his sad eyes.

"I have done wrong, please forgive me."

He looked to Mama Tayyibah, whose eyes glazed with fatigue. He looked to Baba Kareem, who tipped his head to his nephew, pain and pride making his jaw tight. He looked to Imam Hassan, who looked sternly back. Last he looked at Dupe, who looked back with hate-filled eyes.

"I have done wrong, please forgive me."

Without a word to the other men, Dupe stood and walked quickly out of the prayer hall, snatched his shoes, and left. One of the other two men jumped up and followed. The third man, swept up by the sermon, sat unblinking for a moment before he came to and clumsily rose to follow Dupe, an unwillingness to leave revealed in the jerkiness of his gait.

The sweat had dried from Saif's face, replaced by a coolness that came from his soul. Ease coursed through his limbs and numbed his fingers. He touched the pages of the Qur'an but didn't feel them; a pleasant tingle tickled his fingertips. He grasped the sides of the lectern against the lightness in his feet, feeling as if he could float up and away.

After the prayer, Saif slipped quickly out of the prayer hall, not wanting to speak with anyone. He stuffed his feet into his black striped slippers and hurried out the door toward his car, aware that Dupe could be anywhere on the block waiting for him, but not caring, until he heard his name being called. His throat tightened. He turned.

Imam Hassan stood at the gate in a white band-collared shirt with a pen clipped into the shirt pocket, black slacks, and a black domed kufi. Saif moved to walk back toward the imam, but he stopped him with a hand and came toward him. Without stopping he said, "Walk with me," and kept going. Saif took a breath and followed him. Two blocks down and just before Claiborne Avenue, the whoosh of cars on the interstate above them, Imam Hassan turned into a vacant lot with overgrown grass and several pieces of wood stacked along a fence.

"Watch your step," Imam Hassan warned. "Folks been using this space as a bathroom for some time. And for other things too."

He took a white handkerchief from his pocket and dabbed at his forehead. He pointed at the piles of wood.

"Been talking with a few of the businesses around here about getting together and purchasing this lot. Make it a community gathering space. Garden, health fairs, festivals."

Saif nodded, unsure of what to say.

"Something a lot of our younger generations don't understand, can't understand yet. When we talk about rebuilding, revitalizing, the survival and thriving of our people, our neighborhoods, our future and history? Our community, the ummah, has to be at the forefront of those movements. When Allah says He has a trust with us, a promise to the believers, this is how we fulfill that trust. We are the naturally equipped leaders."

He looked at Saif.

"You know how old I am, son?"

"All y'all elders immortal," Saif responded.

Imam Hassan didn't laugh.

"No, we're not. I'm seventy-five years old. I've been leading this community for more than two decades, and when I tried to step down, all hell broke loose. Everybody wanted the position, but nobody could see beyond a foot in front of them. A leader's got to see from all points of view, all walks of life.

"And then you came in. I saw that spark in you that warms people, makes them quiet their minds and listen for a minute, makes them see further into the distance, beyond the traps of this dunya. I thought, 'Here's someone.' Not to try to fill my shoes but make his own footprint, leave his own mark and keep that path clear a while longer. But we can't lead if we're not living the Qur'an and the Sunnah. I saw what happened today. I can't have anyone at the mimbar bringing danger to our community. It's our responsibility as Muslims to stop harm when we see it, and sometimes prayer isn't enough."

"What you saying, Imam?" Saif asked.

"I think you know what I'm saying, son. You've got some wrongs you need to make right before you step in that masjid again. Those people in there are counting on you to bring good."

His face softened. He lifted a hand toward Saif and, after a pause, laid it on Saif's shoulder. Saif's knees quivered. His one last safe space was being pulled from him, and rightfully so. He could do nothing but bow his head. Imam Hassan squeezed his shoulder, then patted him. Each pat was a hammer driving him into the earth. The imam walked away, leaving Saif alone amid the weeds. He could walk in, crawl in, lie and die with nothing and no one to mourn him.

Fatima

FATIMA WOKE LATE TO A BRILLIANT, DECEPTIVE SUN blazing through the half-opened window blinds. Melting ice dripped down from the gutters. The promised freeze had finally come. Baba Kareem and Mama Tayyibah's house, like most homes in New Orleans, wasn't built for cold weather. Fatima's face was numb with cold. She was hungry and had to pee but dreaded coming out from the layers of blankets she had piled on top of her. She didn't know the time but she knew the night nurse, Penny, had likely stepped out for her late-morning break. She sank deeper into the bed and took a breath to brace herself, then threw off the covers and dashed to the bathroom.

Back in the bedroom, she jogged in place as she pulled on sweatpants, a hoodie, and thick socks. She dug out an extra-long crocheted scarf she was grateful she had decided to pack and wound it twice around her neck, the wool tickling her ears and chin. She went to the kitchen and put on water for tea and dropped two slices of bread in the toaster. Baba Kareem's heavy orange coffee mug sat drying on the dish rack. She smiled at it.

Things had improved between Mama Tayyibah and Baba Kareem. A tenderness had returned between them, observed in Mama Tayyibah's caress of her husband's cheek, one finger tracing down to his jaw when he served her tea, Baba Kareem's gentle grasp of her heel in his palm when he helped her put on her slippers. Just the other day Fatima had found him kneeling on the side of the bed next to Mama Tayyibah, holding her hand in his and kissing her knuckles one by one. Fatima had quickly turned away, whispering thanks to Allah for their reconciliation.

She slathered her toast with butter and strawberry preserves. She was just taking a bite of the sweet, warm bread when she heard Mama Tayyibah call her in a croaking voice.

Fatima bent her head back in exasperation, then snapped it quickly back up, catching herself. How much longer would she have to hear Mama Tayyibah's voice calling her? She turned off the kettle.

"Yes," she called, a false tinkle in her voice.

Fatima opened the door to find Mama Tayyibah standing completely naked at the side of the bed, a puddle of discarded clothes at her feet, swaying on her legs to keep her balance. Fatima rushed to her.

"What are you doing?" she tried not to shriek.

"I was trying to get to the restroom," Mama Tayyibah said, her voice a whimper.

Fatima looked down and saw a soiled diaper at Mama Tayyibah's feet. She grabbed a blanket from the foot of the bed and threw it over Mama Tayyibah.

"Come to the bathroom, Mama. Let me clean you up."

Fatima's eyes blurred with tears when Mama Tayyibah whimpered a feeble "okay" in response. Fatima cleaned her with water from a spray bottle and tissue then ran water for the shower. It took a while to warm up. Neither of them could look at each other, confronted with Mama Tayyibah's vulnerability. When the water heated up, Fatima helped her into the shower and onto her shower seat, then washed her down with a soapy rag. Afterward, Fatima dried her with a towel, lotioned her body, and dressed her in a long nightgown, an emerald-green velour dress with gold piping and a

FAR AWAY FROM HERE

zipper at the front. She found thick wool socks and swathed Mama Tayyibah in her favorite raspberry-colored terry cloth robe. Lastly she cupped the back of Mama Tayyibah's bald head in her hand and slipped a black turban over it. She couldn't get enough clothes on Mama Tayyibah to cover up their mutual embarrassment. Mama Tayyibah laid back on the pillows, exhausted. She smiled sadly at Fatima, her eyes tired. Her eyelashes were gone, as were her eyebrows, brow bones smooth, not even a single stray hair.

"Our roles have reversed," she finally said. "I used to change your diapers; now you're changing mine."

She chuckled. Fatima pressed her lips together in a sad smile.

"Alhamdulillah, it's a blessing to be able to care for you," she said, and meant it.

Mama Tayyibah smiled; then her eyes landed on Fatima's chest and her smile vanished. Fatima looked down and her face flushed. She was wearing one of Wakeel's old high school sweaters. The John. F. Kennedy logo in blue and yellow with the lion's head in the center stretched across her chest. His last name, written in black marker right above her heart, was faded but still shone. In her haste to get warm she hadn't noticed what she had put on.

"It's time, Fatima," she said after a beat of silence.

Fatima shook her head.

"Time for what?" she asked.

"Time to give him up," Mama Tayyibah said, her voice rising in strength, growing indignant. "You're a young woman. You got your whole life ahead of you. It's time to give him up, Fatima. He's gone, baby girl. He's gone."

Her eyes were resolute, dry and steady. Fatima stared back, tears pooling in her eyes. Give him up? She couldn't give him up. He was her love, her great love. Fatima dropped her head, and fat tears dripped down on her sweater, Wakeel's sweater, spreading quickly to form dark ovals on her chest.

"Learn from me, Fatima. Life is for living. If I've learned anything from the tragedies and obstacles Allah has placed in my path, it's that. Life is for living. I could be sad because we lost Wakeel, I could be mad at Kareem for hurting me when I was vulnerable, I could be mad at Allah for giving me cancer, but all of that is just life. Not good, not bad, just life. And I want to take my last breath knowing I spent most of my days, most of my time, living."

Fatima sat slumped forward on the bed, her hands in her lap. She bowed her head, numb.

"Aw, come here, girl." Mama Tayyibah patted a spot on the bed next to her.

Fatima crawled carefully over Mama Tayyibah and lay down in her arms, resting her head gently on Mama Tayyibah's bony chest. She'd known deep down all along that though she came back to be with Mama Tayyibah, she'd really come back to be with Wakeel. She didn't want to let him go. She wanted to hold him in her heart, to wrap herself in the memory of him and the love he had promised her.

Her mind went back to when they'd met again as teens at the Treme Center for a Kwanzaa event, after all those years apart. Walking around with Tahani and their friends, as all the teens did, she'd sucked in her breath when she saw him across the room, then quickly looked away, hoping she was mistaken. She'd looked again. It was him, and he was staring back at her openly, a smile on his lips. *He's beautiful*, she'd thought, taking in his shoulder-length dreads and deep-brown skin. Had he always been that beautiful?

Fatima had tugged discreetly at Tahani's sleeve, trying to tell her about Wakeel, but she was too busy gossiping with the other girls. Too quick for her to get her game face on, they reached the spot where Wakeel was standing with a group of boys. She'd made up her mind to just keep walking and pretend she hadn't seen him when he stepped out from the group toward her.

"Fatima, what's up, sis?"

His voice had been smooth like honey on a sore throat. She barely recognized her own name because he made it sound so pretty.

"Heeey. I didn't—how—what are you doing here?" She giggled and put her hand over her mouth, embarrassed. Wakeel laughed, rubbing his faint beard.

He raised his arms, spreading them wide to take in the whole room. "I'm back. I'm home. Couldn't take the cold no more."

Fatima raised her eyebrows and cocked her head, waiting for more.

"Nah, for real. My folks got homesick. Went from Chicago to Indiana to Virginia till they finally realized ain't no place like this city. Took a while for my dad to get a job, but my mama had gotten her degree in nursing back when we were in Indiana and got a job at Touro, so we packed up and came home. Ain't been back but about two weeks."

"Well, my mama will be happy to know y'all are back. Her and your mama lost touch."

"Yeah, from all the moving. I need to get your number." He stumbled on his swagger for a second. "I mean, to pass on to my mama, you know."

Fatima had laughed, leaning in toward Wakeel, then looked around, jarred back to reality. She had completely forgotten about her friends and all the adults that were surely watching them. Sure enough, she spotted Tahani's parents, Mama Sajeda and Baba Musa looking directly at her. They'd both tipped their heads toward her, Mama Sajeda with her usual scowl, Baba Musa grinning like a kid.

It was the ease with which they'd slipped into a life together that stayed with her—the quick courtship, the late-night phone calls, evenings on his porch sharing dreams—as easy as breathing. They talked as though they'd never lost a day of contact.

She had another memory, the one time he had kissed her. It

was at an Eid picnic at Joe Brown Park in late fall, chilly enough for light sweaters. They'd gone off the trail through the trees, their feet crunching on dying leaves. She looked at the splash of skin on his neck above his hoodie and without a thought hooked her pinky around his, tugging him back. He looked frightened, his fingers grazing her hips sending sparks throughout her body. Then he leaned over and kissed her, his lips dry and warm. He pulled away and they smiled shyly at each other. They went back to the trail and walked without saying a word. That was her last memory of him before he'd been killed.

Fatima's tears dripped onto the sleeve of Mama Tayyibah's robe. She watched as they vanished into the terry cloth material. Mama Tayyibah started to fidget. Fatima picked her head up.

"You need something, Mama?" she asked.

Mama Tayyibah looked around the room. "Um, well, it's just . . . *Magnum, P.I.* is about to come on."

Fatima rolled her eyes and grabbed the remote. She left to fix her tea and eat her cold toast, then came back and tucked herself back in the bed next to Mama Tayyibah, who was riveted by the action on the screen. Soon they were hashing out the plot and giving their own suggestions on who Magnum should investigate, and disagreeing over who the criminal was. When Magnum hopped in a boat to chase after a suspect, Mama Tayyibah tsked.

"Mm, mm, mm, I always thought that Tom Selleck was some kind of sexy."

"Mama T!" Fatima shrieked.

"Girl, them dark eyes and all that hair on his chest," Mama Tayyibah chuckled. "Yes indeed."

Fatima didn't remember any conversation after that. Despite the tea, she fell asleep before the episode ended. She dreamed that she and Mama Tayyibah were chasing Tom Selleck in a motorboat with Mama Tayyibah steering. They rammed their boat into Tom's, and just when they jumped into his boat he turned and it was Nurse Penny, her hair wild, yelling words Fatima couldn't understand. She woke to find Nurse Penny standing over her clutching her shoulder, her face distraught.

"Fatima," she said breathlessly. "Fatima, she's gone. Ms. Mujahid is gone."

"Who?" Fatima said, confused and wanting to go back to her dream. She turned to Mama Tayyibah and jumped fully awake. Mama Tayyibah lay sunk in the pillows, her face ashen. Fatima scrambled out of the bed and covered her mouth with her hands. She felt as if the possibility of sound had been sucked from her body. Nurse Penny thrust her phone into Fatima's hands. She looked down at it and then at Penny.

"You need to call her husband. Better he hears it from you."

Fatima dialed Baba Kareem's number, and her knees buckled at the sound of his voice. Years ago that voice had woken her with the worst news of her life. Now it was her turn to do the same.

"Baba Kareem," she cried. "I'm sorry. I'm so sorry . . ."

PART THREE

Fátima

FATIMA'S PHONE PINGED WITH A MESSAGE FROM Tahani letting her know she had just pulled up. She stood at the kitchen counter pouring coffee into two portable stainless steel cups. She added a splash of half and half to each steaming cup and capped them off.

It was just after fajr and the sky was still an inky black with only a milky thread of dawn to mark the transition from night to day. Fatima could smell the clean scent of rain through the slightly opened window above the kitchen sink. Her reflection shone back at her from the window glass. The skin around her eyes was dry and puffy. Her lips were chapped. She hadn't bothered to moisturize. Mama Tayyibah would have clucked her tongue over such neglect.

She took a long sip of the coffee and felt a slight awakening of her senses. She had lain awake in the dark most of the night, despite the steady rain that normally would have soothed her like a lullaby. Alternating between short bursts of choking sobs and quiet whimpers and sniffling, she eventually fell into a heavy slumber just a few hours before the morning adhan trilled from her phone. She tried unsuccessfully to blink away the cobwebs of fatigue that weighted her eyelids, her eyelashes separated like they had been glued shut. This was going to be the longest day of her life.

As she took another, shorter sip of her coffee, a few errant drops of cream dripped down onto the bodice of her dress. She pinched the jersey fabric to shake off the droplets, then wet a corner of one of the white tea towels Mama Tayyibah always kept hanging off the oven door and dabbed gently at the dots of milk. It was Khalilah who, months ago, had quietly pulled the black jersey boatneck dress from the back of the closet and handed it to Fatima while she packed. Fatima had stopped her packing and looked with disgust at the dress, but Khalilah had shaken it gently at her, her eyes down. "You might need it," she had said. Fatima had balled up the offending dress and stuffed it down to the very bottom of her suitcase, only to pull it out last night and find it immaculate and unwrinkled, the reliable fabric rolling out and bouncing back into shape as if it had only been waiting patiently to be retrieved.

Tahani was at the front door when Fatima opened it.

"Hey," they both sighed.

Fatima's eyes immediately filled with tears that she blinked back. Tahani's eyes were equally red and watery.

"I was gonna come down," Fatima said, her voice a croak.

She handed Tahani the second cup of coffee. Tahani shrugged.

"Thanks," she said.

"Yeah," Fatima replied.

She looked up and down the quiet street, the only sound the latent drips of rain from the trees. Light mist covered all the parked cars and dusted the grass and bushes along the sidewalk, all glittering under the streetlights. Fatima took a deep breath and exhaled through her mouth.

"God, I'm not ready for this," she said, expecting fresh tears that now didn't come. She knew they were there beneath her eyelids, just waiting to reappear anew.

"Me either," Tahani said. "Funny how we try to prepare for these moments but we just never can. Every time is like the first time."

FAR AWAY FROM HERE 229

Fatima knew Tahani was thinking about her grandmother who had died just after the storm. She rested her hand on Tahani's shoulder and squeezed. Tahani patted Fatima's hand with her free one, then sipped at her coffee.

"Mm," she hummed with appreciation. "Well, at least we have coffee." She held out her cup and Fatima tapped it with her own.

"Girls gone mild," Fatima said sadly.

Tahani chuckled then nudged Fatima's arm with her elbow as she turned toward the stairway.

"Come on, girl, we gotta do this," she said.

Fatima sighed and followed her childhood friend down the stairs, where the car sat running, the headlights beaming into the gray shadow of the streets beyond. Baba Kareem had arrived quickly after Fatima called, so fast it seemed Fatima had just hung up the phone. He thundered down the hall in his heavy boots and barreled through the bedroom door, his eyes wild, then collapsed to his knees at the sight of his beloved wife, her body small and sunken, her skin already turning ash gray, no longer warm and of this world. The sound he made—the bellow and moan like a wounded animal— it had rung in Fatima's ears through the long, sleepless night, moving in and out of her consciousness like a ghost in the corners of a haunted house. It rang still, causing Fatima to shiver as she dropped into the passenger seat of Tahani's car. She turned instinctively to the back seat, so used to greeting Aliyah and Safia when Tahani picked her up, but of course it was only a dark, empty space, devoid of the joy and laughter the girls brought to her life and that she had come to look forward to. This was no joyride with children, no trip to the lakefront or City Park.

"The girls are at home sleeping. My neighbor Ms. Terri is watching them," Tahani said. "I'll pick them up . . . after."

Her voice trailed off. "After" meant after preparing Mama Tayyibah's body for the janaza. Tahani pulled up at the Charbonnet

Labat funeral home on Claiborne Avenue. Cars whooshed by on the interstate above them, the splashy sound of tires slicing through rain-slicked lanes pocked with dents and cracks.

They walked in through the heavy glass-paned double doors of the front entrance. The women stood in a huddle near the chairs in the front foyer. The soft yellow circles of lights above them ringed their covered heads with golden halos. Sister Amatullah, in a somber gray abaya and white headscarf, was the first to notice Fatima and Tahani. She nodded with her chin toward them, and all the women, about a dozen of them—including Sister Iris, Sister Bayyinah, Sister Sukina, and Sister Maryam—Mama Tayyibah's closest friends and elders, turned to Fatima and Tahani, their arms opening to the two young women in one synchronized movement.

Tahani and Fatima fell into the women's pillowy-soft arms and breasts and wept freely for the first time. They didn't need to pretend to be strong with these women, their spiritual mothers and grandmothers. It wasn't the first time these women had picked them up when they were down. They had nursed stinging scrapes with nothing but the coolness of their breath, pulled tissues like magic from their sleeves in anticipation of a sneeze, wrenched coughs caught deep in the chest with firm pounds from the heels of their smooth brown palms. They had wiped away tears with one thumb swiped across tender cheekbones and had soothed those other aches that didn't have names, the ones that cracked the heart but didn't draw blood. They no longer kneeled to these young women who now stood above them, folding themselves to fit into their sagging arms, but still they held them up against the harsh winds of heartache till the ground beneath their feet stopped shaking.

Sister Amatullah rubbed Fatima's arms vigorously, a sad smile on her face. Grief pulled her eyes down at the corners, but they glowed with an acceptance of what could be neither understood nor changed.

"Inna lillahi wa ina ilayhi raji'un," she whispered, grabbing hold of Fatima's hands and running her thumbs across her knuckles. "To Allah we belong and to Allah we return. It's hard, sugar," she said to Fatima, "I know it's hard. But Allah is with her. Allah has been with her, comforting her through this whole thing, and He ain't about to leave her now. He's gon' send those angels down to be with her in her grave to help her rest easy till He wakes her up and calls her home. We just gon' pray for her soul to be ready to meet Him when the time comes."

"Allah is merciful," one of the women said.

"*Most* merciful," said another.

"Mm-hmm," they all said together, their voices one harmonized hum.

"Now's the hardest part though," Sister Amatullah said, still rubbing Fatima's arms but looking at Tahani too, knowing neither of the young women had ever participated in this ritual. "But there's blessings in this. Let's go on and get our blessings and help our sister and mother Tayyibah go home to God."

Fatima took a breath that shook her to her core then nodded. Sister Amatullah cupped her hand with both of hers, and Fatima reached over and took Tahani's with the other. Together the women turned toward the door that led to the room that held Mama Tayyibah's body.

"Bismillah ir-Rahman ir-Rahim," Sister Iris called as they began to walk.

Whispers of the repeated prayer fluttered through the small group of women: "In the name of God, Most Gracious, Most Merciful." A gust of cold air washed over Fatima's face as they opened the door and stepped into the room. At the back end of the room below wide fluorescent lights, Mama Tayyibah's body lay on a steel table, a white sheet covering her from below her shoulders to her feet. Fatima took in a sharp intake of breath that nearly choked her. Tahani squeezed her hand, her own trembling.

Fatima's knees nearly buckled when she saw Mama Tayyibah's face, the features she knew so well shrunken and decaying. Her lips a sickly blue sagged down toward her ears in a painful grimace. Fatima wished to take her fingers and push up the sagging corners and return them to the mischievous grin she was familiar with, the one that made her smile in turn. Underneath those closed eyelids, thin as wax paper, were dead eyes, not the twinkle she yearned for. Her bald head underneath the harshly bright lights revealed gray, scaly patches of skin she wished to soothe with coconut oil.

Mama Tayyibah's collarbones pointed up prominently from her diminished frame. The bones brittle, like Fatima could snap them between her thumb and forefinger. The delicate brown shoulders soft as baby skin. Her eyes traveled down the length of Mama Tayyibah's shrouded body, naked beneath the seamless white cloth that would later cover her face and head. There would be no silk or gold or diamonds to adorn her body. She would return to the earth as she came into it, till only her bones remained to tell a story of a past life.

Fatima looked at the cloth that hung down past Mama Tayyibah's feet almost to the ground. She lamented the weight of it over Mama Tayyibah's toes, knowing how much the woman hated the feel of her feet covered by blankets, always insisting they remain out. Would it disrupt her comfort in her grave? Did we feel the weight of our bodies while our souls were still caged within them?

The women circled the table and gathered towels and small buckets of water around Mama Tayyibah's body. Sister Bayyinah stood at Mama Tayyibah's shoulder and took hold of one corner of the sheet and nodded at Fatima, who stood at the other shoulder, to do the same. She took hold of it as all the other women grabbed at

FAR AWAY FROM HERE   233

pieces of the hem. Fatima looked at Tahani, who stood near Mama Tayyibah's lower legs. Tahani looked back at her and raised her eyebrows in a way that said, "Here we go." A Qur'an recitation played lightly in the background as the women chanted prayers and removed the cloth that concealed Mama Tayyibah's body.

They pushed their sleeves up above their elbows and dunked the towels in the rose-scented water. They rang out the excess water and flattened the cloths to cover their palms, then proceeded to wipe down the body of their beloved departed sister and mother. The creases in the corners of her eyes, under and around the many curvatures of her ears, around her nail beds, under her arms and breasts, between and beneath her toes. They rinsed and wiped till the smell of roses engulfed the air around their beloved. With their hands and their prayers, they did their best to touch her true self, her soul. Though her body would go into the ground to eventually fall away and become part of the dirt beneath their feet, the ritual cleansing marked the cyclical nature of life. As we are wiped clean of the fluids that cling to us at birth to be brought forth into the world, shedding that which nourished us in the womb, so we are wiped clean of the filth we accumulate in this world to be presented clean to our Lord.

Together they lifted her body, diminished by illness, and laid her gently down on the cloth. They wrapped her tightly in the seamless cloth and, with one last look at her face, shrouded her completely in white. The women laid their hands on her body beneath the cloth and prayed. Sister Iris began:

"Ya Allah, Ya Rabb, forgive our sister. Have mercy on her soul. Accept all her good and forgive her sins. Oh, Allah, comfort her in her grave. Receive her with gentleness and compassion and mercy. Shower her with your all-encompassing love."

Sister Juwayriyah picked up and continued:

"Allah, you are al-Ghafur, The Forgiving, and you love to forgive. Forgive your humble servant, Tayyibah Sabreen Mujahid. Allah, you are Most Generous, and you love to show generosity, so we ask you to be generous in your reward for our sister, Tayyibah, and her family and loved ones. And bless and reward generously all those who cared for our sister in her time of need. Allah, pave the way to Jannatul Firdaus with ease for our sister, and make her soul spotless to meet you."

After each line of prayer, the women called, "Ameen." When Fatima's turn came, she recited Surah al-Fatihah and found herself at a loss of what to ask of her Lord other than His forgiveness and mercy. What would Mama Tayyibah ask for at that moment, if she could? What would she want Fatima to beseech The Creator for? It came to her.

"Allah, in your infinite mercy, have mercy on Mama Tayyibah and reunite her with her son, Wakeel. Have mercy on both their souls and bring them together in infinite reunion. May they be a comfort to each other, a reassurance and coolness for their souls."

The women moaned and wept at the mention of their beloved sister's son, their nephew.

"Ameen, ameen, ameen," the women called, their voices heavy with feelings of loss and grief.

Once the women had finished their prayers, the men came silent and strong and settled her body in the plain pine box to be transported to Masjid Al-Ghafur. Baba Kareem was with them, his head bowed, pain emanating from his rigid posture, his face slack with the burden of loss and an empty heart. Fatima's own heart ached for him. What would he do in that empty house now? What would he live for?

The prayer hall could not contain the number of people who came to attend the janaza. Members of Mama Tayyibah and Baba Ka-

FAR AWAY FROM HERE 235

reem's extended family came, as did Muslims from all over the city and the various masajid. Many of them didn't know Mama Tayyibah or Baba Kareem but had come to pray, as was the obligation of all in the ummah who could, for their departed sister in Islam.

Imam Hassan outlined the ritual for the unfamiliar. The believers lined up in rows at the adhan, their hands at their sides or clutched to their chests, their heads bowed. They stood as they would in any other prayer, but, unlike when they prostrated to Allah, with this prayer there was no bowing or kneeling, only hands raised and lowered in praise of God, heads bowed in respect and prayer. There were many tears shed, a few choked sobs, but the dignified believers stood tall and firm, though some leaned, and some provided shoulders and arms to lean on. It was a day of much sorrow and a reminder of their return to Allah, a reminder of the temporary nature of the body and the dunya, the transitory world in which the believers sought to serve Allah and earn passage to the eternal home, Jannah, the garden of eternal paradise and bliss with Allah and all His beloved, those who had shown steadfastness in faith and worship. Those who had striven to do good in His name, and constantly sought His forgiveness, knowing only His mercy was the key to entering His promised land.

Tahani

"HEY, DARLING," JALISA CALLED AS SHE WALKED UP TO Tahani, who sat at a small table outside of a coffeehouse on Basin Street. She had called Jalisa the day before to talk about her offer. Jalisa suggested they meet up. She was too flighty over the phone. "I need to see a face to focus," she said.

It was a Sunday, their day off. Jalisa had come straight from mass wearing a yellow floral print dress and tan leather stilettos. She took off her sunglasses and placed them above her head, her hair in a sleek bun; her signature black eyeliner and perfectly painted red lips.

"You're looking a lot better, hun. Come here," she said, opening her arms wide.

Tahani stood and accepted her hug, breathing in her scent of White Diamonds.

"Ooh, ooh, ooh," Jalisa cooed, rocking Tahani from side to side before letting her go.

It had been two weeks since they had buried Mama Tayyibah. Tahani had taken a week off to grieve, but on her first day back at the salon she messed up so badly at work—dropping tools and forgetting clients under the dryer, spacing out when she was supposed to be shampooing them, water running aimlessly over their heads— that Jalisa had pulled her aside and suggested she take another week off.

FAR AWAY FROM HERE 237

It was losing Mama Tayyibah, for sure, and being reminded of her grandmother's passing, but it was more than that. She hadn't spoken to Asaad since the proposal, and she saw his face, his sad eyes, everywhere she looked. She ate very little and slept terribly. She went through the motions of her day robotically, getting her girls ready for school and dropping them off, giving them dry kisses on their cheeks. They watched her with hooded eyes and pouted but didn't complain. She lay in bed at night, wide awake, following the slow rotation of the blades of the ceiling fan, playing Aretha Franklin CDs over and over. One late night, after her twelfth rotation of "Do Right Woman," her downstairs neighbor, Ms. Terri, had called her to see if she was okay. "These walls are thin, my dear," she'd said. Tahani had apologized and switched to headphones.

"Here's your latte," Tahani said, moving the drink over to Jalisa.

"Thanks, doll," she said, taking a small sip. "I can't tell you the last time I've been backatown. Back in my day when Canal Street was the place to see and be seen, we didn't go past Rampart. Now we've got coffee shops where there used to be hookers and projects. I got a great-uncle, Jimmy, who played trombone with Buddy Bolden and his band back when this area was Storyville. My great-aunt June claims she met Jimmy at church." She raised an eyebrow at Tahani. "If that man ever stepped foot in a church it would burn down as soon as one of his toes touched the threshold. The devil himself," she muttered. "But enough of my stories."

Tahani laughed. "Ms. Jalisa, you're a Storyville all by yourself. I mean, not like that of course."

Jalisa made a gesture of zipping her lips and throwing away a key, then winked.

"So anyway, doll, how are you? You said you wanted to talk."

Tahani took in a breath.

"Yeah," she started. She looked at the woman who'd been an auntie to her the past three years, dishing out wisdom and wisecracks, teaching her how to be a woman standing on her own two feet, and giving her lots of grace as she navigated young single motherhood. "I appreciate the offer, truly, but . . . I don't want it."

She'd thought she'd say something different, something more layered. That she couldn't take on the responsibility because of her daughters, or that it conflicted with her other pursuits, like her growing interest in interior design. But all she could think was that she was tired, tired of everything, tired of her life. She wanted something else, something she was too afraid to name. She pondered words to soften what she'd just said, but when she looked over at Jalisa she saw the woman was smiling at her without a trace of indulgence.

"I'm proud of you, hun," she said. "I knew you didn't want it, but I wondered if you'd have the guts to say it. Good for you."

"You really mean that?" Tahani asked.

Jalisa pursed her lips. "You ever known me to not say what I mean?"

"Point taken," Tahani conceded.

"Doll, you're not like me," Jalisa said. "I like to think I played a role in shaping you up these past few years, but you're your own person. You work hard, but you've got other priorities, starting with those two lovely girls you're raising. I'm satisfied with my life and the sacrifices I made to get where I am, but I do recognize I made sacrifices that maybe now I see I didn't have to, at least in the way I did. Maybe, you know, maybe I could have made room in my life for a family without it smothering me. I see you and I see how that's possible."

Tahani had a feeling akin to swallowing an ice cube whole. She was shocked and needed a moment for Jalisa's words to thaw in her mind. Sacrifice, possibility, making room for growth. Was she doing any of that? How could anybody see possibility in her if she couldn't even see it in herself?

"Ms. Jalisa, I know you joke a lot about doing things different from how your family would have liked but, wasn't it hard? Weren't you afraid at all?"

"Of course I was," Jalisa responded.

"So what did you do?"

Jalisa shrugged. "I just did it afraid."

"Now the question is," Jalisa continued, "what are you going to do?"

Tahani wanted to be bold in her fear like her mentor, but still she couldn't speak what she wanted.

"I don't know," she said, shrinking back into her seat.

Fátima

FATIMA KNELT ON THE SIDEWALK IN FRONT OF MAMA
Tayyibah's garden in sweatpants and a tattered denim shirt Tahani
had given her. She had moved out of Baba Kareem and Mama Tayyibah's house and was now residing on Tahani's couch. She hadn't
considered Mama Tayyibah actually dying, so she had given no
thought to where she might stay if—when—the woman passed. She
worried about Baba Kareem in that big empty house, air thick with
sickness and death, ghosts of memories flitting around the rooms,
but it wasn't proper for her to continue to stay there. She had
packed her bags, lingering over but ultimately leaving behind all of
Wakeel's old things, and left the house with all and only what she
came with. The knowledge that she would likely never return to
that home that held so many memories, beautiful and tragic, sat
heavy in her gut. But she would honor her promise to herself and
tend to Mama Tayyibah's garden, restoring it to life and color.

She struck the earth with the sharp edge of the spade. It barely
made a dent in the dirt, tight with thick veins of roots sprouting
tough weeds. Various tools and bags of soil surrounded her, overwhelming her in the task she had set for herself. She didn't know
how to grow anything. She had never tried. She pulled off one of
the gardening gloves and tried to press her fingers into the hard
earth, cold and damp from the departing winter. It did not yield to
her touch.

"It's gone take a lot more than that lil bitty spade to break that earth, chile."

Fatima jumped. Sister Amatullah stood behind her on the sidewalk in a brown embroidered jilbab and a tan-colored cotton scarf.

"Sister Amatullah, you scared me," Fatima said. She looked up and down the block. "Where did you even come from?"

"I should ask you the same question," Sister Amatullah replied with a laugh. "I didn't mean to scare you, baby. You must have been working hard to not hear me come up. Or deep in your thoughts is more like it, 'cause it don't look like you got much done," she said, scanning the rigid earth. She knelt down and lifted wilted petals into her palm. "Mm. I think we gone have to start fresh. Dig up all this old stuff and plant some new things." She stood to her full height. "It's a new day."

"I love gardening," she continued, "because it reminds me of what Allah say about how He makes the earth dead and barren to where we can't remember there ever was life there, and certainly don't believe anything can come out of it again, then He plants the seeds and brings the rain down and then what? Flowers and plants shoot up and it's a rainbow of colors. The bees come and the birds come, the caterpillars, all the little bugs, just life everywhere. Subhan'Allah. If the dirt and all that comes out of it ain't a sign of Allah's existence, I don't know what is. Who else could teach so much through something so simple yet so complex?"

She squatted and hooked a thick rope of roots under her finger. She tugged at it, and Fatima followed its snaking path as it revealed rich, brown soil beneath the hard, packed earth.

"On the flip side, some folks see the flowers and think they will always be there, and they come to not appreciate them for the miracle and blessing they are. They stop tending them and then become confused and even angry when they eventually die. But it's both.

Allah says it's both. There are signs in death and signs in life, for those who take heed."

Fatima surveyed the dead and drooping plants, the dried and broken leaves, the tender flower stems that still held feebly to the dirt, or maybe the dirt was still holding the stems up, or both. *It's both*, she thought. *Just like Sister Amatullah said. The stems hold on to the dirt, and the dirt holds on to the old, wilted flower, and they both wait patiently for Allah's truth to come to pass.*

Sister Amatullah rubbed her palms to get rid of the crumbs of dirt that clung to them.

"We gonna clear all of this off and build us something new. That's something Sister Tayyibah knew. You don't just pick up and patch over. You clear the land and start fresh."

"So what do we do first, then?" Fatima asked, still uncertain of the task in front of her.

"Get you a shovel and start digging and turning," Sister Amatullah said.

Fatima stood, renewed. "Okay, I can do that."

"Now where you staying these days?"

"With Tahani."

"She got space?'

Fatima shrugged. "Kind of. I'm on the couch now and we talked about getting an air mattress in the girls' room."

Sister Amatullah tilted her head.

"Yeah, it's not really comfortable," Fatima mumbled.

"Mm," Sister Amatullah sniffed. "I know y'all best buddies and all, and I know she like your help with her babies, but I got plenty of room at my house if you find you need more space to move around. Got whole bedrooms that ain't being used since my step-daughter, her husband, and my grandbabies moved out there to California. You welcome."

"But I guess," she continued hesitantly, "you planning to go

FAR AWAY FROM HERE

back to Atlanta now." She said it as a statement, but her eyes held a question.

Fatima poked the dirt with the toe of her sneaker. She didn't know what to say. Not long ago she couldn't imagine anything worth coming back to New Orleans for beyond a short visit. Now she felt a strange pull toward this place, the only home she had ever known; this homeland that for all the misery and tragedy it held in its roots and in the air she breathed was still as familiar and natural as the palm of her hand. It was so hard to describe.

Her body rested, her breath loosened in this city. At some point she had noticed her breath never tightened in her chest here like it did in Atlanta or Houston, where everything was unfamiliar, no longer to her eyes or brain but to her body. The body remembers. The body knows. It speaks through breath. The even rise and fall of her chest, the slowed, slight heartbeats that she didn't feel but knew were occurring because she was alive, her eyes were open and her mind was working. It was a peace that only came with a feeling of being at home, a feeling of being in the right place.

As she had once, not long ago, looked at New Orleans as a place that had nothing good or beneficial for her, nothing remarkable, now she looked that way at Atlanta. A room in her sister's home, a relationship with a young man who despised her religion, tension and uncertainty, a feeling that she needed to constantly fix some part of herself, fold herself to fit someone else's mold, discard the pieces that held the essence of who she was at her core.

At least she couldn't leave now, she told herself. Not until she finished working on Sister Amatullah's memoir. An idea had begun to sprout, to collect stories from her ummah, bring them together, and make something of them. Show the world, project them out to the world to let people know they existed, they were here, living, praying, loving, and dying as Muslims. It set a fire in her. Like Mama Tayyibah's little stamp of a garden in a tiny section of this small but well-known mythic city that people from all over the world flocked to but knew very little about, truly. She would break through the surface and show the life underneath, show the beauty of it, what grew from it and would continue to grow for generations as long as they had the right seeds, insha'Allah. It would be something not just for others but for her and her generation, and Aliyah and Safia's and everyone that came after. A message to say we are here, we have been here, and we will continue to be here, growing and thriving, by Allah's will. So she had time, or rather she would make time, to build something beautiful.

"I think I'll take that offer," Fatima told Sister Amatullah, who hid the delight that sparkled in her eyes with a short nod.

"Well," she said, "you just come on over when you're ready. I'll have a cup of tea waiting for you."

"Sage?" Fatima asked with a grin.

"With a pinch of mint," Sister Amatullah replied with a wink.

Fatima smiled. She was wide awake and more alive than she had ever been in her life.

Saif

SAIF TOOK THE LONG WAY TO THE PRISON WITHOUT much thought. Time had never been his enemy, but it wasn't his friend either; it just existed alongside him, observing him coolly. When no one was home waiting for you, no one expecting you or anything of you, other than the suffering, addicted folks whose pain he profited from, to his and their detriment, time had an infinite, exhausting quality. All the time in the world to do nothing, to feel the utter fruitlessness of his existence, to wish and wish for death, to imagine his body shriveling and hardening and eventually crumbling to dust, discarded and forgotten. Disintegrated into nothing. Anyone looking at him behind the wheel would have seen a picture of calm and concentration, effortless focus, like a clock between ticks. Beneath the surface was a mind moving in many directions, grief, sorrow, anger, guilt, desperation, anxiety like an itch he could not scratch.

He hadn't visited his father in many months. Shame kept him away, caused him to write short, tepid responses to his father's lengthy, thoughtful letters, filled with his hard-earned life lessons. His father's mind, as shown through his letters, was sharp as ever, not softened or weakened by prison walls, razor focused on one subject: purpose in life. Serving Allah, knowing Allah, seeking knowledge through reading His Book and turning over each word, each letter, and striving to give it its full due. They were two men faced with the expansiveness of time, but where one found it punishing, the other immersed himself in it, letting it guide him and instruct him.

Saif pulled into the gate of the prison parking lot and handed his driver's license to the guard, who accepted it without a word. It was rare that Saif was granted a visit, and it took months to secure it. Despite the exhausting paperwork and phone calls, the long drives and endless security checkpoints, Saif was turned away with little explanation more often than he was let through. He could count on one hand the number of times in his adult life he had seen his father.

Though he wore the same clothes as all the other men, dark-blue pants with a lighter blue shirt, his father stood out from the other men with his full, groomed beard, increasingly more silver than black, and stark-white kufi. It wasn't that he was exceptionally tall, but he held himself in a dignified manner, back straight, head tilted up in quiet dignity that demanded respect. Even the guards who led him in, shackled in chains like the rest of them, respected him in the way they escorted him. Other visitors noticed and studied him. Without knowing him, they knew there was something about him, the way he carried himself with a self-respect that couldn't be touched, that they admired. Saif took in his father with deep pride despite all the sadness he himself carried. He could never be like his father, but he could shelter under the man's enormous shade, if only for the thirty minutes he was allowed, under strict surveillance.

His father raised his arms, wrists bound by handcuffs, and extended his open hands toward his son, both an offering and a beseeching request. Saif returned the gesture, placing his hands in his father's to be engulfed in their warmth and strengthened by their resolute love. He then let go and wrapped his arms around his father, resting his cheek on the solid rock of his father's shoulder. He wanted to cry, weep, and be supported by the solidity of his father's broad chest, but he knew he could not do that. He pulled away and wiped roughly at his eyes with the back of his hand. His father's eyes were wet too, but he let the water run into his beard and stain his dark cheeks, his entire face tender with love and yearning.

"Salaam alaykum, son. Alhamdulillah, you looking good."

It was what his father always said.

"'Hamdulillah you too, Daddy," he replied, after returning his father's greeting.

They sat across from each other at the picnic-style table and took each other in with shyness. Saif noticed the new streaks of gray in his father's immaculate beard and the faintest trace of age softening the sharp lines of his face.

"It's good to see you, man," his father continued. "Thanks for coming out to see me. How was the drive?"

Saif shrugged. "It was good. Fine."

A feeling of restlessness crept in. He shifted in his seat, wanting to be there but wanting to leave at the same time. Escape, flee back to the lengthy, gray indifference of the highway.

They had only just sat down and already one of the guards announced a twenty-minute warning. A wince flickered across his father's face at the announcement. Time flipped, contracting sharply during visitations. Days could go by staring at a gray cinder block wall or a sliver of sky through a barred, meshed window, but minutes picked up and flew away at a maddening rate in these rare moments of human connection. Saif thought he would gladly sit in a cell till the end of time if he could be contained with his father. But he had mere minutes, and much he needed to say. He leaned forward and rested his elbows on the table, his head bowed.

"Daddy, I'm in some trouble."

His father bobbed his head slowly, knowing without knowing.

"This world ain't nothing but trouble for a Black man," he said, his words not forgiving or excusing but stating a painful truth.

"I don't know what to do," Saif said, cradling his head in his hands. "If I stay here, it's a good chance I'm gonna end up dead. I don't wanna leave but I don't know what else to do. Ain't no confessing or making amends."

His eyes shifted around the room as he talked, taking in the huddles of families. At the table to the left of them, a young Vietnamese woman rocked an infant in her arms, her torso swinging back and forth in that way of mothers in all places and times who used their bodies to soothe intuitively, her gaze leveled at the young man in front of her, who looked off at a space beyond his feet, shamefaced. On their right, an elderly Hispanic woman, a wooden cross hanging from a leather cord around her neck, clutched the hands of a middle-aged man as they both whispered prayers intensely, the man openly weeping. Just as Saif looked at them, the man opened his eyes and looked back at Saif, his lips still moving in prayer. Saif looked away, feeling he had seen something he shouldn't. He could feel the man still looking at him as he rocked in prayer. The honest, open pleading in the man's eyes terrified him. He looked back at his father, who lifted his hands to stroke his beard.

"We don't run from our problems, Saifullah. But we don't wait at death's doorstep either." He raised his hands to indicate the prison. "This place is hell, man. Don't lay your neck down at these devils' feet."

"What you saying, Daddy?" Saif asked.

"I'm saying what Allah said, 'Indeed I have made this Earth spacious for you.'"

"You saying I should go?" His voice rose in agitation.

"I'm saying read your scripture. Turn to your Lord and ask Him to open your heart and your mind to His message. Ask Him to show you the path, illuminate it for you. Don't be afraid to set out."

The guard announced a five-minute warning.

"But what about you?" Saif pleaded.

"What about me?" his father responded. "I'm here, man. And likely gonna be here till Allah calls me home."

"But," Saif said, "you all I got in this world. What I'ma do if I can't see you?"

His father reached across the table and grabbed his hands. Saif had never seen such fire in his father's eyes.

"Meet me in Jannah, son, insha'Allah. Go away, far away from here so you can finally live, and meet me in Jannah."

"But where can I go?"

His father let go of his hands and tapped his fist on the table.

"That's for you to figure out. Pray on it, and Allah will answer you."

An alarm sounded and all the guards moved to attention. His father stood, and Saif stood too. He hugged his father to him and let his tears fall freely this time. The guard behind his father extended his arm then pulled it back. He then extended it again and clasped Saif's father's elbow.

"Time," he said in a low voice.

The two men stepped apart. His father turned away quickly, not wanting to see his son's face. Saif watched his father's back as he retreated, those striated muscles depicting a map to salvation. His father never looked back, and then he was gone, back to his cage.

Fátima

'SO HOW DO YOU WANT TO DO THIS?' SISTER ASIYAH asked Fatima.

She sat stiffly on the sofa in her living room, hands folded into her lap. She was in her fifties, a brown-skinned woman with a copper-colored wig styled in a bob with feathered bangs that swooped down just above her gold-rimmed eyeglasses. She wore white linen trousers, a loose white T-shirt, and a quarter-length-sleeve button-down shirt patterned with gold and purple swirls worn open. A delicate gold watch laced her wrist. She was a serious woman, that was how Fatima had always known her; even when she smiled her eyes remained sharp. She wasn't unfriendly but didn't entertain small talk, rolling her eyes or sighing when the women talked about clothes or hair at social gatherings, despite her own meticulous attention to her appearance. Sister Asiyah's outfits were always carefully put together, with earrings that matched perfectly. She had the type of wardrobe that would have been fun for girls to play in, scarves and brooches, pearls and beaded necklaces, lots of high-heel shoes. She had no daughters though; she had raised five sons.

Sister Asiyah was one of the founding members of Masjid Al-Ghafur, "back when it was just a little storefront, one little bitty room," she said, eyes shifting uncomfortably to the camera Hadi had set up. "Wasn't nothing but ten of us in there, but we still had to hold our breath to make space for everybody."

"How many women were there?" Fatima asked.

Hadi shuffled behind her, adjusting the camera. He'd shown her how to do it, how to work the camera, but offered to stay this first time. He sniffled while he worked the camera. Fatima could hear the sound of his tongue scratching the back of his throat trying to relieve the unceasing itch. The pollen was heavy that time of year, in the early spring. Everyone Fatima saw had heavy antihistamine-drugged eyes, their lids rimmed red, noses swollen. So far she had resisted it and held steady, downing packets of vitamin C powder dissolved in water, plus the vitamins Sister Amatullah recommended. Legend had it she never got sick, not even so much as a sneeze, a tale Sister Amatullah neither confirmed nor denied.

"Five," Sister Asiyah stated. "It was five couples."

"So how did you come to the religion?" Fatima asked.

"Oh, well, I suppose it's an ordinary story," she started. "Me and Imam Hassan's wife, Sister Khadijah, we went to school together, back when she was still Claudia. I hadn't seen her since we graduated high school and then I ran into her at a grocery store, the old Schwegmann's on Gentilly Boulevard. I was married two years by then and expecting my first child and she had just had hers, so we got to talking about pregnancy stuff. Now I noticed she looked a lot different since the last time I had seen her. Claudia always had her hair and makeup and her short skirts or tight pants with heels. But now she had on a long skirt and a long-sleeved blouse. It looked homemade. And she had her hair wrapped up. It was plain but she looked nice, real . . . satisfied with herself. So I asked her, you know, what was going on with her, and she starts telling me about Islam, right there in the front of the store with folks walking around us and me with my shopping cart. By the time we was done, my ice cream was melting."

"What did she say?" Fatima asked.

"You know, I don't remember exactly, but what I do remember is she said it had set her free. This was the early eighties and we was coming off the Black Power Movement and a lot of us was confused, you know, going from dashikis and black turtlenecks to button-up shirts and ties. It was a confusing time, and just a lot of us felt like we were losing our way. I know I did. It was nice to see someone who seemed to have regained their footing. Anyhow, she gave me a W. D. Muhammad tape with one of his lectures. Told me to listen to it when I had some time. Soon as I got in the car that's just what I did. By the time I got home I was ready to call her up right then for some more."

"What was the lecture about?"

"Well, it was about everything I had been thinking about really. About where we were as a people in that moment. How to get that fire for revolution going again or redirect the flames, whatever we needed to do. He was talking about the family and community and how what was missing, what we had lost in the seventies, was the spiritual element. That we needed faith and action to liberate ourselves. That's what I remember most.

"Then I got home to my husband and I was so excited to share the message with him, but he wasn't trying to hear it. He'd lost two brothers to drugs and didn't want to have nothing to do with any religion. He was all about working, making money, saving money, thinking that was gonna protect him from his brothers' fate.

"I knew I had enough to worry about, with my baby coming and my husband, but I couldn't stop thinking about what Claudia—Khadijah—had introduced me to, so I kept learning, calling her when my husband was at work, hiding books and listening to Imam Muhammad's lectures. Next thing I was going to her and Hassan's house, where they had jummah in they living room.

"Then came the time when my husband found my books and

tapes and confronted me about them. I was scared a little, because I loved him and didn't want anything to mess us up, but by then I was also a believer. Had taken my shahada over at Khadijah and Hassan's just a few days before then. But I took courage from what I had learned about Imam Muhammad's mother, Sister Clara. She was the one who introduced her husband, you know, Elijah Muhammad, to Fard's teachings, which led to him becoming the minister of the whole Nation. Some folks don't know that. So I did like Sister Clara and told my husband he needed to hear this message and become a Muslim like me."

"And what happened?" Fatima asked.

"He fought me on it. It got to where we was barely talking. I wanted to back down but I couldn't. How do you back down when you believe? Finally I got angry with him and I gave him an ultimatum. I told him he needed to accept Islam or lose me. I had a bag packed and everything. Told Khadijah I might need a place to stay."

She stopped and stuck her chin out at Fatima.

"And then what happened?" Fatima pressed.

"Well, a few months after that, I gave birth to a son and we named him Muhammad after the Prophet and the imam and we went on to have four more sons, and here we are today. I like to think listening to me and taking me seriously was the smartest decision he ever made."

Fatima was quiet after Sister Asiyah finished her story, then she laughed.

"So that's Brother Kasib?" she asked.

She knew Brother Kasib as one of the ones who was always in the front row for jummah, admonishing the congregation to listen with diligence during the khutbahs and demanding straight rows for prayers, calling out, "Shoulder to shoulder, toe to toe," until everyone was in order.

"Yes, child. Who else could it be?"

Fatima shook her head.

"Sister Asiyah, you started off saying you had an ordinary story, but nothing about that story was ordinary."

"Humph," Sister Asiyah laughed. "Well, that's my story." She smoothed a crease in her linen trousers and patted her hair. "Now, honey, I got dressed because you said you was going to take my picture. I hope my efforts weren't in vain."

Outside Sister Asiyah's Broadmoor home, Fatima and Hadi packed the camera equipment into the back seat of Baba Kareem's truck.

"Thanks for letting me use all this," she said to Hadi. "Hopefully I won't have to call you with any issues."

Hadi toed the dirt with his sneakers.

"I mean, I have time if you want me to keep going with you," he said, his cheeks blooming with color.

"I don't want to keep you," Fatima replied.

"No, you can," he said. "I mean, it's okay, I don't mind."

Fatima shrugged.

"Well, okay then."

"So who's next?" he asked.

Sister Rabia lived in Tremé in one half of a double shotgun with peeling white paint and dark-blue shutters, just a few blocks from the masjid. Her daughter, Fatemeh, had let them in. She didn't respond to Fatima's salaams.

"She's not a believer," Sister Rabia explained after her daughter retreated to the back of the house, "but she takes care of me and I pray for her."

They sat in her living room near the open front door, the frigid cold of the morning having loosened to a cool breeze, afternoon sunlight splashing across the worn wooden floorboards. Sister Rabia was a tiny woman with delicate, doll-like features. She sat in an armchair tucked into a corner by a window bundled in a brown cardigan and long skirt, her two-piece headscarf pulled low over her forehead, the edges touching the rims of her black eyeglasses. Her feet were covered in thick wool socks. Small cups of a fragrant green tea steamed on a short round table in front of them.

"Most of the Vietnamese, like me," she said, "came to New Orleans in the 1970s and settled out in the East in Versailles, where they still are, but I spent only a short time there, staying with a white Catholic family. They were nice enough to me until they found out I wasn't a Christian. I was raised Buddhist, technically, but we weren't religious in my family. My father and mother were college educated, professors. I was their only child. They never said it outright, but they didn't believe in any gods. We observed the rituals when necessary, but that was it. I was separated from them when we fled Vietnam. I was twenty years old, newly married; my husband had been killed before I even got to really know him. I had to leave, we all had to leave. We were all supposed to be on the same boat but something happened. I never heard from them again. Anyway, things cooled quickly with the Catholic family when I refused to go to mass with them.

"I got a job working in a gift shop in the French Quarter owned by an Iranian family. They offered me a room and seemed nice enough, so I took it. Easier to get to work and whatnot. They were quietly religious. Prayer rugs on the floor, Qur'ans and religious texts in Farsi and Arabic. They didn't talk to me about it. But they were also intellectuals, lots of books in their house, and I liked reading. From their library I was introduced to the teachings of Ali Shariati, his poetry especially I liked. There was one, "Philosophy of Supplication," that I read often. My favorite line was 'My Lord, give me absolute submission through iman, so that in the world, I may be in absolute rebellion.' So cheeky. I think my father would have loved it.

"I told the family I wanted to learn more about Islam. They pointed me to the mosque, to Al-Ghafur."

"What did you think of the community?" Fatima asked.

"I thought I liked the people there very much. They were . . . serious, but they smiled and called me 'sister.' It didn't matter that I was different from them. They gave me a Qur'an in English. I took it back to my room at the Iranians' house and I read it, and a week later I came back and said, 'Okay, I want to be a Muslim.'"

"What would you say made you want to be a Muslim?"

"Well, I believed, first of all. I read the Qur'an and I recognized it as truth. You see, it wasn't for me so much the early life I had experienced, war, death, losing my family, and fleeing my homeland, it wasn't really any of that. I was already . . . unsentimental, you might say. I've never been a person very interested in feeling. That may be why I've been unsuccessful in marriage. Married, divorced, married, divorced, married, divorced. It's never mattered much for me. I feel with my mind and therefore I can recognize truth very easily. The mind and the spirit are connected. If I am intellectually free, then I am spiritually free. And that is what I took from Allah's words in the Qur'an and what I still take from them. It's the practicality for me. The understanding that the rituals will lead to results. I pray and I fast and I give charity, and my salvation is guaranteed if I continue to do those things with sincerity. There is peace for me in that precision."

"And what about for your daughter?" Fatima asked.

Sister Rabia opened her palms wide.

"It's for her to see it. I can only ask Allah that she sees it for herself. In the end it is only us, individually, and God."

Saif

IT WAS CLEAR TO SAIF THAT HE HAD TO GO, BUT HE HAD one more stop to make before he could begin preparing for his departure. The three-bedroom camel-back house on Almonaster Avenue had never been home for him. The white curlicued awning hung down across the front of the house like lace, the bright white of the trim against the warm ginger of the body suggesting warmth and invitation, but not for Saif. He hadn't called first, not wanting to hear the hesitation and discomfort in his mother's voice, the indefinite pause of finding an excuse to say no, now is not a good time, or for him to fill kindly with a reversal of his request, his own embarrassed disinvitation. So he showed up unannounced at a time he knew they would all be there, because he no longer cared about their discomfort or disdain for him.

He got out of the car and made his way resolutely to the front door. Ferns hung from the porch beams. A wide wooden swinging bench perched in front of the large picture window. In the far corner sat another, smaller white wicker bench and glass-topped coffee table, several newspapers, edges of the worn pages curled and turning brown from the moist air and heat of the sun. Next to the door were several pairs of slippers, three very large rubber pairs in dark colors and one smaller pair of Daniel Greens in shiny matte gold. Saif pressed his thumb on the doorbell, hearing the echo of the ring pulse through the house, then rapped his knuckles once sharply against the wooden doorframe. He heard the shuffle of footsteps approaching, a slight creak as the person leaned against the door to look through the peephole. After a pause the porch light clicked on and the chain lock rattled. His brother James opened the door and pressed his face close to the screen door. He pushed his glasses up with his knuckle and squinted.

"Saif?"

"Yeah, bruh."

James didn't move to open the screen door. Saif's bravado dissolved. He was at a loss of how to continue. The old awkwardness around his younger siblings crept back in. He patted his thigh.

"I mean, I just wanted to come by and say hello," he said.

He gestured toward the screen door but didn't touch the handle. James looked behind his shoulder into the darkness of the house. He was uneasy, clearly unprepared and regretting having answered the door. He couldn't close the door on Saif and ask his parents for permission to let in a blood relation. But he knew his parents would be upset with him. He pushed open the door to Saif, who he had only ever known as a quiet shadow in his young life, someone he often forgot to mention when talking about his family and didn't include even when he did remember him. Still, Saif was his brother, full stop.

Saif took hold of the handle, and James stepped back to let him in. He shut the door and flicked the lights on, revealing a neat living room unchanged from the last time Saif had seen it. His mother had always made sure her home never looked like it was dominated by boys. She ran the home with military precision, beds made upon waking up, sinks rinsed and wiped down after brushing teeth or washing hands. An unflushed toilet or dirty dish left in the kitchen sink could get you banished to your bedroom for an entire weekend. Or you could be Saif and be banished just for being Saif. There were never rewards or praise for chores done well. Her silence meant she was satisfied. Remembering all this, Saif slipped his shoes off and tucked them below a side table next to the front door. He wondered what his mother would say if he reminded her that the removal of shoes was an Islamic practice. She would likely make some noncommittal sound and pretend she hadn't heard him.

Saif stood and faced his brother. James was tall and wiry and looked exactly like their mother, with his eyes that turned down at the outer corners and his thin nose. He looked over his glasses at Saif. He tugged at the hem of his T-shirt, then stepped forward to hug Saif.

"Oh," Saif said, accepting the hug and patting James on the back. The action surprised him; he couldn't remember ever hugging any of his brothers. He smiled and James smiled back.

"So how you doing, man?" Saif asked. "How's, you know, your life and all?"

James rubbed his palms together like he was cold.

"I'm in my first year at Xavier."

"Word?" Saif said. "What you studying?"

"Psychology," he said with an embarrassed shrug.

Saif nodded his head. "That's dope, man. What you want to do with that?"

Saif didn't know what to ask his brother. Talking about school and career was foreign to him. But what he said must have worked. James brightened under Saif's praise and curiosity.

"Um, I'm not sure, but I know I want to work with kids. I'm thinking maybe social work."

"That's cool, man," Saif said. "Sounds like you got a good plan."

Light footsteps shuffled up the hallway toward them. A tenseness filled the space between them. Saif wished he could stay as he was, talking with the brother he had never really known who was growing up and becoming his own person. He wanted to slow the moment down, still time around them, to extend the rare feeling of connection. But all too soon his mother appeared and he knew that little spark of fire he and James had started was out before it could catch on.

She was as beautiful and intimidating as he remembered. Face smooth and unlined, hair pulled back in a neat bun at the nape of her neck. Her face reminded him of Whitney Houston on the cover of the album she used to listen to a lot when she still missed his father and talked wistfully about what the three of them would do when he came home. Except where Whitney's eyes on the cover had been soft and mysterious, his mother's now were stony. Her nostrils flared ever so slightly at the sight of her eldest son. She pressed her lips tightly together and turned her face toward James without looking at him.

"Go to your room," she said.

James looked at his mother then back at Saif.

"Later, man," he said, eyes hopeful.

"Fa sho," Saif responded. He grinned. "Lil brother."

James smiled. They dapped off and James turned down the hall toward his bedroom. It was just Saif and his mother now, the air thick between them.

"Why are you here?" she asked as soon as James's door shut.

She didn't offer him a seat. Didn't say his name or call him "son." Nothing to warm him or make him feel the least bit welcome. He was an intruder to her life, the life she wanted and built, a life of middle-class stability and respectability, a pastor's wife and proud boy mom. Perhaps if Saif looked like her the way James did, her pecan-colored skin and slender build, instead of his solid, husky frame and black skin like his father's, maybe then she could have fit him into her dream life. A child from a previous marriage, quiet as kept, only mentioned when absolutely necessary, the possibility he

FAR AWAY FROM HERE

was their full-blood son cast over them as an illusion of cookie-cutter perfection. But he looked nothing like any of them. He was an ink stain in their picture of perfection that had to be completely washed out.

"May I sit down?" he asked, gesturing toward the sitting room cloaked in darkness.

She took in a slow breath, her chest rising and falling. She tilted her chin up. "Fine," she said, the word coming through tight lips and clenched teeth. She tightened the belt on her robe and led the way into the sitting room. She clicked on a lamp and sat down on an armchair, her posture rigid like the chair was unfamiliar to her. She crossed her legs and laid her hands in her lap. Saif sat down on a love seat on the other side of the coffee table and rested his palms on his shaky knees.

"Is Gene here?" he asked.

"Mr. Gene," she replied. "Yes."

The finality of her response made it clear there would be no further explanation. She had been sent to deal with him, her son. But he hadn't come to see his stepfather anyway. As far as he was concerned, he needed nothing from the man who married his mother and scorned him. He had a father. He had a great love, even if it was caged. And what was more, he had Allah's love, still. Despite the harm he had done, no small thing and nothing that could ever be made right, Allah's love was infinite and ever reaching. Saif only needed to grab hold of it and not let go. He chuckled to himself as the anxiety that had gripped him since he pulled up to his mother's home fell away from him, opening his chest and allowing his heart to expand.

"It's okay," he said. "I didn't come here for him. For true I don't even know why I came. I guess, I don't know, I just want to say I'm sorry."

He glanced at his mother. She watched him impassively.

"I'm sorry I wasn't what you wanted," he continued.

"Saif." She pursed her lips. "I raised you. I did my job. Don't blame me for how you turned out."

"How did I turn out?" he asked. "How do you even know?"

"I know all I need to know." She looked him up and down.

"That's the thing. You don't know anything. You never asked me what I was going through. You never asked me how I felt. You never talked to me beyond telling me to be quiet, go clean, go to my room." He shook his head. "But it's okay. I understand. You didn't know how to love me. And that's not my fault."

She shook her head, not looking at him. "So, what, you want me to apologize?"

Saif laughed and shook his head. "Nah. I thought that's what I wanted. I waited years for you just to look at me, really see me, even just one time. But I don't want anything you don't want to give me. All I want now is to say goodbye. I'm not waiting for you to see me anymore."

He stood. "You don't have to worry about me coming by or calling you no more. I'm done trying to be your son."

He looked down at her. She looked at the floor, her face as blank as a wall. He wanted to tell her he loved her, because he did. He would never be able to stop loving her. But he wouldn't tell her. Knowing it for himself was enough. Better to keep it in his heart, where it was safe.

Tahani

TAHANI STOOD AT HER DRESSER MIRROR, HER FACE CLEAN of makeup, trying to coax her hair into a low bun. Today of all days, the day of her brother Bilal's wedding, when she needed her curls to behave, they resisted the pins she used to try to hold them down, slipping out and springing back to life around her hairline.

She wore a mauve-colored jersey dress with bell sleeves accented in off-white lace. The stretchy fabric was a mistake; she already knew. Her mother's eyes would sharpen at the sight of her curves. The lace headscarf she draped loosely over her head wouldn't help either.

Bilal was the most tolerable of her older brothers, but that wasn't saying much, and their overwhelming presence—all of them and their insufferable wives, disdaining her like her mother—filled her with dread.

Fatima came into the room, Aliyah and Safia trailing behind her.

"Hi, Umi," Aliyah said, hopping toward her on white-stockinged toes.

They had celebrated her fifth birthday with a princess party with some of her friends from school the week before. Having another occasion to dress up for so soon after made her giddy. Safia, copying her sister, hopped up behind her and pouted her lips for

Tahani to kiss them. The girls crawled onto her bed and perched on it like cake toppings, the skirts of their pale rose-colored tulle dresses billowing out around them. They wore matching one-piece hijabs with sequined headbands. Tahani had bought them for the girls to wear to the masjid, but they'd taken to the scarves so much they wore them almost every day.

"My beauties," Tahani cooed, kissing them on their foreheads.

She pinched gently at Safia's cheek, then Aliyah's. Their faces glowed. Their plump arms too. Fatima must have rubbed them down with shea butter; they smelled faintly like cookies.

"Thanks for getting them ready," Tahani said.

"Of course," Fatima said.

She looked at Tahani's dress and pressed her lips together. Tahani raised an eyebrow at her friend.

"What?" Fatima asked, feigning innocence.

Tahani pursed her lips in response. Fatima wore a slate-gray empire-waist dress with a lighter gray duster that reached past her knees. Not a curve in sight. Fatima stood next to Tahani at the mirror and patted her lips with tinted lip balm.

"So," she said, drawing the word out, "is Asaad going to the wedding?"

Tahani flicked her eyes at Fatima in the mirror. She tossed random makeup items into her bag.

"You know he isn't," she said in a muted voice.

Fatima smoothed the edges of her hijab along her jawline and under her chin.

"I thought y'all might have made up by now," she said.

Tahani shook her head. "There's no making up. We're done. I'm done. I don't need a man in my life, and he definitely doesn't need me. He's better off, and soon he'll figure that out, if he hasn't already."

Fatima reached to touch her friend's shoulder, but Tahani shrank back.

"I'll bring the girls down to the car," Fatima said.

Tahani winked at her daughters as they left then turned back to the mirror. She had hoped for a fresh face, but she just looked tired. She grabbed a black eye pencil from the dresser and drew a thin line along each eyelid, then lowered the pencil to study her reflection again. Dissatisfied, she drew a thicker line and dragged the end up into a tail, the way Asaad liked. "Tiger eyes," he called them, growling playfully. Not that she was doing it for him though. She meant what she'd said. They were done. She tossed the pencil down and ran a finger across her brows, smoothing any stray hairs. Now she was ready.

The wedding was at the Hilton by the riverfront. Hadi had told her there would be a band, but she hadn't believed it. It was true though. The faint tinkle of piano keys and the whine of a saxophone hit Tahani's ears as soon as the elevator doors opened to the third-floor ballroom. Leading her girls out of the elevator with Fatima trailing her, she tripped on the thick carpet.

"Damn, you wouldn't even hear the Hulk on these floors," she said, her voice echoing loudly in the hall.

Hadi stood just outside the entrance to the ballroom. He wore a black suit and tugged at the knot in his tie. Tahani smiled and waved.

"Uncle Hadi!" Aliyah squealed.

She and Safia ran and tackled his legs.

"What's up, squirts?" he said, tickling them both under their chins.

Safia patted his coat pockets. "Peppermints?" she asked.

Hadi cocked his head at Tahani. "Man, they don't waste time, huh?"

He gave them each a mint then leaned over them to hug Tahani.

266   AMBATA KAZI

"Look at you looking all clean," Tahani said. "Let me check behind your ears."

She went to pull at his ear but he hopped out of her reach.

"Come on, man."

His cheeks flushed red behind his freckles. He adjusted the lapels of his coat and looked at Fatima. They exchanged salaams and Fatima turned to follow Aliyah and Safia into the ballroom. Tahani and Hadi sauntered in behind them.

Everything was cream and gold. Each table had a floral centerpiece of white lilies on a bed of gold tulle with little candles dotted around them. The chairs were covered in mint-green satin with gold sashes tied in bows at the back. Chandeliers hung from the ceiling. The whole room was bathed in a rich honey glow.

"This lighting is incredible," Tahani said. "It even makes you look good."

"You got all the jokes," Hadi said. "I thought your boy was the comedian."

She ignored the reference to Asaad. She touched the edges of her brother's golden hair, cut into a high top fade. "Seriously though, I see you with your fresh cut."

He'd worn his hair in a short Afro as long as she could remember. The new cut was surprising, and Tahani suspected it had something to do with Fatima, but she decided to spare him and not ask. His face was already rosy enough just having seen her. Always too skinny, he was finally starting to fill out a little. His suit actually fit him. He tilted his chin up and stroked his measly facial hair with the back of his hand, then stopped suddenly and ducked his head.

"Heads up," he said.

"Umi?" she whispered.

"The Beardy Bunch."

She turned to see four of her brothers approaching. They wore dark-colored thobes and white turbans wrapped around their

FAR AWAY FROM HERE 267

heads. They were dark-skinned and muscular like their dad. All of them had full beards that grazed their collarbones. The brothers took turns giving Tahani stiff hugs.

"You look . . . healthy," her second brother, Walid, said.

Tahani rolled her eyes and smiled weakly. Her weight had been one of their favorite jokes growing up. Their teasing had hurt her to the point of tears as a child, hiding in the bathroom or her bedroom until she had calmed down. They didn't know that though, just like they didn't know much of anything about her now.

"Shampoo girls must be making good money these days," Omar, the oldest of her brothers, said. "Buying shrimps and steaks."

"I have my own booth at the salon, thank you very much," Tahani replied.

"Speaking of shrimp," Shaheed laughed, and he reached for Hadi's head.

Hadi stepped back and patted his hair.

It was good to see her brothers all laughing together, but Tahani knew the camaraderie wouldn't last long. The jabs would start to hit harder, and she had a long night ahead of her.

"I gotta go find the girls," she said.

"They're probably with Namira," Shaheed said. "You're at the table with the sisters-in-law."

"Perfect," Tahani muttered.

The women were seated on one side of the room. Tahani recognized many of the guests. She stopped and exchanged greetings with several people, giving updates on herself and her daughters and confirming that, yes, they were getting so big and growing up way too fast. The table with her sisters-in-law was toward the front, close to the dais. Two chairs on the dais faced each other, with a long table a few feet behind them. The bride and groom would sit there with the parents during the ceremony. Fatima and the girls were already seated. There was one seat left next to Namira, Shaheed's wife.

"Salaam alaykum," Tahani greeted the women.

"Walaykum salaam," they chimed back.

The women smiled weakly as they looked her over. They all wore black abayas and tightly wound headscarves, their faces unadorned. Namira wore a face veil and black satin gloves. She bounced a chunky baby boy in her lap. Tahani reached to pull him into her lap, but he shrieked and lurched back toward his mother.

"Sorry," Tahani said, gently squeezing the baby's foot.

Namira waved her hand at Tahani. She looked around and flipped up her veil. She had deep, brick-brown skin and high cheekbones.

"He's just fussy because he's hungry."

She laid the baby across her chest and draped a blanket over him. His kicking and flailing ceased when he began to nurse.

"I like your dress, Tahani," Walid's wife, Ruqiya, said.

"Thanks," Tahani replied, hesitant.

"I love the color," Azizah, Omar's wife, said. "And that stretchy fabric looks so comfortable. It would be great to wear to a ladies' get-together. You know, inside the house, of course."

The women all nodded. Tahani's jaw tightened. Aliyah and Safia giggled in their seats. Tahani had brought them each their own coloring book, but they preferred to draw in one, making a game out of coloring in the same spaces.

"They're so lovely," Namira said, looking longingly at them. The baby was her third boy.

"Their arms should be covered though," said Shadia, the wife of her fifth brother, Muhammad.

"Aliyah's only five," Tahani replied, trying to keep her voice even.

FAR AWAY FROM HERE 269

"It's never too early," she responded with a saccharine smile.

Namira slipped her veil back over her face. The room was filling up with people. Waitstaff in black pants and crisp white shirts moved around making last-minute adjustments. At the table across from them, Tahani's brothers sat down.

"I guess Hadi's the next in line now," Ruqiya said.

The other women giggled.

"Well, Tahani's older than Hadi though," Fatima added.

The table went silent. The women glanced sideways at each other. Fatima shot Tahani a look of pleading apology. Tahani shook her head slightly to let her know it was okay.

"Insha'Allah khair," Namira said.

Her words of encouragement set off a flutter of disapproving glances her way. Under the table she laid a gloved hand on top of Tahani's and squeezed her fingers. Tahani looked over at her sister-in-law, who gazed down at her now-sleepy infant and cooed at him. She'd never spent much time with Namira, lumping her in the same category with the others. Now that she thought about it, though, Namira had never contributed to the other's veiled insults of her. She squeezed her sister-in-law's hand back.

The sounds of the band rose as they switched to a traditional bridal march. Everyone turned in their seats toward the doors. Bilal was the first to walk in, flanked by their parents. Their father wore a black suit and an ivory-colored shirt with a mandarin collar. He beamed at the crowd, waving and grinning, every bit the proud father. Tahani could tell by the way he tapped the lapels of his jacket and pointed at a few close friends that he was eager for the post-ceremony party to begin.

He had always been kind and gentle with her, combating her mother's harshness with his own easygoing sweetness. Tahani remembered when her mother had ordered her to start wearing a headscarf. She had run to her father, pleading with him. He had held her in his lap and wrapped her in his arms, cocooning her. "Let the girl be a child," he'd said to his wife, but she had been unyielding. Her boys could run wild, but her girl had to be reined in. He was no match for her.

Her mother stood to the right of Bilal, her arm looped in his, not looking at anyone. She wore a black satin abaya with copper-colored beading accenting the lengths of the sleeves, a matching head scarf wrapped tightly around her head. No makeup, of course, only her amber eyes decorated her face, but that was all it needed. She was an effortlessly beautiful woman whose face waned whenever someone complimented her looks. As Bilal and their parents passed Tahani's table, Bilal nodded to her. Her mother's eyes flickered toward her, flat and unseeing, then turned back to the dais. Her father was the last to notice her. His smile grew. He winked at her, and a familiar thrill ran through her. It was a gesture she associated only with him, a surreptitious action that had always soothed her.

Imam Khalil of the Westbank mosque stood on the dais in front of Bilal and Jamilah in a charcoal-gray three-piece suit with a matching kufi that sat high above his head. His snowy white beard seemed to glow against his dark-brown skin. Where Imam Hassan was stern and serious, Imam Khalil loved to joke, even in his sermons.

After Bilal and Jamilah recited the shahada, Imam Khalil launched into the responsibilities of the married couple, mostly directed to Bilal.

"It's not her responsibility to cook for you nor clean for you, unless out of the kindness of her own heart. You understand that, young brother?" he asked.

"Yes, sir," Bilal said.

FAR AWAY FROM HERE 271

"And you understand, young brother, that your money is her money, and her money is her money, yes?"

"Yes, sir."

"And if you come home looking like Sloppy Joe with your pockets hanging inside out and she decides to drop you like a hot potato, that's her right?"

"Yes, sir."

"And you *still* want to get married?"

"Yes, sir!" Bilal's voice boomed.

The guests laughed. Jamilah blushed and ducked her head.

He talked on about the man and woman being each other's garments, covering and comforting each other, and about a blessed union being a completion of faith. Tahani couldn't see her brother's face, but from the way Jamilah stole shy glances at him and smiled into the folds of her hijab, she could tell he was as smitten as his new bride.

Tahani blinked back tears and wished they were for the happy couple and not for herself. She thought of Asaad and the two of them sitting across from each other under chandeliers sharing anxious looks. Her sisters-in-law had confirmed for her what she already knew. Marriage in front of an imam and a happy, supportive crowd was not to be for her.

There were two lines leading to the buffet table, one for men and one for women. Tahani held two plates, one for her and one for the girls, and tried to figure out how she would juggle both. Her father came up and patted the back of the man standing across from Tahani.

"You don't mind, brother?" He gestured at Tahani. "This is my daughter."

The man chuckled. "Go ahead, brother. Congratulations."

They shook hands and he turned to Tahani.

"Hey, honey bear," he said. He took the second plate out of her hand.

"Thanks, Abi."

"Mm-hmm." He extended the plate toward her while she placed chicken wings on it. He chuckled to himself in a way Tahani knew well.

"What's up, Abi?"

"Hm? Oh, nothing. Just been hearing 'congratulations, congratulations' all night and it got me thinking about you. You know the story, right, about your name?"

Tahani rolled her eyes and shook her head. She ladled lamb and gravy over the brown rice on her plate. Of course she knew the story, but it didn't matter, he was going to tell it like she didn't anyway.

"First time in my married life your mother let me do anything. So you came out, right?—we didn't know what we were having—and the doctor says, 'Congratulations, it's a girl,' and so, you know, after six boys, I had to ask, 'Doc, you sure?' Saw for myself and yep, sure was. So I told your mother, that's what we should name you. Congratulations. Tahani."

He looked at her expectantly. She raised her eyebrows.

"Yeah, I don't know how to explain it," he continued. "It's just, I don't know, six kids, all boys, and then you came, and . . . well, it was like that's the moment I became a father."

Pain bloomed in Tahani's chest. She blinked back tears for the second time that night. She loved her father and she missed him, and she hated that she had disappointed him and run away the way she did. She had hurt him and abandoned him and yet he could still speak with such love and pride in her. What had she ever done to earn that? She plopped food mindlessly onto both of their plates.

FAR AWAY FROM HERE 273

"I think that's enough mac and cheese for the girls, huh, honey bear?"

"Sorry," she croaked.

"It's okay."

She shook her head.

"No, it's not, Abi."

He looked at her and saw her tears. His shoulders dropped.

"It's okay, honey bear, really."

His own eyes began to tear, and she regretted deflating his mood.

"Let's talk more later, okay?" he said.

"Yes, Abi," she responded. "I know we have a lot to talk about."

He nodded then gestured toward his plate with his chin.

"Put a lil more wings on there for me since your mama's not around."

He smiled and winked at her, and the world was right again, at least in that moment.

After dinner they sat through awkward apple cider toasts and music that only the children danced to. Aliyah and Safia had long since discarded their shoes and slid around the dance floor with the other kids. Guests mingled and clustered around tables and various pockets of the room, but Tahani stayed in her seat. She looked around for Fatima and spotted her in the line for cake talking to Hadi. He said something that must have been funny for the way Fatima clutched her belly and leaned forward. Hadi smiled and his eyes never left Fatima's face. Tahani blushed and turned away. Was everybody falling in love? She tugged at the browned edge of one of the lilies in front of her. A wilted petal fell off into her palm.

The girls ran up and hopped into the seats next to Tahani.

"Well, hello, my little party animals," Tahani said. "What brings you to my lonely table?"

"Sitti got us cake," Safia said, bouncing on her knees in her seat.

"Sitti?"

Tahani turned to see her mother coming up carrying three plates with delicate slices of cake. She set two of them down by the girls then rested the third in front of Tahani. Tahani looked at the plate like it might be explosive.

"I figured you would want some," her mother said. "I know how much you like your sweets."

Tahani thanked her mother and slid the plate away from her.

Her mother shook out fresh linen napkins and tucked them into the bodices of the girls' dresses.

"I cut them small slices. I hope you're watching their sugar consumption."

"Yes, Umi."

She turned to walk away. Tahani was surprised at how her breath caught in her throat.

"Noooo," Safia crooned. "Sitti, stay with us."

A flicker of softness passed across her mother's face.

"Well, all right."

She perched on the seat next to Safia and rested her folded hands on the table.

Safia moved to dig into her cake but Aliyah stopped her.

"We have to say the dua first."

Safia put her fork down and mimicked her big sister's moves, cupping her hands in front of her face and bowing her head. "Allahuma bariklana . . ." Aliya began. Safia attempted to follow along, catching the ends of the words.

Her mother shifted in her seat and looked at Tahani.

"They know the dua. Who taught them?" she asked.

"I did," Tahani replied.

Her mother nodded.

"You should enroll them in Sunday school," she said.

FAR AWAY FROM HERE

"They're already enrolled. Aliyah started when she was three, and Safia just started."

"Good."

Aliyah placed her fork on her empty plate and wiped her mouth with her napkin.

"All done!" she said with a flourish. "Can we go play?"

"Sure," Tahani said.

"Bye, Sitti!" they called.

They hopped out of their seats and ran off, sliding across the dance floor on their stockinged feet. Tahani's mother turned to rise from her seat.

"Umi?"

Her mother stopped with her palm still resting on the table. She looked plainly at Tahani, waiting.

"Why?" Tahani asked.

Her mother cocked her head. "Why what?" she asked impatiently.

"Why were you always so mean?"

Her eyes sharpened. "Excuse me?"

"You've never liked me."

"Oh for God's sake, Tahani." She sat back in her seat like she was exhausted.

"You never said a nice thing to me."

Her mother huffed. "I can't say what I don't see."

Tahani's chin quivered. She willed herself not to cry.

"You didn't want me," she said, her voice choked.

"No, Tahani, I didn't. But you were what Allah sent me."

She paused and looked around the room, disapproval brimming in her eyes.

"I was afraid for you," she said, not looking at Tahani. "The second the doctor told me you were a girl."

"Why?" Tahani asked.

Her mother paused for a long time, her gaze fixed on the table. She took a deep breath, then looked at her daughter, her eyes pained.

"The world isn't always kind to girls, can I just say that?"

Tahani looked at her mother. She shook her head.

"No. No, you can't."

Her mother closed her eyes, shutting her face to her daughter and to everything. She opened them slowly.

"I had an uncle. My mother's younger brother. He was funny. He always made me laugh. That's what I remember most about him. He did magic tricks, card tricks and pulling coins from behind my ear. Nothing amazing but I liked the attention, how he made me feel special because of his attention. He was always asking me what I wanted to be when I grew up. I had all sorts of fanciful ideas and I told them all to him. He indulged me. No one else in my life did that. He was . . . someone I loved. Someone I trusted."

She shook her head. Tahani sat cold, watching her.

"I went to his house one day after school. He lived not far from my school, not on my way home but not far off it. He was always telling me to come by if I wanted a cold drink or a snack. I don't know why I went that day. I probably just didn't want to go home. I didn't get along with my mother. I was sixteen. So naive. So innocent. No one knew where I was. But he was my uncle. He was my family. I was safe."

Her mother's face flushed the same way her own did when she was about to cry, splotches of pink blooming around her eyes. She blinked hard several times, her face a contortion of restrained emotions.

"I told my mother," she continued. "We didn't have a great relationship, but I had to tell her what had happened to me, what had been done to me." She sighed and shook her head. "She didn't believe me. She called me a liar and . . . other things. I blamed myself. I became ashamed of myself.

"Later, when I became Muslim, I thought I had found a way to be in a healthy relationship with shame. I didn't have to be ashamed of myself for what happened to me. It wasn't my fault. I thought I was healed from it, I thought I was done with it." She waved her hand like she was shooing away a fly. "It was like something from another life." She sighed.

"But then you came along. Every time, every pregnancy, I prayed for a boy. I was prepared to be a mother of boys. But not girls, not you. Your father was overjoyed. I was distraught. Almost angry. I cried. The doctors thought I was depressed, and I guess I was, but not for the reasons they thought.

"Your father reminded me of the story of Hana, the mother of Maryam. She only wanted boys, too, and God showed her through Maryam that a girl could serve God too. So that's what I set out to do with you, in my own way. I wanted to keep you straight on the path and I thought the best way to do that was to be strict with you, keep you observing the rituals and away from the world. I wanted to protect you, keep you out of the lion's den, and there you went, right into his mouth." Her face flashed with anger. "The shame I carried wasn't healthy, but there is such a thing as healthy shame. That is what keeps us away from the actions Allah dislikes. I believed that then and I believe it still."

Tahani bristled at her mother's assertion. She had always struggled with this concept of praiseworthy shame.

"I know I had a relationship with Darius that I shouldn't have," she said, "but that relationship also brought me Aliyah and Safia."

"That was Allah's mercy on you," her mother said. "He took the lemons you picked and still made something sweet with them. And you learned from this to savor the sweetness through teaching them our beautiful way of life.

"I'm not saying you have to live in shame, Tahani. What's done is done. We ask Allah's forgiveness and we move on, as you have done. But it's your responsibility as those girls' mother to teach the whole lesson, not just the parts that make them feel good about themselves. Allah's truth is greater than anything we can imagine, and it's not always pretty. But the more closely we accept the fullness of Allah's truth, the more self-discipline we'll gain to stay on the right path."

Her breath caught then.

"I do recognize, though, that in my determination to teach you the right way to be in this world, I neglected to do it with the type of love you needed. Your brother is helping me to understand that."

"Hadi?" Tahani asked, incredulous.

"Yes, he gave me quite the talking-to the other day." Her face was stern as always, but a hint of pleasure twinkled in her eyes. "I didn't know whether to be angry or proud of him for showing some backbone."

"Tahani," she said, her voice firm again. "I only ever want for you what I want for all my children, to live in a way that pleases Allah. Are you doing that?" she asked.

"I am, Umi. I mean, I'm getting there, I'm trying," Tahani answered. "But," she hesitated and looked her mother in the eyes, like looking in a mirror that showed her future self, "I think there are *ways* that please Allah, not just one way."

She fought the urge to look down in fear and kept her gaze on her mother's. Her mother looked back. She nodded once in concession. Tahani's heart quickened. Had she really challenged her mother, and won?

Her mother rose from her seat and looked down at her daughter. She hesitated then rested her hand on Tahani's.

"You're doing a lovely job raising them," her mother said.

Tahani blinked back tears. Her face flooded with warmth.

"Thank you, Umi. It means the world to me to hear that from you."

Her mother patted her hand and nodded toward Tahani's plate.

"Eat your cake, Tahani," she said.

"Yes, Umi."

Tahani stepped out of the hotel clutching her phone. She'd left the girls with Fatima, promising to be right back. She crossed the front passageway toward the riverfront and stopped at the railing. A cargo ship passed by slowly. Lazy waves lapped the rocks along the shore. Moonlight reflected against the water in shimmering lines.

She unlocked her phone and tapped the green call icon. Seeing Asaad's name still near the top of her recent-calls list reassured her. The phone rang three times before he answered.

"Hello," his voice rumbled.

"Yes," Tahani said.

She waited, her heart thudding in her chest. She took a deep breath.

"Yes, I'll marry you." She bit her lip; her voice broke. "If you still want me."

The line was silent. She closed her eyes and prayed he didn't hang up. She prepared herself for the click. She opened her eyes at the sound of his laughter crackling through the line, the smile in his voice.

"I knew you was gonna come around. Lucky for you I ain't been snatched up."

She let out a breath, and a fresh pool of tears rose in her eyes. She sniffled and laughed.

"Boy, shut up."

"Nah, my roommate will be happy though," Asaad said. "Can finally turn off the Al Green. Went down to Peaches and bought up all they Al, they Luther, and Billie too. Ol' dude at the counter saw my stash and asked me if he needed to call somebody for me. I told him, 'Man, the only person I wanna talk to don't wanna talk to me.'"

He laughed, but she heard the sadness in his voice. They both went quiet again. She didn't know what to say. Finally she heard him breathe.

"For real though. Tiger, you my girl, I love you."

She opened her mouth and paused, terrified of what she was doing.

"I love you too."

Fatima

FATIMA'S FIRST THOUGHT AFTER COMMITTING TO THE idea that had been forming in her head over the past few months was that the event had to be held at Umoja Bookstore in Mid-City. She had grown up in that bookstore, spent many Saturday afternoons and random evenings during the week slouched in the aisles reading. Once Mama Josephine, the matriarch of Umoja, had caught Fatima with her nose buried in a Terry McMillan novel. She'd swiftly plucked the book from Fatima's hands and stuck it back on the shelf.

"Ooh, chile, you not ready for this one," she'd said, eyeing Fatima's chest. "Ain't even got mosquito bites yet. Come on, girl."

She'd hustled Fatima out of the adult section toward the middle-grade books and pulled *Song of the Trees* by Mildred Taylor off the shelf with barely a glance and handed it to Fatima.

"How about we start here?" she'd said. "Ain't gone have no parents coming in here fussin' at me," she'd mumbled as she stalked away.

Mama Josephine's daughter, also named Josephine, had answered Fatima's call. Ms. Jo was far less chatty than her mother. Books were for gaining knowledge, and knowledge was serious. Whenever Fatima came to browse, Ms. Jo would list the teachable qualities of each of Fatima's choices in an even, emotionless voice.

Ms. Jo didn't talk; she asserted. Fatima was intimidated by the woman, always feeling like she needed to respond with something equally smart and insightful but knowing nothing she could come up with could measure up to Ms. Jo's quiet brilliance. She usually just nodded and smiled and felt utterly stupid. Every book was a good choice, though, at least at Umoja.

Ms. Jo had an intimate knowledge of every book they carried, from graphic novels to books of poetry and obscure, dense historic and scientific texts. She had studied literature in college, Fatima knew, and was a writer herself, but she didn't talk about those things. And any questions related to herself or her personal life were disregarded as if they had never been asked. On the phone with Fatima she had gathered the necessary information about the event Fatima was planning with brisk efficiency. Her only personal comment had been, "Our communal history is essential to our survival and prosperity."

Now the evening had finally arrived. It was a balmy Saturday night. It had rained heavily throughout the day, worrying Fatima that no one would show up. Rain made everyone sleepy and lazy. But they came. The room was filled to capacity with people, many faces Fatima knew well, others complete strangers. She stood toward the back watching everyone take their seats, stopping to hug and kiss or shake hands, waving across the room at others.

Tahani had put her flair for decorating to work. She had strung rows of soft white lights from the ceiling's exposed wooden beams, creating long threads of light. Behind the large screen that would project the movie, she'd draped sheer ivory curtains, and she'd erected a trellis of vines around and over the screen. With the dim lights and vases of lilies perched on small tables around the room, it gave the effect of a secret garden in evening time, perfect for the intimate storytelling experience Fatima hoped to achieve.

At the front of the room, Hadi adjusted wires and tested equipment while Asaad waited to take the mic. Asaad had been the obvious choice to emcee the event. He was funny, but more so it was his charm, his way of making everyone in the audience think he was speaking directly and only to them. The baggy jeans and T-shirt that seemed to be his uniform were gone. He wore a black suit with a fresh white shirt and black tie, his dreads tied back with a band. Fatima noticed something new in him in the way he kept smoothing down his tie and stealing shy smiles and glances at Tahani across the room, busy greeting guests and keeping an eye on her girls, all the while discreetly stealing looks back at Asaad. Fatima was giddy to see her childhood friend immersed in her first real love. Since accepting Asaad's proposal, Tahani bounced around with a contagious energy. She was the sun, and everyone kept turning toward her with admiring eyes, basking in her glow, though her radiance was only for one. It was amazing what love could do.

Fatima's parents and Khalilah and her family had come down for the event. Fatima had teared up when she saw them, her mother and sister first, then her father holding Khalilah's daughter's hand, followed by Khalilah's son and her husband. Fatima hadn't realized how much she missed them till she saw their faces, the pieces of them she saw in the mirror every day that she thought were just her own. This part of growing up, breaking away from her parents and sister, her first home, her roots, was painful. There was nothing and no one that could ever replace or fill in for them.

Fatima fought to keep herself together before they reached her, lest her mother assume something was wrong and interrogate her, unconvinced by any assertions and insisting Fatima return to Houston. In her parents' arms, she felt safe and reassured. She had people, she had family, in the truest sense of the word. People who would never turn their backs on her, never leave her to figure things out on her own. A thought dropped down into her gut like a smooth stone slipped into a bucket of water: she hadn't lost that when she lost Wakeel, despite how it had seemed at the time.

And then there were the elders, seated prominently in the front rows. Sister Amatullah in a dark-purple embroidered jilbab and a lavender hijab pinned under her chin with a pearl clasp. She clutched her purse in her lap and rocked in her seat, a small smile like a secret on her face, tilting her chin in acknowledgement of all the people around her who smiled and glanced discreetly and outright stared at her. They hadn't seen the film yet, but already they recognized her from her picture. Fatima and Hadi had developed the photographs they had taken of all the documentary participants and blown them up. Tahani had hung a large white sheet covering one of the walls of the bookstore and hung the portraits from the ceiling beams in front of the sheet.

Sister Rabia, seated next to Sister Amatullah, wore a cream-colored suit jacket and a long black skirt, tailored to fit her small frame, and a matching black two-piece hijab tucked into the collar of her jacket, with her daughter Fatemeh, who this time had smiled at Fatima.

Sister Asiyah sat toward the end of the row, her copper hair covered partially by a gold lace scarf. She had called Fatima a few days earlier, nervous about how she would be portrayed in the film. Before Fatima could attempt to calm her doubts, she had doubled back on her concerns. "You know what, never mind, I'm being silly. Us old folks have to learn to trust you young people," she'd said, then hung up. Thankfully she looked at ease as she sat talking with a few other women.

Brother Abdullah stood near the door in a dark-blue suit and a silvery-gray mandarin-collared shirt, a matching domed kufi atop his head. He stood with his hands folded in front of him, a large onyx ring with a silver band gleaming from his right hand. He peered at the crowd with his chin lifted, studying everyone from under his glasses. "All right, all right," he said to no one in particular as more people shuffled down the aisles to claim the few remaining seats.

The elder women took up the first few rows on the left side. They huddled together talking in snippets, laughing and nodding in shared understanding, legs crossed at the ankles, clutching fat leather handbags in their laps in the same way they had once held babies. The men congregated on the right side. They were louder than the women, leaning with their elbows on their knees to talk from one end of the row to the other, or with arms folded into solid chests, thrusting their chins out to emphasize certain words.

At the front to the left of the screen, Asaad tapped the microphone, jolting Fatima back to the present and silencing the audience.

"All right, folks. Welcome, welcome," he began. "Thank you all for coming out this evening for an important community event. I greet you all, and I do mean all, with the best greeting to humankind, As salaamu alaykum wa rahmatullahi wa barakatuhu. Peace to you all and God's mercy and blessings." The audience, even many of the non-Muslims, returned the Islamic greeting.

He talked about the importance of community support and telling our own stories in our own voices. The audience leaned in, nodding appreciatively. Those familiar with his comedy raised their brows, surprised at his seriousness. Others shot him knowing looks, waiting for the punch line. He didn't disappoint. He stopped and furrowed his brow at the crowd.

"Of course some of y'all bums just came for the free food and gonna try to dip down into your phones once the lights go dim, but I'ma be watchin' y'all."

He narrowed his eyes and pointed his fingers at his eyes and then to the audience. Laughter tinkled around the room. Someone in the back laughed extra loud, causing a second round of giggles.

"That better not be Malik," Asaad grumbled, bringing more laughter. "Let me find out," he warned with one last squint around the room. He let the laughter die down for the last time and then resumed his serious posturing.

"All right, folks, we gon' start the film shortly, but before we do, I want to introduce the young woman whose creativity and passion brought this whole project from idea to fruition. Fatima Jabbar is a home-grown New Orleans girl, a Seventh Ward hardhead, and a talented, creative, thoughtful individual dedicated to collecting and preserving the legacy of our community. Without further ado, I'm gonna pass the mic on to her."

Fatima walked unsteadily toward the front, lightheaded and with her heart quickening. She was actually doing this. It was too late to run out the door and pretend this moment wasn't happening.

"Come on, girl," Asaad called.

Fatima took a deep breath and grabbed the mic.

"Thank you, Asaad, for that warm introduction, and thank you, everybody, for coming out. There's a lot of other places you could have been on this wet Saturday night, but you came here, and I appreciate you all for that."

She held her gaze on a spot on the floor in front of her. She took another breath and forced herself to look up and out at the crowd. As she looked out at the faces looking kindly back at her, her body began to relax, tension releasing from her shoulders, her belly, and down to her feet. The faces that beamed back at her welcomed her home. Tahani, her family, Sister Amatullah and the elders, faces familiar and not, even Mama Sajedah sitting stiffly but with no hardness in her eyes, only curiosity and appreciation.

Far in the back stood Saif, sedate in a dark-gray polo and black jeans. She smiled at him, though she couldn't see much of his face. She parted her lips to speak again when she spotted another face lah's face, his chin tilted up as he looked down out of his eyeglasses. He sat still in his seat in one of his immaculate suits, his signature onyx stone with Allah's name written in silver Arabic script pinned to his lapel above his heart. His hands rested calmly in his lap. He leaned back in his seat, eyes fixed on the camera.

"Now see for me, the hallmark of my childhood—and it's an unfortunate one—the hallmark of my childhood was fear. I was born in 1935 in a lil town in Georgia with itchy feet. My world was small, much too small for me. I yearned to run. But folks around me told me to slow down, walk, be quiet, stay small. Because they had fear. They were afraid of everything outside themselves and the world beyond the fields they worked. But I saw, as a consequence, how that fear creeped inside them. Took up residence in their minds and hearts and didn't pay no rent. They accepted it, that fear, let it inside so they could survive.

"But I didn't want to just survive, I wanted to thrive. My talent was I could play ball. I was quick with a ball, moving around the court so fast them fellas couldn't catch me. So soon as I could I ran with that ball outta Georgia. Before I left I took a piece of notebook paper and wrote the word 'fear' in big letters on that paper. Folded it up and put it in my shoe right there under my heel. Why? 'Cause I planned to stomp that word out of my existence.

Went up to North Carolina to play ball. Studied physical education 'cause I had to keep moving. Kept moving and made my way up to New York City. First thing I got there a brother in a clean suit and tie handed me a paper. In big letters it said, 'ISLAM WILL SET YOU FREE.' They was talking my talk 'cause 'free' is my absolute favorite word. That word has all the letters a body need. You take the 'f' out and that leaves 'ree' and don't nobody need to *re*peat that you are free. You take the 'r' out and that's a fee you gotta pay, and Islam tell you don't sell your soul to nobody. Your soul belongs to Allah and you are free on this Earth to worship Him.

"I set off as a young man to outrun fear and I succeeded with 'Ash'hadu an la ilaha illallah.' I am Abdullah, servant of the one God Allah, and I am *free* because I live with no *fear* of any man or any thing. All right."

There were other stories included, Imam Hassan and his wife Khadija, Brother Kasib and others from the earliest days of Masjid Al-Ghafur. The last story of the film brought gasps throughout the audience. It was the moment Fatima had been anticipating and dreading. Mama Tayyibah sat propped up on her sofa with several pillows, dressed in a black abaya with a gold silk scarf over a black turban. Nothing could hide the sickness that shone in her ashen skin and sunken cheeks, but her eyes blazed with life.

"I could tell you about how I came to Islam, but truthfully that's not much of a story, certainly not one I'm proud of. Truth is I became a Muslim for a man I was dating, a man who became the father of my child but didn't stick around long enough to even meet him. I could've left the Muslims like he left me, but they told me I was their sister then and their sister now and they were gonna take care of me and they did. So I stuck with them and actually learned about the religion and eventually accepted it for myself.

"I could talk about that. I could talk about my life, reflect on it, but my life is ending. So what I want to talk about, what I'm reflecting on, is my soul.

"That time in my life, pregnant and abandoned, wasn't the first trial I faced, and it certainly wasn't my last, but what sustained me then and sustains me now is knowing that I am both profoundly alone and profoundly connected. I am alone, but with Allah. That came to me when I was pregnant with my son, before I met Kareem, the man who would become Wakeel's true father.

"You know the story of Mary, Maryam, the mother of Jesus? She was pregnant, alone, and afraid, and her comfort came when Allah came through the angel Gabriel and reminded her that while, yes, she was bereft of human contact, she wasn't alone. Her body may have needed that contact, that human care and concern, but her soul was connected with Allah. He was caring for her. He had always been caring for her.

"I'm standing here, or sitting here rather, and all the hurts I've endured, all the pain, all that's behind me now. I'm on the threshold of death and I'm seeing, it's an exit and it's an entrance too. I'm leaving with what I came with, I'm leaving with my soul. I am alone, and I am in the best of company too."

After the screen faded to black for the last time and the lights came back up, there was a moment of stillness in the room, like everyone was holding their breath, then the slow expansion of their chests as they took in air. There were sniffles and the rustle of tissues and napkins.

"Allah have mercy," Sister Amatullah said, breaking the silence.

A flutter of whispered prayers followed. Fatima stood and returned to her position at the front of the room. She thanked everyone for coming and all the elders who had participated in the documentary and Hadi for his technical and production support, then opened the floor for questions and comments. There were many, mostly from people who weren't Muslim but were moved to learn of their community's history and be exposed to the depths of its existence, and wanted to learn more. They emphasized the importance of the Black Muslim community to the city. One person, an older woman, marveled at their long presence in New Orleans, Louisiana, and the greater South.

"Y'all have *been* here," she kept saying. "From the very beginning, from even before the beginning. More people need to know that, like really know and understand that."

Her words lingered in the air and nurtured a feeling of comfort that seemed to settle into everyone's hearts. Fatima took note of the vibe and closed on it, thanking everyone again and inviting them to mingle and view the photo displays. She relinquished the mic with relief and wished to disappear, though she knew in many ways the night was just beginning. There would be many people to greet, many questions to answer, many compliments and congratulations to receive. She was exhausted and exhilarated, wanting to lie in a dark, quiet space and release the emotions her mind was immersed in, but that would have to wait. She smiled through tears and fatigue and dove in.

There was one confrontation she wasn't prepared for but knew was inevitable. She felt his presence behind her as she accepted congratulations from another guest. The fluttering in her belly made her feel lightheaded and slightly nauseous. She took in a breath and turned, feigning an indifferent smile as she took him in.

"Hey," she greeted Ishmael.

He looked good, as good as when she first met him at the bookstore a year ago that now felt like a lifetime ago. Except he wasn't wearing jeans and a T-shirt this time. He had dressed casually for the occasion, brown corduroy pants that hugged his thighs and a brown-and-orange-plaid button-down. Fatima had a sudden urge to grasp a piece of his shirt near his collarbone to feel the fabric that touched his skin. To feel, full stop.

He grinned at her, that smirk that sent an electric shock through her body every time. But there was something different in his eyes now, a heaviness and warmth, a hint of sadness. He missed her, Fatima realized with a jolt. She was embarrassed by this new emotion in him, this vulnerability. Humility looked good on him.

"How've you been?" he asked.

Fatima shrugged. "Okay." She sighed heavily. "It's been a lot, you know? Mama Tayyibah dying."

Fresh tears flooded her eyes. She willed the rush of loss and

FAR AWAY FROM HERE 293

grief to fall back. *Why now?* she thought. She had held herself together so well. She blinked back the tears, shook her head as if she
could turn them away, and took in a ragged breath. She cleared her
throat and waved her hand at Ishmael, not ready to speak. Ishmael
watched her with unease, his arms stiff at his sides.

"I'm okay," she finally said, sniffling. She forced a smile.
"Thanks for coming."

"Thanks for inviting me," he replied. "The show was . . ." He
looked off and around the room, at the people who milled about,
the elders tall and beaming, the younger Muslims, the teens and
young adults mingling with the other non-Muslim guests, the
youngest ones in their kufis and headscarves modeling the coolness
of the young adults, hands in pockets or on hips, their feet itching
to run around. "It was incredible. Y'all have a rich tradition. I . . . I
admire that. I see where you come from." He shrugged and smiled.
"I wouldn't want to leave that either."

"Yeah," Fatima said, smiling wistfully at the fullness of life that
surrounded her, held her close. "It's pretty special."

She looked back at Ishmael. She wanted to rest her palm on his
face. She felt a tenderness for him she had never felt before. It was
over between them, whatever "it" had ever been. Despite all the
times Ishmael had angered her and left her distraught, he had also
expanded her vision and helped her grow. In trying to pull her from
her deen, he had actually pushed her deeper into it, forcing her to
confront her faith and accept it as her way of life, not just the tradition she had been brought up in. This, she now knew, was her
world. Not just in New Orleans. Her global Muslim community.
These were her people, and she would know them in her soul and
gravitate toward them wherever in the world she happened to be.
There could be no love or partnership with someone who didn't
have that same feeling in their core. Fatima stood taller and looked
Ishmael squarely in his eyes.

"Thank you," she said.

He looked back at her, for once not smirking.

"Thank you, Fatima. Take care of yourself."

"You too," she said, her voice trembling.

She knew they were being watched, had been since the moment he walked up to her. She could feel the stares, but she didn't care. She watched him walk away.

Tahani sidled up to her, a sleeping Safia in her arms, her head tucked into the space between Tahani's neck and shoulder. She slid into the spot Ishmael had just occupied and faced Fatima. Her hazel eyes sparkled with mischief. Fatima rolled her eyes.

"Ishmael?" Tahani whispered.

Fatima nodded.

"Girrrl . . ." Tahani hissed through her teeth.

Fatima laughed. "Whatever."

"Mm-hmm, whatever," Tahani teased. "That's a fine whatever. But that had 'temporary' written all over it. Trust me, I have a radar for these things now."

She hoisted Safia up higher on her waist. Before she could complain about her child's weight, Asaad was there, his hands extended to take Safia.

"I pulled some chairs together at the front," he said. "Let me lay her down."

"Oh," Tahani said, startled. "Okay, thanks."

"Yeah, fa sho," he said.

He nodded at Fatima and she nodded back, fighting the smile that tickled her lips.

"All right, now," she teased after Asaad walked away.

"Girrrl . . ." Tahani repeated, watching Asaad lay Safia down like she was made of porcelain. She snickered. "I don't know if I can get used to this."

"Um, you better," Fatima retorted. "Love's in need of love

today," she sang. "Seriously, I'm happy for you. Not just Asaad but you going to school to study interior design. You're, like, living your dream."

Tahani scrunched her brow. "Yeah. This shit is scary. I mean, I'm excited, of course. But then a part of me is like, *Girl, who do you think you are?*" She flung her hand out dismissively.

Fatima grabbed her friend's wrist.

"No. Stop," she said. "This is good. Full stop. And you're not acting alone this time. You and Asaad are doing this the right way. With your family's blessing. And you have me and everybody else rooting for y'all." She bumped her friend with her shoulder. "You're gonna be sick of us, watch."

Tahani grinned and bumped her friend back.

"Us, huh?" She raised an eyebrow.

"Yes, us," Fatima said, tilting her chin up.

"Word? Okay. But look, my brother's been over there eyeballing you like crazy. No pressure, but maybe go talk to him?"

Fatima glanced over at Hadi, wrapping up cables, and sure enough he hurriedly ducked his head back down. Though Fatima's dark skin hid the blush that crept up her cheeks, her friend still recognized the fluster in her expression. She nudged Fatima again with her shoulder.

"Don't play that shy-girl routine with me. I been seeing those looks y'all keep giving each other. You know you can't keep no secrets in this ummah. Go 'head." She thrust her chin toward Hadi.

Fatima rolled her eyes. "Okay, Ms. No Pressure. Dang."

Tahani tossed a laugh over her shoulder. She was already making her way over to Asaad.

Fatima walked across the room to Hadi, who was pretending he didn't see her coming, badly. He had already dropped the cables twice. Fatima wasn't much better. The flutters in her belly practically lifted her off her feet and carried her over to him.

"Heeey," she said, trying and failing to sound breezy. She was very aware of her hands. She folded them behind her back to still them.

"Hey," Hadi responded.

Unlike Fatima, there was no hiding the pink flush of his cheeks, so bright his freckles seemed to glow.

"Yeah, I just wanted to say thanks for all your help with this. Everything came out great. I couldn't have done any of this without you."

"Oh, yeah, fa sho. It was fun. We, uh, make a good team."

His face was full-blown raspberry. He winced at his words.

Fatima laughed. "Yeah, we do. I hope you're not tired of me just yet." She raised her eyebrows. "We've got more work to do. The website and all? Teammate?"

Hadi looked at her, his eyes heavy with tenderness that flooded her with warmth. He smiled, then frowned.

"What?" Fatima asked.

Hadi scratched at his temple.

"It's not my business, but, uh, that guy you were talking to. Is he, uh, a friend of yours?"

Fatima's eyes widened.

"Not . . . like that. We knew each other for a while—not *knew* knew—but it's . . . it's over. I mean, it was barely anything."

She let out a frustrated breath. She was babbling. Hadi was silent. She felt him drifting from her.

"I like you," she blurted out.

Her eyes grew wide. Had she really said that? Out loud? She hadn't even thought it through.

"Like, want to get to know you like," she stammered.

"I like you too," Hadi said, looking at her under his golden eyelashes that she wanted to count one by one.

"Well," Fatima said, embarrassed and wanting to hide. "Okay."

"Okay," Hadi replied. "So I guess I'll . . . call you?"

"Yeah. You have my number."

"That I do."

They locked eyes. His stare was intense, like he could see inside her heart. She turned away sharply, feeling dizzy. That was enough of men for the day. She felt the heat of his stare as she walked away, fighting to still the quaking in her body.

The bookstore was pretty much empty, with a few stragglers chitchatting in huddles or lazily browsing books. Fatima took this as her moment to slip away. She walked outside to look for her parents. Khalilah had just sent a text saying they were parked around the block. Fatima stuffed her phone in her bag and hurried down the street, her mind twirling. She wanted to raise her arms and spin on her toes right there under the streetlights. She was smiling and traipsing down the sidewalk when a figure stepped out of the shadows at the back alley behind the bookstore. She gasped, slamming her palm over her racing heart.

"Saif!" she wailed.

"My bad. I thought you saw me. You need to pay attention walking down these streets, you know."

"Apology accepted," she snapped.

She was embarrassed because he was right. She'd been so caught up in the moment she had forgotten where she was.

"You need to announce yourself. Hiding in corners like that. What are you doing?"

He was facing her but his eyes roved the street.

"I'm a marked man. I gotta watch my back."

Fatima frowned, resisting the urge to look over her shoulder.

"But I had to come see your show," he said.

Fatima perked up, surprised.

"And say goodbye."

Fatima blinked and shook her head. "Wait, what?"

298 AMBATA KAZI

"I gotta get out of here, Tima. It's too hot for me."

"But where?"

He took in a breath and smiled sadly at her, but there was a gleam in his eyes.

"Senegal."

Fatima put her hand on her hip.

"Sene-what?"

Saif laughed despite himself.

"You can take the girl outta New Orleans . . ."

Fatima smirked and took her hand off her hip.

"You know what I mean. Senegal? As in Africa?"

"You know another one?" he asked.

"Shut up. Why are you going so far away?"

Saif shrugged and scratched at his neck.

"I don't got to, but I got to. I could go to Houston, Atlanta, shit, even New York or California, but it's gon' be the same thing, eventually. Ain't a whole lot for a nigga like me. Imam sending me to study with the sheikhs. Why not? It's probably the best thing for me. Really study my deen. It's scary but . . ." He looked around him and shook his head. "Ain't no living here for me. Whether I'm physically alive or not. I don't know," he shrugged. "Could be living there for me, you know? At least give me some time to breathe."

Fatima raised her eyebrows. "Wow, Africa." She tilted her head up toward the darkening sky, moonlight hitting her chin. "You know Wakeel would be proud of you, right? And a little jealous."

They laughed then grew quiet. It was the first time Fatima had mentioned him in that way, so lighthearted yet with the permanence of his absence from her life, their lives. He had faded into the sepia space of memory.

"I'm proud of you, Saif." She looked at his watery eyes and smirked. "I might even miss you a little bit."

He laughed and rubbed at his eyes with his fist. "Shut up, Tima.

Now stop crying and come on, let me walk you down the street with your absentminded self."

"Whatever," she said, giggling.

At the next corner Fatima saw her brother-in-law's car idling at the curb with the lights blaring. She turned back to say goodbye again but Saif had already crossed over to the other side of the street and was halfway down the block. He turned at the corner and was gone like he'd never even been there.

Fatima's family came to Sister Amatullah's house the following day for breakfast. The food Fatima and Sister Amatullah made was spread out over the large table in the dining room. Sister Amatullah buzzed around setting down bowls of fresh-cut fruit and plates of biscuits and waffles. Fatima sliced small sweet peppers and added them to a glass bowl with arugula, kale, and butter lettuce. She spooned feta cheese on top and sprinkled in handfuls of chopped pecans and dried cranberries. Sister Amatullah insisted that every meal should include leafy greens. She had also balked at Fatima's parents' suggestion that they go to a restaurant for breakfast instead, to save Sister Amatullah the trouble.

"I never eat out," she'd said. "I have to know the hands that prepared my food, and what better than my own?"

Perhaps that explained how she moved about like a woman half her age. In the short time Fatima had spent with her, she had been awed by the woman's energy. There was no frenzy to it; she moved from task to task with ease and precision and no fatigue. She was up an hour before dawn every morning and in bed by nine.

Fatima had begun to operate on the same schedule. Just that morning she had woken up a half an hour before fajr without an alarm, despite how tired she had been the night before. She had slipped out of bed and prayed tahajjud and read Qur'an with an ease and serenity she had never felt before. No feeling of rush or a sense of duty to complete a task, only communion with her Creator. The quiet time before the sun began to announce the day held a sweetness that lingered in her soul. By the time the official morning prayer began, she heard the birds twittering in the trees and smiled at the thought that she had awakened before them. Now as she did the final preparations for the family breakfast she felt more prepared than she usually felt, calmer and more focused.

She heard her niece's and nephew's voices ringing like windchimes and car doors being slammed, then Khalilah's sharp voice commanding them to walk. The children burst through the front door with the fastest walking feet possible, their bright smiles and eyes displaying their itch to run. Sister Amatullah would have none of that restraint. She knelt down and flung her arms wide.

"Come here, my babies," she called.

They squealed and ran to her. She pulled them in and smothered them with kisses. Fatima stood behind Sister Amatullah waiting for her turn to snuggle with them. They all hugged like they hadn't just seen each other yesterday. After the hugs the children's roving eyes took in the toys set up in a corner of the living room.

"I brought out all the toys for us to play with," Sister Amatullah said. "Y'all go ahead and take them shoes off now, y'all done trampled my carpet enough. Take them shoes off and let's come on and play, yeah?"

Sister Amatullah kept a closet full of toys and books and puzzles. Fatima had pulled them out earlier that morning and dusted them off. She had recognized one large box that held a miniature jungle playset with slides and swings and a catapult. Fatima recognized it as the same set she had played with as a child. All the original pieces were there and intact, the hard plastic jungle animals, trees and rocks, and the little play people

FAR AWAY FROM HERE 301

in safari clothes. She ran her thumb over the one brown girl figure and smiled, remembering it as her favorite.

With that nudge from Sister Amatullah, the kids fixed their gaze on the toys. Khalilah's daughter made a beeline for the jungle playset. "Come on," she called to her brother, who stood shyly back. With a grin at Sister Amatullah, he inched over and collapsed to his knees. Soon they were immersed in the toy. Sister Amatullah kneeled on her haunches and launched into a play act with the animals, giving them dialogue and voices that had the children giggling. By that point Fatima's mother and father and her sister and brother-in-law had sidled in unnoticed by the kids. Sister Amatullah nodded at them and kept up her play act.

Fatima walked over to them and whispered salaams.

"Why are we whispering?" Khalilah whispered.

"Why are you whispering?" her husband whispered back.

They all laughed and resumed their normal voices.

"Masha'Allah, look at this spread," Fatima's mother exclaimed. "You all have outdone yourselves."

"For real," Khalilah added. "I see why Sister Amatullah doesn't want to eat out. This is better than any restaurant."

Sister Amatullah grinned from her spot on the floor.

"Alhamdulillah, it's my pleasure. Y'all help y'all selves and sit wherever you wanna sit. Table, floor, sofa, don't matter. Dig in."

Khalilah pinched a slice of turkey bacon and took a bite, shimmying her shoulders. "Mmm," she squealed.

Her husband looked over at her, his eyes wide. "You don't even have a plate yet. I've never seen you like this before . . . You're not—?"

"No!" Khalilah stopped him. "I'm just . . . home."

They all laughed.

"New Orleans will do that to you," Fatima's father chimed in.

He handed plates around. Fatima had planned to tell them of

her plans after they ate, but she took Khalilah's comment as her cue.

"Speaking of home," she started.

"I knew it," Khalilah cut in, not unkindly.

Fatima frowned at her sister.

"Let your sister speak," their mother interjected.

Their father looked pointedly at Khalilah's husband.

"Some things never change," he said.

Khalilah's husband smiled and glanced at the two women. Fatima wanted to be upset at her bossy older sister interfering in her moment, but really she was glad that Khalilah had opened the door.

"Okay, well, yes," she started again. "I've been thinking, and I think I want to stay in New Orleans for a while longer. I've still got a lot to do with the oral history project, and I've learned of a few grants I could apply for, if I want to grow it. There's a lot I could do with it. A gallery exhibit at a museum, bringing the film to schools, maybe even a book..."

She stopped and looked at them, aware of how quiet they had grown. She was worried they would disagree with her choice. Khalilah's face revealed no emotion, but her eyes showed genuine interest and a hint of impression. Her parents beamed at her.

"I think someone has found her passion," her mother said.

Fatima ducked her head. "Maybe."

"You know Xavier has a good journalism program," her father added, his eyebrows raised. He looked at his wife. "We should look into scholarships and other funding possibilities. With a project like this under your belt, they just might come knocking at your door."

Fatima's eyes widened. She hadn't even considered that far, but why not?

"Yeah, yeah," Khalilah interrupted. "How much of you wanting to stay has to do with Tahani's brother?"

Fatima's eyes grew wider. She avoided looking at her parents. She tilted her head at Khalilah.

"I'm just kidding," Khalilah said, though she clearly wasn't. She softened. "But no, I think it might actually be a good idea to stay and continue your work. For now, at least."

Fatima smirked.

"Our Tooma, growing up," Khalilah said, grabbing a biscuit and settling it on her plate.

Fatima rolled her eyes then looked away. The mention of her childhood nickname made her think of Saif, of all people. He had never had this joyful annoyance of family banter that she took for granted. They were all growing up now, for real for real, and also growing away.

"Now what's all this about Tahani's brother?" her father asked, snapping her back to reality.

Fatima held up her full plate. "Let's eat, yeah? We can talk about that more later."

"Oh, so there is something to talk about though?" her mother asked, delight sparkling in her eyes.

"Bells will be ringing," Sister Amatullah sang from the living room.

Fatima turned to look at Sister Amatullah. *Not you too*, she thought. She cut her eyes at Khalilah for starting this mess. Khalilah grinned back with a shrug. Their mother was likely already thinking of color patterns and venues, a calendar of possible dates running through her mind. She wanted to be angry but all she could do was laugh.

She sat down to eat and watched her family eat and talk, the kids running in and out, pecking at food then returning to their play, Sister Amatullah keeping them entertained while also conversing with the adults. She thought about what Ishmael had said, how she had something special here and how he wouldn't want to leave it either. She took his words in with guilt and shame.

Leaving was all she had wanted to do after Wakeel died. She

had blamed them for his death: the ummah, her city, everything and everybody that hadn't been able to save him. She had deemed them too accepting of his death, too resigned. "Inna lillahi wa inna ilayhi raji'oon," they had said. "To Allah we belong and to Allah we return." Like his death was a natural thing, like it couldn't have been prevented. Maybe there had been some resignation in their attitudes, some concession to powerlessness, but the answer hadn't been to abandon them all. They were grieving. They were all grieving. And carrying a heavy burden. They needed life and energy, the kind that came from youth, not more departure. It was up to them, Fatima's generation and the ones to come, to repair and build up from the foundation the elders had lain for them, with love and endurance, with fear and anxiety they fought against and never let stop them. They didn't give up. They had not, still, given up. And she could not give up either. It was her turn to build something for the future, for their continued survival and prosperity.

Epilogue

IT WAS FATIMA'S IDEA. SOMETHING SHE HAD DONE WITH her family as a child. The four of them, her, her mother, father, and Khalilah, giddily piling into the family car in the early morning and driving to the lakefront to watch the usually calm water grow fitful, before the real storm came. She had texted Tahani and Saif late the night before.

You crazy, Tahani had texted back.

Come on . . . Fatima had begged.

Huh??? had been Saif's response.

Come on . . . she'd pleaded. *Please . . .*

Despite their initial skepticism, Tahani and Saif had warmed to the idea by the morning, or maybe it was the doughnuts Fatima brought from Tastee's. They devoured them on the ride over, licking glaze off their fingers and laughing. Lauryn Hill's "Doo Wop (That Thing)" came on the radio.

"Ooh, turn it up!" Fatima shrieked from the back seat.

They all sang the opening lyrics together, "*Don't forget about the deen, the siraatal mustaqeem . . .*"

"When she say 'saying you a Muslim sleeping with the jinn'? Lawd, I felt that," Tahani said.

"Lauryn know she need to go on and take her shahada," Saif said.

Fatima and Tahani laughed.

"But can we talk about how this is playing on the classics station though?" Tahani asked.

"Ouch. We're getting old already," Fatima said.

How you gon' win if you ain't right within? Uh-uh, come again, Lauryn sang. They took in those words with a collective deep breath.

"Insha'Allah, we just gettin' started," Saif said.

This would be the last time they were all three together for none of them knew how long. Saif had a plane ticket for a flight leaving in a few days. Every morning he looked at it on his nightstand and his heart fluttered and his stomach churned. He wouldn't breathe until he was on the plane and it was lifting him in the air with the wheels folding up. Then he could relax and feel safe. No one but Imam Hassan and Fatima knew he was leaving. It took everything in him to keep doing deals for Dupe. In his head he was already writing the letter he would send his father once he was on African soil. He would take some of that dirt and put it in the envelope for his father to rub into his palms. He could see his father smiling in his prison cell, and it made him feel good and sad at the same time. He thought he knew loneliness until he thought of his father, locked away and slowly dying, unknown and not thought of by anyone except his son and Allah. With this opportunity, Saif would live and make his father proud, remembering his father's name on his tongue and in his heart so Allah would remember him in return.

Tahani and Asaad were to be wed. She had surprised everybody, herself included, when she declared she wanted a simple ceremony at the masjid with a reception under the pergola in the courtyard. She didn't think too much about how the wedding she envisioned was almost exactly the type her mother deemed best. Of course it would have the Tahani touch, though, with lights, lace, soft colors, and flowers. Asaad said he didn't care where or what they did as long as they did it soon. "Before you change your mind," he joked.

He was starting graduate school in the fall, and Tahani was starting her design classes too. The past weekend she and Asaad had gone to her parents' home for dinner. Her brothers and their families had come too. Asaad had diverted any jokes headed her way with his own charming banter. Even the corners of her mother's mouth turned up a few times. He'd been delighted by her large family, confessing to Tahani that being the only Muslim in his family left him feeling lonely and was the main reason he started doing comedy. "Laugh to keep from crying, ya know?" he'd said. He would take a meddling Muslim family over none at all.

And sure enough, Aliyah and Safia had warmed quickly to him. After the family dinner when Tahani was tucking her girls into bed, Aliyah had shyly asked, "If you and Mr. Asaad get married, does that mean then I can get a brother?" Tahani had smiled at the memory of her daughter's question so many months ago. "Maybe, insha'Allah, but Umi's got a few other plans first, if that's okay with you." Aliyah had looked away and then back to her mother and nodded. "Okay. But not too long." Tahani had gone to bed feeling like she was being carried by butterflies. The way her life now felt like puzzle pieces coming together made her dizzy with joy.

Fatima was weightless too but for opposite reasons. She had no set plans, no clear path or next steps. There was journalism school, possibly. There was her oral history project and all the possibilities for growth within it. She was thinking of partnering with schools and community groups to work with kids to gather their own communities' stories. Maybe even starting her own nonprofit. Wakeel would be proud of her, she knew. She remembered their reunion at the Kwanzaa festival in Tremé those five years ago that felt like a lifetime ago. She remembered the joy in his voice when he said he was back home, the joy in that one word, "home." The energy and serenity of it. She understood that now. There was no place like their home.

And there was Hadi, possibly. But they were going to take it very slowly, she had cautioned him over the phone the other night. She needed time to explore who she was and what she wanted for herself in life first. Hadi understood. That was what she liked about him. He was steady, quiet and reassuring, and seemingly endlessly patient. He could make a good companion, and for now she was enjoying just getting to know him. She had time. That she knew now. She had time to just be.

By the time they got to Lake Pontchartrain they were quiet; the sugar rush had ebbed. Tahani parked away from the waterfront, one of a few cars sprinkled around the parking lot. They stepped out and the wind almost knocked Fatima's loosely wrapped scarf off. She grabbed the hood of her sweatshirt over her head and pulled the strings tight.

"Oh!" she squealed.

"You wanted to come out here," Saif shouted over the roar of the waves, though he was happy to be out in this weather, not thinking about the past, the present, or the future, just observing Allah's might. The wind whipped around him like an embrace from God, and for once he could welcome it without feeling like he hadn't earned it.

Tahani had smartly tied her hair up in a tight turban, but she was grumpy for other reasons, restless to take her vows with Asaad. The girls had spent the night at her parents' house, their first time. Tahani had woken early to the wind creaking through the floorboards and whistling through the cracks around the window frames. She had tossed and turned with it, wishing she could snuggle under the covers in Asaad's arms. Fatima's call in the morning reminding her of their ridiculous plans had not been what was up, but she laughed now to watch her friend struggle to keep her hair contained under her flimsy scarf.

"Serves you right," she mumbled as they linked arms and tried to fight the wind to get across the street toward the lakefront.

Halfway across, Saif stopped and turned back, motioning with his hand for them to go back.

"Nah, this too crazy. Let's go up on the hill," he said.

It was still just wind, so the grass was only damp. They climbed up the hill with ease. They watched the waves rise up and crash into each other, mesmerized by the force of the water. To think this was the same water that lapped lazily most days with seagulls rippling the surface with their beaks as they searched for food. The same water people fished in on the weekends and where the brave or foolish waded. It was beautiful and terrifying, as so much of life is.

"We should go," Tahani finally said. "I gotta go get my babies."

They made their way down, and Saif walked toward a small patch of sidewalk covered with tarp and held up by wooden poles. He knelt and lifted it up and smiled at them.

"Still wet," he grinned. "You know what that means."

He tramped around in the grass and found a sturdy stick. He pulled back the tarp and wrote his initials in the top left corner, then handed the stick to Fatima, who wrote hers in the top right. Tahani followed, writing hers in the bottom left corner. Fatima tilted her head at their work.

"It's missing something," she said.

Saif reached for the stick.

"Let me see that," he said.

Tahani handed it to him. Saif kneeled over the patch of wet concrete. In the empty fourth corner he wrote, "W. T. M." Wakeel Tauheed Mujahid. Then in the center he wrote in all caps, "STILL HERE." Fatima thought of all the initials they could add, all the blocks they could fill with loss and life.

Saif re-covered the concrete slab with the tarp, then stood and tossed the stick. He stuffed his hands in his jacket pockets and stepped back. The three of them stood over it for a minute, their heads bowed; then they turned back to the lake, its water roiling, black foamy waves rising up and moving slowly toward the shore, the water tossing over the steps in big splashes onto the street.

"We should go," Tahani said again.

"Yeah," Fatima replied.

But none of them moved. They stood shoulder to shoulder, watching the waves, rainwater sprinkling their faces. Fatima felt a tug at her left hand. It was Tahani taking her hand. She looked down then up at her friend, and smiled. She reached for Saif and slipped her hand through his. She felt his surprise at her touch, the tightening in his muscles, then the slow release. His warm fingertips pressed into the back of her hand.

Fatima held tight to Saif's and Tahani's hands. The three of them had grown. They had survived. They had futures waiting for them. And for the first time it felt to Fatima like something she was ready for, not something she dreaded or feared. They looked with steady eyes at the water raging in front of them. They breathed as one and braced themselves against the coming storm.

Acknowledgments

"Whoever has not thanked people has not thanked God."
—attributed to Isa ibn Mariam/Jesus, son of Mary

My gratitude, first and foremost, is to my Creator, Allah. I prayed for this moment, prayed throughout this four-year process for guidance and success. I asked You to allow me, if this project pleased You, to complete it. I have, so I can only thank You for making it so. Any good in this book comes from You, any bad comes from me and me alone.

I thank Brooke Warner, Lauren Wise, Shannon Green, and everyone at She Writes Press. Thank you for putting writers first and making an effort toward equity in publishing with the STEP publishing award. Thank you to Marissa DeCuir and the BookForward team for much-needed and appreciated pro-bono publicity support to amplify my work.

Mil gracias a mi hermana, book coach extraordinaire Maceo Nafisah Cabrera Estévez, for your gentle and thorough editorial feedback and guidance in making this book better, and for getting what I'm trying to say in it.

I thank my writing teachers at University of New Orleans. Barb Johnson, thank you for your clear-eyed professionalism and dedication to craft. Your reminder to always ask what's serving the story and what isn't guides my writing. M.O. Walsh, aka Neal, the story, this novel, started in your classroom, where you nicely ripped it to shreds. I am grateful for your comment, "This isn't a story; I think you're writing a novel." Indeed I was, though I didn't know it yet.

I also thank my first true writing community, Melanated Writers Collective, for nurturing me into audaciously claiming the title "Writer" and staying true to my voice and perspective.

I thank my literary foremothers. Toni Morrison, your books, essays, and speeches will stay teaching me for all my days. You are an immortal gift. Leila Aboulela, finding your book *Minaret* randomly at a bookstore in Kentucky was a gift from Allah. It showed me it was possible to be a Muslim writer, that we have stories to tell and we can tell them our way.

Eternal and innumerable gratitude to my parents, Kuumba Kazi Ferrouillet and Ua Dumas Kazi. May Allah have mercy on your souls. I miss you both every day, but I hope you know your guidance and love is holding me up and keeping me going. Till Jannah insha'Allah.

Thank you to my stepmother, Sandra Pierre-Kazi, for teaching me the value of hard work and owning my strengths. Thank you to my siblings, Shujaa, Zijazo, Mandela, Ahmad, and Jathiya. You all are my day ones. Thank you for loving me as I am.

Alhamdulillah, all praise to God, I have a big and loving family, biological and inherited, that has been cheering me on from the beginning. I would love to name you all individually, but that would compete with the length of this book. Thank you to all the members of the Dumas, Ferrouillet, Nance, and Keyes families—all my aunts and uncles, grandparents, and cousins, family that are friends and friends that are family too. You are all and individually special to me. Thank you for telling me stories and for encouraging mine. Because of you all I can say with confidence, "I got people."

I thank my ancestors, those I know by name and those I don't, those whose origins I can trace and those I can't. Your lives and stories live in me. I hope I'm making you proud.

The sisterhood of female friendship is special and sacred. I am blessed to have too many to name in this space but I must mention my soul sister, Amane Hamdan, and my sister friends Aleshia, Kristin, and Malika, who've held me down these last few years. Your friendship is a lifeline.

Thank you to my Sapelo Square family; with you all my Blackness and Muslimness merge beautifully, no explanations or code switches needed.

Thank you to Nasr Nance, friend and first reader, for the valuable feedback and encouragement through the long process of writing and publishing. And thank you to my buddy, my sonshine, Idris. I thank Allah every day for blessing me with you. Thank you for the love and warm hugs, and for telling anybody who will listen that your mama's an amazing writer.

And to my readers, thank you thank you thank you! I hope you loved this book and I hope to bring you more. Thank you for reading.

ABOUT THE AUTHOR

AMBATA KAZI was born and raised in New Orleans, LA. She is a graduate of the University of New Orleans Creative Writing Workshop with a master of fine arts. Her short stories have been published in *Carve, Muslim American Writers at Home, midnight & indigo, CRAFT,* and other journals and anthologies. *Far Away from Here* is her first novel. She lives in Oakland, California.

Looking for your next great read?

We can help!

Visit www.gosparkpress.com/next-read or scan the QR code below for a list of our recommended titles.

SparkPress is an independent boutique publisher delivering high-quality, entertaining, and engaging content that enhances readers' lives, with a special focus on commercial and genre fiction.